Praise for *Sisters*:

'A moving and compelling tale ⟨
impulsive lie can cause, breaking apa.. ....y. ..ei. ana contident,
this book has it all: emotive and gripping in equal measure. Had to
stop myself gulping it down in one go!'
Louise Mumford

'I love everything about this book. If you like character-led novels,
then they don't come finer than this, with its beautifully developed
personalities reacting to changing circumstances. Amongst the
shocking revelations are touches of humour and lightness that
balance the grief and darkness... "I couldn't put the book down"
may be a cliché, but I read this in one session that stretched into the
early hours of the morning, from the shock of the opening to the
ultimately satisfying conclusion.'
Alex Craigie

'Judith Barrow is such a skilled storyteller I was completely
immersed in the narrative, living alongside the characters as the plot
played seamlessly out. It is hard to say too much about the story
itself without including spoilers, but take it from me, *Sisters* is a first
class read.'
Jane Cable

Judith Barrow grew up in a small village on the edge of the
Pennines, but has lived in Pembrokeshire for over forty years.
She is the author of several novels and has had poetry
and short fiction published. Judith has degrees in literature and
creative writing, makes regular appearances at literary festivals,
and presents talks on research and creative writing.
She is a creative writing tutor and holds workshops on all genres.

Her novel *The Memory* was shortlisted for
Wales Book of the Year 2021.

judithbarrowblog.com

Connect with her on Facebook:
www.facebook.com/judith.barrow.3
or Twitter: @judithbarrow77
https://www.instagram.com/judithbarrow2912/
https://www.pinterest.co.uk/judithbarrow/

Also by Judith Barrow from Honno:
Pattern of Shadows
Changing Patterns
Living in the Shadows
A Hundred Tiny Threads
The Memory
The Heart Stone

SISTERS

Judith Barrow

HONNO MODERN FICTION

First published in Great Britain in 2023 by Honno Press
D41, Hugh Owen Building, Aberystwyth University, Ceredigion, SY23 3DY

1 2 3 4 5 6 7 8 9 10

A catalogue record for this book is available from the British Library.

Published with the financial support of the Books Council of Wales.

ISBN 9781912905768 (paperback)
ISBN 9781912905775 (ebook)

Cover design: Liz Gordon, Madapple designs
Cover photograph © Archangel.com
Typeset by Elaine Sharples

Printed by 4edge Ltd

For David

Prologue

I never wanted to be in Micklethwaite ever again. Yet here I am. And meeting the one person I never wanted to see again. Sisters don't do what she did to me. I'll never forgive her. Ever.

Part One

Chapter One

'Thanks, love, he's not settled all night.'

I know, I heard him. Robert's in Mum and Dad's bedroom, next to mine, and the walls are thin. But I don't say anything, I love my little brother and I'm proper chuffed that Mum trusts me to take him out in his new pram. They bought all new things for him because they'd got rid of everything after me: the pram, a cot, one of those seats that bounce when Dad lays him in it. And loads of clothes – Mum was knitting all the time before he was born. Most of the wool was yellow because we didn't know if the baby would be a boy or a girl. When Dad came back from the hospital, after Robert was born, he kept repeating, 'a son', and that he was, 'over the moon'. I think my sister was a bit jealous. She said it showed she was special, being the first girl, and that I was a disappointment because I wasn't a lad. I don't care, I get to play with him more because Angie says she has better things to do. I'm guessing she means dolling herself up and putting all that muck on her face.

Mum tells people Robert was a total surprise. I can't think he was that much of a surprise, seeing as how she must have known there was a baby in her tummy, seeing as how she got fatter and fatter. Anyhow, I know she loves him because she smiles all the time and laughs at everything he does. She says he'll be sitting up before he's six months old. I can't wait – it'll be good to show him all the birds and things in the garden.

'I'll just take Robert round the avenues, Mum. I'm going to call for Belinda. We won't go off the estate. Promise.' I grip the handle of the pram; it's a bright and shiny blue with little letters that spell out 'Silver Cross' on the rim of the hood. I love pushing it around the avenues. 'I'll look after him. Cross my heart.'

'I know you will, Mandy. I'm not worried.'

Robert whimpers. I jiggle the pram.

'Go on, then, before he starts again. Off you go. It'll give me a chance to get the washing done.'

We both look up at the sky. There are no clouds, and the brightness hurts my eyes.

'It's a good drying day,' I say. Mum laughs and gives me a quick hug. It's something she always says on washdays like this. I walk steadily along the path, through the gate and onto the pavement. I know she'll be watching to see how I'm managing; she always does.

When I go round the corner to the next avenue, I go a bit faster. Robert's muted grumbles mean if I stop, he'll be in full throttle in no time. I take no notice when I hear someone clip-clopping behind, because I can tell it's Angie in those daft wedge-heeled sandals she insists are 'the fashion'.

'Give us a go, our Mand,' she says, catching up with me.

'Why?' She's never wanted to before. 'You always say you wouldn't be seen dead pushing the pram outside.'

'If I stop in, I'll get lumbered with the washing or stuck doing some boring weeding on the vegetable patch for Dad.' Angie tugs at the handle of the pram, jerking it. Robert lets out a loud cry.

'Stop it!'

'Go on, our kid, and I'll buy you some sherbet from my spends.'

I'm still cross with her for leaving me to wash and dry the pots on my own after breakfast. But when I look at her, I feel a twinge of guilt. Angie's eyelashes are clumped together with mascara; I'd seen her spitting on the black block earlier and peering into the mirror while she used the little brush. The same brush I'd swished around in the toilet after I'd peed. Just to get my own back.

I shouldn't have done that, so to make me feel better, I give in. 'Okay then, just for a bit. And a liquorice stick to go with the sherbet, mind?'

6

'And a liquorice stick to go with the sherbet.' She's mimicking me, but I don't care. It's a bargain. And one thing about Angie is she always keeps her promises.

She turns the pram to go along the next avenue.

'I'm not going that way. I'm calling for Belinda.' I try to catch hold of her arm. She dodges away and the pram jerks. Robert gives a wail of protest.

'Does it matter?' She walks faster, though how in those stupid sandals I don't know. 'You can call for your little best friend after.'

'She'll be waiting for me. I told her on our way home yesterday I'd go round to their house. Stop! I'll tell Mum.' I bump into her when she suddenly halts.

'You'd better not tell Mum.' She glares at me.

'Well, all right, I won't. But I know what you're doing.' I glare back. 'You're going to meet that lad off Victoria Avenue, aren't you?'

'How do you know?'

I'd heard her giggling about him with her friend, Sally Sedgemoor, but I can't tell her I had my ear pressed to the wall between our bedrooms. So I just say, 'That's why you want the pram – so if his mother sees you, you can pretend you're only walking the baby.'

She glances at me. 'You won't tell Dad, will you?'

'As if.' He'd only go off on one of his, 'It's not you I don't trust, it's the kind of boy you'd attract,' talks. I snap, 'I don't know how've you managed to get out of the house with all that stuff on your face.' She's also wearing blue eyeshadow and pale pink lipstick. She's so pretty and has lovely, thick, dark brown hair that swings around her face like that singer's, Sandie Shaw. Not that she can sing like her; her caterwauling in the bath is like cats fighting. I can sing, but I take after Mum's side, with my ginger hair, horrible pale green eyes and the freckles.

She shrugs. 'He didn't see me. I nipped out when he was in the back garden.'

'Well, you'll have to put up with me being with you. Because as soon as you see that lad, you won't want the pram...'

'He's not just a lad, he's lovely. He's called Stephen – Stephen Birch.' She flushes and leans forward to tuck the knitted blanket closer around Robert.

'Soppy.' I make a gagging noise. 'Anyway, what about Ben Watson?' She's been seeing my friend Belinda's brother on the sly from Dad for months. 'Does he know you fancy this Stephen lad?'

She goes redder. 'No, and you won't tell him. Will you?' She narrows her eyes at me.

I shrug; I don't really care. Except that Belinda's my friend and I don't want anything my daft sister does to spoil that. Ben's always nice to me when I go to their house. Friendly. And Belinda's family are like us – normal. They live on the cul-de-sac at the end of our road. Not like that stuck-up lot off Victoria Avenue.

'Will you?'

'I like Ben...'

'Oh, shut up, and mind your own business. Anyway, I don't have to go past Stephen's house. He's meeting me at the bottom of Beggars Ginnel...'

'And, like I said, as soon as you meet him, you'll want to get rid of Robert.'

She grins.

I keep on following her as fast as I can. I'm not happy. I promised Mum I'd look after Robert. We turn into the narrow passageway and I see Stephen Birch standing down at the other end, looking up at us.

Angie glances at me, just the once, before shouting, 'Catch!'

I try to grab at the handle as she lets go of it. I'm not fast enough. The ginnel's steep and cobbled. The pram bumps and lurches, going faster and faster. My legs won't move. Don't understand. Don't believe it. I push past her. Run.

Robert's screaming.

Stephen Birch is yelling, panic in his voice. He dodges from side to side of the ginnel, arms outstretched. The pram careers into him and tips over onto its side. He's underneath it. The cobbles are bumpy. I slip. Pain. Pain in my ankle. I scream. Still running. Crying. Can't breathe. Can't breathe.

'Robert!'

He's not screaming now. Not crying. I tug at the pram. 'Help me,' I shout at the boy. He's curled up, moaning. 'Angie. Help!'

She's standing at the top of the ginnel. Staring.

I'd heard Robert when the pram was crashing around. Now he's quiet. Totally quiet.

Angie's helping at last. I'm dizzy. Hot. Cold. Feel sick. Hate her. Hit out at her. 'Hate you. Hate you!' She doesn't hit back.

The pram's on its wheels. The blankets are bunched up in the hood. Can't untangle them.

'If anything's...'

My little brother's not moving. His face is pale. His eyes shut. His little mouth is open a bit. He's not breathing.

Chapter Two

Angie

The tears have dried, salt-tightened, on her cheeks. Angie hunches her shoulders and rocks, ignoring the sharp branches of the beech hedge pressing against her back. No one can see her here from the house, she knows that, and she needs time to think what to do. The pulse in her neck has gradually subsided to a steady beat.

She shouldn't have run away, shouldn't have left Mandy on her own to bring their baby brother home. The thought torments her. But she'd panicked when she hadn't heard him cry. He should have been crying. She mustn't think about it. Was he hurt? No, he couldn't be. She *had* heard him cry. Hadn't she? That makes her feel better for a second before she remembers how he'd looked. So still.

She can't think straight. She rocks harder, wrapping her arms around her knees. Wishing none of the last hour had happened. If she could just go back...

Chapter Three

Mandy

Everything's happening at once. I know they're talking, but all I can hear is this loud, rushing noise in my head. My face is hot, wet with snot and tears. I wipe it with my cardigan sleeve because I don't have a hanky. No one's taking any notice of me except Dad, my dad, who's usually really kind, keeps glaring at me, the skin around his mouth white because he's pressing his lips so tight together.

The ambulance outside on the road still has blue lights flashing. I can see it out of the corner of my eye. Two men in green uniforms bend over Robert. Mum's kneeling next to them. Since that horrid woman pushed me and the pram through the front gate, with all those other people behind us, she hasn't made a sound. But she's shaking, so I know she's crying too. I'll never forget the way she held onto the front door. The way she ran towards me, her arms out in front of her as though she was pushing at the air to get to the pram, her eyes stretched as wide as her mouth.

There's a policeman talking to Dad. I'm guessing he's telling him what happened. Not what really happened, because I haven't told him the truth. I don't know why, really. I don't know where Angie is, but I can't tell on her. I'll let her tell what happened.

I can't get my little brother's face out of my mind.

The policeman and Dad are looking at me. I don't know what else to say except, 'I'm sorry.'

All at once, a lady is standing at the living-room doorway. Her smile makes me take in a deep breath that sort of turns into a gulping sob, and I hear her say, 'Carol Hudson, from social services,

Mr and Mrs Marsden. I'm here to help in any way I can.' She looks at me. 'You must be Amanda?'

Mum doesn't move. The two ambulance men don't look up. They're still leaning over my brother, but they're not moving anymore. I don't know what that means. Dad's eyes are flickering everywhere but at me. There's a strange silence in the room. Nobody calls me Amanda unless they are cross with me. Unless I'm in trouble. And I know I'm in trouble now.

Mum starts to scream.

I cover my ears, shut my eyes.

I wish Angie was here with me. She'll make it right.

Chapter Four

Angie

Angie stops rocking, rests her head on her knees. She has to think, think what to do, what to say. Mandy's probably in the house, telling them what happened. Telling on her. They'll be in there, waiting for her to show up. To blame her.

Or they might have taken Robert to the doctor's, just to get him checked over. Make sure he's okay. Yes, that's probably it. But there's a tremor rising from deep inside her; she saw the stillness of her brother's face, the trickle of blood on the pillow. She knows.

The shaking grows. The branches of the hedge dig deeper. Angie welcomes the pain. But she can't stay upright any longer and she sprawls sideways onto the ground, the smell of freshly cut grass all around her. Dad's been mowing the lawn. Dad! What will he say? Do? Oh God, what will he do?

She can't get it out of her head – that moment when she realised that Mandy couldn't catch hold of the pram, that it was going too fast. Seeing it bounce and jolt over the cobbles.

The shrill scream from Robert. The moment when the pram

bounced over, the metal screeching against the cobbles, the wheels spinning. And then the quiet few seconds when there were only her own sharp intakes of breath inside her head.

Slowly, she sits up, wipes her hands over her face and pushes herself to her feet. Fragments of cut grass stick to her skin. She still feels wobbly, but she must go in; she must face up to what she's done. She needs to know what happened after... If Mandy is all right. The guilt is like a weight pressing down on her head. Walking unsteadily, she crosses the lawn. At the back door she stops, hears a voice coming from the hall, a deep voice, not her dad's. And then she hears her mother. Screaming.

She staggers backwards, crossing her arms over her head. Falls to her knees. Whimpering, she crawls back to the beech hedge. Hides.

Chapter Five

Mandy

I know that Mum will be blaming herself. She'll be thinking she shouldn't have trusted me to look after Robert. And it isn't my fault, it's Angie's.

They've taken my baby brother away. Mum's still on the floor, all crumpled up. The lady from the social services has told Dad she's phoned our doctor and he'll come as soon as he can. She's sitting next to me, her arm around my shoulder, and the policeman keeps asking me to tell him what happened to Robert.

I close my eyes so I can't see the policeman. I don't want to think about pushing the pram home with my dead baby brother in it. Me crying. Noisy, snotty, gulping sobs. Me standing on the corner of our avenue, just out of sight of our house, not knowing what to do. Rocking the pram, hoping Robert would wake up. Not be dead.

My breath's shuddering in my chest. I don't want to say the words, make it all real again. But they're waiting. And I have to try. I think back to when that woman stopped at the side of me...

'Eh up, it's young Mandy, in't it? It's me, Mrs Ormorand, love. Now then, what's up?' The woman spoke through the cigarette pressed between her lips.

I couldn't speak. I wiped my cardigan sleeve across my nose, then pointed at the pram.

'What is it, love?' She leans over me; her breath smells of the cigarette.

'Nothing... I mean...'

'It's your little brother, init?' The woman pats the hood of the pram. 'I'd recognise this fancy pram anywhere.'

'Yes. No. I mean, yes, it's...' My voice cracks. 'It wasn't my fault.'

'What wasn't, pet?' She frowns as she pokes her head inside the hood. I make myself not look. Make myself stare at the bright red smear of lipstick on the end of the cigarette she's now holding above her head. 'What's happened then...?' Her voice trails off. She steps back, dropping the cigarette. 'Oh, good God!'

'I couldn't help it.'

'He looks...' She leans forward again, puts her hand inside the pram. I see her touch my brother's face.

I look up at her. 'Honest, I didn't do anything.' The swallowing hurts my throat. 'I mean I couldn't...'

'What happened?' She's a funny colour now.

I shake my head, a finger of cold stabbing my insides. I can't stop the shaking.

'What have you done, lass?' She's almost whispering. Looking at me as though she's as frightened as I am. I'd thought that somehow, because she was a grown-up, she'd know what to do.

She doesn't.

'It was an accident,' I say again. 'It was in Beggars Ginnel. It was rolling so fast I couldn't catch it.'

'What do you mean, it was rolling so fast? Weren't you holding it?'

I shake my head. I don't know why I said that. My mind's a muddle. Why had Angie run away? Why had she left me, when she's always the one who knows how to make things right? She always gets us out of trouble. But she's not here. I'm on my own.

The woman shakes me by the shoulder, her bony fingers digging in. 'What have you done to the babby, eh? What did you do?' Her voice gets louder.

'It was an ... accident ... honest ... honest.' There's a great lump in my throat. I can't get the words out properly.

'I don't believe you. That's blood on that babby's head.'

I hadn't seen any blood. 'N-no...' I'm going to be sick. I cover my mouth with my hand.

When she talks, it's through a screwed-up mouth, her thick black eyebrows pulled together.

'We'll need the police to decide that. Wicked! God above, your poor mother.' She pushes at me with her shopping basket, her other hand on the pram.

I'm trying to keep up with her as she strides out. I stumble, trip, twist on my ankle again. Cry out in pain.

'No point in skriking, my girl.' She nods without looking at me, her voice loud. The way she's speaking, it's almost as though she's now enjoying what's happening. Even as I'm thinking that, she says, 'You're for it...' It doesn't sound right coming from a grown-up. She sounds like Angie when she's won an argument.

'I can't ... I'm sorry ... please...'

'Shut up!'

The shout brings people to their doors. Some women follow us along the avenue. They crowd around, asking questions she's not taking breath to answer. I don't want her to answer. I don't want to hear the words. I'm so frightened I can hardly see where I'm going.

But then I do see. I see Mum running towards me...

Angie should be here. Where is she? I need her.

'Mum? I can't...' I'm going to be sick again, but there's nothing left in my stomach. When I swallow, I think I'm going to choke. I can't think about anything except seeing Mum's face after she'd looked into the pram at my baby brother. Touched him. And then looked at me as if she didn't know me.

'Mum? It was an accident. Honest.'

But I'm not being honest. And it's as though Mum knows. She's still sitting on the carpet, legs stuck out in front of her, her hands lying limp on her lap. Now she shakes her head slowly. Large tears run down her face and onto her skirt, making splotches on the yellow flower pattern.

Behind her, I see Dad's Adam's apple rise and fall in his throat. He doesn't speak. His eyes aren't like Mum's. He's never looked at me like this before. He keeps running his fingers through his hair. They're trembling.

'Is there anyone we can contact for you? A member of the family? Friends?' The social services lady says to Dad, squeezing my shoulder. He shakes his head. I hear her swallow before she says, 'This is not something you have to deal with on your own, Mr Marsden. I can arrange for someone to be with you?' Dad shakes his head again. 'Amanda will need a lot of support—'

'*She* will?'

'Eric!' Mum raises her head. 'Don't.'

His eyes are shiny with tears. I've only seen him cry once before. When he was telling Angie and me we had a baby brother. But this is different. He keeps screwing his eyelids tight together.

'*She'll* need support?' He's shouting. '*I've* lost my son. My only son...'

'Eric. Don't. Please.'

'I understand, Mr Marsden. Of course I do—'

'Oh, do you? You understand why my son is dead? What happened? Because I bloody don't.'

He pushes past Mum and comes to tower over me, his lips drawn thin over his teeth. His face is really red and the two lines between his eyes are almost together. 'What *I'd* like to know, madam, is what you were doing anywhere near that ginnel?'

I don't know this dad. This isn't my lovely, gentle dad. I want my proper dad back.

He jabs his finger at me. 'Eh? Eh?'

Spit lands on my cheek but I daren't wipe it off in case he thinks I'm being cheeky. I try to sit as still as I can. Anything to stop him shouting.

'Why? Why did you leave the estate – when you were specifically told not to? Well?'

Mum hadn't actually told me not to go off the estate; it was me that said I wouldn't. But I don't say that. I shouldn't have told them where we were, where I was when it happened. I should have made something up when the policeman first asked. All I wanted to do was to tell him, tell Mum and Dad, that it was an accident. And I didn't want to get Angie into trouble.

'Well?' He's breathing big, loud breaths. My legs start to jiggle. He lifts his hand, all his fingers clenched. I duck down. I don't look at this man who looks like my dad but isn't. Dad's never hit me, but I think he's going to now.

I'm weeing and I can't stop. The warmth between my legs goes on and on. I try to hold it back by putting my hand there but it's no use and my fingers are wet through. When I look down there's a patch of damp on both sides of me on the seat.

Dad drops his arm to his side. He walks out of the room.

Mum shuffles over towards the settee. The lady moves to make room for her and, still on the floor, Mum puts her arms around me. 'Oh, love,' she whispers. 'Oh, love.' Her body is limp and heavy on mine. She moves back and forth so the two of us are rocking.

The policeman clears his throat. I see him exchange a glance with the lady, move his head slightly. See her nod. He leaves without saying anything.

'I'm going to go now, Mrs Marsden, ' the lady says. 'But I'll be back tomorrow. PC Radon – and some other people – will need to talk to Amanda again. When the doctor comes, Mrs Marsden, please let him give you something to help you to sleep.'

'I should be with my baby.'

I can't keep still. The wet underneath me is cold now.

'There's nothing you can do – not today. Your baby is being looked after. If you want to, you can see him tomorrow. Would you like me to stay with you tonight? I can do that; I don't need to go. Or is there someone you'd like me to contact?'

'No.' I feel Mum shake her head against mine.

'Well, as I said, your doctor will be here soon.' She puts a piece of paper on the arm of the settee. 'I'll leave my number at the office here. If you need to ask me anything... I'll be back tomorrow.'

The lady stands and smiles at me. 'It was an accident, Amanda, we all know that. Try not to worry.' But I can tell from her eyes that I should be worrying.

When she's gone Mum sits back from me, her forehead wrinkled, her jaw slack. 'Oh no, Angela! Mandy, we need to find her. Tell her what's happened. Do you know where she is, love?'

Chapter Six

Angie

Angie waits for a long time, unable to go inside. When she peers around the corner of the house, she sees the blue lights of the ambulance. Her stomach jumps. The sudden terror, the realisation that this is the worst thing that has ever happened to her, makes her retch.

She should run away.

The choking sensation in her throat, the tingling in her arms and legs, last for a long time.

The sky holds a faint shadowing, a pale orange and blue, when she finally pushes herself forward. The slow unsteady walk to the door is still too fast, takes her too soon to a house, a family, where life has changed forever.

Angie listens to the harsh sobs coming through her sister's bedroom door before pushing it open. 'Mandy?'

Her sister has the covers over her head. When she peeps out, her eyes are pink and swollen. 'Where were you?'

Angie flinches at the accusation.

'Why didn't you come home. Why?'

'I'm sorry. I was scared.'

'And me.' Mandy raises her voice. 'And me. I was scared as well. A woman dragged me here. There were loads of people following. No one believed me when I said it was an accident.' Mandy covers her eyes with her forearm. 'Because it wasn't, was it?'

'It was, Sis, honest. I thought you were closer when—'

'You let go of the pram. And now Robert's dead.'

Hearing his name spoken out loud shocks both of them. After a long, stretched-out minute, Angie mutters, 'Yes.' She's jumpy. And frightened. She's going to throw up. 'Why didn't you say what really happened?'

'I don't know.' A hoarse whisper. 'I thought you'd come home, that you'd tell them. You'd look after me.'

'I'm sorry, Mand. I am, really.' Angie's voice cracks. She's crying again. She knows she should own up. She should have the minute she walked into the house. But to admit to killing her own baby brother is something too awful, too unbelievable.

Mandy sits up, her face blotched. She scrubs at her nose. 'You could tell them now what happened. That you were pushing the pram?' She nods a few times, her eyebrows lifted in a plea. 'You could say the handle slipped from your fingers. Like I said. But your fingers, not mine.' There's a hopeful quivering around her mouth. 'Please?'

Angie looks around the door to the stairs. 'There's no point now.

You didn't tell them, so if we do now they'll know you lied. And they'd only think I was lying – covering up for you.'

Mandy slumps back down under the covers. Her voice is muffled. 'They might not. You could try? Please?'

Her desperation makes panic lurch in Angie's stomach. 'I can't. It'd be worse for me, being older, like. You're only thirteen – they'll think the pram was too much for you to control.'

'How do you think that would make Mum feel? She'd blame herself for letting me take Robert out.' Mandy snaps the covers off her, lies with her arms straight down on them and stares at her sister. 'She'd blame herself.'

'You don't know that.' Angie closes her eyes. But she knows her sister's right and that their mother will blame herself.

How can she make Mandy stick to her story? 'Didn't you say you tripped? That it was an accident? Can't you just stick with that?' She can see the fear on her sister's face, hear the shuddering breaths, and she hates it. 'I'm sorry.' Crossing to the bed, she sits, taking hold of Mandy's fingers. 'You're freezing!'

'I can't get warm. I can't stop seeing...'

'Don't.' Angie pushes away the same image, along with the guilt. 'Just a minute.'

Running to her room, Angie drags the eiderdown from her own bed and carries it across the landing. Spreading it over Mandy, she says, 'How's your ankle?'

'The doctor said it's sprained. Mum put cold cloths on it and then one of her knee bandage thingies. She sent me to bed to rest it.'

Angie knows her mother sent her sister to bed to get her away from their father. He'd come back downstairs when she'd plucked up enough courage to come into the house. He hadn't looked or sounded like their dad; Angie didn't know the man who paced the room, loomed over her sister. Shouted.

She'd felt Mandy's eyes on her all the time their mum was holding her, telling her what had happened to their little brother. She could feel Mandy's silent pleading that she tell the truth. And she hadn't.

Shame sweeps through her again when she thinks of the way their father had thrown those nasty words at Mandy. It had made Angie feel sick. And yet she'd been relieved it wasn't her he'd vented his hatred on.

'What will happen, Angie? What will they do to me?' Mandy plucks at the covers.

'I don't know.' Angie kneels by the bed, covers her sister's hand. 'I'm sorry, Sis.'

Mandy pulls her fingers away. 'Get out.' Anger makes her voice rough. 'I don't want you in here.'

Angie pushes herself off her knees. At the door she stops. 'I am, Mandy, I really am sorry.'

'Get out!'

When Angie hovers at the top of the stairs, there are no voices downstairs. For a moment she listens to her sister crying, then she creeps into her own room.

Chapter Seven

Mandy

They're waiting for me again. Third time this week. There's seven of them tonight; Karen Webb has got two more in her gang now. There's no way I can get to the school gate with them circling.

I hang back, trying to get into the middle of a group of other kids, but they drift off, giving me dirty looks and leaving me on my own. It's all over the school that I killed my little brother. Glancing over my shoulder, I see that the teachers who were standing at the main doors, making sure there was no pushing and shoving on the steps outside, have now disappeared. The school is dark. Empty. We're not allowed back inside after the end-of-day bell, unless there's a good reason. Is being pushed around for the third time this week a good reason? Being scared to death?

I wish I'd asked Angie to come to our gate to meet me. But I don't want anything to do with her. I can't believe she's letting me take the blame for something so horrible. She's always stuck up for me in the past. I haven't spoken to her since she came into my room to persuade me it was best to stick to my story. Best for who?

Dad ignores me. I think he hates me. And Mum's just sad. Sometimes I hear her crying in the night.

I'm thinking all this while I'm watching them watching me. There's a strange smile on Karen Webb's face, like she's won something. And I suppose she has. She's won and I've lost. I lost that first Monday I went back to school. The whispers started as I walked past groups of girls outside school: 'Murdered her own brother.' 'Killed her little baby brother on purpose.'

And my best friend, Belinda, was one of them.

The social services lady, Miss Hudson, told me not to talk to anyone about it, to ignore anyone being nasty, but it's hard. No one will sit next to me in class. Not even Cecilia Atherton, the cleverest girl in the class, the one they always call a dork. They ignore me, talk over me when I try to answer a question. They bump into me in the corridor, pull my satchel off my shoulder, hiss words: *baby killer, bitch, murderer.*

The teachers try to help; they're extra kind. But it makes things worse.

I try hard to push the names to the back of my mind. But they fill my head in my sleep, in the nightmares. I see my brother's face, sometimes smiling up at me, more often how he looked on that horrible day. I blame myself; it doesn't matter that it wasn't my fingers on the pram handle.

I feel like I've been standing here forever, my satchel digging into my shoulder, the grit on the drive grinding under my shoes as I move from one foot to another. I should run. But Karen always beats me. She'd catch me, no bother. Behind me car doors click shut, wheels crunch. I should run after them; one of the teachers might see me, stop for me. Or I might make it to the vehicle entrance.

The girls are nudging each other, goading one another on. Grinning. They start to take sudden steps towards me and then jump back. Each time my heart leaps. I'm shaking inside; that feeling like on Sports Day just before the gun goes off. That wanting to run. That instinctive movement.

It overwhelms me. I turn and I'm running across the grass towards the open gate. The caretaker hasn't closed it yet. I'm running and running.

The whooping and shouting behind me is loud. My legs are burning. The thump of my shoes on the ground shudders through me. My chest hurts each time I try to drag in air. There's a strange, horrid taste in my mouth.

And now I'm flat on the ground, winded. A weight of bodies lands on top of me. They're tugging at my hair so hard it stings, and banging my head on the ground. I've bitten my lip. I taste blood. I try to cover my head with my arms, but they're dragging at the straps of my satchel, wrenching my shoulders. It's so hard, not to beg them to stop, but that didn't work last time. They don't speak. All I can hear is the sound of their breathing, my breathing.

Until there is a shout and all at once I'm lying face down, alone.

'You okay?' The hands that lift me up are gentle. I keep my head lowered but I recognise the man's voice.

'I'm all right, Mr Jessop.' I wipe my hand across my mouth, look at the blood. My lip already feels swollen. 'My satchel...' I look around for it. My books are scattered everywhere, trampled on, ripped.

'Here, let me 'elp.' The caretaker drops to his knees and as he picks each book up, he tries to flatten the pages with his big hands. The arms of his glasses push his ears forward. He has a boil behind his right ear. I wonder if it hurts.

'You okay, lass?' He looks over his shoulder at me.

I nod. The movement makes my lip hurt more; it feels as if it's getting fatter all the time.

'You've got a fair old scrape on your knee.' He struggles to his feet, holding the books.

My leg is throbbing.

'My satchel?' There's blood in my mouth and it splatters out when I speak.

'I see it.' He points to one of the small trees that the sixth form planted as part of their project last summer. My bag is hanging on one of the slender branches. The branch is broken. 'I'll get it.' He hesitates, takes a white hanky out of his jacket pocket. 'Here, use this on that cut.'

The handkerchief is surprisingly clean compared with his overalls.

My lip stings. I want to cry. But I don't want him to report what's happened, so I say, 'Thank you. I'm all right. Really, Mr Jessop. It's nothing.' My words are muffled by the hanky, so I take it from my mouth and say again, 'It's nothing.'

'Didn't look like nothing to me. I know bullying when I see it.' He places my books carefully into the satchel and hands it to me. 'I know that girl of Barry Webb's. She's a nasty piece of work...'

'Karen? You know her?' I'm looking across the field for my shoe but can't see it.

'I know 'er father. Went to this school, same time as me. He were the same. A bully.' He frowns. 'I should report this. It's happened on school premises.'

'No. Please don't, Mr Jessop. It'll only make things worse.'

'Aye, 'appen you're right; always did in my time. Perhaps I won't, then, if it bothers you that much, Amanda.'

I'm surprised. 'You know who I am?'

He shuffles his feet, stares around the field before answering. 'Everybody knows who you are, Amanda. And what's 'appened to your baby brother...'

I feel the heat creep up my throat and into my face. 'It was an accident.'

'Aye, that's what I 'eard.' Even though his eyes are kind, there is doubt in his voice.

I just want to get away. 'I'd better get home. Mum will wonder where I am.' I say that, but I doubt she'd notice if I never went home again; it's like she doesn't even know where *she* is.

He dips his head towards me. 'She'll wonder what's 'appened when she sees the state of you. And your blazer.' It's ripped on the shoulder. I shrug. 'And you've lost a shoe.' Turning a half circle, he surveys the ground around us, saying, almost absently, 'I really should report it, you know. '

'Please don't...' I feel really sick now. I try to hand his hanky back to him, but he shakes his head.

'Keep it.'

'I'll get my mum to wash it for you.'

'It don't matter.' He sweeps her offer away with a wave of his hand. 'I'll look out for your shoe as I'm closing up.'

He won't find it. Karen's lot will have taken it. 'I have to go,' I say again.

And I'm running. At the gate I turn around. He's still standing there.

'Please don't report it, Mr. Jessop,' I shout.

He shakes his head but I'm not sure what that means.

Chapter Eight

Angie

Angie is sitting on the back doorstep trying not to hear the stifled grief in her mother's voice, the despair in her father's. They're in the living room. Sometimes the words are so loud she has no choice; she can't shut them out.

'It makes no sense. He was only a baby, for God's sake. We – you shouldn't 'ave let her take him out. Or made sure Angela was with her '

'What could she have done?'

'She would have made sure they stayed on the estate. She has more sense in her little finger than Amanda. *She's* always daydreaming – always away with the fairies. I've told you. 'Ow many times have I told you? How many times 'ave I said, she's only thirteen, and she's got no sense...' He sounds to be spitting the words out.

'So you're blaming me?'

'Yes. No. I don't know. We're ... we were his parents ... we should have looked after him—'

'You mean I should.' Her mother is sobbing. Angie can picture her mother twisting her handkerchief in her fingers. The sobs become muffled.

Angie stands up, steps into the kitchen, head turned to hear better. She moves forward until she can see them on the settee. Her father has his arm around her mum. There's a long pause. When he next speaks, he's quieter.

'I'm sorry, love, but we only 'ave her word for what happened. What the 'ell was she doing at Beggars Ginnel?'

'I don't know. But it's doing no good, keep having a go at her. She's in such a state. She's distraught, Eric. She's a child. Please...'

'I just want to know the truth. She's lying about summat, I can tell. We 'ave a son lying in the—'

'Don't! Don't say it. I can't stand it.'

Angie twists around when she hears movement, sees her mother, hand to her mouth, run up the stairs.

And then she hears deep sobs. Her father crying.

When her dad wished she'd been there, her mother asked what she could have done.

And what had she done? The thought makes Angie sick. She grabs her cardigan from the back of the chair and runs from the house.

Angie's heard what happened to Mandy at school the day before. Saw the state she came home in. Too late to help her. And her help's

25

not wanted anyway. Her sister won't talk to her. Won't even look at her.

Sometimes, at night, the guilt keeps her awake. Often she imagines she can hear the crashing of the pram over the cobbles in the ginnel. Hears her baby brother crying. But it's too late to own up. Too late to say sorry to Mandy. Just too late for anything, except to cover her own back. And live with the awful feeling that turns her stomach every time.

Crossing the field and following the path along the line of trees, Angie has only the glimmer of an idea about what she's about to do. But she knows she needs to do something about Stephen. She pushes the image of Ben's face from her mind; she can't think about him now, and, anyway, he's not really her boyfriend. She climbs over the stiles onto the narrow footpath and stands looking towards the row of low, stone cottages. Two women walk towards her, baskets over their arms. On the opposite side, an old man sits on the bench outside the Swan, a pint pot on the table in front of him. A cluster of girls still in school uniform perch on the wall by the war memorial, swinging their legs and laughing. She recognises them in a vague sort of way, but they're younger than her, unimportant.

The sense of urgency that forced her from the house is almost unbearable. Biting her lip, she hops from one foot to the other, spins around and scans Mickle Road leading away from the village. The women pass her. She's conscious of a backwards glance from one of them, a whispered, 'That's the sister...' as they walk away. She glares at their backs. Shivers.

Pushing her arms into the sleeves of her cardigan, she dithers, nibbles harder on her lip. She's looking for Stephen. He won't have gone home yet; there's a good chance he'll still be hanging around the village. She knows where most of the boys usually go at this time of night. Working up her nerve, she peers over the hedge at the cricket field, hearing laughter. There he is. But he's with two of his mates.

She knows they're watching her when she pushes open the cricket club gate. They're sitting on the wooden steps of the pavilion. She recognises the lads with Stephen: John Gibson and Alec Holroyd. They nudge one another with their shoulders as she gets closer, and she wonders what he's told them. The thought makes her stomach lurch. If he has said anything, it's all too late. She falters. Lifting her head and pulling back her shoulders, she makes herself move forward.

'Stephen.' He turns his head away, leaning on the railing at the side of the steps. She sees a dotted line of blood, a cut healing on his forehead. 'Can we talk?'

His hand goes to his arm below the sleeve of his t-shirt; there is a large bruise and a red scabbed-over graze from his wrist to his elbow.

'About?' The word is drawled. But she'd seen the way his shoulders hunched when he first saw her.

'Please?'

An explosion of sniggering from the two lads contrasts with the nervous way his eyes dart towards her. But he shrugs. 'Watson know you're here?'

'This is nothing to do with Ben. Please, Stephen?' Angie hears the desperation in her voice and wants only to spin on her heels and walk away while she still has some pride. But she can't afford to do that.

'So he doesn't.' Stephen twists around to grin at his mates, who are still snorting behind their hands. Pushing at John Gibson, he laughs a loud, punctuated laugh. When he looks back at her, he narrows his eyes. 'I'm here. Talk.'

A flicker of nerves runs through her. 'On our own.'

More laughter drowns out Stephen's words.

'You're in luck, mate. Watson loses out...' John Gibson stands, jabs his foot into Alec Holroyd's side. 'Come on, let's go. Leave these two love-birds to ... er ... get on with whatever.' He grins.

Inside, Angie is cringing but tries not to show it. She tells herself she doesn't care what they think.

'S'open.' John gestures with his thumb to the door of the pavilion, jerking his hips at the same time.

'Go to hell.' Angie glares at him.

They walk away laughing, but not before Alec, clutching his crotch, makes the same jerking movement.

Her fear melts under the humiliation. Angie knows what's said, what happens next, she'll never be able to undo.

'Can I sit down?'

He shrugs.

'I haven't seen you in school?' Careful not to touch him, she balances on the edge of the step.

'Looking for me, were you? Worried what I might say when I found out you'd landed your kid in it? You're bloody unbelievable.'

'I'm sorry.'

'You told anybody I was there?' He faces her, his brown eyes narrow.

'No.'

'Has she?'

'Mandy? No.'

'Why not?'

'I don't know. She won't talk to me.'

'You surprised?'

She swats at her quick tears. The growing distance between herself and Mandy is horrible. Yes, they fought, like any of her friends fought with their brothers or sisters. But she's used to Mandy looking up to her.

'You going to own up?'

'I can't.' Bile swells in Angie's throat. She swallows, unable to say any more.

'So? What now?'

She waits, pushing down the fear, willing her voice to work. In barely a whisper she says, 'You haven't said anything to the police?' She closes her eyes, afraid of the answer.

'No. But I told my dad.' She gasps. 'Oh, don't worry, he hates the cops. Keeps his head down from that lot. Told me to do the same. He's more bloody annoyed this is keeping me out of training with the county football team.' He puts his hand flat on his thigh. 'Tore a muscle, thanks to you.' Neither speaks for a few moments.

He drops his chin to his chest, looks sideways at her. For the first time she sees the deep shadows under his eyes. 'I've hardly slept. I keep seeing that bloody pram coming at me, hearing the kid screaming.' He screws up his face. 'What the hell did you think you were playing at?'

'I don't know.' Angie takes a deep breath, laces her fingers. 'But I do know I'll have to live with what I did. And I know I've been a coward.' Her heart is beating so fast the noise is pulsing in her head. 'But I wanted to ask you...'

'What?' Without giving her a chance to answer, he lowers his voice. 'You killed your own brother. What do you want from me?'

'I want...' She speaks in a rush. 'I want you to tell the police that it was Mandy, that it was an accident—'

'No bloody way.'

'Please, Stephen. I thought you liked me—'

'Not that soddin' much. And Dad'd kill me. I'm doing what he said. Keeping out of it. He's taking me on in his business next year. He won't want me if I get into trouble with the police. Mustn't do anything that's bad for the family reputation.' He says it in a bored voice, as though it's something he's heard a lot. 'So I'm not about to bugger that up for *you*.'

Standing, he slowly makes his way down the steps and limps across the pitch.

She can't let him go. He must listen to her. Help her.

Catching up with him, her words tumble out. 'I'm frightened, Stephen. It'll be worse if I own up. Our kid will get away with it because she's so young...'

He walks faster, the limp more pronounced. 'You're bloody unbelievable.'

'If they find out it was me...'

29

'What? You'd have to face what you've done?' He throws the words over his shoulder.

Angie ignores the image of Mandy's face in her head. 'Please?' What can she say? 'If you do this for me, I'll do anything for you.'

He slows down. 'Don't ask me to do this, Angie.'

'I wouldn't ask if I wasn't sure it'll be okay for our Mandy. Honest.'

'I told you, Dad'll go mad.'

'It'll be all right. You always say you can wrap him round your little finger.'

He's wavering. She can see it.

He stands still. Studies her. 'I could get Mum to tell him.'

She sees the flicking of his tongue against the inside of his cheek. A habit she's noticed he has when thinking.

'Please. Stephen. I'll do *anything*.'

'Anything?' He raises his eyebrows.

'Yes.' If he can get her out of this, she'll do whatever he wants. 'Anything. Honest.'

'That desperate, eh?'

'Yes.'

'Let me give you one?'

Her throat is tight. She swallows. 'What?'

'You heard.'

'Yes.' The word is out before it has hardly formed in her head.

'You mean it?'

'Yes.' Her voice is low.

'You done it with Watson?'

'No.' She won't – can't think of Ben now. Her heart is thumping.

'So I'll be your first?'

'Yes ... yes, you will.' She lets her breath out in a long quivering sigh.

When he turns to look at her, his face is strange, his jaw set. 'Okay.' He nods slowly. 'Okay. I'll do it. I'll lie for you. After we... All right?'

'Yes. After...'

Chapter Nine

Mandy

'I think it will be better for all concerned if Mandy stays home for the time being, Mrs Marsden.'

The sun from the large window slants across the room, an elongated rectangle, making Mum squint. The glare shows up the lines around her eyes and mouth. I haven't noticed them before. I can tell from the way she's screwing her hanky between her fingers that she's struggling not to cry. I feel bad. I shouldn't have lied. Now it's too late. But Angie is Mum's daughter as well; she would be in this state even if my sister had owned up. Our brother would still be...

Mrs Lestor rests her elbows on her desk and steeples her fingers. I know what she's doing: she's getting rid of me. Pushing me, the problem, onto someone else until the police decide what they are going to do. Pain cramps in my stomach.

'I've talked with the governors, and they've agreed. We can arrange home schooling for her.' Mrs Lestor smiles down at me. 'Is that all right, Mandy?'

We're sitting on chairs that are lower than hers. I bet that's to make her feel good. I decide I've never liked her.

What's she going to do if I say no? I know I won't. I can't keep pretending I don't care when I hear the whispers, when I get pushed or pinched on the corridors. When no one will sit by me. When I see Belinda in Karen Webb's gang. I keep thinking Belinda will remember she's my best friend. But she hasn't been to see me. I thought, at first, that she didn't know what to say to me, because she loved our Robert as much as I did. But then I saw her with Karen Webb.

So I shrug and answer, 'Yes, Mrs Lestor.'

'Good. That's decided then.' She pushes herself away from her desk. The chair squeaks on the wooden floor. Mum hesitates when

Mrs Lestor stands and holds out her hand. When she gets up, she forgets her handbag is on her knees and it falls to the floor with a thud.

'It's okay, Mum, I've got it.' I pick it up before she moves. When I hand it to her, I see her fingers are shaking and I realise she hasn't spoken a word since we came in. She looks as though she hasn't a clue what's just happened. She looks frightened. For the first time ever, it's me that needs to protect her. I grab her arm. Don't let her shake hands with Mrs Lestor. 'Come on, Mum.' I hustle her to the door. I leave it open.

'Head up, love,' I hear Mum whisper.

That makes me feel better. 'Yes, Mum,' I say. 'But can we go a bit quicker, I'm bursting for a pee.'

'Yeah, me an' all. Where's the loos?'

'Down here, on the left.' I don't care if the Head can see us going into the lavvies, but I'm glad that lessons are still going on and there's no one else in here.

The sound of my rushing pee is nothing compared to that of Mum's, and I giggle when she says, 'Bloody 'ell, how the hell does anyone fit into these places. There's no room to move. I hope to God I can get up again.'

But she does and we're out of the school doors and down the drive whippet quick.

I see Mr Jessop and he lifts a hand, waves, but I lower my head and pretend not to see him. I'd rather forget the time he picked me up. He might have helped me, but I knew he hadn't believed me when I said what had happened to my baby brother was an accident. Then I regret it. He was right that I am lying. But when I turn to wave back, he's gone.

'I'll never come back to this school, Mum. Not ever.'

'No, love, you won't have to.' Her fingers tighten around mine. 'Ever.'

Chapter Ten

Angie

Following Stephen's instructions, Angie goes through the gate in the middle of the long, perfectly trimmed privet hedge and into the garden of the large, red-brick detached house. She hasn't been to his home before, although she's walked along Victoria Avenue plenty of times, hoping to catch a glimpse of him, way before he noticed her in school.

Ben Watson noticed her eyeing up Stephen at school though. Angie tries not to think back to the hurt and bitterness on his face when he'd challenged her.

'You must think I'm bloody stupid.' Ben folds his arms, the bulk of him almost blocking the narrow passageway to the school gym. Middle-school girls, kitted out in netball gear and boots, shuffle past them.

There's a knot in Angie's stomach but she lifts her chin, tosses back her hair.

'What you on about?' She copies him, folding her arms.

'You, all cow-eyed over Birch. Following him round every day. I've been watching you.' His jaw juts forward. 'Why Birch? Why pick him?'

A wave of guilt makes Angie blink; she knows the two lads have hated one another since primary school, vying for the same places on the school and county football teams. But still she says, 'It's a shame you've nothing better to do than spy on me.'

A girl hesitates before passing them. Angie glares at her. 'Yeah? Want a photo?' The girl scurries away. 'Look Ben, I'm sorry—'

'Don't bother. I'll say it for you.' He locks his hands on the top of his head, looks at two girls who are walking towards them, heads together, whispering. 'We're finished. You're dumped.'

Angie sees hurt and bitterness in his eyes before he turns away.

Watches him following the two girls, sees them glancing back at him, smiling. Wonders if she's made a mistake.

Now here she is, knowing that she has to keep her side of this deal she's made with Stephen. Angie takes in a long breath. If she doesn't go through with it he won't lie to the police for her. She's terrified. Even after going together for all those months, she and Ben haven't done it, haven't gone all the way.

She stands, looking around. Although early in the year, she sees some of the shrubs already have buds fat enough to burst open. The large flowering cherry tree in the centre of the lawn is in full bloom. The black tarmacked drive edges a large, immaculate lawn, as her dad would say 'cut to within an inch of its life'. She tries not to think of her dad. Knows what he would say if he could see her here.

'What're you doing?' The hissed question makes her jump. Stephen is standing by the corner of the house.

'I didn't see you there.'

'Stop bloody shouting. I don't want the whole bloody neighbourhood to hear. Come on. Get over here.'

'What?' What neighbours? Angie spins around. All she can see are the roofs of the houses on the other side of the avenue over the high hedge at the end of the lawn.

'I'm not supposed to be here. I told my parents I'd be at a mate's place.'

'Your parents aren't here?' She goes towards him.

'What do you think?' He walks away, leaving her to follow. 'They play golf every Saturday. They won't be back until tonight.' He adds, 'And they'll be too pissed to notice whether I'm here or not.'

A jolt goes through Angie's body. Of course she wouldn't be here if his mother and father were home. And she's under no illusion; they'd be none too thrilled to see their precious son meeting a girl from the Carrbrook council estate.

Stephen doesn't look at her as he walks through the kitchen into a long hall. The walls are painted a dark maroon and seem to close in around Angie. She follows him.

'Upstairs.' He takes the pine staircase two treads at a time.

She catches her top lip between her teeth. There's still time to leave.

'Steve...'

'What?' Leaning his forearms on the railing at the top of the stairs, he looks down at her. His face is flushed, and she can see her tension reflected in his face. 'You know why you're here. Don't pretend you don't. This is what we agreed.' He frowns.

'And you'll do as I asked? You'll talk to the police?' She must make sure.

'I've said so, haven't I?' He straightens and drags his t-shirt over his head. 'You're not backing out now, are you? 'Cos if you are...' He shrugs.

'No. But...'

'Come on up, then.' He walks off.

Angie follows slowly. He's right, this is her choice; she has no choice; she needs to feel safe.

On the landing only one of the five doors is open.

'In here.'

When she goes into the room, Stephen Birch is lying naked on top of the covers of a large double bed.

Hardly an hour later, Angie is running along Victoria Avenue, trying not to think about anything. All she knows is that she is sore. It must have been his first time as well. It hurt, but it was over in minutes. When he rolled off her, he turned on his side and wouldn't answer when she'd asked him when he was going to go to the police.

Chapter Eleven

Mandy

'PC Radon.' The policeman introduces himself as though I could ever forget. He wipes his feet on the doormat and takes off his helmet. It drips on the carpet where there's also a line of rain from the bottom of the front door.

I look out onto the avenue. A car swishes by, spraying an arc of water onto the pavement. The leaves on the trees opposite droop with the weight of rain. The sky is grey, the same grey colour as the school gates.

'We've found a witness.' He's still wiping his feet.

The relief is like a huge wave all the way through me.

'Close the door, Amanda. You're letting the rain in.' Dad's using that new voice, the one he's used since it ... it happened. When I turn to him, he doesn't look at me. He fixes his stare on the policeman. 'A witness? Who is it?' He's got that funny expression again, eye-flickering, head bobbing. He doesn't make me feel safe, like he did before. I used to talk to Belinda about how our dads looked after us when we had nightmares. I'm in a nightmare now.

The policeman moves to let me close the door and unbuttons the top pocket of his jacket to take out a small notebook. Tapping it flat onto the back of his hand he gives a heavy sigh. 'Or rather he found us.' His glance takes us all in. Mum puts her arm around my waist and gives me a squeeze. 'Though why it took him so long, we've yet to find out.' He frowns.

I don't look at Angie, but I wonder if she's as scared as me. Yet it feels wonderful, knowing it will be all right. Whoever it is will say it wasn't me. I feel sorry for her. They will have said what she did.

I peep at her out of the corner of my eye, trying to let her know I'll help her all I can. But when she meets my gaze, the relief in me falters. There's something in her face that isn't right.

'It's a young lad called Stephen Birch. Not sure why he waited so long – said something about not knowing he needed to...' He studies the notebook. 'Said he thought everybody knew what had happened. I'm going to interview him again this afternoon, just to clear up some details, you know.' He nods towards me. 'I'm afraid this lad has said your daughter lost control of the pram because she was,' he reads, '"acting the fool, and messing about at the top of the ginnel."' He pauses. 'Er... "and seemed to give it a push, as though to see how fast it would go. But then couldn't catch it."'

He closes his notebook and slides it back into his pocket. 'The lad said that once she let go of the pram, because the ginnel was so steep, there was nothing she could do to stop it...' He waits to let us take in what he's just said.

I don't understand.

Angie won't look at me. Dad turns away, shaking his head. Mum moves away from me. I try to catch hold of her fingers, but she sits down with a flop onto the settee. She's crying.

'I wasn't... I didn't...' I stop, try to steady the quivering in my voice. 'Angie?'

She frowns, lifts her head a fraction. 'It's okay, Mand.' She comes to stand next to me, taking Mum's place. Takes hold of my hand. I try to shake off her fingers, but she holds firm. And then I know. Somehow Angie has got Stephen Birch to lie for her. To blame me.

I hate her.

I will always be blamed by everyone for what happened to Robert. Big gulps come out of my mouth in squeaky breaths.

'Mum?'

There's this twisty feeling inside me. I'm frightened. What will happen now? What will they do to me?

'Mum?'

She's got her face in her hands. Won't look at me.

'Mum, I didn't...'

The policeman closes his notebook and slides it back into his pocket. 'My condolences to you both...' He leaves the words drifting in the air.

There's another knock at the door. After a moment's hesitation Dad goes to answer.

The social services lady follows him back in and turns to the policeman. 'Can I have a word, please? In private.'

He goes red, pulls his shoulders back, runs his fingers around the inside of his collar, tugs at it. Then, nodding, follows her out to the hall.

My legs sort of crumble under me. I'm on the floor. Dad has gone over to the window and stands, staring out, his back all stiff. None of us say anything. We're all listening to the quiet words being said in the hall.

'Your sergeant said I was to meet you here, PC Radon.'

'Not what I was told, Miss Hudson.' He gives a small cough. 'I was told to pass the information on and that's what I've done.'

'With about as much tact as I've seen you show before in other circumstances. I should have been here. To support them. What's happened is the worst thing that can happen to any family. My greatest concern is for the younger sister.' I hear her sigh. 'And I hear the witness is a young person as well. I should have been there when you spoke to them.'

'There appears to have been some sort of breakdown in communication, Miss Hudson. I just do as I'm told. I still haven't told them that a post-mortem examination will need to be carried out and the report submitted.'

Mum cries out.

'Oh, for God's sake!' Dad shouts. He strides across the room. I hear the front door bang back against the wall. 'Get out. Both of you. Leave!'

'I'm sorry, Mr Marsden. I'm here to help—'

The policeman clears his throat. 'Mr Marsden, I'm sorry but we need to present all the information to the coroner. And we will need to re-interview Amanda—'

'Just go. Leave us alone.'

'Eric...'

Dad turns to look at Mum. His face is all crumpled. He's clenching and unclenching his hands.

'Eric, let Miss Hudson stay. Please.'

He moves quickly. Across the room to the kitchen. There's a draught of cold air and the back door crashes.

The policeman leaves without saying anything. The lady comes to sit on Dad's armchair.

'Girls, let me speak to Miss Hudson on my own.' Mum's voice is shaky.

I run upstairs. I don't wait to see what my sister does.

I don't know how long I've been lying on my bed, my pillow over my head, when there's a knock on my bedroom door. I sit up, rubbing at my eyes. They're itchy, sore.

'Mum?'

Miss Hudson peers round the door. 'Can I come in?'

I nod. I know she's only being polite. I have no choice.

We sit in silence for a minute or two. She holds my hand. I want to tell her what really happened. I will tell her. I will make her believe me. I pull in a deep breath...

But she speaks first. 'It will be all right, Amanda. Try not to worry.' She sounds like Mum does when she's pretending everything's okay. And I don't believe her, anymore than I believe Mum.

Chapter Twelve

Angie

'Why has he lied?' Mandy stands by the door of Angie's room.

'Who?' Angie doesn't look up from the history textbook she's pretending to read.

'Who do you think?'

Angie shrugs. 'Suppose he thought he was helping.' The intensity of her shame rises in her throat, choking her. Stephen has gone too far, saying Mandy was acting stupid at the top of the ginnel. It isn't what she asked him to say. But still she shrugs again.

'You know what happened. You know I wasn't messing about. If anybody was messing about it was you. You did it.' Mandy points at her.

Angie sees how her sister's fingers are shaking. She pats the bed.

'Mand, come and sit here.' She tries to stifle the pleading tone in her voice. 'Come on.'

'No.' Mandy's face is distorted with tears.

'Come on, our kid.' Angie has agonised over what to say. It's as though the guilt of what happened to her brother and of letting her sister take the blame has taken on a life of its own, like some horrible snake-like thing wrapping itself around inside her. She holds out her hand. 'Please...'

'Stephen Birch has lied. It's horrible. Why would he do that?' Angie watches Mandy's mouth slacken as something occurs to her. When she speaks, her words are slow. 'He's lied because he fancies you. That's why, isn't it? Did you know what he was going to do?' She takes a couple of steps into the room, her fists clenched.

'I didn't know he was going to say all that. Honest.'

'You did!'

Angie lets the textbook drop to the carpet, ready for whatever will happen next. 'Mand...'

'You knew!' She leaps on top of Angie, knees on her chest, taking clumps of hair in her hands and pulling, pulling. 'You knew.' She speaks with clenched teeth.

Angie squeezes her eyes tight against the pain. She'd thought she would fight back if this happened, but she doesn't; it's what she deserves.

It stops. The weight of her sister lifts. She opens her eyes. Mandy is standing by the bed, breathing heavily through flared nostrils.

They stare at one another for a long time. Angie wonders if what just happened has been heard downstairs.

'I hate you.' Mandy's voice holds no emotion. She doesn't look like her little sister anymore; she looks older.

'I'm sorry.'

'I hate you.'

Mandy doesn't look back when she leaves Angie's bedroom.

Chapter Thirteen

Mandy

I'm not going back to school. Miss Lestor has decided to expel me. Of course, she doesn't call it being expelled. She says I would 'be better having a new start' at a different school. The trouble is no one seems to know where.

I don't care. Everything's horrible. I don't go out. I don't come out of my room except when I'm made to for mealtimes. That's horrible as well. Dad doesn't talk, except for, 'Please pass the salt,' or something like that; Angie stares at me, and Mum keeps crying. I stay quiet and ask to leave the table as soon as I can. Even then Dad just grunts.

I don't know how I feel. Alone. And sad. And frightened.

I hear *her* come home. I hear her stop outside my bedroom door. I close my eyes, hold my breath, wish her to go away. I hate her.

I hear Dad come home.

Before long the shouting starts again. Well, not proper shouting; it's horrid talking, like being so cross they don't listen to what the other is saying. Like they talk as though they don't love one another anymore. Last night I had an awful thought: what if they're going to get divorced, same as Cecilia Atherton's mum and dad?

I shuffle on my hands and knees onto the landing. There's no sound from my sister's room. I slide halfway down the stairs, stopping where I can hear them. I've been doing this every evening.

Mum's crying. I hear him say, 'I don't want her here. I just can't forgive her, Eve. I've tried, I just can't.'

I know he means me. My stomach clenches.

'She's your daughter, Eric. How can you say that?'

'It's how I feel. I can't help it. I don't want to feel like this...'

I can hear him crying. I wrap my arms around my knees and rock. The stair carpet becomes all blurry when I hear Mum pleading.

'You can't leave her out of it, Eric. You can't...'

Suddenly, I know they're talking about my baby brother's funeral. My hands are all sweaty. I rub my palms on my pyjama front and move further down the stairs.

I'm sitting on the bottom stair, and I can hear them both crying.

'I'm sorry, Eve...'

'It's too cruel. Letting Angela be there and not...'

I don't wait to listen anymore. My stomach tightens again and I'm cold but sweating at the same time. I hold onto the banister, make myself stand, and pulling on the rail, drag myself up to the bathroom. I'm on my knees in front of the loo, heaving.

When it finishes I slide across the lino to the door and lock it. And curl up between the basin and the bath.

'Mandy? Are you in there, love?'

Eventually I say, 'Yes.'

'Can I come in?'

I wipe my nose on my pyjama sleeve. My hands are shaking. 'Yes.'

Mum sits next to me, shuffling up against the bath, and strokes my hair. It sets me off crying again.

'You heard Dad?'

I nod.

'I'm sorry, love. I know it's hard, you're so young, and it's all been so ... but try to—'

'Don't, Mum. Don't say it.' I manage to get the words out. 'He hates me.'

'He doesn't. He loves you. But he's hurting so much, he doesn't know what he's saying.' Mum stops stroking my hair and dabs at my eyes with her hanky.

42

'No! I heard him. You both hate me.'

'Oh, love.' She puts her face next to mine. 'We don't.'

'Nothing's going to be the same. Ever again.'

'No.' She kisses my forehead. 'No.'

We sit together for ages, hugging. But it changes nothing.

Chapter Fourteen

Mandy

It's been days now and Mum hasn't said anything else about the funeral. We're on our own in the house. I'm watching her from the kitchen door.

'I want to go to the funeral. Please, Mum?' I try hard not to cry. 'He was my brother as well.'

'I know, love.' When Mum turns toward me, she's sucking in her top lip. It's her thinking-what-to-say face. 'But it would be too difficult for you. You're too young—'

'That's not why. It's because of Dad, isn't it? It's because he doesn't want me there.'

She crosses the kitchen, pulls me to her. 'Try to understand, Mandy.'

'No!' I push myself away from her. 'I want to go.'

She catches hold of my hand between hers, leads me to one of the chairs at the table. Pulls her chair near to me. Waits a moment. And then she says the words that will change my life forever.

'I want to talk about something else, Mandy. Your dad and I, we've been talking ... and ... we think it best that you go away.'

'What? No! Why?'

'Just for a while ... maybe ... just until we all feel a little ... better...'

I can't take in what she's saying. 'You're sending me away?'

'No!' She squeezes my fingers. 'Not like that. We've talked to

Miss Hudson. You know, the nice social worker? She thinks it's the best thing for *you*.'

I don't answer.

'So, your dad and I have decided that you should go to stay with Auntie Barbara in Wales.'

'I don't want to.' I make myself talk as calmly as I can. The last thing I want is to leave my mum. The thought makes my heart thump until I think it's going to burst out of my chest.

'Just for a short while. Just until after the funeral...' She gives my hand a little shake, smiles at me. Smiles with her mouth, but not with her eyes. 'Perhaps a little longer. Just until everything is sorted out. Please, Mandy. Try to understand.'

I don't know what she means by *everything*. All I can think is that they are sending me away because I remind them too much of Robert. 'You just want me out of the way. Dad wants me gone.'

'No. It's not that. I'm ... we're ... thinking of you. It's just for a couple of weeks.'

'But *she* stays?'

'Angela? Well, yes. Because she'll have her exams soon.'

Because they think she hasn't done anything. That what happened to Robert is nothing to do with her.

I hate her more and more. And that gives me a nasty feeling inside me. A sad feeling.

Mum's waiting.

I want to argue. To shout. To say I won't go. Instead I hear myself say, 'You'd come to see me?'

'Of course.' She leans towards me, puts her forehead against mine. 'Of course I will. I'll miss you so much.'

I've lost. 'Do Auntie Barbara and Uncle Chris know?'

She nods.

'And they've said yes? They want me to stay with them? Just for a bit?'

'Of course they do; they love you.'

Not like Dad then.

'Okay,' I say, eventually. 'Okay. As long as you promise that you'll come to see me, I'll go.'

Chapter Fifteen

Angie

When Angie gets up on Saturday morning, Mandy has gone.

She doesn't understand at first. The house is strangely silent. Putting one foot on the stairs, she stops to listen. Nothing. No clatter of crockery in the kitchen, no voices, no aroma of coffee, Mum's essential initial hit of caffeine for the day. She glances at Mandy's bedroom door. It's closed, but that's nothing new these days. The treads creak slightly under her feet, and she feels the first tremor of nerves.

'Mum?'

Nothing. But even that isn't unusual, her mum seems to be in a world of her own since... Angie closes her mind to the image of the pram rattling down the narrow ginnel.

In the hallway, the post – three buff-coloured envelopes and a leaflet – is still on the mat. She pushes at them with her toes, listens again, glancing through the door to the living room, and walks slowly into the kitchen. No one in the garden. No note.

Taking a glass from the cupboard, Angie fills it with water and perches on the edge of the table. The quietness of the house is unnerving, contrasting with the muffled radio music from the neighbours' connecting wall. She looks up at the ceiling, considers running back upstairs to fling open her sister's bedroom door.

She hears the harsh sound of the key being pushed and turned in the lock of the front door. Her father stands back to let her mum step into the hall.

'Mum?' Her mother looks at her but says nothing. 'What is it? What's happened?' Angie puts the glass on the table. She's cold. 'Is

45

it Mandy?' Why does she ask that? Why should she think this strange feeling is anything to do with Mandy? Yet she knows it is.

All at once her mother moves, unbuttoning her coat and hanging it with a sharp movement on the hook of the stand. She walks past Angie to fill the kettle.

'Mandy's gone away for a bit.'

And Angie knows not to ask anything else.

Part Two

Chapter Sixteen

Mandy

I step off the train's only carriage into another world. Compared with Manchester station, its crowds and noise and smells, the platform here at Ponthallen, with hanging baskets filled with pink flowers, is small and empty. Well, almost empty.

'Here, petal. Here.'

Auntie Barbara waves. Her multi-coloured scarf around her hair flaps in the backdraught from the train. She's wearing matching culottes, an embroidered peasant blouse draped around her plump chest, and flat red flip-flops. I can see the scarlet toenails from here.

In contrast, Uncle Chris is in an old dark jumper and jeans.

I am so happy to see them. I wave back. I'm still waving as she gathers me in her arms, into the soft comfort of her chest.

'Hello, little one.' Uncle Chris strokes my head. 'Welcome to Ponthallen.'

'For as long as you like,' my aunt says, with emphasis.

Just two or three weeks, I want to say. But it might seem rude. I breathe in her scent: lily of the valley. It's how I bring her to mind, always have for as long as I can remember.

'Come on, Chris, let's get her back to the house.'

They lead me away from the station.

'Fancy seeing the sea on the way?' Uncle Chris loads my small bag into the back of an old blue Land Rover. He cocks one eyebrow at my aunt before looking at me.

'Please.'

'Good idea.'

We answer together, my aunt and me. It feels good.

It's only a few minutes before we're driving past the low wall that separates the beach from the road. I lean forward to gaze at the water shimmering silver in the sunlight. The tide is in, and the waves creep up to the shingle. The calmness of the sea comforts me.

'Oh, I'd forgotten...' is all I manage to say. When I lean back in my seat, I see they are smiling.

'Come on, then.' Auntie Barbara slaps her hands together. 'Home.'

They live in an old cobb cottage on a smallholding they've built up over the years. It's only a five-minute walk to the sea. We've been here on family holidays. This time, it's different; this time I'm on my own.

We bounce along the narrow lane, all squashed together on the front seat, with Auntie Barbara yelling, 'Yay!' every time we hit a pothole.

She has her arm around me, holding me close. For the first time in weeks, I feel safe. Loved.

'It'll all be okay,' she whispers in my ear.

I believe her. Why do I believe her? I don't know. But I do.

The first thing I hear when I jump out of the Land Rover onto the gravelled path at the side of the house is the muted clucking of hens.

'You have hens! I'd forgotten the hens!'

'We do. And lots of eggs.' My uncle nods towards the back of the house. 'Go and see if you like. But please, don't open the gate. We don't want them escaping.' He laughs.

I'm not sure why he laughs until I see them. They strut. Slowly. Very slowly, heads nodding. They don't run. There are two kinds. I count five who are a deep red, with dark red eyes and white legs, but there are more of the white ones with black tails and black in their wings and necks.

'They're Sussex hens.' Auntie Barbara rests her hand on my shoulder. 'Good layers.'

I don't know what she means. I glance up at her.

'We get lots of eggs from them. Want to go in the hen house?' She points to a long wooden building at the farthest end of the fenced-in square.

'Please.'

It's dusty inside the hut and quite dim. My aunt rummages around on a shelf. If I stand on tiptoe, I can see eggs on top of straw. When she hands one to me, it's still warm. I'm not sure I like it.

'You could have it for your tea?'

'Hmm...'

She laughs. 'Come on, then, let me show you to your room.'

My room. I love the sound of that.

We leave the hens, closing the tall mesh gate. 'To keep the fox out,' my aunt says. We follow Uncle Chris into the house where he's made tea for them and poured some lemonade for me.

'Homemade,' he says. I can tell he's quite proud of himself, so I make lots of appreciative noises as I drink.

It's been so long since I was here, I'd forgotten what the room I'll be sleeping in looked like. The walls are so thick that the windowsill is lovely and wide. I can sit and look out for miles over the fields behind the house.

'I like this room, Auntie Barb.' I put my arms around her middle. My hands don't meet at the back. She's lovely and squishy when I hug her. There's an odd feeling inside me, like I'm going to cry and laugh at the same time.

Aunt Barbara is younger than Mum. And, like me and Mum, she has ginger hair, but hers flows down her back. I think I'll ask Mum if I can grow mine when I get back home. I'm sad when I think of my mum. But she has promised she'll come to see me, even though I'll only be here two or three weeks. And she'll write as well. She promised.

I know my mum and aunt keep in touch by writing letters; they don't often see one another, with my aunt and uncle having the smallholding and Dad working and not keen on travelling to Wales anyway. Mum told me once she missed her sister.

I don't want to think about sisters. I won't think about sisters.

My aunt and uncle have never had any children of their own. I know it's wrong but I'm glad. There's no one here to get me into trouble, to tell lies about me. I have them all to myself in this lovely house. I pretend it's like a holiday.

Auntie Barbara pats me on the back. 'Would you like me to show you around the garden? We've done a lot on it since you were last here.'

'Please. I'd like that.' I take in one long sniff so I can breathe in her scent.

Chapter Seventeen

Mandy

Right at the back of the smallholding there are six rows of tall purple plants with silvery leaves. Auntie Barbara (she says her name is too much of a mouthful so I should call her Barb like Mum does) says it's called lavender. It smells like the scent one of my teachers used to use, but I didn't know what it was called before.

In front of the lavender rows are patches of all kinds of vegetables. Dad only grows potatoes and those beans on sticks. Auntie Barbara – Barb – says they sell the vegetables to people in the village, as well as the fruit. The fruit trees are separate, through a gate, next to the hens.

Barb says for us to sit on the bench in the orchard. She looks serious. Has she changed her mind and wants to send me back to Micklethwaite?

'Chris and I were talking earlier...' She takes hold of my hand. 'And I need to say something to you.'

This is it, I think. They've decided they don't want me here after all.

She says, 'I'll believe and try to understand anything you tell me.

But it must be true. You have to be honest, Mandy. Do you promise?'

I'm so relieved I just nod.

She breathes in so deeply I think her bust is going to pop out of her v-neck embroidered blouse. I think that even while I'm worrying what she's going to say. 'I want you to tell me what happened,' she says, at last. 'What really happened with your brother.'

I don't pretend not to understand. So I tell her.

She doesn't say anything when I stop. I wipe my eyes, blow my nose. Wait.

I've almost accepted that she doesn't believe me, when she gives a deep sigh and puts her arm around me.

'Thank you, Mandy.'

'You believe me?' There's a lightness inside me. My aunt believes me. Believes me without any questions.

'Of course. I said I would, didn't I?'

'You're crying. Why are you crying?'

'Because it makes me sad. That your baby brother died. That this had to happen to you. And that Angela hasn't had the courage to own up.'

I don't want her to talk about Angie; I don't want to think about her at all. So I don't like it when my aunt says, 'What do you feel about your sister? About what she's done?'

'I hate her.'

The words are out. Stark and cold. I don't care.

She tilts her head. It's almost a nod. Almost. 'And how does that make you feel?'

The breath I'm holding in comes out as a burst of noisy crying. When I stop, I shake my head. 'I don't know.'

'You do really, though, don't you?'

I shake my head. I wish she'd stop asking.

'I know if I fell out with your mum, I'd be very upset. I can't think of one thing that would make me hate her.'

'Even if she did what Angie did to our Robert? Just because she wanted to look clever in front of a lad? Even if Mum did to you what *she's* done to *me*? *Lied*. Got the lad to lie? Made Dad *hate* me? Made *this* happen?'

My aunt doesn't answer right away. Then she says, 'By *this*, do you mean having to come to stay with us for a while?'

I meant me taking the blame. 'No, I'm glad I'm here. I love it here.'

'So, something good has happened from something truly awful?'

I see my little brother's face.

'Let's leave that for now, eh?' Barb gives me a squeeze. 'There's something I want to ask you. Okay?'

'Okay.'

'Do you want me to talk to your mum? To tell her what you've told me?'

'She won't believe you.'

'She will.' She says it in such an unwavering voice, I almost believe her.

'I don't think it will make any difference.' I shrug. 'I think she'll want me to stay here until after...?'

'Yes, well, that's okay, isn't it? No use worrying about it, petal. Let's make the most of you being here.'

'Thank you, Aunt ... Barb.'

She laughs. It's a wobbly laugh, as if she feels as unhappy about everything as I do. 'I'm sure things will be all right in the end, Mandy. It just might take a little while.'

'Even with Dad?'

She doesn't hesitate. 'Yes. Even with your dad.'

We sit for a while. There's a bird singing on one of the branches of the tree.

'A blackbird,' says my aunt. 'Isn't that lovely?'

It is. I've never taken much notice of birds before. Hadn't thought about them at all, really.

There's a full moon that lights up my room and makes strange, shadowy shapes. The weird outlines of the things in the room don't frighten me. Dreams frighten me. Dad not liking me anymore frightens me. I'll never forget what happened to Robert and how he looked in his pram after ... after it happened. And that frightens me – that I'll never forget.

I like looking out at the sky. I think the moon has a smiley man's face. I wave at him. All around the moon are stars. I've never seen so many. They shine like white jewels.

I turn onto my side, and lift and shake the pillow to make it more comfy. There's something under it. A handkerchief. When I hold it to my nose, it smells of lily of the valley. A piece of paper drops from the folds. Scrambling out of bed, I go to sit on the windowsill, holding it up so the moonlight shines on the words.

Welcome to Ponthallen. Sleep tight. Love, Chris and Barb xx

Chapter Eighteen

Angie

By the end of the week, Angie is getting used to the bubble of silence that greets her whenever she enters a classroom or walks along a corridor. From the sideways glances, she knows Stephen Birch has bragged about what happened between them.

Has he said why? She doesn't know. But she knows she's the subject of the hot gossip going the rounds.

One morning in the English class, it isn't until the teacher comes in that she realises the desks on either side of her are empty. Looking around, she sees the other girls squashed two to each desk, two rows back.

'What's going on?' Miss Earnshaw glares at them. 'Move to your usual seats.'

They don't move.

'We'd rather not, Miss.'

'Don't be ridiculous. I said move.'

'We'd rather not sit next to that slag.'

The gasp is followed by stifled sniggers.

Angie waits. The mortification is unbearable. She's always been popular, never having any trouble making friends. She's taken it for granted all her life, unlike Mandy, whose self-doubt always holds her back. A wave of heat moves from her throat to her face. Grabbing her bag from the back of her chair, she stands. The chair crashes to the floor as she shoves her way past the teacher.

'Sorry.'

Flinging the door open she runs along the corridor, down the staircase to the front doors, faster and faster, out of the school to the school gates.

Her life is being blown apart.

She doesn't stop until she reaches home. She can't get the key in the door. Dry gasps burn her throat, the iron taste of blood in her mouth. She pounds on the glass panel.

'What the...?' Her mother staggers back when she opens the door, when Angie pushes past her. 'What is it? What's happened?'

'Leave me alone.' Angie stumbles up the stairs and into her room. She flings herself on the bed. 'Leave me alone,' she screams into her pillow.

Angie has decided she won't go back to school. Even Ben calling at the house to see if she's all right hasn't changed her mind. She refused to see him, shamed because he's obviously heard what had happened between her and Stephen Birch and she hates that.

Mandy still hasn't returned home. By eavesdropping, Angie's discovered her sister is staying with their aunt and uncle in Wales. To get her away from their father. She suspects he will never forgive Mandy. The thought makes her cold.

Her mother comes into her room and sits on the end of her bed. Angie grits her teeth, wishing she would just go away.

'Your dad and I need to know what happened in school, Angela.'

'Nothing. I've finished with that place.'

'For no reason? What about your A-levels?'

'When is Mandy coming back?'

Her mother doesn't answer, smooths out imaginary creases in her skirt.

Well, two can play at that game. Angie turns onto her stomach, her head resting on her folded arms. She hears her mother's sigh, feels her get off the bed.

'I know this is about your brother.' Angie hears the small catch in her mother's throat. 'But you can't hide away. It wasn't your fault. You can't let it affect your future. We will all miss Robert ... always. We won't forget him. I'm not telling you we'll forget him. Just that we can't go back –'

'I'm not going back to school.' Angela interrupts. 'Ever! So stop talking about it.'

'Please don't be rude.'

'Oh, good God!' She shoves her arms under the pillow and folds it over her head. 'Just go away, Mum. I've told you I'm not going back to school; I hate it. And anyway, there's only a few weeks before the end of term.'

'A few weeks that are important. And then it'll be your last year.' Mum moves one corner of the pillow, uncovering Angie's ear. 'If you don't do your A-levels, you'll miss out on university.'

'I won't, I'll study at home. You could arrange with Mrs Lestor for me to take the exams somewhere else.'

'No, you can't. And I won't.'

Angie moves her shoulders in an upward shrug. 'Won't be my fault then. If I don't get into uni. Will it?' She listens to her mother leave her bedroom, before burrowing her head into the pillow and screaming.

It's like winter, cold and wet. The wind moans through the edges of the window, where the frame sits uneven. In bed, Angie crosses her arms over her chest, hugging the anxiety inside her. She stares into the darkness, just as she has done most of the night. Floorboards creak every now and then, the door rattles slightly. Normal sounds.

But today is not normal. Today is Robert's funeral. Almost three weeks since that day... She won't go. They can't make her.

She wonders how Mandy is. If she knows it's today.

Chapter Nineteen

Mandy

When I wake up, it's cold. I have a horrid skin-prickling feeling all over my body and I stare into the dark, unable to move. I listen to my heart banging in my chest.

Yesterday was Robert's funeral. It rained hard all day here. Like 'stair rods', Mum once told me my Nanna Hall, her mum, used to say. Miserable. Just like winter again, which feels right. I don't know if it rained in Micklethwaite but I imagine it did.

And even though I'd wanted to be there, I'm glad I wasn't. I don't even care that *she* was allowed to be there.

I didn't get up yesterday. Barb kept coming to see me at first. But then she left me alone.

Chapter Twenty

Angie

Sometimes Angela thinks it might have been better to stay in school, if only to stop the whispering thoughts that fill her head. They echo around her bedroom, fill her dreams with shifting shadows. At least in school, the stupid gossiping would drown out the nightmare she's living in. Distract her from the guilt.

Ben hasn't called at the house again. None of her so-called friends have been near. The loneliness she's imposed on herself is almost unbearable. She needs to do something. But what?

Chapter Twenty-One

Mandy

I'm sitting on the wide windowsill looking out at the blue-grey hills in the far distance. Knowing Barb and Chris know the truth and still love me makes me feel better. They are spoiling me: taking me walks on the beach and through the woods just outside Ponthallen. Barb is making my favourite meals. Chris takes me around the smallholding, finding butterflies, teaching me the different kinds of bees, the different wildflowers. He likes to talk into this thing he carries around with him called a Dictaphone, for keeping records of the place, he says. Sometimes he lets me use it.

But even though I've felt safe since I came here, I've had bad dreams. I dream about Belinda who is ... was ... my best friend since infants. There wasn't a day we didn't play together. We used to pretend we were sisters. I miss her. I miss being part of her family. Does it bother her we're not friends anymore?

I'm beginning to worry about going back to Micklethwaite. What will I do if I see Belinda on our avenue? Or in the park with the other girls? What if they all turn their backs on me? Which school am I supposed to be going to? The nearest one is ten miles away in Oldfield. How will I get there?

I often wake Barb or Chris with my bad dreams, my screaming. I don't have a baby brother anymore. That thought always brings a hard lump in my throat that I can't swallow. Before long, now the funeral is over, Mum will either come or write, to say I can go home. I don't want to.

The blackbird flies down to a branch on the tree outside. Twisting its head, it flaps its wings, giving out a harsh clattering sound. Chris says that's its warning cry. Something's wrong. I know the feeling. I wish I could squawk and flap.

'May I come in, Mandy?'

Barb's peering around the door.

'Of course.' I blow my nose. 'The blackbird's upset by something. Look.'

Barb comes to sit by me. She glances at the bird. 'He's certainly making a noise.' When she looks back to me, she says, 'Are you all right? You've been awfully quiet today.'

I nibble on the skin at the side of my thumbnail. Should I tell her?

Everything has been so open here. I've been able to say how I feel, what I want to happen. But this isn't the same. What if they are counting the days till I go home?

'There is something. Come on. I can't help unless you tell me.'

The blackbird flies off.

I think what to say. She's waiting. 'I'm not sure I want to go back.'

'To Micklethwaite?'

I nod.

'You sure?'

'Yes.'

'You want to stay here?'

I nod again. I don't raise my eyes.

'Well, I guess we need to talk to you mum then, eh?'

After a rainy week it's beginning to feel like June again. The sky above the hills in the far distance holds only a few wispy clouds. I'm in my favourite place, on the windowsill in my bedroom. I'm watching the hens pecking at the ground. Charles, the cockerel, parades around, king of his world. I imagine I can smell the lavender in the air.

The blackbird is back on the branch of the tree outside. Chris says it had a nest in the hedge at the back of the allotment, but the babies have fledged. I wish I'd seen them. Perhaps next year.

60

I'm glad I'm here, but I miss Mum. Barb hasn't said if she's written to her yet. It's my birthday today – I'm fourteen – so I was hoping I'd get a card, but nothing came. Perhaps Monday.

'Mandy? Can you come downstairs, please, petal?'

Lunch is ready. I'm starving. But when I go into the kitchen, I see Chris standing by the back door. He's pulling his ear lobe. I've learned over the weeks, it's a sign he's a bit bothered by something.

'There's a visitor for you,' he says.

I follow the direction he's looking, to see Barb linking arms with Mum.

'Hello, love.' Mum's voice quivers, uncertain. 'Happy birthday.'

I fly into her arms. Yet, at the same time, I'm hoping she hasn't come to take me home.

Chapter Twenty-two

Mandy

We've had our dinner – Barb calls it lunch – all sitting at the wooden table in the front garden under the pergola, which is covered with cream and pink flowers. Meat pie and new potatoes from the garden, which I loved. And salad, which I didn't.

Now Mum and me walk between the rows of lavender. The heat of the sun has brought the scent out.

'Barb says you'd like to stay here?'

Does she sound sad? Or angry? I decide it's sad and feel a bit upset. 'I'm sorry, Mum. I just feel...' How do I feel?

She stops and takes hold of my shoulders.

'If that's what you want, love. You were very brave, coming here on your own. I know you didn't want to, and were frightened after what happened.'

I can't talk about that. I see my brother right away, so I interrupt her. 'Only because I didn't want to leave you, Mum. I love you.'

'I know.' Her eyes look all shiny. 'But I want what's best for you. And if you're happy here, then that's what I want too.'

A huge wave of relief washes inside me. She's letting me stay.

'Let's sit down for a minute, love. There's something else I need to say.'

There's a quivering in my tummy. We sit on the bench, surrounded by white roses. Mum leans over to sniff one. 'Mm, lovely. Barb always was the one for her garden.'

This isn't what Mum meant when she said she had something else to say. I fold my hands in my lap and sit very still.

'Your aunt has told me everything about what happened to your brother.'

I can't help starting.

She chews her bottom lip. 'I can't say I understand, but I respect what you did. I guess you had your own reasons for covering for Angie. I'm disappointed, no...' She bites again on her lip. 'I'm angry, that she hasn't owned up, let you take the blame. And that she got the Birch lad to lie for her. Neither of them should get away with what they've done.'

'You won't say anything though? You won't say anything to her ... or Dad?'

'Your dad should know, love. I don't think he'll ever get over what happened. But he should know the truth. Then he won't...'

'Hate me.'

'Oh, Mandy, love, he doesn't hate you.'

'He does.'

'But he shouldn't.' She hesitates. I wait. 'You're both his daughters. He shouldn't hate...'

Would he hate her? I'm not sure. I've always known she's his favourite.

'I'm happy here, Mum. Please don't tell Dad. He'll want me to go back. I don't want to go back...' I almost say home. But it's not my home. It stopped being my home that day. 'I don't want to go back to Micklethwaite, ever.'

62

I see the way she flinches when I say that and I'm sorry. But she needs to know. I couldn't stand living in the same house as my sister.

'If it's what you want, love...'

'It is.'

Nothing will ever be the same again.

'I don't belong in Micklethwaite anymore.'

'Oh, love, don't say—'

'It's true.'

'I'm not forcing you to come home with me, love.' She looks around the allotment. 'It's lovely here. And with the sea nearby...' She takes hold of my hand. 'I'm just so sorry I didn't listen to you. Didn't see what was really happening, Mandy.'

'It doesn't matter. Not now you know. Thank you, Mum, thanks for letting me stay here. But you will come and see me? Come and stay sometimes?'

'I'll come to see you when I can.'

'Just you?' I don't want her bringing Angie with her. Or Dad.

She sighs. Her eyes are sad. 'Just me.'

'Good.' I ignore the sigh and the sad look. It brings back what Barb said about sisters and I'm sorry that nothing will ever be the same between Angie and me. But it doesn't stop the anger. I've lost Dad because of her.

'Let's go tell Barb I'm staying,' I say, standing up. 'And hope she hasn't changed her mind and wants me to leave.' I giggle, but there's a little thread of fear that Barb might.

'Your aunt loves having you here.' Her eyes are glistening again but she smiles. 'Listen, let's have a look around Ponthallen before I go back. It's a long time since I saw the place. And let me buy you something for your room.'

'You don't have to do that, Mum.'

'I'd like to. Please.' She swallows. I hug her.

We've reached the hens and she stops to peer at them through the fence.

'The black ones with the bright red things on their heads are my favourite,' I say. 'Not so keen on the cockerel, though.' I point at Charles. He's strutting around, shaking his shiny black tail feathers. 'He chased me yesterday.' He lets out a great shriek.

'Goodness.' Mum covers her ears. We laugh. I think Charles is offended because he pecks at one of the hens before marching off to the other side of the pen.

I can see Barb peeping through the kitchen window. I wave. 'I'm stopping,' I shout, and laugh at the mock horror on her face as she holds her hands to her cheeks.

I'm happier than I've been for weeks.

Before Mum catches the train back, we go to the beach in Ponthallen. There are quite a few families around, with it being the weekend. We walk along the water's edge with our shoes off. My aunt's culottes, bright yellow and blue today, get wet on the hem but she doesn't seem to notice. Mum's taken off her cardigan and tied it around her neck over her matching pink jumper. She keeps her tights on, and I think how uncomfortable that must be with the sand in between the material and her toes. But she seems happy enough, just to be holding my hand and swinging our arms.

We don't say much. What needed to be said has been said.

We've been in nearly all the gift shops, and I've chosen two pictures: one a photo in a frame of the sea from the harbour, and a print of two girls on the beach with their backs to us. I'm not sure why I chose that. Mum also bought me an ornament of a rabbit dressed in clothes.

When she gets on the train, she asks if I'll try to forgive Angie. I shake my head. I can tell that upsets her but I won't lie. There's been too much of that. And if she thought I'd forgiven my sister, she might be tempted to bring her to Wales one day. And this is my home now. I don't want Angie here. Ever.

I watch the train disappear behind the tall trees and follow the curve of the line. I'm sorry she's gone. But I'm glad I'm staying.

Chapter Twenty-three

Mandy

Barb and I finish locking up the hens for the night. I sit at the kitchen table, drinking my cocoa and nibbling on a biscuit, trying to make it last while I summon up my courage. She catches me watching her.

'Okay, what is it?' She laughs. 'Come on, spit it out. You know I don't bite.'

'It's...' I wonder if it's wrong to think about this, let alone say the words. 'It's my name. Can I change my name? Be someone else?'

'What do you mean, petal?'

'I don't want to be called Amanda Marsden anymore. I want to change my name.'

'Oh...'

'I mean, if I can have a new start, like you said, I'd like a different name. I've thought of one.' I clear my throat. 'I've seen the name in a book I read. 'Lisa Brooks. I'd like to be known as Lisa Brooks.'

Barb understood straight away. So I'm registered at my new school, Ponthallen Comp, as Lisa Brooks. It surprises me how easy it is to be a different person.

And my bedroom is different now. Barb and me painted the walls and ceiling. It's all pale blue. Barb let me choose it. I have a new wardrobe for my clothes and a new bedside table for my books. The curtains, bedding and the cushion on the window seat all match – white with navy stars. I chose all those as well. I love this room.

But I still have bad dreams. It's like there are two of me. Neither is real. There's the girl whose name I've left behind. The girl Dad hates. And then there's the girl who's as much of a stranger to me as to anyone, even though I chose her name. Does Lisa Brooks like the same things: running, drawing, the colour blue, the same books? Or still hate maths and stupid cartoons?

Perhaps it will be better when I start school tomorrow.

Chris drops me off outside the school. I'm terrified. I stand to one side, waiting until nearly everybody has gone in. One or two of the girls, who look about my age, smile at me.

The school is smaller than at Micklethwaite and very sixties: blue panels between big windows; an entrance of five glass doors that open automatically. The whole building is surrounded by sports courts and playing fields. I hope they have a hockey team.

Everyone's being nice to me and I'm hanging around with a group of girls from my class at break time. I'm not saying much, and it's taking me all my time to tell what some of them are saying. I don't mind that they say the same about my accent. We laugh about it. I feel accepted.

Once or twice this morning, I've forgotten to answer to my new name, and I almost cry when one of the girls shows me a photo of her new baby brother. I think she thought I was just being soft, and that's okay.

I'm glad the uniform is blue and grey, unlike the maroon and white at Micklethwaite. One more thing to make my new life different. My new friends all wear their clothes in the same way: blouses, under their blazers, open at the neck, ties slightly loosened at the knot, skirts with the waistband rolled up once, so the hem is just above their knees when they stand. The only difference is the shoes. Five wear slip-ons but one girl, who's being really nice, and showing me around and explaining how things are done, wears lace-ups like me.

I'm going to go into the lavvies at lunchtime to alter my uniform, so I look the same.

I'm on my own. The others have gone into Ponthallen; it's only five minutes' walk and there are two cafés and a chip shop. I've not gone because Barb's packed a sandwich and some crisps and an apple for

66

me. I didn't know where to sit in the dining room because some were having school dinners and some who have their own lunches were sitting at two big round tables, one all boys, the other girls. So I'm outside sitting on a low wall on the edge of the playing field and thinking about everything that's happened this morning.

I think I really like the girl who wears the lace-up shoes. She's called Jayne Williams and, like me, has ginger hair. I won't say she might become my best friend; I'm not sure I'll even have a best friend again because you're supposed to tell them everything and I can't do that. I don't think I could trust anyone enough to tell them about my brother. Ever. But I like her, and that's enough for now, despite the lonely and uneasy feeling that lurks inside me. I wonder if that will ever go away.

Well, that's the first day over. Barb's picked me up.

'How did it go?' she asks, all casual-like. But I know she was worried this morning before I left because she gave me one of her special big hugs.

And I see her shoulders drop when I say, 'Great. I made some friends, I think.' I wait a few moments until she manoeuvres the Land Rover into the traffic outside the school. I see Jayne getting into an old black car with a lady at the wheel, and we wave at one another.

'The others went into Ponthallen at lunchtime,' I say.

'Is that what you want to do?' Barb takes her eyes off the road to glance at me and smile.

'Would that be okay?'

'Of course. I'm glad you're making friends. Tell you what, I'll give you money for the week, then you can choose what you have.' She changes her voice into a pretend seriousness. 'As long as it's nutritional and not junk food.'

'I promise,' I reply, in the same sort of voice.

We laugh. She reaches over and pats my arm. It's good.

Chapter Twenty-four

Angie

Angie carries her loneliness around with her like a heavy coat on her shoulders.

She misses Mandy, the closeness they sometimes shared, despite the rivalry and occasional jealousy. It was her sister's birthday last week. Angie wonders what she did, if she had a party. Probably not. Not this year. She would have liked to have sent her a card, but she knows it wouldn't have been welcome. Probably be ripped up.

When she can bear to think about *that* day and everything that happened afterwards, it's as though a crack appeared in the family, letting secrecy and bitterness creep in, making the rift between the four of them wider and wider. And it's her fault.

Sometimes she wishes that the truth would come out. When she looks in the mirror, she sees the downward line of her lips, the bleakness in her eyes, revealing the terrified stillness inside her. She's just waiting to be found out.

There is nothing else.

Since she came back from Wales, Mum is different. Angie catches her mother studying her, mouth slightly open, as if she's about to say something, and then stopping herself. Angie is sure something's happened. Or been said. But she's too scared to ask. She has no one to talk to, no one she can confide in.

There's only one thing she can do. Each night, lying on her side, clutching her knees against her chest, Angie agonises over it. But as far as she can see, there is only the one choice. The thought terrifies her, but it's the only answer.

Swinging her legs over the edge of the bed, Angie crosses her bedroom and opens the wardrobe, halting at each creak, listening for any noise from her parents' room. Taking out the rucksack she packed the night before, she drops it on her bed and dresses in jeans and jumper.

She's going to leave it all behind: the worried stares of her parents, the furtive conversations she only half hears, her father's bitterness about Mandy, the way she's destroyed his family, her mother's silence. Something happened in Wales, something was said. Her mother knows the truth.

So she needs to leave. Perhaps then, without her here, Mandy will feel able to come home.

She gets on the first bus of the day out of Micklethwaite. The only other occupants are weary shop and office workers on their way to Manchester.

Angie huddles on the back seat, hood pulled over her eyes, feet pressed down on the rucksack. There is no one she knows. And, as far as she can tell, no one to recognise her. It's as she wants it. Her escape from all the guilt.

Chapter Twenty-five

Lisa

The sun is peeping over the top of the hills. I pull my knees up to my chin and wrap my arms around them, thinking back to yesterday. Earlier in the week Jayne asked if I wanted to go to her house after school to catch up on the reading list for English, which is different from the list at Micklethwaite. There, we were told it would be the *Strange Case of Dr Jekyll and Mr Hyde* and *Much Ado About Nothing*. Mum had already bought the books to bring with me, and I'd read them, determined to be ready, whichever school I finished up at. But Ponthallen have chosen *Pride and Prejudice* and *Antony and Cleopatra*. Jayne's given me all her notes and I have all the summer holidays to catch up. With her help.

She lives in a big shabby barn of a house, all beams and old furniture, but her bedroom is small and cosy, like mine at Barb's, with loads of book shelves and boxes of jigsaws. I've never been interested in jigsaws but, to please her, we sat and did one with a picture of Black Beauty. Jayne's mad on horses, apparently, but has no chance of ever having one; her mum and dad aren't well off. Bit like Barb and Chris, which cheers me up, because it makes Jayne and me even more the same. And she had a bottle of Corona Cherryvale that we drank out of, and two huge bags of Fruit Pastilles and Cheery Lips that she told me to help myself to.

We had sausage and mash and peas for tea, sitting at the kitchen table with her mum. The floor was stone-flagged with rugs everywhere, but there was an old sort of built-in oven that kept the kitchen warm.

I like her mum, she's small and plump and jolly. And she said I could come to tea anytime. I'm not sure about her dad, who is a very big man. Cheerful. Just like Dad used to be.

My blackbird is on the branch of the tree outside again. He's singing and I'm sure he's looking at me with his little beady yellow eye. We stare at one another.

'Hello, Mr Blackbird.' I attempt to whistle. He flies away. I don't blame him. He's free to do as he likes, with no worries. No guilt.

Chapter Twenty-six

Angie

At Manchester Piccadilly bus station, Angie hitches her rucksack onto her back and, her head lowered, follows the other passengers through the stands lined by the bright orange buses spewing out exhaust fumes, engines rumbling.

Crossing Piccadilly Gardens, barely noticing the flower beds filled with white astilbes and bright yellow marigolds, Angie wonders what her mum and dad will think when they discover she's left. Will they realise she's gone for good? Last night, she thought it would serve them right to have to worry about her. But now remorse, knowing they will be devastated, mixes with a swell of panic; she's also hurting herself. She thought she would soon get a job in one of the stores, find a bedsit, but reality is kicking in. Manchester's a big place and she hasn't a clue where to start looking for either.

Taking a deep breath, she weaves her way around people, leaves the gardens onto Market Street. It's been some months since she last came to Manchester: an outing with a group of friends, exploring the underground market for bits of tat and cheap clothes, before going to the Gaumont to watch *The Sound of Music*. Angie had thought the film a bit soppy but went along with what most of them had wanted. Just being in the city was an exciting novelty. And safe.

But safe isn't what she's feeling right now. Her eyes smart when she thinks how easily those friends shunned her. How lonely she's felt, in school and at home. Could it have been any worse if she'd owned up to what she'd done? She brushes at the tears with the back of her hand, stopping to stare blindly at the furniture in Kendals' window, conscious of the flow of people behind her, all with somewhere to be. She's scared.

But she has to follow her plan: find a job and somewhere to stay. She's seen this programme on the telly called *Take Three Girls,* about girls clubbing together to rent a flat. Why couldn't that be her? The idea sounded simple enough, but now unease swills around in her stomach. She allows herself to drift with the crowd into the market. Perhaps she should first ask for some sort of temporary job.

Tucking herself by the side of the first stall, where the savoury aroma of fresh bread, meat pies and warm fat is filling the air, Angie swallows, already hungry. But she must be careful with her money, and it's too early to eat the tuna sandwich she packed in her rucksack.

One of the two women behind the counter, making bacon sandwiches for the growing queue, glances towards her.

'Sorry, love, we've nowt to give away yet. End of the day, okay? Come back then.'

'No, I don't want anything ... well, not to eat, anyway.'

Embarrassed, Angie shifts her rucksack from one shoulder to the other. 'I'm looking for a job and I thought you looked busy. I just wondered if you needed any help?'

'No, sorry, love. Can't afford to pay anyone. Times are 'ard. Try the fish stall. I think they've just lost someone.' She straightened up, one eyebrow lifted, a smile hovering on her mouth. 'If you think you can 'andle wet, cold, slimy fish.'

'Thanks.' Angie ignores the grinning nudge the one woman gives the other. 'I'll try there then.'

Overhead fluorescent lights flicker – white flashes that make her blink. She pushes her way through the lines of stalls towards the smell of fish.

It's the same answer, there, and at every other stall she asks; no one is hiring. Leaving the market, Angie stops by the bakery stall, thanks the woman for her suggestion.

'You got taken on, then?'

'No, but thank you anyway, for your help.'

'No probs. You just come into town, then?'

'This morning, yes.'

'Where're you staying?'

Angie hesitates. 'Haven't decided...'

''Ave you got money for a B and B?'

'Yes.'

The woman sees her uncertainty. She studies Angie. 'Okay. But if not, don't go to the hostel on Mount Street; you get real rough sorts there. Try the charity one on Top Chapel Lane. It's run by some friends of mine.' She reaches under the counter and rummages in her bag. ''Ere, I'll write down directions.'

Glancing at the other woman, she takes a meat pie from the warming cabinet and drops it into a bag. ''Ave this.' She hands it to Angie. 'An' look after yourself.'

The gesture fills Angie with humiliation and gratitude. Her cheeks burn. 'Thanks ... you don't need ... you shouldn't, er...'

'Nancy. The name's Nancy. And no worries, it's one that fell on

72

the floor.' She cackles with laughter, seeing the dismay on Angie's face. 'Only joking, love. Go on with you, and mind what I said, the Top Chapel Lane hostel. It's your best bet.'

In Debenhams, Angie munches on the last of the pie, lingering by the cosmetic counter and trying the samples of lipsticks with a sweep of the colour on the back of her hand. She's hoping to be offered a makeover by the skinny saleswoman dressed in black, her hair swept back into a tight French pleat. But when she turns to look at Angie, taking in the pie, her denim jacket, overstuffed rucksack and trainers, the woman's expression is contemptuous. Angie glares at her and moves away.

By the time Angie finds the hostel on Top Chapel Lane, it's full for the night. The man in the reception area suggests another place to stay, but when she gets there, they're not taking in any more people either. Rising alarm churns inside her. She's sent to another two hostels before giving in to the inevitable and, not knowing what else to do, she wanders back to the shopping centre. The stores are closed but the windows are still lit and there are still people around. They pass her, lost in their own worlds.

Chapter Twenty-seven

Lisa

When Barb is feeding the hens and Chris collecting the eggs, I overhear them talking. It's about Angie. She's run away from home. Barb says Mum is going out of her mind, but Dad won't call the police. Not yet. He says she's looking for attention. Typical of Dad: don't make a fuss. Even when it's his favourite daughter who's missing.

I'm not sure what to do. Do I tell Barb I've heard what they've said?

I don't know how I feel.

Chapter Twenty-eight

Angie

There's someone lying next to Angie in the shop doorway. She lifts her head, opens her eyes. It's still dark and it's raining. The ground under her is cold and hard. Her hips ache and the rucksack is digging into her neck.

Whoever is next to her groans, snorts, shuffles closer and flings a heavy arm across her chest.

'Get off! Get away from me.' She jumps up and stumbles from the doorway.

The man curls up tighter, coughs. Beer fumes and a fetid odour of sweat and unwashed clothes. She curls her lip in disgust. But when she sniffs her jacket, she realises that, after three nights sleeping rough, she smells the same.

Grabbing her rucksack and pulling her hood over her head, she hobbles along the street. Her trainers are still wet from yesterday's rain. They're beginning to rub the back of her heel and they make an odd squelching noise as she walks. It's loud in the early morning silence. Abuse is thrown at her from hunched forms under sleeping bags and layers of cardboard as she passes.

The tremor in Angie's throat threatens to escape as a whimper. Wrapping her arms around her rucksack, she holds it close to her chest. At the next empty doorway, she sits, pressing her back against the wall and rocks from side to side. Desperation is filling the hollowed-out sensation inside her. When she pushes her sleeve up to check the time, she stops, unable to move. Her watch has gone. Sometime over the last few hours, it's been stolen. Someone has unfastened the strap and taken her watch.

The idea of a stranger touching her without her knowing fills her with horror. What else had they done? Would she know? She doesn't know she's screaming, until she takes a breath.

'What's the matter, miss? Come on now, you can't do that.'

It feels good to scream.

'If you don't stop, I'll have to arrest you for disturbing the peace.'

The policeman's threat makes her laugh: at least she'd have a roof over her. But when he takes hold of her arm and gets her to her feet, she makes herself calm down.

'Sorry. I'm sorry. Okay?'

'How old are you?' The terse question holds a glimmer of compassion. 'What are you doing here in this state? I think you'd better come with me, miss. Get you checked out. Yeah?'

'No. I'm fine. Honest.'

She's scared he'll make her go back home. She won't go back. She shifts her arm, taking him by surprise. Freed, Angie runs, pushing past people.

He shouts, but she doesn't stop. Not until she's streets away. Her breath comes in gasps and her throat is burning. In the entrance of the underground market, she stumbles to a halt, her hands on her knees, dragging air into her lungs.

'You again!'

Still bending over, Angie shakes her head. 'I'll go.'

'It's me, Nancy. You look bloody awful. I'm guessing you didn't get in at the shelter. 'Ang on.'

Angie slumps against the wall. Hears some rustling.

''Ere.' A bag is thrust into Angie's hand. 'It's only bread and marg. It'll be a while before the ovens heat up. But it's something to fill your belly.' Nancy glances up at the enormous clock hung high on the outside wall of the hall. 'Now you'd better go. It's nine o'clock, nearly time for the market superintendent to unlock this place and do his morning round. We're not allowed to be open to the public yet.'

Not knowing what else to do, Angie walks slowly to Piccadilly Gardens, nibbling on the bread, making it last. She's trying to eke out her money; yesterday the only thing she ate all day was a bag of chips.

The benches are already crowded with people chatting, drinking coffee from paper cups, reading newspapers. She finds a small space on the end of one and balances on it, ignoring the irritated glance from the elegant, green-suited woman next to her, who is smoking, her lips pursed.

The woman shifts, slightly turning her back on Angie. It gives her more room to place her rucksack on the ground between her feet.

'Hiya.'

Angie starts. She looks around at the girl standing behind the bench. She's slender and dressed in flared black jeans and a tight black polo neck top. 'I just got this in the market.' From the bag on her shoulder, she pulls out a purple-and-black-check miniskirt. 'Great innit?' She grins 'Only two quid.'

'Yeah.' Angie forces a smile.

'I know. I gorrit for you.'

'Bought it for me? Why?'

'I didn't say I bought it.' The girl gives a shout of laughter. ''Ere, nudge up.' She squeezes onto the bench next to Angie.

'Don't mind me!' The woman stands, glares at them, drops her cigarette onto the ground and grinds the sole of one black stiletto shoe onto it.

'We won't.' Without taking a breath, the girl says, 'I'm Tracy.' Nodding at the woman striding away, she adds, 'Snotty cow.' She prods Angie with her finger.

Thrilled as she is with this cheerful offer of friendship, Angie says, 'I can't take the skirt, you know.'

'Why not? It's free, and I don't want it. I gorrit for you.' Tracy looks down at the rucksack. 'Holiday or runaway?' That snort of laughter again. 'I'm guessing...?'

'Just got here.'

'Naw, I saw you hanging around yesterday. You looked a bit lost...'

A sudden pinch of caution makes Angie say, 'I'm fine.'

'Course you are. But, guessing again – got nowhere to kip?' The girl folds the skirt and pushes it onto Angie's lap. 'Here. And you can doss down with me if you like? Till you find a place of your own? I share with a couple of other girls.' She pauses. 'Yeah?'

'I don't know...'

'Your choice.' She stands.

'Oh, why not!' Angie ignores her niggle of fear. 'Okay. What the hell!' She's trying to sound nonchalant. She's on her own now, it's up to her what decisions she makes. 'Thanks.'

'We can do a bit more...' Tracy gestures in the air with her forefingers. '*Shopping*. Or I can take you there now?'

'I don't mind.' Angie only just stops herself saying that a bed and a bath would be good.

'Come on, then.' Tracy holds her at arm's length, her head to one side. 'Oh, bugger it, let's have some fun first. Kit you out a bit. Then I'll show you our place.' Linking arms with Angie, she adds, 'The girls will love you.'

Chapter Twenty-nine

Lisa

I'm watching a man dragging a screaming boy along the pavement so fast his little legs are barely touching the ground. It looks as if he might pull the child's arm out of its socket.

'No! Mummy?' The child is looking back over his shoulder. 'Mummy!'

They're coming towards me. I look up and down the street. There's no one else around, nothing's moving, no traffic. Just one old car parked further along. I freeze. Should I do something? But I'm only fourteen and perhaps the man's the boy's father.

But something's wrong, I can feel it.

'Is everything okay?' My voice wobbles.

The man stops at a car and opens the back door. He sees me looking at him, and glares. He jerks the arm of the child. The action swings the boy forward and he screams louder. 'Mummy.'

I don't know why I'm doing this; I run towards the car.

'Hey,' I shout. 'What's happening? Why is he crying like that?' When the man scowls at me, I'm scared. I stop a few feet away. 'Why is he crying like that?' I repeat, quieter now I'm so close to them.

He grabs hold of the boy under his arms and tries to lift him into the car, but the child is squirming and kicking, his face all screwed up in panic and fear.

'Mummy, Mummy.' His voice is hoarse. 'I want my mummy.'

'No. Please.' I move closer, try to make myself heard. 'He doesn't want to get in.' This is all wrong. I wish an adult would come to help. But there is no one. Just me. 'Can I…?'

'I'm his dad.' The man's mouth twists into a sort of weird grin. 'He's only having a tantrum.' He nods at me. 'No need to worry, missy. Run along.'

'I could help…'

'Look, I'm taking him home. I'm taking him to his mum.'

The little boy suddenly stops fighting. His breath comes in shudders but he's quiet. He looks over his shoulder at the man, then at me.

'I don't believe you.' I hear myself say the words. I hear how calm I sound. But my heart is trying to burst out of my chest. 'I think you're lying. I don't think you're his dad.'

'Sod off. Mind your own business, interfering little bitch.'

'This isn't right.' I know I must do something. I push into the space between the man and the door. The man smells strange, musty like the inside of the hen house at Barb's. I drop to my knees and wrap my arms around the child's waist. When the boy looks at me, his eyes are huge. I can see my reflection in the pupils.

'It's okay,' I say, even as the man starts thumping my back and shoulders. 'It's okay, I've got you.' The man grabs my hands, trying to prise my fingers away. His nails are dirty and dig into my skin.

'Stop it,' I pant, wincing with the pain. But I won't give in. 'Let go of me!'

He kicks me so hard I fall over onto my bum. But I'm still holding on to the little boy and I pull him close, scrambling to my feet. I stumble into a run. I'm running as fast as I can towards the end of the street where I can see traffic and people passing.

'Help! Help!' I yell as loud as I can, clutching hold of the boy. He's sobbing, his face hot and wet against my neck. But he's heavy, he's slipping through my arms. I hear a deep roar of an engine, a squeal of brakes. When I glance over my shoulder, the old car is driving away.

'Help! Help us. The man in that car tried to take this little boy.'

Faces turn towards us. A woman is running. She's shouting. People are following her. Then there's a swell of noise around us, voices loud, asking questions I can't hear. The little boy is pulled away from me, despite my efforts to hold on to him. Hands grasp my arms. Rough fingers pinch. Shake me. All I can see are angry faces.

Chapter Thirty

Angie

Angie has lost track of how many streets Tracy has hurried her along. The terraced houses all look the same. Closed doors. Boarded up windows. She wouldn't know how to find her way back to Piccadilly Gardens. What she does know is how tired she is. How grubby. How hungry.

She's following Tracy so closely that when the girl stops in front of an end house, she bumps into her. 'Sorry, I didn't...'

'Here we are.' Tracy squeezes Angie's arm. 'Home from home.' Her giggle is high-pitched.

The door is opened by a tall man wearing a dark duffle coat. He pulls the hood over his head and shoves past them without speaking.

Angie looks inside and knows, deep inside her, if she goes into this house something terrible will happen to her. And there'll be no going back.

'I'm sorry. I shouldn't...'

'Oh, don't worry about him. Boyfriend of one of the girls.' Tracy pushes Angie toward the uncarpeted flight of stairs in the hall. She closes the door and flips a light switch. Angie sees the flaking plaster on the pale green walls, the bare lightbulb, fly-speckled. Tracy presses her knuckle into Angie's spine. 'Go on, it's okay. You can have first go in the bath. Bet you're ready for a bath, eh?'

Two girls stare down from the landing.

'Who's this?' one of them asks. She wears a loose flimsy dressing gown. Black bra and knickers reveal an almost skeletal figure.

'New girl.'

It's all Tracy says, but with those two words Angie knows what she's let herself be led into. Faltering on the stairs, she half turns. 'I should...'

'You should ... what? Go back to another night on the streets, another night of being hungry?'

From behind one of the bedroom doors, she can hear muffled grunts, a small cry.

'Yes. No...'

Another girl pushes past the two who are watching. Her thin legs are bare but she's wearing a silver tracksuit top that she pulls close and zips up. When she speaks, it's with a broad Scottish accent.

'She okay? On her own?'

'Yeah. Just arrived.' Tracy stands next to Angie, puts her arm casually across her shoulder. 'She's good, aren't you, pet?'

'I don't...' Angie is desperate to get out of this house, but the girls are crowding around her now, smiling, ushering her along the landing.

'I'm Vanessa. You can share with me,' the girl who hasn't spoken before says. 'There's a spare bed in my room.' She's tiny with long black hair and huge eyes. She smiles, oblivious to Angie's fear. 'Here.' She leads her into a small square room with two single beds in the corners.

'I don't know...'

'We watch out for each other, keep one another safe.' Obviously trying to be reassuring, Vanessa continues, 'It'll be lovely to have someone to share with.'

'I can't.... Tracy?'

Angie's trapped. The three girls crowd her.

'You're not thick. You must have known?'

'No! I mean, sort of...'

'If you don't like it, go back to where you came from.' Tracy shrugs, her stare hard. 'We're not forcing anything on you. Up to you...'

'But you need to know,' the Scottish girl interrupts, 'we all pay our way. If you decide to stay, we expect you to help out with the rent and what-have-you.'

She stops, as a man appears at the top of the stairs. She lifts her chin, jerks her head towards an open door and watches him go through it, before fixing her gaze back on Angie. 'You pay your way. How you do that is up to you.'

Angie looks at them, one by one. What choice does she have?

'I'll stay.'

Chapter Thirty-one

Lisa

'What you did was very brave.'

Barb has her arm around me. I can't stop shaking and my legs are like jelly when we walk out of the police station on Templeworth Road. I'm so glad to be in the fresh air.

'And very foolish,' Chris added. 'But we're both very proud of you.'

'I want to go home.'

All those people had thought I'd taken the little boy from his mother. Remembering how they all crowded round me makes my insides all jittery. It wasn't until the police arrived that they stopped prodding and shouting at me.

'Can we? Can we just go home? Please?' I see they're upset. 'I'm sorry I worried you.'

'You haven't. We only want you to be safe.' Chris's smile looks forced, so I know they've been worried. Looking at his watch, he adds, 'It's six o'clock!' I'm surprised by how long we've been in the police station. 'Fish and chips? Let's see how much more they cost in this new daft money the government has inflicted on us, eh?'

Barb and me give a little cheer. We're all pretending today hasn't been too bad.

'We'll get them on the way home. And later, I think, we should let your mum know what a wonderful daughter she has.'

The way Barb's saying it tells me it's a question, so I jump in. 'Oh no, she mustn't know; she'll only worry. And she has enough to worry about.' My aunt and uncle exchange glances. 'I know,' I say. 'I know Angela has run away.' I want to ask if there's any news of her, but something stops me; if I ask, if I show I'm mithered, then they might expect me to go back to Micklethwaite. And I'm not going back there, ever again.

Chapter Thirty-two

Angie

There was a moment when Angie had a chance to change her life: that first time she stepped through the door of that house, that first night, that first week, that first time, that first man…

But she didn't.

Chapter Thirty-three

Lisa

That day with the little boy, I knew I'd never have a choice if I saw a child in distress. And I knew what I wanted to do with my life.

Part Three

Chapter Thirty-four

July 1977
Lisa age twenty-one

Today has been one of the happiest of my life. I must savour every moment. I've graduated; I've got my degree in social work for child welfare. First class. Everything, all the hard work, the self-doubt, disappeared when I saw the proud faces of Barb, Chris and Mum. Yes, Mum made the journey from Micklethwaite. I didn't ask where Dad was when she stepped off the train. I'm glad he's not here. I push away the quick thought that he doesn't care.

The three of them have gone back to Ponthallen. I could tell Chris was itching to get back. Ever since all those power cuts three years ago, and even though they bought a generator, he frets about the heating in the greenhouses and the lights outside to keep the dreaded fox away from the hens.

And even though I've enjoyed living in Cardiff, I'll be glad to go home as well. I've got an interview lined up with the social services committee in Ponthallen. I'm keeping my fingers crossed, even though my insides flip when I think about it.

I can't stop going over everything that's happened today. Next to me, my old friend, Jayne, snores in her sleeping bag. I'm grateful that she stayed for my last evening in the house.

Today has been wonderful, but for one uncomfortable moment with Mum. Only a few words, but I can't shake them off. She'd looked at me with a wistful sadness. I knew she was weighing up whether to ask me a question. And I knew I didn't want her to. It was selfish of me, but I hadn't wanted my day spoiled.

'Have you heard anything from Angie?' Mum sat forward and twisted her fingers together, glanced at Barb and Chris, who were chatting to some of the tutors. I wondered if they'd decided she should ask this.

'No, I haven't, Mum.' I wanted to say I hoped I never would.

'If I just knew she was all right, you know?' Mum paused. 'Just to settle my mind, you know. I keep thinking – hoping she's okay...' She seems to want reassurance. I'd none to give. 'How would I know if she wasn't?' Her voice trembled. 'If she was...'

The unspoken word hung between us. We wouldn't know if Angie was still alive. I felt an unexpected desolation. I nodded. At the same time, I couldn't forget that my sister robbed me of any proper relationship with my parents.

Being a parent must be so complex; whatever a child had done, there must still be love. Not that I'd ever know. I decided long ago I'd never have children.

I just hugged her. 'I'm sure she'll turn up like a bad penny,' I said, my tone light but firm enough to let Mum know I didn't want to talk about it.

She nodded and patted my hand.

'It's been such a lovely day.' Forcing a smile, she went to join the others.

Leaving me guilt-ridden.

I need to sleep but my head is spinning from that last glass of Cinzano and lemonade and the plaintive notes of Dylan's *Mr Tambourine Man* that one of the other girls living here keeps playing on her cassette player. I can still hear it. Even above Jayne's snoring!

Chapter Thirty-five

July 1977
Angie age twenty-four

'If you don't stop pawing me, I'm leaving.' Angie digs her nails into the man's hand.

'I've paid for you.'

'And you've had more than your money's worth, Jack. I'm telling you, you try to stick your hand inside my top once more and I'm off.'

'Aw, Angie, come on, be a sport.' His words are slurred. He leans against her. 'Be kind. Just a little feel?' His fingers tap a rhythm from her waist to her breast and he giggles. 'Lovely tits.'

Angie pushes him away and stands. He slides down on the leather settee until he's almost horizontal. She doesn't need this.

Being an escort is undeniably preferable to what she had to do in the early days. And her apartment in Manchester is a thousand times better than that first house she shared with those girls when she first arrived. Girls, now women, that she hasn't seen in four years. But this is humiliating in front of all these people.

Jack is struggling to get to his feet. Angie moves away from him. She's leaving. And yet she feels a tinge of regret. When she was booked for tonight, she'd looked forward to it; this is just the kind of place she loves to be seen at. The reception room of the hotel is ultra-chic: crystal chandeliers, floor-to-ceiling windows draped with plush red curtains, the floor a highly polished veneer. Classy.

The room is crowded with men in dinner suits and bow ties, the women dressed like Angie in glamorous evening wear. In her figure-hugging but elegant silver gown, her long hair softly waved to fall to her shoulders, and her immaculate make-up, she knows she fits in. She sees the open admiration of the men, the speculative stares from the women. She's used to it. She knows that the hours in the gym, the expertise she's learned with cosmetics and hairstyles, have paid off.

No one would know her profession. Her carefully cultivated story of herself as a PA to the sales executive in a flourishing interior design firm is totally believable.

But Jack's behaviour is attracting unwelcome interest. Swaying, he grabs her arm. 'I've paid for you.'

Angie tries to shake him away. 'Let go. Please.'

'All right here?' An impeccably suited man is by her side, his head tilted to one side. 'May I help at all?' He has an air of authority.

And Angie knows him. The sudden shock of seeing Stephen Birch makes her catch her breath. His deep grey eyes hold a steely purpose. He reaches out his hand to Jack. 'Everything okay, old chap?' When Jack clumsily returns the handshake, Stephen doesn't let go. He turns and clicks his fingers towards a burly man nearby. 'Time to leave, I think.'

'You can't tell me when to leave.'

'I can. This is my show. A gesture of appreciation to all my business acquaintances and employees over the last year. Remind me, which firm are you representing?'

A slow wave of red covers Jack's face. 'I... I...' He shakes his head. Grins sheepishly.

'I thought so. Definitely time to go.'

Angie needs to go as well. As quickly as possible. Even though she looks nothing like the girl who first came to Manchester, she can't chance Stephen Birch recognising her.

'I'm sorry,' she says quietly. Over the years she has smoothed out her northern accent, lost the broad vowels, but she knows the tone of her voice hasn't changed very much.

'No, please stay. I insist.' He rests his fingers on her arm, watching the security man unobtrusively lead Jack out. He gives a grunt of satisfaction. 'Good. Let me introduce myself. Stephen Birch.' When he looks directly at her, his expression changes from courtesy to confusion.

Angie turns to pick up her stole. Sliding her eyes sideways, she sees Jack shove the man's hand off when they reach the hotel entrance, wave his arms in the air, and glare at her. 'I'm sorry, I had no idea—'

'And I'm sorry to interfere,' Stephen Birch interrupts. 'But your friend looks worse for wear, and I presumed you needed rescuing. I hope I wasn't wrong, Miss...?' His voice suddenly uncertain.

Angie avoids the question. 'No, thank you. And I don't know him that well. Business acquaintance really...' She just wants to escape.

'Let me get you a drink?' He dips his head to get a better look at her face.

'No. Honestly, this is so embarrassing.' She wraps the stole around her, keeps her face turned down.

'I insist.' Stephen summons a waiter. 'What may I order for you? Er...?'

'Angela.' Damn. She should have lied. Given another name.

'Angela.' Seconds pass before he gives a shout of laughter that draws curious glances in their direction. 'Angie Marsden! I knew it.' He grins, a mouth-wide-open grin that shows perfect white teeth. 'Well, good God! Bloody hell, you've changed...'

'Well, good God, Stephen Birch, it is over seven years, just in case you've forgotten.' Panic and annoyance make her curt. 'Now, if you'll excuse me, I apologise again for gate-crashing your party...' All she wants is to get away.

'No. Please. Sorry, that came out all wrong. I was just so surprised. What I should have said was that you look stunning. Abso-bloody-lutely drop-dead gorgeous.'

Stephen takes hold of her elbow, leads her firmly towards a table in the corner and waits until she sits down before sitting next to her. 'So?' He studies her, ignoring the waiter, who discreetly places a bottle of white wine and two glasses in front of them. 'What have you been doing with yourself?' He touches the bottle. 'Dry white wine?'

How does she get out of this? 'I shouldn't. Really.'

'Oh, come on. I haven't seen you for ages. For old times?'

91

Angie winces. 'Old times' sake?' Has he got a clue what he's just said?

He pours the wine into her glass. Tilting the bottle over his, he pauses. 'I knew you'd left Micklethwaite. I asked around but no one knew where. Or why. I always wondered...' He shrugs. 'Well, I guessed...' He fills his glass and places the bottle back on the tray. 'You don't ever go back?'

'No.' He's playing games with her. Her anger grows. 'You must know I don't.' She half-rises in the chair. 'I'm leaving now. I'd be grateful if you told no one in Micklethwaite that you've seen me. I left that life behind a long time ago. By choice.'

This time he lets her take a few steps before saying, 'I'd like to see you again, Angela ... Angie ... if you'd agree?'

'I don't think that would be a good idea. I have a new life now.'

'Well, at least let me get my chauffeur to drive you home.'

'No, I'll be fine. I'll get a taxi.'

'Nonsense. Don't be daft. I insist.'

Only when she steps out of the chauffeured Jaguar at her apartment does she realise that, by allowing herself to be taken home in his car, she has revealed her address. In the dark, restless night that follows, she knows that if Stephen Birch is the same as he was as a boy, he'll make sure he gets his own way. He'll take what he wants. Her life is going to change.

Chapter Thirty-six

Lisa

'How's work?' Jayne slides her arms out of her coat and unwraps her scarf from her neck. 'That's better,' she mutters, hanging both on the back of her chair. 'So, tell me. How's it going?'

We're sitting at our usual table in the Cwtch, a tiny, old-fashioned café, squashed between a shoe shop and a clothes shop on Castle

Street in Ponthallen. It smells of warm cakes and coffee. The mullioned window next to us is steamed up from the contrast of the warm room and the cold outside. Blurred figures hurry past, and occasionally someone slips on the icy cobbles of the narrow street.

I leave my coat on; I haven't been able to get warm all morning.

'Good. Well, mostly good.' I'm tearing the edges of the white paper napkin that had come with the coffee, thinking back on the morning. 'Not today though, today's been difficult. I'm working with Melanie, my boss, with a family that's just lost a baby boy.'

The old wound has opened; the memory of what happened to my baby brother made me feel vulnerable, less professional, when I sat opposite the couple grieving for their two-year-old, who'd died in an accident. Back at the office, I'd gone into the ladies' loo and cried. 'The father crashed the car; the child was killed instantly. He blames himself...'

As I always do, when I picture our pram bouncing down the ginnel, I remember how my father is still not speaking to me.

'That's awful.' Jayne slowly stirs the spoon through her cappuccino, mixing in the chocolate sprinkles. 'Does Melanie know? How it upset you?'

I look down at the napkin I've demolished, roll the pieces into tiny balls. 'Yes. But I should have been more professional. I don't think I helped the family. I left it to her to talk to them; I couldn't find the right words...'

'You haven't been in post that long, don't be so hard on yourself.'

I bite my lip, open my eyes wide. I won't cry, not here. I won't.

'You need to talk it through with her. That's what a line manager is there for, to show you the ropes. To support you.' Jayne leans across the table towards me, rests her hand on top of mine. 'That's what I do in school, if I can see there's something wrong with one of the children, especially first thing in the morning. If I think they're distressed about something at home, I talk to the deputy head.'

Jayne started teaching at the local primary school in Ponthallen in September, a few weeks before I got my job in the council's social services department. She's a natural. Whereas I often wonder if I'm capable of helping families who seem to need more than I can give. I'm doing what I've wanted to for so long, but what if that's not enough? What if my guilt about my baby brother will always affect my judgment?

'Look, I've known you long enough to see when you're struggling, Lisa. There's something else, isn't there?'

I pick up my cup of coffee, put it back in the saucer, look over my shoulder around the café. No one is looking our way. The hum of conversation forms a bubble around us. Jayne's hand is still on mine. Her eyes hold a concern that somehow reminds me of Barb.

'There is something,' I say at last, waves of apprehension inside me. 'I probably should have told you years ago...' I stop. I'm going to cry.

'Go on.' Jayne's voice is soft. 'I'm listening. And, whatever it is, I'm here for you. I'm your best friend. You can tell me anything. Yes?' She tilts her head.

'Yes.' She is my best friend. I can trust her. 'The reason I came to live with Barb and Chris... Something happened ... that changed everything for me – and everyone in my family.'

I tell her about Robert. I tell her the truth.

Chapter Thirty-seven

Angie

'It's late.' Angie pushes back the sleeve of her negligee to check her watch.

'Play me something on the piano.' Stephen gestures to the small keyboard in the corner of the room. 'It soothes me and I like to watch you play.' He makes playing movements with his fingers.

'No, sorry.' She forces a laugh. She's tired and he's overstayed his welcome. It's been the same, ever since the first time he showed up at her apartment. Perhaps she should have turned him away then. But one minute he'd been at the outside door, the next at the apartment door, and then inside.

And he always overstays his welcome.

'You said you had a meeting in the morning, so you'd better leave soon.'

'I'm tired of all this going backwards and forwards between here and Micklethwaite.' Stephen yawns, lolls back on the white leather settee, one arm slung casually across her shoulder, his eyes half-closed. 'Move in with me.' It's the same demand he makes all the time.

There was no intentional decision on her part to have a relationship with him. It started with the occasional overnight stay, his rushing off home in the morning, to a gradual appearance of his spare shirt in her wardrobe, pants and socks in one of the drawers, his toothbrush and shaver on the bathroom shelf. His choice.

But when he repeats, 'Move in with me,' she has the answer. She shakes her head.

'I can't.' The thought brings a hard lump to her throat. In her most desperate times, she's craved the security of the home she once knew. But now it's too late. The thought of her parents finding out how she's been earning a living in Manchester terrifies her. It's safer to stay away. 'I keep telling you; what you're asking is impossible.'

'Why?'

She sighs. 'You know why.'

As usual, he pretends not to understand. 'It's not as though we don't know one another, Angie. We have a history together, remember?'

Unbelievable! She turns her head to look at him and lifts her eyebrows. Does he really think what happened is a nostalgic memory? A shared history that makes everything all right?

He seems to understand her silent question. 'Aw, come on, that's all in the past. I've always liked you, and I know you like...' He pulls a face back at her and laughs. 'Well, at least you don't hate me anymore.'

But he'd hate her if he knew how she'd lived before he'd arrived to take over her life with his gifts, his insistence on paying for everything. The places he takes her are more select than the ones her past clients ever took her, even the wealthier ones. But there's still a chance she could be recognised. Then what would he do?

What would happen if she agreed to move to Micklethwaite with him, made things right with her parents? Might that work?

But what if her past came out? It doesn't bear thinking about.

'Forget it, Stephen. It wouldn't work.'

'Look.' He frowns. 'I want to settle down, have kids.'

His last words send a huge jolt through her.

'Then you wouldn't want to settle down with me. I can't have children...'

'What?'

'I found out years ago I'm unable to have children, Stephen. I was in hospital once... I was told I will never be able to carry a baby...' It's the nearest to the truth she'll tell him. Or anyone.

'Why? What happened?'

'Please, Stephen, It's too personal, too upsetting. Can we just not talk about it?'

She doesn't want to think about the worst day in her life. One that changed her forever.

'That's the only choice. I'm sick of your sort coming to me and demanding an abortion.'

Angela didn't meet the doctor's gaze; she looked at a point just above his head. A thin strand of grey is plastered across the bald dome of his skull. The girls had told her to play the game: the doctor expected it, and it eased his conscience if she cried and pretended her boyfriend's condom split. They'd warned her not to admit what she did for a living in case he was one of the doctors who refused to help. But he wasn't fooled by her story; he knew right away what she was.

She felt vulnerable, lying on the couch, her knees still flopped to the sides, her legs pale, thin, like the rest of her. The curtains on the screen shivered in the breeze from the open surgery window. She shivered too; goosebumps crept along her skin. But it wasn't just the cold that made her shake. It was fear. This man had the power to change her life

He stared down at her. He had small brown eyes, almost hidden by thick, grey, wiry eyebrows.

'Just get dressed.' He pushed the curtained screen to one side and went to his desk. If someone opened the surgery door, they would see her. Quickly swinging her legs over the edge of the couch, she reached for her knickers and jeans. She could hear him tapping his biro on the surface of his desk. Tap. Tap. Tap.

She shoved her arms into the thin sleeves of her coat, his words on a loop inside her head. She swallowed. She wouldn't cry. She needed to think. She felt nauseous. She'd felt ill for weeks, refusing to believe what was happening inside her body.

Her legs took her as far as the chair in front of his desk before they gave way, and she sat down with a thump.

'You've got yourself into this mess. And there's no doubt it will happen again.' He pointed the pen at her. 'So you have two options. Have the ... er ... procedure and sign this consent form to be sterilised at the same time. Or I can't help you—' He reached down to his desk drawer and took out a sheet of paper.

'What? No!' Angie's heart knocked inside her chest so hard it was difficult to drag air into her lungs. 'Please...'

'That's the choice. In your line of business, this will happen again. And I'm not here to sort your mess out every time.' He pushed the paper towards her, leaned back and steepled his fingers. 'Reluctant though I am to give you permission to have an abortion, I will give it – if only for the sake of a child avoiding the kind of life you would provide.' He jutted his forefinger at her. 'Women like you should never have children.'

The shame has never left Angie. It wove itself around the deep roots of guilt planted when her baby brother died. She'd had no choice.

Now, trying to hide her distress, she moves to the piano. Seeing his uncertainty, even disbelief, at what she's just told him, she says, 'How about *Woodstock*?' She begins to play.

But he's raising his voice above the music.

'Since I – *we* found one another again, I've known what I want.' He takes a last gulp of whisky, clunks the glass down on the coffee table, and walks over to her. 'We can work all the kids business out...'

Angie doesn't look at him. Hasn't he taken in what she's said?

He gives her shoulder a squeeze. 'You must know how much I care about you? I can get the best doctors.'

Angie shakes her head. 'No point, Stephen. Please...'

'I'll look after you.'

'Have you heard a word I've said?' She stops and stares up at him. 'I can't have children. And I can't move back to Micklethwaite.' She closes the lid of the piano.

He's not listening. 'It's all in the past...'

'Not for me.'

'Okay, forget the kids thing for now. No one in Micklethwaite will even remember what happened...'

Angie shakes her head; he has no concept of the devastation to her family. 'I do. My parents do. Have you thought what my parents would say? Me turning up, after all this time? With you?'

'With or without me, I should think they'd be over the moon. At least they'd have one daughter living nearby. Don't you think it's about time?'

She used to wonder if her leaving home meant Mandy had moved back. When Stephen told her it hadn't happened, it made her sad.

'And I bet it would buck your mother up. I see her around the village, Angie. She looks pretty miserable – and rough,' he adds. 'Lost weight and everything. I heard she has problems with the old ticker.'

'You haven't said anything to her? Told her you know where I am?'

'Of course I haven't.' He flings himself back onto the settee. 'But I have been thinking you should get in touch with her.' He grins, snaps his fingers. 'Tell you what! Let's get married. That'll square things with them.'

And there it is, his final throw of the dice. His trump card. Dangling the carrot; bait to the fish; any other cliché you can think of, she tells herself, panic making her move away from the piano to the window. The city is so anonymous, safe, she thinks before turning to face him.

'No. I told you; I can't give you what you want—'

He shrugs.

'Why is my moving in with you so important? We're all right as we are.'

He doesn't answer.

'Aren't we?'

He sits upright. 'Are we? We spend a part of almost every day together, but you always come back here at night. I want us to be together all the time; I want to wake up every morning next to you. I want to know what you're doing every moment of every day. Isn't that what you want? For us to be together?'

Is it? Has what's happened over these last months been a relationship gaining momentum without her even realising? 'It's a nice thought, but impractical.' Angie moves to sit next to him, her mind in turmoil. 'There's my work—'

'There'd be no need for you to work anymore; I have more than enough for us to live on. Business is good. I've got plans for a big estate in Barnsgate in the pipeline.' He puts both arms around her, crushes her to him. 'What d'you think, girlie?'

Angie hates it when he calls her that but forces a smile, and decides to appease him. 'I don't know; I like being independent. Let me think about it?' Giving him a swift kiss on the cheek, she stands.

He's scowling.

'I thought you'd jump at the chance, Angie. Wife of a man with a successful building firm. Influential in all the right places. Prospective Tory councillor. *Youngest* potential Tory councillor, I might tell you!' He puffs his chest out, pointing his thumb at himself. He grins, making a joke of it, but she knows he's deadly serious when he says, 'Don't take too long to decide.' He pushes himself off the settee with a grunt and makes a mock-sad face. 'I'll go back to my lonely house, then.'

It's two o'clock in the morning. Sleepless, staring out at the city lights, drinking a second glass of red wine, in the hope that it will help her to finally get to sleep, Angie thinks back to Stephen's final words.

'You'll love my house. You'll be in your element. Knowing what you do for a living...'

A ripple of shock had run along her skin when he'd said that. 'What do you mean, what I do for a living?'

'You know, your interior design stuff. You could have a free hand. Do as you like. And,' he'd added, triumphantly, as though it will be the one thing to sway her, 'I'll buy you a grand piano, so you'll be able to play all day if you want to.'

He gave her a wink before leaving, but there was a warning in his voice. 'Don't keep me waiting too long, Angie. I'm not a patient man, and I'm offering a life you can only dream of.'

Can she overcome her fears? She can't return to the life she had before in Micklethwaite. Would it even be possible to begin a new life there?

Part Four

Chapter Thirty-eight

Lisa, June 1981

I never wanted to be in Micklethwaite ever again. Yet here I am. For my mother's funeral. My conscience tells me I should have come years ago, despite Mum's insistence it would only bring back bad memories. And it does. Over the last two weeks, since she died, the nightmares have returned. And knowing I have to meet Angela has brought back the resentment of her I buried a long time ago. Sisters don't do what she did to me. I don't want to see her, and I'll never forgive her.

I stand, hold on to the rail, wait for the bus to stop, and peer through the window. It's dirty and smeared with rain but, already, I can see Micklethwaite is run-down, shabby.

The doors squeal open, but I can't make my legs move. I can sense the driver's impatience and curiosity, and worry he's recognised me. He's older, but I know he used to be the school caretaker. I can't remember his name but when I see he's going to speak, the old, familiar fear prickles my skin.

But all he says is, 'On or off, miss?'

I step down, clutching my only luggage, my small, blue suitcase. I'm not intending to stay long. Standing on the edge of the flagged square, I look around at what used to be the new shops and flats. It's depressing, exactly as Mum described it last time she was in Ponthallen. She'd said it had deteriorated beyond recognition and she was right. Most of the shop fronts are boarded up; the windows of the flats above are covered in yellowed net curtains or wrecked blinds hanging lopsided. Empty crisp packets and torn, greasy chip cartons wrap themselves around the iron railings that were fixed to protect the young saplings, now fragmented twigs.

Except for a group of hooded youths slouched in front of an off-licence, with windows plastered in red and orange posters offering knock-down beer and wine prices, there's no one around. What had been there before?

It comes to me: it was the hairdresser's, Mavis's Waves and Curls. Mum used to come out of there once a month with the same tight perm all the other women had. And each time, red-faced, with an embedded line from a hairnet across her forehead, Mum swore she'd find a different hairdresser. Each time it had taken until the evening for that line to fade.

Angie and I used to tease Mum about it.

The thought makes me feel wretched, broken. As broken as I was when I left Micklethwaite, carrying a burden that would be with me all my life.

My father didn't want me here. His recrimination drove me from the only home I'd known up to then. I'm dreading seeing him again.

And I've told myself I just have to manage how I feel about Angela for the short time I'm here. It'll be the first time I've seen her in over eleven years. We're grown women now. But then there's a small voice that keeps saying it's the first time I'll speak to her since her lies, and the lies she let Stephen Birch tell, completely altered my life.

The last thing I said to her was, 'I hate you.' I wonder if she'll remember that.

On the journey today, a strange fear of seeing Dad has grown inside me. I wonder if my sister has told him I'll be at the funeral. He'll expect me to be there, surely? The ready tears smart.

I take a minute to calm down. Wipe my eyes, blow my nose. I'm not as brave as I thought I was. What was I thinking coming here alone? Because I thought it would be less uncomfortable for Barb and Chris. If there was any trouble, I didn't want them to see it. Because I need breathing space to get used to being in Micklethwaite.

I'll feel better when Barb and Chris arrive tomorrow.

The rain has stopped. I push the hood of my coat off my head and look up. The thick metal-grey clouds are clearing, but it's still not warm for late June. I've lost track of time and push my sleeve back to check my watch. Almost four o'clock. I'm not sure what to do. I don't like standing here with that lot loitering over there, staring at me. My case is getting heavy but I'm not putting it down on all the grit and cigarette ends. If Angela doesn't arrive in five minutes, I'll go to her house, presuming I can find it. Irritation makes me tap my foot. She said she'd booked us into rooms somewhere. I should have asked for the address.

Why the hell did I leave anything to her? But I didn't, did I? I left it to Barb. First to contact Dad and then Angela. They'd sorted out somewhere for us to stay, worked together on the funeral arrangements. I'd gone to pieces when Mum died. I told Barb I couldn't work with Angela. How could we agree on our last goodbye to Mum when we'd had such different relationships with her? She loved someone I hated and yet, even though the person I hated was her other daughter, she still loved me as well.

'Mandy?'

I don't turn around at first. The accent is different, but the voice is the one I remember.

'Mand.'

'Lisa. My name's Lisa. You know that already.' Barb or Mum will have told Angela that I changed my name as soon as I went to live in Wales. It's who I am. It's been who I am for over a decade. Her calling me by my old name has turned fear to anger. I turn.

It's a bit of a shock to see her. It must have shown on my face because she says, 'Don't recognise your own sister, eh?'

The words are precise and clipped, the accent wrong, false.

She doesn't look anything like I remembered. There's nothing of the girl I'd once known. Or even the woman I'd imagined she'd be. At twenty-eight she hasn't a wrinkle in sight; her cheekbones and forehead are so smooth, so taut. Has she had a facelift? And her mouth is different somehow. Despite the dull weather she has fashionable sunglasses on top of carefully arranged, long blonde hair, obviously bleached. She's wearing what I recognise as a Donna Karan coat with huge shoulder pads.

'Well, you do look different from when I last saw you. It's a long time.' My voice is steady, and I look her straight in the eye.

She is the first to look away. But then she straightens her shoulders and turns to face me. Her voice is equally calm.

'And whose fault is that?'

I don't give her my first answer. Over time I've learned to control my deep-rooted antipathy towards her, except when I have the nightmares that leave me staring into the darkness for hours, wondering if she ever has such dreams. Convinced she doesn't.

My hatred must have shown because I see something flicker across her face.

'I'm here for Mum, that's all, Angela.' I deliberately use her full name. 'I'm here for tomorrow and then I'll be gone again.'

'You could have come before now. You could have come when she was ill.'

I bite my lip. Mum hadn't wanted me to, even when she was ill. Should I have insisted? The thought makes me defensive.

'Like you did, you mean? Disappearing for years, then coming back with *him*? Married to *him*?' Hopefully that's turned the tables on her. 'Why, Angela? Why suddenly decide to come back, without one word as to where you'd been?'

'You know nothing about me. I told Mum why I went. And why I came back. None of which is any of your business.' She clears her throat. 'So, we'll go back to our house before checking into the place where you'll be staying. Obviously there are things we need to talk about...'

'There are.'

'Things that need explaining.'

'I'm not sure there's any explanation for what you and your husband did to me.'

'About Dad,' she says.

106

'What about Dad?' Is she going to tell me he doesn't want me here?

She doesn't answer, walking away from me to a posh, silver car. She looks at me in a pointed way; I know she wants me to say something about it.

I don't. Sheer bloody mindedness, I know, but her refusal to explain what she means has rattled me.

I slide into what she tells me is an Audi something or other. Cars don't interest me much. Working in and around Ponthallen, my beat-up Mini gets me about well enough. I feel a twinge of envy for the leather seats, more than enough room for my long legs (unlike the Mini), the soft purr of the engine. I clutch my case to me like a barrier.

When we turn into a street of large, detached houses, we still haven't spoken.

Chapter Thirty-nine

Lisa

A path leads to the front door with immaculate long narrow lawns on either side.

'Please take off your shoes. The carpets...' It's a request, yet not a request.

She opens the front door. Stairs rise from the long hallway. There's a row of polished wooden hooks on the wall. When she takes off her coat, I see how thin she is under the silk blouse and black pleated skirt. She pushes open the door on the left and waits, deliberately, until I press at the back of my heels with my toes to slip off my shoes.

'Please mind the wall with your case.'

The room she leads me through has a cream carpet, a two-seater Ercol settee in brown, a matching chair and a glass case with three shelves, each holding a decanter. The slate fireplace is filled with a large crystal bowl of pale mauve silk flowers and green ferns.

'What needs explaining, Angela?'

'In a moment. Come through.' She walks through a dining room, bare except for a large oak table and six chairs, and I follow. My heels pad softly on the oak floor.

The kitchen surprises me. It's so ordered. I think of Barb's kitchen with the shelves of cookbooks, plants and seashells, sea glass she's collected over the years, the worktops cluttered with kettle, toaster, bread bin and a hundred and one other bits and pieces she doesn't put away because she says she would never find them again. Pride of place on the back door, the slate sign engraved 'A Messy Kitchen is a Happy One'. A present I found for one of her birthdays. I smile, remembering her raucous laugh when she unwrapped it.

'Tea?' Angela stands in front of one of the white cupboards, her hand on the door handle. She doesn't smile.

'Thanks.' She's making me wait for whatever she wants to tell me.

This kitchen looks as if it has never been used. There is nothing out of place. The worktops hold nothing. The black tiled floor gleams, not a mark or a scuff on it. It's a show kitchen.

I watch my sister take a teapot and a kettle from the cupboard, fill it with water, plug it in, switch it on. In silence she begins to dry a splash of water on the sink. I don't know what to say. Still holding my case, I cross to the window. The back garden is as immaculate as the front. A straight, flagged path splits two lawns, leading to a green shed at the far end. Behind it, a long stone wall reaches to the neighbours' gardens.

'Oh, you have a flowering cherry.' I push my annoyance to one side. 'It's beautiful.' Small pink petals float past the window, settling on the sill. Others have landed on the path and on a stone ornament of a fox. It looks so pretty.

Angie draws in a sharp breath. Without speaking, she pushes past me, takes a pair of canvas gardening gloves from a drawer and flings open the back door.

I can't believe what she does next. She's trying to sweep up all the blossom with a brush and pan. Petals float down; she's squatting, frantically brushing at them, trying to keep them on the pan. I can see every bone of her spine through her thin blouse. Her face is screwed up in anger and frustration.

'Let me help, Angela.' I put my case on the doorstep and look around for a proper sweeping brush. 'Can I help?' I feel an unexpected wave of compassion. Now I think I understand the clinical appearance of the kitchen, the bareness of the other rooms. It's obsessiveness.

'No. No. You go inside, you've nothing on your feet.' I'm just going to say the same thing to her when she adds, 'And please make sure you don't take any dirt in with you.'

'The kettle's boiled. Shall I brew?' I stand on the doorstep, checking the soles of my feet.

'No!' From the anxious hiss Angela makes through her teeth, I can tell she begrudges me asking. 'You don't know where anything is. I'll do it now.' She goes around the corner of the house. I hear the bang of a dustbin lid.

At the door she reaches around to take a cloth and a bottle of cleaner from a small cupboard just inside the kitchen and sprays and then dries her feet. Her movements are agitated.

I know she's watching me, challenging me to say something. I don't. Instead, I go over to the window. The blossom is still floating down. Must drive her up the wall.

'It's hopeless,' she says. Her mascara is smudged into a black shadow under her lower lashes.

'Does it matter?' I go to what's on my mind. 'What did you mean about Dad?'

'In a minute.'

When the kettle switches off again, she opens the cupboards and takes out teabags and cups and saucers. Pouring milk from the fridge into a jug, she arranges everything on a tray, handles, spoons, all in the same direction.

Tipping a bleach bottle onto a cloth, she wipes the worktops. 'Do you take sugar?'

'No.'

'Good. No need to get it out then. Leave your case where it is; it'll be fine there. Please...' She waves a hand at me. 'Go. Sit down in the dining room.'

My impatience is making me clench and unclench my fingers, but I wait until she's fussed around, arranging everything on the table and me on the right chair, before she sits back and folds her hands in her lap.

'So, what's there to explain about Dad? Tell me.'

'First, the funeral.' There's no expression in her face at all. 'There's nothing for you to bother your head about. It's all sorted. Everything to the last detail.'

'I know. Barb told me.'

'Aunt Barbara and I have organised it all.' There's a disapproval in her words that echoes across time: her older sister voice. But when she stands and pours the tea, her hands shake and the cup rattles in the saucer as she passes it to me.

'Thanks. Yes, don't worry, Barb said.'

'I don't know why she's suddenly Barb.'

'She's been Barb since I moved in with them.' I can't help adding, 'And Chris, not uncle.' I'm glad that's annoyed her. 'But never mind that. What about Dad?'

'Stephen says we need to decide what's going to happen to Father.'

First *Mother*, now *Father*. 'Dad?' I say. 'Why?' I take a sip of tea. 'And what's it got to do with your husband?'

'He can't stay in that house on his own. Stephen says...'

'Why?' I'm not interested in what Stephen says. There's something odd going on here.

'It's his blood pressure. He's had those couple of scares, small strokes, over the years, you know that.'

I don't. Mum never told me Dad had anything wrong with him. I stay quiet.

110

Angela's waiting, but when I don't answer, she says, 'So, we need to decide what to do.' She's studying her fingernails. They are long, bright pink. Reluctant though I am to admit it, she's kept herself looking good, even though she seems to be a bag of nerves.

'When?' I ask after a long silence.

'When what?'

'When did he have these "couple of scares", as you call them?'

She moves the jug to one side of the tray and arranges the handle so it's facing the same way as the teapot handle.

'Angela! When?'

She taps her nails on the surface of her cup. The clicking annoys me.

'Well, of course, there was the one just after you...'

'Just after I...?'

'Left.' She picks up her cup, raises it to her mouth but doesn't drink. Her fingers still tremble. 'Mum said it was just after you left home.'

The remorse makes me turn away, look out of the window. When I face Angela again, I see my guilt reflected in her eyes. 'And after you left as well, if I remember rightly.'

'Yes.' She bites her lip. 'Just after I left as well.'

'Only you had a choice.'

'Did I?' The slight movement of her head turns into a nod. 'Yes, I suppose I did.' She looks directly at me. 'I didn't think so at the time.' Her voice is low. 'I thought if I left, you could come back.'

That shocks me.

'I wouldn't have wanted to come back.'

'No?'

'No. I hoped I'd never have to come here ever again.' But I should have done. I should have come when Mum was first ill. 'You didn't know either? About Dad?'

'Not until I came back here four years ago. I ... I lost touch with Mum and Dad for quite a long time...'

I knew that, but I don't say anything. I remember my graduation,

111

when Mum had asked if I knew where Angela was. How resentful I'd been that she was thinking of my sister on my big day. How selfish I'd been.

'Where did you go?'

'Manchester.' Her tone terse.

'What did you do there?' It's like pulling teeth, but I persevere.

'I was working for an interior designer.' She holds her cup with both hands in front of her mouth. She's blinking rapidly.

'That must have been fascinating. What was the firm called?'

'You're in social services, Dad says?' She puts the cup down, brushes imaginary crumbs off the table into her palm, goes into the kitchen. Above the sound of a tap running, she calls, 'What exactly do you do?'

Nicely avoided, Angela, I think. Her reluctance to tell me about her life in Manchester intrigues me, but that can wait. I go to lean against the kitchen door.

'You said Dad had more than one of these episodes?'

'Yes, there was another just after I came back,' she says, strangely vague. 'And then, last March, I had a call from a neighbour who'd sent for his GP. He said he'd had a suspected slight stroke. But he wouldn't go into hospital because of Mother being ill.'

'So what happened? What did you do?'

'The doctor said he couldn't force him to go and told him to rest as much as possible. He increased his medication. There was nothing for me to do.'

'Except look after the two of them.'

'Like you, you mean?'

I wince. 'I didn't know.' A thought strikes me. 'Did Barb know? Did you telephone Barb?'

'No. Father said not to. And Mother. They were both adamant you were not to be worried.'

'You didn't think to tell me?'

'When did you and I last speak?'

It's there again, that accusation. But she's right, of course: I cut

112

her out of my life. With good reason, the small voice at the back of my mind reminds me, trying to give me an excuse. But the thought of my parents struggling on their own over all those months heaps more regret on me.

'So we need to decide what to do.'

I'm still trying to take in everything Angela's said. 'Do...?'

'He can't stay in that house.' She deflects any argument by saying, 'Would you bring in the tea things, please?'

'Right-oh.' I'm not going to quarrel with her. After all, it's Dad's decision whether he stays there. Not her's. Or her husband's. 'You mean because of his health?'

'No!' She takes the tray from me, takes it to the sink. 'Well, that is a consideration, I suppose. But it's a three-bedroom house. A family house. The council want him out.'

I take in a long breath. They're kicking Dad out of his home. 'It's barely over a week since Mum died, Angela. How have they found out so soon? What have they said?'

'Stephen's on the council.'

'What?'

'He was elected a year ago. Took the seat from Labour. He's doing well. Youngest Conservative councillor for Barnsgate.' She sounds defensive. I lift my shoulders; I couldn't care less. I do care why Dad's been told he must move.

'What's Stephen being on the council got to do with what's happening to Dad?'

She squirts washing-up liquid into the water. 'He said it was his duty to tell the housing department—'

'He did what? When? When did he tell them?'

'On the day—'

'The day Mum died? Good God, Angela, and you don't think that was despicable?'

She lifts her hand, scattering soap suds. 'Like I said, he can't stay there.'

She's right. We can't leave him on his own if he's not well. But what

113

Stephen's done is spiteful. I shake my head. 'We shouldn't be talking about this now. We haven't even had Mum's funeral yet. And what Stephen's done to Dad is so wrong, Angela. Surely you must know that?'

A mottled red rises up her neck. 'He said ... I'm only saying...'

'Well, don't.' I swallow down my anger and try to be civil. 'I can't discuss this now, Angela. I'd better go to wherever you've booked us in.'

'I'll drive you there.' Her tone is as stiffly polite as mine. 'As soon as I've put these away.'

I don't offer to help. Crossing to the back step, I pick up my case. I put on my shoes and walk down the path to wait by the car. We don't speak again until she parks in front of a large hotel.

'The Grove.' I read the sign above the elaborate front entrance. 'I thought we were in a B&B?' Neither Barb and Chris nor I can afford fancy prices.

'It's okay. Stephen's paid. He insisted.'

'No. I don't ... I can't accept...'

'You'll have to.' She twists in her seat to face me, a strange expression in her eyes. 'There's some folk festival going on this week, outside Barnsgate; Stephen says everywhere else is full.'

Stephen says, Stephen says. I'm sick of hearing what Stephen says. I don't know what to believe. Nothing since I arrived in Micklethwaite is as I imagined. I don't move.

'Do Barb and Chris know we're all staying here?'

'I telephoned them this morning. Gave them directions from the station.'

'You're not meeting them?'

'I won't have time to pick them up. Stephen's arranged a meeting with the bank manager and I need to be there. With Stephen...' She revs the car and pushes up the sleeve of her coat to check her watch. 'And...' Now she looks at me. 'Stephen will be home soon, and I need to make his tea.'

I have no choice. I shuffle out of the car with my case. Before I close the door, she leans forward and peers up at me.

'Auntie Barbara told you the time tomorrow?'

I nod.

'Right. I'll pick you up at two o'clock. Get it over with.'

I watch her drive away before I turn to look at the hotel door. Her words echo in my head. 'Get it over with.'

Chapter Forty

Angela

Driving away from the hotel, Angela's unsettled by the talk about her return to Micklethwaite. Those first few weeks are not ones she choses to remember: people's speculative stares, the nosy questions (so difficult to swerve), the fear of what she'd done, what she'd been, in Manchester being discovered, had sometimes made her physically sick.

Stephen hadn't understood, of course. But there again, he didn't know the truth either.

Standing on her parents' doorstep had been the most terrifying moment. She had no idea how they would look at her, what they would say.

Angela glanced back. The road was empty of cars and passers-by. She could spin on her heel and run, leave what Stephen calls 'the reunion' for another day.

But he'd be disappointed in her; he'd been nagging for her to come here ever since they arrived in Micklethwaite. Insistent that she saw her parents as soon as possible. 'Better they find out from you you're back,' he quite reasonably said, 'than from some neighbour sticking their beak in.' It was Mum he seemed most anxious she saw, for some reason.

She held a trembling finger over the doorbell and fixed on a smile. But however much she'd practised her first words, they stuck in her throat when the front door slowly opened.

Any words were forgotten, of course, when she saw her mother. They both began to cry. Not loud blustering sobs, but quiet weeping. Mum stepped forward and embraced her. Standing in the doorway, they rocked side to side.

'I'm sorry,' Angela mumbled into the soft skin of her mother's neck. 'I'm sorry.'

'No. You're back, that's all that matters.'

'Who is it, love?' Angela's father pulled the door open wider. She felt him put his arm around her mother's waist as though supporting her, and noticed, for the first time, how slender her mother was, how paper-thin her skin. She stepped back a little, still holding onto her mother's arms.

'It's Angela, Eric. It's Angela.'

Mum buried her head into his chest and he stroked her back, making soothing, shushing noises. Angie couldn't remember seeing such tenderness from her father before. A gentleness she'd never experienced from any man, even in these early days of marriage with Stephen. She felt ashamed.

'You'd better come in.' Her father nodded at her. 'Your mum can't stand 'ere at the door forever. It's too cold.'

She followed them into the living room. He supported her mother to the armchair by the fire, pulling a blanket over her knees, and straightened up. He stared at Angela. 'Cup of tea?'

'Please.' Her voice shook.

'Sit down then. I won't be long.' He gave her a warning look. 'Yer mum's not too good, so let's take things slowly, eh?'

'Oh, Eric...' Her mum waved her hand. 'I'm fine.' Her lips turned up in a small smile. 'Our daughter's back home. I'm fine.'

'Let's take things slowly,' he said again. 'We can talk when I come back with the brew. Then Angela can tell us what she's been doing for the last four years.'

Angela gave them the same version of her life in Manchester that she has given to anyone else who has asked.

She knows that her father hasn't really forgiven her for the grief she caused her mother. That he blames her for her mother's rapid decline.

She's dreading tomorrow. And after the funeral, Mandy ... Lisa ... will start asking questions. And demanding answers.

Chapter Forty-one

Lisa

I'm not sure how Dad will be with me, but I need to see him before the funeral to settle my mind.

During breakfast, I decided I would leave a note at reception to let Barb and Chris know I've gone to his house.

It looks a bit like rain again. The sky's filled with wavy lines of light and darker grey clouds. No sign of the sun. But it's warm enough and I reckon I can find my way to the house, once I'm on the main road to the village. It can't be that far.

I'm shaking. I had a shock when I first turned off Mickle Road onto the estate. The first few avenues were bad enough: the tarmac full of holes, the pavements uneven and crammed with weeds. But further into the estate, it's worse. The houses are so scruffy, with the paintwork on the doors and window frames peeling, most of the gardens untended. Children playing in the dirt which used to be lawns. They look neglected and the adults sitting on the doorsteps stare with disinterest as I walk past. I try smiling at one or two but no joy, so I stop making eye contact.

It feels strange, not speaking to anyone. In Ponthallen I can barely walk anywhere without having to stop and chat, or at least greet someone. I love that.

I turn onto the avenue where I'd played as a kid and walk towards Dad's house. The house I'd grown up in. There's no gate anymore, but the hinges are still there, red-rusty and hanging. I head up the path. The pulse in my neck throbs and my heart is in my mouth.

There's no bell, so I knock on the wood and step back to look first in the living-room window, and then up to the bedrooms. I see the curtains move.

When he opens the door, his eyes widen. 'You're back then.' The words sound harsh but he gives me a tentative lift of his lips. Relieved, I return the smile. 'Come in then,' he says, turning back into the house. His baggy trousers trail over the back of his slippers and there's a hole at the elbow of his maroon jumper.

I straighten my shoulders. Now I'm here, I'm more anxious than ever.

Inside, the smell is awful – a mix of stale tobacco smoke, sweat and rotting food. When I look through to the kitchen, I can see plates piled high in the sink, pans on the cooker.

'Sit down.' He gestures to one of two armchairs. I swear they are the same ones that were here when I lived here. No settee though, just two wooden kitchen chairs under the window, one with a tray holding a plate of what looks like the remains of egg and chips.

'You just arrived?' He picks up the plate of congealed food and takes it into the kitchen. I watch him add it to the already toppling pile of crockery, look away when he returns to the living room. A transistor radio is playing classical music. It's whistling, as though slightly off station. He turns it off.

I blink a few times, hope he doesn't feel he has to do something, like hold me or pat me on the arm. I'm not ready for that, yet. If ever.

'I thought we should talk before ... this afternoon.' I don't know what to say next. This isn't the man I've been remembering all these years; this is an old man with dark pouches under his eyes and grey whiskers on his jawline. He's worn down. 'How are you?' Stupid question. I try again. 'I thought it time we made peace with each other, Dad. That's all.'

He huffs, sits, shuffles about, rubs his hands on the arms of the

118

chair. The material is shiny black, as if this is a habit he has: sliding his palms along them.

I perch on the other armchair, resisting the urge to brush the seat, thinking I'll regret it if my one and only coat is stained afterwards. Looking around, I see four deep dents in the carpet making a rectangular shape under the window.

He sees me looking. 'Your mother liked 'er bed down here. First, on her bad days. Then later...' He sniffs. 'So she could see what was going on outside.'

'I remember her telling me that, once, on the phone.' She sometimes managed to give me breathless running commentaries on the 'goings-on', as she called it. I smile, remembering her giggles, then bite the inside of my cheek to hold back the sobs.

'Did she have many?'

'Bad days?'

I nod.

He rubs his chin. 'Some. Before she started on the new tablets. She rallied for months after they sorted out 'er medication.'

'She said that in a letter last year.' Suddenly I can see the shaky handwriting. 'She sounded on top form.' Or did she always pretend for my sake?

'I didn't stop her writing,' he says.

'I know. You wouldn't.'

'Yes, well... I posted the letters an' all. Sometimes took me an hour, there and back, to the postbox in the village.' He waves vaguely at the window.

'Thank you.'

'For ages we thought, yer mum and me...' Dad shakes his head. 'An' the doc did as well – that the new medication was working fine. And then...' He sucks in his lower lip, his eyes bleak.

I almost reach over to grasp his fingers, but there's still that resistance in me. So I only say, 'What happened?'

'She insisted on going on 'er own to see Angie. She wouldn't let me go with her because of... But I did walk with 'er to the bus stop, just to see her on the bus. I insisted on that. But you know how strong-willed yer mother was.' He gives a short breathy chuckle before his face tightens in grief. 'She knew how much I 'ated 'im – Birch.'

That he's actually said that surprises me. It gives me permission to ask, 'How did Mum feel about her marrying him? About her just turning up after all that time? With him?' I'm curious. And, I reluctantly admit to myself, a little envious of the way my sister slotted back into life in Micklethwaite.

Dad says, 'I won't lie, at first she took it better than me. She told me she were just glad one of you were 'ome.' He pulls an apologetic face. I suppose he thinks I'm hurt by that, and I am.

'I'm glad she was happy.'

'Oh, not about her being with 'im.' He's rubbing the palms of his hands along the arms of the chair again. 'Don't get me wrong. I think she 'ated him as much as me. In fact I know she did; right from the beginning she told your sister she didn't want 'im in the 'ouse. And Angie agreed. I was surprised she was so easy about it. Couldn't work out why.' He pushes his lower lip out.

I nod, wondering how my sister had felt about her parents refusing to acknowledge her successful husband. Angie didn't know that Mum knew the truth about my brother's death.

'But things changed, you know. Something 'appened between your mum and Angie. And Angie changed as well.' He shrugs. 'Perhaps it was because yer mum was so poorly. To be honest, all I was bothered about then was yer mum. I should have gone with 'er that day though...'

He lapses into silence, then says, 'But me and Angie, well, we'd 'ad a bit of a fall out some time back. I've tried, but to be honest, I've not really got over it.'

'What about?'

He hesitates. 'Another time, eh, Lisa?' He wipes his hands over his face.

I know to leave it alone. Instead, I ask, 'Do you know what Angela did in Manchester. Her job?'

'She did say the day she came back. Summat to do with doing up 'ouses.'

'Interior design. Yes, she told me that. I don't suppose you know the name of the firm?'

'No. She's never said much about it. But she looked the part. You know, 'er hair, 'er clothes. I remember your mum saying the outfits she wore must 'ave cost a pretty penny...' He blows out his cheeks in a huge sigh. 'I dunno.' He suddenly repeats, 'I should ... I should 'ave gone with yer mum...' There's this great sadness in his eyes.

'You weren't to know.' Even though I feel this awkward tenderness towards him, I still push for answers. 'What happened?'

'As far as anybody can make out, she got off the bus near your sister's and was outside on their street ... when it happened. Massive 'eart attack,' he says, then, answering the question I'm about to ask, 'she didn't come round.' He breathes out a long wobbly sigh. 'Some neighbours called an ambulance. By the time they got 'old of me she'd gone. Died instantly, they said. No pain, they said. But how did they know?' His voice rises, tight with grief, with anger. 'How did they know?'

This time I don't think twice. I take his hand. Just for a few seconds, before I pat his fingers, let go.

'It wasn't me that stopped you coming back home ... coming back 'ere...'

'I know. Mum said she didn't want me to come back.' I take a long breath. 'She said she knew I was happy in Wales.'

He nods. 'Aye, she told me that an' all...' He wipes a hand over his head. I notice the thick blue veins running from his fingers to his wrist. And, for the first time, see he's wearing a hearing aid. 'You said you're only staying the day?'

'Until after tomorrow – I have work.'

'Yer mum said social work?'

'Yes.'

'You enjoy that? Sorting out folks' problems?'

'I do.'

'Ah, well, each to their own.' He looks puzzled.

I can't help smiling. 'I like helping people, Dad. You know, when awful things happen.'

I freeze. Close my eyes.

He clears his throat.

What happened to my baby brother is always going to be between us.

'Barb and Chris are here as well,' I say brightly. I look around for the clock that stood on the sideboard at the back of the room. No clock, no sideboard. So I glance at my watch. I'll have to leave soon.

'It'll be good to see them. 'Ave a catch-up, like.'

'Yes.' The unease has returned. 'I'm glad I came, Dad.'

'Aye, me too. I'm glad you came an' all, lass...' He sits back in his chair. 'It's been lovely seeing you.'

'Yes.' The uncomfortable moment has passed. No need to go back over old ground. It's more important to help now. 'Angela says the council have told you to move out?'

He blinks. 'They didn't waste much time, did they?'

'No. It's a disgrace.'

A ginger cat strolls into the room, leaps elegantly onto Dad's lap and settles down, purring. It amazes me. I don't remember him liking cats, but he's stroking it and it's lifting its head, pushing at his fingers.

'What's it called?'

'Cat.' He shrugs. 'I got it for yer mum, last year, but it were me it more or less adopted. Your mum used to laugh about that.' The slight lift of his mouth diverts the tears running down either side of his nose.

I manage a smile. 'I bet she did.' She hadn't mentioned the cat, but our phone conversations had mainly been me talking, telling her about my days, my work, what was happening on the smallholding, and her listening, her laboured breathing.

'So Dad, what will you do? About here?' I glance around the shabby room.

122

He stiffens. 'Dunno.'

I shake my head.

'There's a new estate being built t'other side of Barnsgate,' he says. 'They told me there's a flat for me, but as *I* told the chap last week, they can all bugger off, I'm going nowhere...'

'This estate's in a really bad way though.'

'Aye. Since this last lot got in the council, they've done nowt. Bloody Tories. You can ask anybody. Owt goes wrong, anything wants doing to the house, yer can tell them till you're blue in the face and yer get nowhere.'

'Some of the houses do look in a state, that's for sure.'

'Well, like I said to 'er next door...' He dips his head to the far wall. 'Sod the council, we need to keep our houses in good nick on our own. I've tried to do what needed to be done myself. But these last years — it's been hard. With your mum an' all, you know?'

'I can imagine.' When I really look, the dust, the pots in the kitchen sink, the stale smell, do seem to be recent neglect. And I can't blame him; bereavement can bring on lethargy.

'It's all down to Birch, you know...'

'You know?' I don't pretend I don't understand.

'Course I do.'

'Did Angela tell you?'

'Did she 'eck. 'Er and 'im think I haven't cottoned on, but I have. Thinks he can bully me like he does other folk. Bastard.' His laugh is bitter. 'But they'll have to drag me out from this place. That or wait until I'm six foot under.'

Chapter Forty-two

Lisa

There's no service in church before the cremation. I had no idea which chapel we were going to, so I hadn't questioned the route.

But when the car stops at the crematorium, I look first at Barb and then at Chris.

'I thought...'

Chris leans forward. 'Barb?'

'It's not what we discussed. Angela said there would be a service first at the Methodists.' She looks as bewildered as I feel. And as upset. She puts a hand on the driver's shoulder. 'Excuse me.' Her voice quivers. 'Are we at the right place?'

He glances at us in his mirror. 'I just go where I'm told, madam. Is there a problem?'

'I'm not sure.' She opens the door. 'Let me have a word with Angela.'

Angela's wearing what looks like a black Dolce & Gabbana dress under her fur coat. (I remember almost – almost – buying a similar one in a sale. Still couldn't afford it). She and Stephen Birch are standing by the hearse. He's taller than I'd imagined he would be and fills the black suit he's wearing. There's also a hint of a double chin above his collar. He keeps pushing back his thick black hair and looking around, as if he thinks people are watching him. Which I am, of course. His other hand grips Angela's arm. My unease after I'd seen the anxiety in Angela yesterday was right: this is a man who likes to be in charge, especially of his wife, I suspect.

I can't see Dad. I presume he's still in the car in front of us. The one my sister and her husband have just got out of. How must he feel, having to sit in there with them, after everything he told me this morning? Has he even had a choice, despite his show of bravado?

It's strange. I'd thought I was only going to see him to make this afternoon as bearable as possible. After all, my last memory of him was his back turned to me when I went to say goodbye. I hadn't expected to feel sorry for him. And I certainly hadn't expected to feel any responsibility for him. It makes me angry to think what the council is doing to him. And Stephen Birch's part in it.

I don't understand why Angela married Stephen Birch. She keeps looking towards us. She's pale, and she isn't saying much to Barb. But he is.

'This is ridiculous. I'm going to find out what's happening.'

Chris squeezes my hand. 'Stay calm, *cariad*. Let's just see what Barb says about it.' I can see the muscles at the side of his jaw moving, and I know it's just one more thing that has angered him today. When he found out Stephen had paid the hotel bill, he'd told Barb that he would write him a cheque to pay it back. Now he nods towards the windscreen. 'See, she's coming. We'll find out now.'

Barb slides into the back seat. 'Well, according to Angela, there was a mix-up at the chapel. Apparently, there's a new minister there and he double-booked the funeral with a big wedding. She says there was nothing they could do about it and she hasn't had time to tell me – us...'

'I don't believe that. And why not another chapel? Why here? Did Dad know?'

'I don't know. Didn't he say anything to you this morning?'

'No. Not about this. I don't think he was thinking straight.' I was so shocked, we didn't talk about the funeral. I haven't told either of them yet about Dad being kicked out of the house. There hasn't been time.

I try to remember what he said when I was leaving. I'd hugged him for the first time since I was little, and I was upset by how skeletal he was. 'I asked him was he going to be all right at the funeral, did he want me to do anything? He said everything was sorted.' Saying it out loud, it sounds odd. Why hadn't we discussed the funeral? Were we treading on thin ice and didn't want to upset one another? 'So why here? Did she say?'

'Stephen's suggestion. According to him, she was panicking, so he contacted the funeral director who'd said it was best to come straight here. Well, actually, he said there was no choice; it was too late to do anything else.'

Chris looks at me. 'What do you want to do, Lisa?'

People are milling around in groups, staring at our car, curious.

How did they all know to come straight here? Who'd told them the change of plan?

Our driver, who got out to give us some privacy, is standing with the other two drivers, looking bored. Angela is talking to Dad through the open door of his car. Stephen is moving around the groups shaking hands and chatting as though it's something he's organised. Which, when I think about it, it is.

'What can I do? Did Mum ever say anything to you, Barb?' I know how hard this has been for her. 'About what she...?'

'Wanted?' I can tell by the long breaths she's taking that Barb is trying to stay calm. 'She didn't want to talk about it, said it didn't matter what happened.' She shakes her head. 'All she said was to make sure you were all right, not to put any pressure on you to make any decisions, and if Eric wasn't up to it, to let Angela sort things out. That's how she put it: "sort things out".'

Even in her last illness, Mum was trying to protect me. I shouldn't have been such a coward. I should have faced up to things, made sure her funeral would reflect the kind, gentle woman she was.

There's movement outside. Dad is getting out of the car. He holds onto the roof, steadying himself. People are watching him, but no one is going near. He looks confused, vulnerable. A pathetic old man.

Angela is walking towards us.

'We need to go in,' she says, when she gets back to us. 'There's another funeral in less than an hour.' She doesn't quite meet my eyes.

'Lisa?' Barb turns to me.

'No choice,' I say. Now I think I know what my sister meant when she said 'get today over with'. She thinks I'll just up and leave. But things have changed; I won't be going home as soon as the funeral is over. I need to make sure Dad's all right before I go back to Ponthallen. And, because I'm not the frightened little girl I was last time I was in Micklethwaite, I've decided there is a lot more I want to say to Stephen Birch.

Chapter Forty-three

Lisa

We wait until the pallbearers have lifted Mum's coffin onto their shoulders and entered the crematorium through the large glass doors. I'm shaking as we follow my sister. She's linking arms with Dad. Stephen is slightly apart from them, his tall, bulky frame held stiffly, as though uncomfortable, even though this is all his doing. Chris is between Barb and me, his arms around the two of us.

There's a song playing. It's The Seekers' *I'll Never Find Another You*.

'Your dad's choice,' Barb whispers. 'Angela must have told them to play it.'

I sob. My sister turns to look at me, apprehensive. I nod and try to smile. I'm grateful. Mum adored The Seekers. Angela turns back but not before I see her faint smile.

It's light and airy inside the crematorium, almost like a chapel. That comforts me. The windows are high and wide; I can see the tops of trees, leaves swaying black against the pale blue mid-afternoon sky. There's only a hint of wispy cloud. The benches, the walls, the lectern are all in gleaming golden pine. Against the wall on the right, there is a tall vase with white roses and ferns. I'm guessing this is also something my aunt and sister decided between them, even if they meant it to be in the chapel. The men quietly place Mum's coffin on the large flat table at the front.

For the second time, Angela surprises me. Reaching into her handbag, she takes out a photo frame and places it on top of the coffin. It's a photo of Mum. She's standing slightly sideways, hand on hip, head tilted back, laughing. A large oak tree is in full leaf behind her.

Barb leans past Chris and says in a low voice, 'It's the one I gave Angela for the chapel service, the one I took the last time she was with us in Ponthallen before she was ill. I've got a copy of it for you as well.'

It's a memory I treasure. My eyes sting. 'Thank you.' We wait until

Angela joins Dad and Stephen on the other side of the aisle before we sit. There's a brass cross on a small table directly in front of us. I'm not in the least religious but I can't stop myself staring at it. It's catching the light from one of the windows, shining multi-coloured reflections onto the cream wall that bounce back onto the wooden floor.

I hear the rustle of people and glance back. The place is packed. I don't know anyone, but I didn't expect to. I wonder if some of them are old neighbours. If they recognise me. The thought makes me shift in my seat. I'm irritated with myself. Why should I care? I wouldn't be here if it wasn't for the one thing I've been dreading for months: losing Mum forever.

The service is short. No music. The celebrant looks around, waits until everyone settles down and then reads from a prepared script.

'Welcome, everyone. We are here today to celebrate the life of Eve Marsden. Eve lived the whole of her life in Micklethwaite, as her parents had before her. She had many friends.' He looks over our heads. 'As is shown today by so many of you being here.' I feel, rather than hear, the ripple of agreement moving over the rows. I bite the inside of my cheek. The only thing I can think of is how many of them stayed away from our house when she lost her baby son. Or was that because of me? Because I was there? Did it all change once I'd gone? When 'the problem' disappeared, did they all come to see the grieving parents? Were all these people at Robert's funeral? It was something I'd never asked, and Mum didn't speak about home when she was with us in Wales. I should have asked when I was older. I shut this place out of my mind. I'm sorry, Mum.

The celebrant allows the air to settle around us again. He smiles at Dad. I see Stephen shifting, scratching his nose, looking upwards.

'Eve was the loving wife of Eric, mother to a son, Robert, who sadly passed away as a baby...'

My throat tightens. I close my eyes; I won't look at Angela.

'And to her daughters, Angela and Lisa...'

I hear a murmur from the people behind: 'Who? Who did he say?'

Chris squeezed my hand. 'It's okay. It doesn't matter.'

I drop my chin on my chest, wait for the whispers to fade away. The celebrant raises his voice. Does he know what happened? Is he looking at me?

'Eve and Eric married soon after Eric completed his national service. Their love remained strong during those eighteen months they were separated and remained strong during their marriage, through many ups and downs...'

Was that how it was, their marriage? Ups and downs? Am I misremembering the quarrels, Mum trying so hard to protect me, him so bitterly against me that there seemed to be no way back? Did Mum stay in the marriage because that's what she was expected to do? To keep up the pretence? Is that what marriage is?

But then I think of the way Chris looks after Barb, the gentle teasing between them. It's clear they care for one another in the things they do, the looks shared. Sooner or later I would have seen over the years if it had been a façade. I know that.

I've yet to meet anyone I could envisage spending the rest of my life with. I sigh.

Barb looks past Chris at me, her forehead furrowed. I give a small shake of my head, concentrate again on the celebrant's voice.

He looks back at me. His next words stab into me.

'During the last two years of Eve's life, she struggled with pain and illness with courage and stoicism. She is at peace now.'

He mutters something I don't quite catch and then nods. A low whirring noise starts up, two purple curtains I hadn't noticed before slide around the table. I keep my eyes on the photo of Mum, glad I'd refused when Angela asked me if I wanted to see Mum in the chapel of rest at the funeral director's. The last time I saw her she was hanging out of the train window waving like mad at me, blowing kisses, her hair, no longer permed into tight curls, flailing around her head because of the speed of the train. The further away the train went, the younger she looked, in my mind. That's what I want to remember. I don't blink once until the curtains close with

129

a low swish. Then the only thing I can think is, Will they give the photograph back?

I try to make my mind blank; I won't cry, not here, not in front of strangers.

There is a collective sigh, some sobs. I see Dad bent forward. Angela's crying, but she has her arm around him and I'm glad she's comforting him. Chris does his best to comfort Barb and me by pulling us close to him.

A door opens near the tall vase, the breeze rustling the petals. The celebrant lifts his arms a little, palms upwards, his eyes moving across us. 'Please stand whilst the family leaves.' Stephen is already standing.

The celebrant encourages us to move with another tilt of his head and a smile. He straightens the lapels of his suit, as if to say, 'There, that's done,' before giving a short cough. Encouraging us to go a bit faster, I suppose.

We file out. Stephen strides past with purpose, patting his hair with his fingers. He's already some way along the path before he looks back and sees the rest of us have stopped in an untidy line by the viewing area, where wreaths and floral tributes are laid along a low stone wall topped with planters.

People file past with murmurs of condolences, speaking first to Dad, whose hearing aid is giving out a low whistle that everyone ignores, and then to Angela. They give a louder greeting to Stephen when he returns to squash in between my sister and dad to shake hands, with little quips and low laughter as though this is just a social gathering. Most of them have a moment of hesitation in front of me, a muttered word or two. I can feel their relief when they can move on, to stop when they see Barb.

When almost all have gone, with just a few grouped around my family, all at once I'm self-conscious. Alone. I remember seeing the Chapel of Remembrance as we came through the gates of the crematorium. Following the signposts, I soon find the small building, feeling better for having a purpose.

It's cool and dark inside. Small blue curtains are closed over the six tiny windows, set in alcoves. Three on each side of the chapel. Only one pool of light shines onto a large, golden-edged book on a raised lectern in one corner. I can see columns of names in cursive handwriting. It must be the Book of Remembrance. Is this where they will print Mum's name? I walk over to look at it, running my forefinger over one page.

My scalp tingles when I hear a small cough.

A figure moves in the shadows at the front. A man. He stands.

'Sorry if I startled you.' His voice is deep yet holds that slight hoarseness of recent tears.

'No, that's fine. I didn't see you.' My voice is too loud, too harsh for this place. I move towards the book and the light, a little apprehensive, hoping to see him better, but he's walking away, carrying something in his arms. A child.

He doesn't speak again. There's a slant of light across the darkness when the door opens. Then he's gone.

Chapter Forty-four

Lisa

'We've all been directed to go back to the Grove,' Barb says, tipping her head towards Chris, who's standing by the car looking distinctly irritated.

'Who by?'

'Who do you think?'

'Stephen?'

'Yes.'

'I thought you said we'd just have a small family gathering at Dad's local, the Swan, in the village?' At least it used to be his local before Mum's illness.

She sounds weary. 'Change of plan again, for some reason.'

The reason becomes clear when we arrive at the hotel. Stephen leads the way, leaving Angela and Dad to follow. Dad looks as pleased as Chris about yet another change in a day that should have been all about his wife. And exhausted. Stephen strides over to a large group of men standing by the bar and, from what I can make out from his flapping arm gestures, he orders another round of drinks for them, while, at the same time, offering cigarettes.

'Friends of his from the golf club; a couple of them are on the council with him,' Angela says. 'They usually meet today for lunch.' She ushers Dad across the room. 'There's food been put on over here.' A waiter opens a red door that matches the carpet.

'I wonder if he'll be joining us or them,' Chris mutters, glaring at Stephen's back.

A large table in the centre of the room is laden with oval platters of sandwiches, fruit, cakes, and other nibbles. At the far end is a bar. Two young girls wearing black and white uniforms and suitably sombre expressions stand behind the counter.

'A large G&T, please, Chris,' Barb says. 'And whatever Lisa wants.'

'Same, please. And can you get Dad a pint of bitter?' I hope that's still his tipple. 'And perhaps you'd better ask Angela what she wants, please.' She's looking as uncomfortable as I feel. 'I'll pay.'

'You won't,' he says.

The room is filling up. There are a few curious stares being cast our way. Barb chooses a round table far from the bar and pulls a few extra chairs around it.

'Do you mind if I ask Mildred and Fred and Bill and Mary to join us, Lisa?' she asks. Dad looks relieved. They are old friends of his and Mum's. 'And Sandy's here with her hubby, Clem?' Sandy is Barb's best friend from her younger days.

'Of course,' I say.

Angela looks surprised she hasn't been asked. But I know what Barb is doing; she's making sure Dad's okay, and that I'm shielded from the people who are now crowded in front of the bar. I sit with my back to them.

'There aren't any speeches,' Dad mutters, to no one in particular. 'I'm not going to do any speech, whatever yon mon thinks.'

'Don't be like that, Father.' Angela takes off her black fur coat and drapes it over the back of her chair. 'Nobody expects you to do anything. Stephen just thought it would be considerate to put on a bit of food for all these friends who came to pay their respects to Mother.'

'I don't know most of these folks.' He lets his gaze move around the table at us all. 'The only folk I do know are sitting here.'

'Don't be silly.'

She's treating him as though he's senile. Despite being grateful for the touches at the crematorium, the music and the photo of Mum, I'm more and more annoyed at the way the day has been ambushed by Stephen. The way my sister has let him.

I say, 'Dad's not being silly, Angela. In fact, I think he's been extremely tolerant, given that your husband has hijacked all the arrangements. Dad wanted what Mum wanted. Today hasn't been that, so far...'

I become aware of the silence hanging over our table. Everybody except Dad and Angela are busy studying the pictures on the walls around us. 'What Mum wanted, as far as I understand, was a quiet, simple ceremony where those she loved, her family...' And just in case I was about to offend them, I added, 'And her friends could get together to show how much *she* was loved.' I force a smile. 'Sorry, everyone.'

Barb pats my hand under the table. Dad smiles at me at the same time as he's weighing up Angela out of the corner of his eye. Chris arrives just at the right time with our drinks on a tray, followed by a waiter carrying five bottles of wine and holding a notepad.

'Any orders other than these, please, ladies and gents?'

The awkward moment is immediately dissipated in the confusion of voices.

Angela pushes back her chair and leaves the table. I watch her cross the room to the door marked 'Ladies'.

'I'll go,' Barb whispers. 'After all, it's the arrangements she and I made that have been completely, as you said, hijacked—'

'No, please, let me.' I look at my father. 'Sorry, Dad.'

'Ah, lass, after today, nowt else can surprise me. She had it coming, but I don't want any fallouts, not on your mum's day. You go and sort 'er out.' He looks up. 'Hey up, his lordship's in the room.'

That produces a low chorus of laughter. I watch as Stephen does what Chris sarcastically calls 'glad-handing', when we see politicians on the telly on voting days, as he crosses the room. It occurs to me that the people at the table know Stephen better than me. And share the same opinion.

Chapter Forty-five

Lisa

Angela is drying her hands. Her sleeveless dress reveals how skinny her arms are, how thin she is. She could use some of the extra pounds I'm carrying. But it's the misery on her face that really hits me.

I glance at the rows of open cubicle doors; there's no one else in here.

'Satisfied?' She glares at me, digging into her handbag and dabbing beige panstick on her reddened nose.

'No.' I'm trying to keep in mind what Dad said, that today isn't the day for any quarrels. But today hasn't gone the way it should have. 'I'm sorry if I upset you in front of everyone. But Dad has a right to say what he wants, you know; he's not a child to be told not to be silly.' I stress the word. 'He's put up with all the changes with Mum's funeral. Not made a fuss.'

'Why should he? He's not paid for a thing.' Her voice is so monotonous, it's as though she's rehearsed those words. Or they're words that have been drummed into her.

'That's a nasty thing to say. Is that what you really think? Or are you a mouthpiece for that husband of yours?' I can't stop myself. 'Why change what you and Barb and Dad agreed on? I don't understand, Angela. Without telling Barb? Her sister. Or me? My mum—'

'Your mother...' She spits the words out, glowering at me through the mirror. 'Whose funeral arrangements you wanted nothing to do with.'

It's true but it hurts. That's how it must appear to her. 'Still my mum as much as yours, whatever you think. And to change everything, without telling Dad, for God's sake. The funeral of his wife?'

I see the slow flush rise from her throat to her face. 'You don't understand...'

'So tell me.'

A tap drips into one of the hand basins eight times before she answers.

'Stephen said it was my fault, that I made a mess of the date. He said I hadn't confirmed the service with the vicar, and so the vicar had booked something else in at the time we wanted.' She stops, shakes her head, just the once.

We're still watching one another in the mirror. A glimmer of sympathy lights inside me. I nod to encourage her.

'I thought it was all sorted.' She looks bewildered. 'But after we'd been to the bank yesterday, he told me how much I'd messed up, but that he'd managed to sort it out. It was too late to tell you and – well – I didn't know what to do.' She presses both hands flat on the edge of the hand basin, her head hanging down. 'I really don't understand. I'm usually so organised. Always have been.'

'I guess you had to be in your job.' I can't help it; even today, I'm still fishing to find out who she worked for in Manchester.

She doesn't seem to hear me. Or chooses to ignore what I've said. So I just say, 'I'm sorry, it's partly my fault, I should have helped you and Barb.'

As I'm saying it, I know that Barb wouldn't have made a mistake.

She would have checked everything to the last detail. No, what's happened is all down to Stephen Birch, I know it. I just don't know why.

'It's understandable. You're upset. I can't even begin to think how awful it must have been, finding Mum in the street.'

'Oh.' She is struggling to speak. 'I didn't. I was out at the supermarket. Some of our neighbours found her. I feel so guilty about that.'

I shut out the image of Mum being alone in pain on the hard ground, surrounded by strangers. It hurts too much. I need to concentrate on what's happening now with Angela.

'You weren't to know. And I know you were good with Mum when she was ill, she told me.' She hadn't; she hadn't mentioned my sister since the day I graduated. She knew I didn't want to talk about Angela. But when I see the small, quivering smile on my sister's lips, I'm glad I've lied.

'Did she? I've sometimes worried that my leaving the village started her being ill.'

'No. Though I don't know why you didn't keep in touch? She'd have been glad to know you were safe with a good job...'

She rummages around in her bag, her long hair hiding her face.

'Perhaps talk to Barb about today? Explain?'

'I will. Stephen said it was time of the month.' I see her neck mottle with embarrassment. 'Actually he's right—'

'He's not.'

'He is.' She nods. 'I was on a period, as it happens. When I was organising everything. It probably was that.'

I've heard these kind of shit comments from controlling men before. 'Have you talked to your doctor about it?'

'No. Stephen says it's natural to get a bit woolly-headed then. I don't need to see the GP...'

What does he know? 'Well, have you talked to any friends, then?'

She gets a comb out of her bag, gives the crown of her hair a quick backcomb. Not looking at me.

'Angela? What about friends?'

'No.'

'Why not? My friend, we talk all the time about all sorts of stuff. Things that are bothering us. Everything.' I remember how Jayne held my hand and how much better I'd felt after telling her about my part in my brother's death.

That tap drips a few times before Angie drops the comb into her handbag and finally answers.

'I don't have any friends. I'm too busy, don't have time. There's too much to do at home.'

'That's rubbish.'

'Stephen likes things done a certain way.' She glares at me. 'And so do I. I need order. Everything tidy. Clean.' I remember that obstinate set of her mouth from childhood.

No friends? Angie was always surrounded by friends when we were kids. 'So, has this started since you were married? This "being disorganised" business?'

She straightens up, pulls out a lipstick. 'Hmm?' She cocks her head to one side, staring at her reflection as though considering the question. 'I suppose.' She gives each lip a careful application of pink. 'I don't know. Anyway, we'd better get back out there. Stephen ... people will wonder where we are.' She pushes her hair back, adjusts the diamond studs in her ears. 'Right?'

'Right. We good then?' We should have a long talk, but I'll leave all that for now.

'We're good.' She smiles – a smile that trembles a little.

I don't get a chance to talk to Angela later. In the confusion, while Barb, Chris and I make sure Dad has seen everyone he wants to see and decide how to get him home safely, Stephen must have whisked her away.

Chapter Forty-six

Lisa

'Stay as long as you need to,' Melanie Grimshaw, my line manager, said, when I telephoned to tell her I'd be in Micklethwaite for another two or three weeks. She's a good friend. She's also the only one in work who knows my personal background. 'You're owed a lot of leave,' she'd added. 'I'll get cover for you.'

She knows how much courage it's taken me to come back. When Barb came into my bedroom that awful morning, to tell me Mum had died, as well as the terrible loss, I was also afraid, knowing I would finally have to return and face everyone. Standing in line at the crematorium I saw the furtive glances, the whispering behind their hands.

I didn't stay in that hotel; I couldn't afford to. And I refused Angela's tentative invitation to stay with them. I couldn't bear to be in the same house as Stephen Birch.

Still, it feels strange that I'm here in this house, living with Dad, who disowned me.

We're on old, faded, red-and-cream-striped deckchairs in his back garden, outside the back door. No vegetables now; the square of land is overgrown with tangled grass and nettles, the hedge a mix of privet and brambles. The air is still, humid. The sheep-filled fields and the meandering stone walls above the village shimmer, distorted in the heat. Beyond them, the moors are indistinct from the colourless sky.

We were always told to keep out of those fields and leave the crops alone. Now the land is left to nature: wild flowers, tall grass, rippling in a breeze I can't feel here, sheltered by the sun-warmed wall of the house.

Those fields were where we played when the crops had been safely harvested. All the kids off the estate would hold our own 'sports day'.

Angela was in charge, of course; she was the oldest, so we all deferred to her. She organised us into teams, decided what races were to be run, and in what order. I can see her now, bouncing on the balls of her feet, holding the pause between 'get set' and 'go' for so long some of us fell over, and the race needed to be started all over again, with groans and complaints. And laughter.

Dad and I haven't spoken for a while. It's enough that we're sitting together, if not in complete harmony, at least not in the resentment I was dreading before I came. But he's fidgeting, uncomfortable. He's tried to light his pipe a few times, sucking and puffing, while the stem makes that whistling sound I remember from my childhood. I pull myself back to the now.

'Want a cup of tea?'

'No, lass, I'm fine.' He talks through the pipe clenched in his teeth. It waggles around.

The endearment 'lass' makes me cry. It's sad that Mum can't see us; even though we didn't talk about it, I've always known the estrangement between Dad and me upset her. And yet there is still this gap, this unspoken thing that has haunted me since I was a child, that wrecked our family.

I feel the touch of his fingers on my hand. 'You okay, Mand-Lisa?'

'Yes.' I turn and give him the best smile I can. 'Memories. You know.'

'Aye.' He waves the stem of his pipe towards the garden. 'They can be the death of you.' He stops.

I pull down the sleeves of my cardigan against the sudden shiver that puckers my arms. 'I'll make tea, anyway.'

'Okay, I think I will join you, after all.'

When I'm on the top step, the doorframe warm under my palm, I look back at Dad. What he said about memories makes me wonder if he's ready to listen to me about Robert.

'Can we talk, Dad?' I rub at the peeling paint on the frame. Flakes drift downwards, like tiny green leaves. I'm trying to put what I'm thinking into words. 'Dad...?'

He's very still, as though waiting.

Now I've asked, I don't know what words to use. I'll need to think about it. I tap on the doorframe, loosen more flakes. 'I'll make that tea.'

I hold the kettle handle, feeling the water heating inside and gaze through the window. Cat snakes through the long grass, stalking something.

In the week since I moved back, I've got the house as spotless as I could make it. I've gone through the place as my gran apparently used to say, 'like a dose of salts'. The memory of Mum once telling me this makes me smile and the movement of my lips feels strange, as if I haven't done that for a long time. Which is true.

Chapter Forty-seven

Lisa

'Tea up.' I'm trying to sound casual, but my heart is thumping so hard.

I've found Mum's favourite tray, decorated with red roses. It feels reassuring in my hands. 'And biscuits – digestives.' I set it on the step next to my deckchair and hand Dad his mug. His fingers are shaking. I wonder if he's as nervous as I am. But, thinking about it, he shakes most of the time. I wonder if he's seen a doctor about it. 'Biscuit?'

'Ta.' He takes one off the plate and dunks it in his tea.

Sitting, I reach for my mug and dunk my biscuit as well. It's ages since I've done that. He notices and snorts a chuckle. It gives me the confidence.

'Is it okay? Can we talk, Dad?'

He goes red in the face, as though struggling with the memories. The look that passes between us is perplexing. I don't understand.

'Sorry, lass.' He's so quiet I'm not sure I've heard right. He clears his throat. 'I'm so sorry for what 'appened. You know, what I was like with you. Afterwards...'

'Everything turned out for the best, Dad. Honest. I've had a good life with Barb and Chris, they're lovely people. I couldn't have wished for better. And I have a good job, friends. I'm fine.' With every sentence, he winces. 'Don't.' I reach over to pat his shoulder. 'You couldn't help how you felt.'

'No. I was wrong. I shouldn't have blamed you. I should have looked after you...'

My throat closes up. I swallow. There's a pause between us, waiting to be filled.

'I know,' he finally says. 'I know what really 'appened.' He's blinking, blowing out his cheeks with each juddering breath.

My stomach turns over and over and I'm not sure if it's because I'm convinced if he carries on like this, he'll have another stroke, or because I'm afraid of what he's trying to say. When he does speak, everything tilts in front of me. 'I know the truth...'

'The truth?' I look away. Dark clouds are bubbling up over the moors in the distance. The stillness in the air has intensified.

'About the accident.' Dad places his mug on the ground. 'About what really happened.'

I remember again what Barb first said to me when I went to live with her. She told me that there are some moments in life which will never leave you. When one can look back and think, *that's when it changed.* She said what happened to my brother, I would never forget. But I mustn't let it ruin the rest of my life; I should reflect on it, learn from it and move on.

I can't wait for Dad to start speaking again. I can't stand it. 'Did Mum tell you?' She'd promised she wouldn't. I hadn't wanted to come home. But if she had, why hadn't he written to me, to tell me he knew it wasn't my fault?

'Dad?'

'No. She got our Angela to admit it. Years after, sometime after

141

she came back. Brought her here to tell me. Must have been around '75. Or '76.'

Give him his due, I thought, irritably, he's keeping eye contact. 'And you knew? All these years? You knew the truth?'

'I did.' He raises his hand in a weary, fluttery gesture. 'But it was too late, yer mum said. She told me to let sleeping dogs lie. That you were settled in Wales. Happy.' He rubs his nose with his palm. 'And I agreed. I thought, why rake up bad feelings. Old gossip.'

'Old gossip!' The anger erupts. 'You were so horrible to me. You made me move away from everything I knew. I was thirteen, for God's sake.'

All because I'd covered up for Angela, thinking she would own up, and she hadn't.

And then, at last, she had. At least to Mum and Dad. And neither of them had told me. Given me a chance to talk about it with them. With Angela. Shared the grief, the nightmares.

I've been here over a week and my sister's had time to tell me this. And not a word. Not. One. Word.

He holds out his hand to me, but I don't take it.

'You could at least have told me. Told Angela to... Bloody hell!' I struggle to get out of the damn deckchair. I need to get away from him. 'You made me feel you didn't want me here. Do you know how abandoned I felt? How ashamed? Even though it wasn't me that caused the accident?'

He's trying to get up now. His pipe falls from his lap to the ground with a clatter, but he doesn't notice. His eyes don't leave me.

'I'm sorry.' He takes a step towards me. I back up until I feel the rough stone step at the back door against my calf. 'I promised your Mum ... before she died. She said I 'ad to tell you that we, that *I* knew. She said, when you came back for her...' He gulps. 'For the funeral ... I 'ad to tell you. Set things straight between us, like.' Taking a large grubby handkerchief from his trouser pocket, he scrubs at his eyes. 'I'm sorry. I'm that sorry for everything.'

'And me.' The words explode out of me. 'Sorry none of you

142

thought to let me know.' I'm even angry at Mum. Why wouldn't she realise I'd want to know the truth had come out. Why had she not made Angela write to me? 'I need some time on my own. I'm going upstairs for a while – if you don't mind?' I can't keep the hard sarcasm out of my voice.

'Right,' he says. He doesn't take his eyes off me. Frowns.

Running up the stairs it occurs to me that he thinks I'm going to pack and leave.

I think so too.

Chapter Forty-eight

Lisa

It's almost dark when Dad taps on the bedroom door.

'Lisa...'

At least he remembered what to call me. I can hear his wheezing as he waits for an answer.

'I'll be down in a minute, Dad.'

'Ah, okay.' There's relief in his voice.

Back in the living room, I ask him, 'Where's the piano gone?' Totally irrelevant, but I've been meaning to ask all week. I want to break the tension a little.

'Mum stopped playing after you both left. She gave it to Angela when she came back. Birch promised her one of them big fancy pianos, but it didn't 'appen, so your mother gave 'er hers.'

'Does Angela still play?'

'She did. But after a few months she stopped.' He shook his head.

'I don't remember seeing the piano at Angela's house?'

'Angela told your mum she went home one day and it wasn't there. That's all we knew.'

'It was Mum's piano; they should have given it back.'

'I don't think Angela had a say in it. Your mum said to leave it.'

Something else not talked about. 'Horrible man!'

'Aye.' There's a mixture of anger and sadness in the word.

'Do you remember how Mum set all the nursery rhymes to music for us to sing to? She used to hold her hands high in the air before bringing them down onto the keys...'

'To make the crashing noise for when Jack and Jill fell down the hill, or Humpty Dumpty falling off the wall.' We smile at one another. But we're putting off discussing the bombshell Dad dropped earlier.

'That reminds me.' Dad grunts as he pushes himself out of his armchair. 'I've kept something. Your mum said she'd meant to give it to you every time she came down to Wales, but kept forgetting.'

The floorboards creak above me as he crosses their bedroom. I hear the opening and shutting of drawers, more creaks, his laboured tread on the stairs.

'Here.' He hands me a large brown envelope. It's soft and crumpled with age.

I slide out the sheet of paper inside. It's the sheet music for 'Mazurka', a piano piece by Chopin, Mum's favourite.

There are handwritten notes in the margins, just comments on how she wants to play a certain passage, but seeing her writing makes my heart stop. All I can say is, 'Thank you.'

Should I feel a small stab of triumph? Satisfaction that she saved this for me, her tone-deaf, non-musical daughter, and not for Angela, the talented piano player? I hold it close to me, the sheet music that my mother held so many times.

The gas-fire flames sputter yellow and blue, giving off little heat. Not that it matters; even after the deluge of rain earlier, when it pelted on my bedroom window until it trickled through the frame and pooled on the windowsill, it's still humid.

'Makes the room a bit cheerful,' Dad says, seeing me stare at the fire. He points at the sheet music with the stem of his pipe. 'I kept it for you.' He nods. 'I hoped you'd come. Not to the village. Not just for your mum's funeral. Here...'

144

He sits in his armchair. 'Here, to the house.' His voice is husky. The cat sidles in and jumps on Dad's lap. It rubs its head against his hand, and he strokes its ears with the back of his forefinger. 'So I could tell you ... how sorry I was. How sorry I am.'

My anger has drained away, but I'm unsettled; I feel out of place in this house. Yet I know I must stay. There are things I need to understand, to put behind me once and for all. Since I stepped off that bus, I have known that all the old secrets have been festering inside me, worse now I'm here. Why was I never told that Mum and Dad knew the truth?

I perch on the arm of his chair and stroke the cat's back. It turns to look at me and blinks slowly, and purrs.

'I'm trying to understand why you and Mum didn't tell me, Dad.' I can't let it go. 'Even if you decided to keep it secret from everyone else, you could have let *me* know. All these years, I've thought you blamed me for my brother's death.'

I hold my breath. Saying this brings a rush of anxiety.

'If I'd just known...' I twist to look at him. 'I wouldn't have asked to come back to Micklethwaite, you know. No...' I hold onto his arm when he begins to speak. 'No, and I'm not saying you wouldn't have wanted me. I understand how awful it must have been for both of you. But you could have told me...'

'I know, lass. I know. It was a bad mistake.' He shakes his head. 'And yer mum did say we should make Angie write to you. But you know what she's like, mind of her own, that one. Or had, before...' He stops. 'But in any case, you're right.'

A thought comes to me, and I feel slightly sick. 'Did you tell Barb Angela has admitted it was her?'

'No, we never said a word to anyone. And for that I'm ashamed, an' all.'

Relief rushes through me. I couldn't bear to think I couldn't trust Barb and Chris. 'I'm glad you didn't. I'm glad they didn't know. By then I knew where I belonged. Where I was happy.'

The chair shakes. He's crying.

Chapter Forty-nine

Lisa

Angela's cleaning the dining-room window when I arrive. She might have yellow Marigold gloves on her hands and a floral apron tied around her tiny waist, but she's fully made up and her hair is immaculate. She's wearing a bright blue pencil skirt, with a pair of white stilettos that wouldn't look out of place in a dance hall.

'Are you going out?' I know I'm being sarcastic, but she is *so* overdressed for housework.

The sarcasm goes right over her head. 'No, of course not. Monday's washday.' She doesn't stop rubbing at the smears of Windowlene. 'I'm just trying to get this done before it rains.'

I glance up. 'It won't rain, Angela.' The sky is as clear as any June day can be. Not a cloud. The humidity of the previous day ended with a storm of crackling lightning and ear-splitting thunder. It was a relief. Dad and I sat in the kitchen and watched it through the window as rain swept through the fields behind the house, Cat trembling on Dad's lap.

I want ... I need to see Angela's face when I tell her Dad finally admitted she'd told them the truth about Robert.

'You've been avoiding me since the funeral. Why is that?' Can she sense the tension in me?

It's only the slightest hesitation, a momentary pause as Angela bends over the bucket of water.

'I haven't. I've been busy. We used to have a cleaner, Mrs Beech. But she left.' The words are clipped.

'I've called here twice with no answer.' Last time I came, I could have sworn I saw movement behind the bedroom curtains.

'You could have phoned.'

I cross my arms. She has no right to be so offhand. I force myself to be calm when I speak. 'You don't go out to work, so I took a chance.'

No answer. She rubs at one corner of the window.

'I know you told them.'

'Told who what?' She keeps unfolding and folding the chamois leather, still keeping her voice cool.

'Mum and Dad. About Robert. About what really happened to our baby brother. About Stephen lying for you. About letting me take the blame.'

Just for a second, she stops.

'Old news.'

Almost the same words as Dad. But the same sentiment?

'Is it?' Anger forms a lump in my throat. 'Well, it's not old news for me, Angela. Have you any idea how I felt coming back to Micklethwaite? Facing Dad?'

The chamois leather is swished around in the bucket again.

'Look at me! Well?' I say.

'Well, what?'

'Have you any idea how I felt coming back here?'

She doesn't answer.

'I waited until after Mum's funeral. I was going to go back home, but I decided not to, after what you said about Dad and the house...'

Still staring at the window.

'I thought – was hoping, I suppose – that you'd have the decency to want to talk about what happened?'

She shakes her head, scrubs at one pane of glass.

'I think that's the least you owe me.' I cross my arms, stifling the urge to slap her. 'Okay. How would you feel if the truth came out?'

She half turns. I see her neck move in small swallows.

'You wouldn't...' Her voice trembles.

'Why wouldn't I?'

'Stephen...'

'What about him?'

'He'd...You can't.' Her face is mottled pink. 'Please, Mand ... Lisa. Please.'

'He'd what?'

'You don't understand.' Her voice rises, thin and breathless.

'No, I don't.'

'You'll be going back to Wales soon. There's no need to say anything, is there?'

'When Dad told me he knew, I was so angry, I almost went back home there and then. You got away with what you did. Because of your lies. *His* lies, his wicked lies. If you'd told me that you'd been honest with Mum and Dad, however late...' I stop. 'It might have changed things.'

She says something. I can't make out the words.

'What?'

'I said, I'm sorry. I really am, Lisa.'

Even though an apology is something I've needed from my sister, I feel flat. I'm not sure the damage that's been done can be repaired. But I'm conscious that the bitterness I've held onto for too long is lessening.

'Why did you tell them?'

'After I came back from ... Mum and me, we never talked about you. I knew she'd been to see you over the years, she said so, but she never told me anything about you. I guessed it was because you didn't want me to know?'

'I didn't see why you should know.' The words are cruel, but I try to say them softly.

'And I understood. You were angry with me because of ... because of...' She's shaking, twisting the cloth round and round in her hands.

'The lies.'

'Yes.' She breaths out. 'But then, one day, Mum came to the house after ... after something had happened. Stephen ... we'd had a row ... I was upset. You need to understand, Lisa, while I was away, I managed to push it all from my mind. Well most of the time—'

'Lucky you.' I can't help the automatic resentment, even though her words, 'something had happened' are hovering at the back of my mind.

'I know. I'm sorry, I didn't mean it like that.' She drops the cloth into the bucket. 'But once I was here again, it wouldn't go away. So, when Mum came that day, when Stephen had...'

It's there again. 'When Stephen had what?'

'Nothing. I meant when Stephen and I had quarrelled – and she was so kind – I told her everything.'

'She already knew.'

'Yes, I know. She said you'd told her, and that she believed you. I was so ashamed. I wish I'd known before...' Suddenly she picks up the bucket and brushes past me, clip-clopping in those heels to the kitchen. I follow.

'How did you feel? That she knew and believed me?'

'Like I said ... ashamed.' She turns the tap off, leaves her hand on it, sighs. 'But relieved as well, I suppose.' It's as if she's talking to herself. 'Yes, relieved. Then I went to Carrbrook with her and told Dad.'

'And Stephen doesn't know you told them?'

'No. No, he doesn't know.'

'Why?' I'm sure I know, but I need to hear her say it.

'Because...' She's wiping the sink and worktops. 'Because I can't.'

'Why? What would he do?'

She points. There's a note pinned to a noticeboard by the door. *Windows this morning.* Large flamboyant letters, followed by a capital S. Not her writing. Well, not how I remember her writing, anyway. A note from him? An order? Thinking back to what she told me in the toilets at the hotel, and her fear just now, it sends a shiver through me.

She goes to the front of the house, starts cleaning the living-room window. I'll make her tell me; I can't help unless she does. 'What time will Stephen be home?'

She freezes, her hand lifted to the window. I see a trickle of water run down her arm. 'Why?'

'Well, I think he should know the truth. And I'd like to see his face when I tell him. You never know, Angela, it might stop him—'

'Stop him what?'

149

'Stop him treating you like he does. Make him give you some respect?'

'It wouldn't. You can't talk to him. If he thought you would tell people, I don't know what he'd do... Please. He's built up this public figure, his reputation, the business, getting on the council. He won't let anything – anybody take it from him.' She looks at me over her shoulder, her eyes wide, and I see the terror. 'I don't know what he'd do...'

She gives up on the window and, wiping her hands on her apron, glances at her watch. 'You've made me late.' She locks her fingers together at her waist. 'Please don't tell him, Lisa.' She looks anxiously towards the avenue. 'Look, please go. Stephen comes home for his lunch. He likes it on the table for one o'clock.'

She said something similar the day I got here, when she dropped me off at the hotel. She doesn't add *exactly* but the word hovers around the 'one o'clock'.

All my instincts were right: she's terrified of him.

Chapter Fifty

Lisa

I'd listened to Angela at the hotel on the day of Mum's funeral, figured out how Stephen played mind games with her. Why it hadn't occurred to me that she was physically afraid of him as well, I don't know. He'd changed my life when I was a child. And if he was manipulative enough at that age to lie to the police, what's he capable of as a man?

But I need to get back to Dad. When I left, he looked drained, even though he insisted he was only tired. It worries me. Perhaps I shouldn't have left him.

Standing at the bus stop in full sun is uncomfortable. The air seems to have been sucked out of the day. I look around for shade.

A high wall runs the length of the main road, hiding the houses and gardens behind it. I step back and lean on it, grateful for the cool stone, thinking again about the conversation I had with Barb before she and Chris left.

She was cramming clothes into their suitcases on the bed in the hotel. It was good to see her in her usual multicoloured maxi skirt and a long-sleeved purple top, her hair carelessly tied back with a yellow ribbon.

I asked her what she thought I should do.

Typical of her, Barb turned the question around and asked what I wanted to achieve. I knew she was worried about me.

'I don't want you to be hurt again, Lisa,' she said. 'You should think about what could happen if you confront him. Making it public would really upset the applecart as far as his public life's concerned, and there's no knowing what he will do to stop that. From what I've seen of Stephen Birch in the short time we've been here, he's the spit of his father, out for himself and trampling on anyone who gets in his way.'

'What can he do to me that he's not already done, Barb?' Seeing him after all these years, I knew I was strong enough to face up to him. 'I think he should understand I could ruin his life. Like he almost did mine.'

'And there's Angela as well, Barb. I know things are difficult between her and me – and probably always will be – but I'm sure she's scared of him. I'm sure he bullies her...'

She straightened up, rubbing the small of her back and grimacing.

'Be careful, petal. If she won't tell you, there's little you can do, and she might not thank you for trying to find out.'

'I'll be careful.' I wasn't sure what I could do, but I couldn't let it go. 'I just want him to know—'

'He'll not admit it, Lisa, any more than he'll admit to lying about you.' The little worry lines across her forehead deepened. 'You'll get yourself in a state all over again. Is it worth it?'

I shrugged. 'And then there's what Stephen's doing to Dad. I need to be here for him...'

'I've had a word with your dad's friends, you know, and they've promised to keep an eye on him. Mildred's said she'll get Fred to take him fishing next time he goes, and Bill and Mary said they'd ask him to go to their house for Sunday lunch every other week or so. There's not a lot you can do until he finally has to move.'

I knew she was trying hard to persuade me to go home with her.

'I'll just feel better if I hang on a bit longer, Barb. If only to build a few more bridges with Dad.' I hugged her, feeling the familiar reassurance from her softness.

'Just be careful, Lisa. And come home as soon as you can.'

The bus comes around the corner at the end of the road. I move away from the shade, still thinking about confronting Stephen Birch. Over the years I've wondered if I ever would. But one way or another, I am determined to. But what will that do to Angela? There's something badly wrong in my sister's marriage.

Chapter Fifty-one

Lisa

When the bus stops at the beginning of the estate, I glance at the driver. It's the man who was the caretaker at Micklethwaite school. He pushes the button to open the doors and smiles.

'Welcome home,' he says. 'Bet your dad's glad to see you.'

I smile back. So I'm not totally a pariah. 'Thanks. I think he is.'

Walking home, I feel a little lighter inside. Even the neglected houses don't upset me as much. I smile when I pass people and some even smile back. Whatever's facing me with Stephen Birch, I can deal with it.

But when I turn the corner, I see Dad waiting at the front door, looking along the avenue. I walk faster. His face is grey.

'What's wrong? Are you okay?'

'I didn't know where you were.'

'I said I was going to Angela's. What's the matter?'

He waves a piece of paper at me.

'What is it? The notice to quit the house?'

'What? No. No!' He dismisses my question with a flick of his hand. 'Come in, come in. See. Came in the post...' He thrusts it towards me.

It's a letter, the heading in embossed print.

Chapter Fifty-two

Lisa

Angela's outside, cleaning those bloody windows again.

'You only did them yesterday?'

'They weren't clean enough. What's the matter?' She stops. 'It's not Dad, is it?'

'No. No,' I say. 'We've had a letter from a solicitor in Barnsgate. Asking Dad to call into their offices. Apparently, Mum left a will. I'm presuming you'll want to be there?'

She pulls a duster from her apron pocket. 'I'm not sure. What day?'

'We thought Friday. Well, Dad says that's the best day for him, because he's got an appointment at the doctor's for ten o'clock. We can go after that. I'll try for eleven?'

She begins vigorously polishing the glass. 'I'm not sure. If I'm there, I'm there. Can't think what Mother had to leave anyway.' She says it in a kind of offhand, flippant way.

'No?'

'No what?'

153

'I don't know; it's just that you said it in a weird way. As though you know something.'

'No.' She pulls a face.

I can tell she's not going to say anymore. 'Well, no doubt we'll find out.'

'Is there something else? Because I need to get on.' She's looking down at the cloth, folding and unfolding it.

'The solicitor's Banner and Banner...' I glance at the note I'd made of the name earlier. 'On Whitworth Street in Barnsgate. We'll be catching the nine-thirty bus to get there in time for Dad's appointment.'

She glances up at one of the upstairs windows. I follow her gaze and see Stephen staring down at us.

'I have to go in,' she mutters.

'Angela—'

'Sorry, I have to go in now.'

'See you on Friday, then?'

She doesn't answer.

Chapter Fifty-three

Angela

Angela watches Lisa walk down the path and onto the road. *There's going to be trouble*: it's the thought going through her mind over and over again during their short conversation. And now she feels Stephen standing behind her.

'What did she want?' He lights a cigarette.

'Nothing. Just checking I, we, were okay.'

He doesn't believe her; she knows by the scowl. She's been tiptoeing around him since her mum's funeral. He's been in one of his moods for days. Now her skin crawls in readiness.

'Pull the other one.' Stephen grabs hold of Angela's wrist.

She looks at his hand, the carefully manicured nails that cut into her skin. She tries hard not to show he's hurting her but fails. He grins when she winces.

'It's just that Mother's left a will.'

'A will?' With the cigarette in the corner of his mouth, he speaks through tight lips. 'And?'

'She asked if I wanted to go with her and Dad to find out about it. Some solicitor, Banner and Banner on Whitworth Street in Barnsgate.'

'You do.' It isn't a question. 'You will go. When?'

'Friday, eleven o'clock. I can't see the point, Stephen. Whatever is in it, I'll ... we'll find out soon enough.'

'The point, you stupid bitch, is, we know what's in it: that land, that farty little bit of land she had no use for but knew I wanted – needed. That you were supposed to get for me. But like everything else, you were bloody useless. I need to know what happens now. So think on, you're going.'

He takes the cigarette from his lips, holds it between his thumb and forefinger. She can see he's thinking of stabbing it into her arm. He breathes heavily. 'Not worth the fucking effort.' He turns away. Angela doesn't watch him leave.

She remembers the first time he'd sent her to ask her mother about that plot of land. 'Ask' wasn't the right word; Stephen had demanded that she tell Eve to sell it to him and Moorland Investments. She'd known she was treading on thin ice as soon as the words came out of her mouth.

'Stop right there, Angela.' Her mother flushed with anger. 'I'm not discussing this with you. And I'd advise you not to get involved.'

'Why? Stephen just asked me to ask if you would sell the land to him—'

'Enough!' Eve held both hands out, palms facing Angela. 'I will not talk about this...' She sighed. 'Look, I've loved having you back home; you can't imagine how awful it was not knowing where you were. But seeing you arrive back married to Stephen Birch...'

'Why? What's he ever done...?' Angela stopped, the rush of panic making her scalp tingle. There was only one thing that would make her mother hate her husband. But she couldn't know that. Surely? His lies, *her own* lies, had split their family. 'Mum?' She waited, dreading what her mother would say next.

'I'm not going to discuss it with you ... or him. Ever. You tell him that.'

Angela took in slow breaths until the fear faded. 'Okay.' It couldn't be that; it couldn't be what happened. But it was something her mother didn't want to talk about.

'I'm sorry, Mum. I know he can be—'

'Enough! Enough, Angie. Best leave it. It's for your own good.' Eve put her hand to her throat. 'And if you want everything to be all right between the two of us, you won't bring the subject up ever again.' She coughed, a long dry wheezing bark.

'Are you all right?'

'It's just a cough.'

'It's my fault...'

'No. I'm fine. Honest. I think I'll go for a lie down.'

Angela waited until her mother was almost asleep before she left. Whatever was wrong between her husband and her mother had nothing to do with what happened that awful day. But, she suspected Stephen wasn't going to be very happy.

When she told him what her mother had said, she saw the narrowing of his lips, of his eyes. He didn't say a word. She wasn't ready for the slap that left fingermarks on her face. Then he didn't speak for over a week. He watched her, the same expression on his face, but said nothing.

But each night he clambered on top of her and forced himself into her.

There's going to be trouble. Angela stands by the kitchen window, staring out, seeing nothing. The quivering begins somewhere deep inside her and swells. After Friday, there's going to be trouble.

Chapter Fifty-four

Lisa

I've decided to walk to Dad's. It's only about three miles, the weather's decent, and I need to think.

I hurry through the square, trying not to look at the empty shops. It's as depressing as it was when I got off the bus two weeks ago. There's a group of lads in front of the off-licence. I can't tell if they're the same ones as before and, this time, there are a couple of girls with them, wearing denim jackets, black leggings and scrunched-up purple leg warmers. One has extremely short, bright orange hair and when she catches me looking, she smiles. I smile back and for a moment I envy their self-confidence; I spent most of my teenage years trying to blend in with the crowd.

The road isn't too busy: a bus passes, belching out petrol fumes, a few cars, one with the windows open and music blaring, a motorbike, a couple of cyclists. But I'm glad when I turn onto the side road that lead to the estate, stopping every now and then to admire the white blossom against the dark branches of the blackthorn. These hedges have been here for as long as I can remember and, unlike most things in Micklethwaite, are as unchanged as the undulating black moors in the distance.

Walking, I've been going over the earlier scene with Angela: the uncertainty in her face, the way her body shrank into itself, her tone of voice when she said, 'If I'm there, I'm there.' When I saw him watching us, I knew she wouldn't come. I could always tell what she was thinking, whatever she said. It surprises me how quickly that instinctive knowledge has come back to me.

I've enjoyed the walk, despite the turmoil in my head. When I'm almost at the avenue, I pass a bench; it's badly in need of a lick of paint but looks solid enough. I sit on the edge of it. A group of children on scooters and roller skates clatter past. Most of them wave.

'Hiya,' one boy shouts, before wobbling off his scooter. He laughs and pushes off again with one foot.

'Hiya.' I can't help laughing as he puffs off.

The bench shifts slightly under me as an elderly woman sits at the other end. She grins a toothless grin at me.

'Hello, love,' she says, 'It's Eric and Eve's lass, in't it?'

I can't help my frown. I wait for the attack. 'It is.'

'Aye, I heard you were back.'

I don't doubt it. I've heard, since Mum's funeral, word has gone around about me being back in the village. I've already been shunned or glared at in the street by some of the older residents on the estate. I start to move away.

'Hey-up,' she says, 'Don't go. I just want to say how glad me and my hubby were to hear you were back for your dad. I know your sister's been back a while, but she doesn't come onto the estate that much, with her fancy clothes and being married to that useless piece of Tory muck. Pardon me for sayin', like,' she adds. 'But I calls a spade a spade. And your sister hasn't had much time for the likes of us since she came back from wherever she went. But you – well I always had a soft spot for you...'

I shake my head. 'Sorry?'

'Harriet Buckley?'

'Oh, yes. Hello.' I smile, pretending I know who she is.

'When I heard you were 'ere, I said to our Sid, my 'ubby, I'm going to tell her. I was that sorry about what happened to your baby brother and that you had to go away. Accidents 'appen, love, and we 'ave to live with them. I know, I've made enough in my time. So, you just think on. We live wi' 'em and we move on. I've no doubt you've had many a night going over it but there's nowt you can change. And I'm that glad you're back with your da. It's nice for 'im to have you here. He must miss your ma. Such a lovely woman.'

She reaches over and pats my hand. 'You make the most of the good memories. That's all I can say.' She holds onto the arm of the bench and pushes herself to her feet. 'Think on.' She smiles, her tongue moving over her top gums. 'And if anyone says any different, well, you just tell 'em to piss off.'

I laugh. 'Thank you, I will.' I watch her waddle away, giving a wave to the children on the scooters and roller skates in the road.

I sit back, savouring the comfort her words have brought me.

Memories have been forcing themselves into my mind since I returned to Micklethwaite. Thoughts lost down the years, and unwelcome. Yet insistent. All are happy memories. And all are of Angela.

As children we argued. She was the eldest, so assumed she knew best and could make the decisions. As far as she was concerned anyway. Sometimes I accepted that, because I knew she was looking after me. I knew, however much she grumbled, that she was in my corner. I can't help smiling at the memory of one of the Sunday School anniversaries. And that awful dress my mother had bought for me.

'She knows I hate green.' I pluck at the skirt of the horrible dress and glare with envy at Angie, who is wearing a similar dress but in blue. My favourite colour. 'It's not fair.'

We're standing in a line waiting to go on stage to sing. Some of the other girls are humming the first song for Miss Harding, our Sunday School teacher. 'Jesus Wants Me for a Sunbeam.' Well, Jesus would be well disappointed in me today. I kick the toe of my shoe against the edge of the step and get a frown of disapproval and a pursed-lipped shush from the teacher.

'Here. Quick!' Angie grabs hold of my arm. 'Come on.'

She's stronger than me so I have no choice when she pulls me down the steps, through the line of bored boys behind us, and into the girls' lavvy.

'Take it off.'

'What?'

'The dress. We'll swap.'

'You're bigger than me.' I say, grinning and dragging the horrid thing over my head.

159

'Doesn't matter, we'll tuck it up with the belt. You want it, don't you?'

Did I! It took only a minute or two before we are dashing back up those stairs to follow the last of the boys slouching onto the stage.

We're partly hidden by the curtain, but I watch my mother's eyes move along the line as she looks for us, see the frown when she spots us.

'She's mad,' I whisper to Angie.

Her fingers grip mine. 'So? Nothing she can do now.'

When we file off that stage half an hour later, I see how daft we look. The hem of the green dress barely hides her knickers and the buttons down the back look as if they will pop any minute. How she's breathing, let alone just been singing, I don't know. And when we go back into the lavvy to change, I see the blue dress has come away from the belt on one side and is dangling down to my shoes, while the other side is bunched up under my armpit.

It's a struggle to get Angie out of my dress. By the time we're on the front steps of the chapel everyone's left. Including Mum and Dad.

We didn't hurry home that day. We did get a row, I remember. But I also remember my sister's hand squeezing mine behind my back. It was a small thing. But it's one of many that have started to chip away at my long-held hatred towards her.

Chapter Fifty-five

Angela

Closing her eyes, Angela lets herself sink down in the bath until her head is under the water. She's alone. Stephen has gone to work without speaking.

It's warm and comforting; she's floating. The water echoes,

hollow sounds when she moves her fingers, touching her skin, sore where he'd twisted her arm. How long can she hold her breath? What would happen if...? She feels a tightening in her chest. Holds on... Holds on...

Coughing, choking, she thrashes to the surface.

Hands slipping on wet tiles, Angela clambers out of the bath, water sloshing around. Still coughing, she crawls across the landing into the bedroom, pulls herself onto the bed and lies on her stomach, dragging in air. The covers are scented with the familiar jasmine fabric conditioner. But nothing else is familiar. Nothing normal.

Nothing has been normal since her mother died, since Lisa's arrival in Micklethwaite, bringing so many memories with her. They're forcing Angela to see what kind of life she's let herself be drawn into over the past four years. But dare she change it? Has she the strength to face the consequences? She'd walked away from her life once before. Why not now?

From here, she can see her dressing table, the wedding photo Stephen insists she keeps there. So she can never forget he's in control.

She huddles under the duvet, pushing her wet hair away from her face, and turns the pillow onto the dry side.

She should have left Stephen after her unsuccessful attempt to get her mum to sell that land to him, and that first slap. She still doesn't know what happened between the two of them. She's been too scared to ask; Stephen's temper flares without warning. He's usually clever with the pushes or full-fisted thumps. He makes sure it's on her chest, her back, her shoulders – anywhere where it won't be seen.

In her head Angie often plans her escape. But she does nothing. He'll never let her go.

She's cold. Each breath shudders in her throat. She rolls over onto her side, pulling the duvet close... remembering the day the violence escalated.

Angie's waiting for Stephen to come home. Restless, she paces from room to room, ignores the unwashed crockery in the kitchen sink, his note, telling her to get the steak he wants for his tea from Robson's the butcher's, ignores his discarded shirt and socks on the bedroom floor that need washing. She needs answers. She's terrified, but determined to get them. In the dining room, she sits, shakes the large white envelope open again and lets the contents spill out. Bank statements in her name, a bankbook in her name, cheque book stubs in her name. But the writing on them is not hers. It's Stephen's.

'How was your meeting?' Angie's planned her strategy, and the envelope is safely back in his desk. She'll wait until he's had a drink before she asks about the contents. Although, from the smell of whisky coming from him, he's had quite a few already. Instead of the usual grunt of satisfaction, he says nothing. 'Stephen?' He walks towards her. She sees a flicker at the corner of his eye, his tongue jabbing inside his cheek. 'What's the matter?'

The back of his hand connects with her cheek, jerks her head sideways. She falls onto the floor.

'Met someone today. Bloke who said he knew you – took great delight in telling me. Works in Manchester Council and belongs to a different lodge. Couldn't believe who I was married to...' His spittle sprayed Angie's face as he leans over her. 'Says he was a regular of yours once.' The laugh is bitter. 'Interior design, my arse.'

In disbelief, she watches him unbuckle his belt.

She should have left then, but go where? Not back to Manchester. She couldn't do that again. Not back to her parents. Stephen threatened to tell them how she'd earned her living over those years and she couldn't bear to see the disgust on their faces.

So she stayed.

This room used to be her favourite. The cream carpet, the pine wardrobes, drawers and dressing table, the loose-woven linen curtains, all carefully neutral, were her choice. But, over time, she's come to hate what it stands for.

The room is split into her side and Stephen's side. Her bedside table holds only a lamp, a small coaster for her cocoa at night, the tiny pill box for her sleeping tablets, a novel she's struggling to start, let alone finish. His table is piled high with folders for work, a tall anglepoise lamp and the ashtray that she empties every day before flinging the windows wide open in an attempt to rid the room of the stale smell of cigarette smoke. To Angela, this divided room epitomises all that is wrong in her life.

Angela's breathing steadies into an even pace. She closes her eyes, desperate to sleep, to escape. There is nowhere to go. No one to help her.

Chapter Fifty-six

Angela

'It's today, isn't it?'

Angela is perfectly aware what Stephen is asking. She feels some small satisfaction when she puts on a puzzled expression. 'What is?' A feeling that shatters when he catches hold of her hand as she reaches over for his empty cereal bowl. He places his knuckle at the base of her thumb nail and presses down.

'Don't. Please.' Angela pulls away. 'That hurts.'

'Well, stop playing stupid games. You know full well what I mean. The solicitor. You're going.' He stands, throws his white napkin onto the table. 'We need to know...'

He takes his jacket from the back of the chair and stands in front of the mirror to fasten his tie. Pulling the green and yellow knot straight, he gives a satisfied nod to his reflection. 'And I'll want a full report when I get home tonight.'

Angela goes to the solicitor's office in Barnsgate. She parks her silver Audi two streets away, walks to Whitworth Street, and stands in the doorway of an empty shop, watching, until she sees her father and sister go in.

Even then she dithers whether or not to go in, until she tells herself it's too late; she's missed the chance. She walks quickly back to the car. She'll make something up to tell Stephen. At least it'll be true that she went to the office.

Chapter Fifty-seven

Lisa

When we arrive at the solicitor's, we are shown into a gloomy office, with magnolia walls covered in framed black-and-white photographs of severe-looking men, the casement window partially hidden by a white vertical blind.

The high-backed chair Dad sits on creaks each time he shifts. He runs his finger around the inside of his collar, coughs, uncomfortable in these surroundings. 'Bit miserable, isn't it,' he whispers.

'Just a lot.' I nod.

He gives a low laugh.

The large round clock on the wall ticks, loud in the silence. I jump when the door opens in a sudden whoosh of air. A man, a bit older than me, I'm guessing, pushes his way in backwards, a pile of folders in his arms.

He crosses to the desk in front of the window, dumps the files down and pulls on the cord of the blind.

'Let's have some light in here,' he says, smiling at us. He sits down, flicks back a lock of blond hair from his forehead and straightens in the chair. 'Oh!' He stands again and comes around his desk to shake hands with Dad. 'My name's Richard Bolton.'

Dad clears his throat. 'I'm not sure why I'm ... we're 'ere. This is my daughter, Lisa. My other daughter was supposed to be here, but she 'asn't arrived yet.'

'Well, when she does, one of the girls in the office will show her in.' He pauses. 'Ah, right.' Looks down at the files. Says something I miss about houses.

Sitting behind the desk, he opens a black box file and riffles through some papers before taking out an envelope.

Dad gives his hearing aid a jiggle. It whistles, then stops. 'Your letter said my wife made a will?'

'Indeed she did. And other matters—'

'She said nowt about any matters or a will to me.'

'Let Mr Bolton finish, Dad.'

The man picks up a sheaf of papers and shuffles through them. 'Of course...' He nods slowly. 'It seems the last time we were in actual contact with Mrs Marsden was...' He puts on a pair of black-rimmed glasses. 'Was the tenth of February eighty-one. On her request, one of the partners here went to your house to see her...?'

He glances at Dad, who shrugs, looking bemused.

'I don't know. I can't think where I'd be, but I'd 'ave known if I'd been home.'

'Well, the will was made then. Mrs Marsden did have a copy.'

'There wasn't one in any of the papers she kept.' Dad looks at me. 'She kept all that kind of stuff in a box in the bottom of 'er wardrobe. I saw nowt like that.'

I touch his arm. 'Don't worry about it, Dad, you know now.'

The solicitor hands the opened envelope to my father. 'It's straightforward; she leaves it all to you.'

'Leaves what?' Dad flaps the envelope around. Doesn't open it.

I take it from him, slip out the stiff sheet of paper and unfold it. *The Last Will and Testament of Eve Sylvia Marsden.* The date rings a bell: 10th February 1981. I am sure that was when Mum had her first heart attack.

Holding this stiff sheet of paper, I remember the blue Basildon

Bond Mum always used to write on, the carefully formed letters, hardly changed from those she'd learned in school. I can see the sentence she wrote to me now: 'So, they told me last Monday the attack has left me with a weak heart.'

The same day Mum made her will. And told no one in the family. So, whatever she's left to Dad must have meant a lot to her.

I make myself listen to Richard Bolton.

'Mrs Marsden had some land, inherited from her parents. It's a tiny plot on the border of Barnsgate and Micklethwaite. Two acres or thereabouts. Apparently, it was a small market garden at one time, owned, according to the records, by a distant relative of your wife's father who had no family of his own, so eventually it was passed to your father-in-law, Mr Rigby.'

Dad says, 'I never really knew him, he were a carpenter; both 'im and Eve's mother emigrated to Australia under that Ten Pound Pom scheme they ran for years.' He looks at me. 'I were tempted myself.'

'Anyway, they went when we were courting. We brought our wedding forward so she wouldn't be alone. For some reason we more or less lost touch with them, except for the odd letter.'

I hadn't known any of this. I must ask Barb what happened. Why hadn't they given Barb the land; it was more her thing than Mum's? Why not share it between the two of them? I wonder if Barb had kept in touch with her parents.

'Indeed.' The solicitor delves into the box file again and produces a form he holds out to Dad. 'As you can see, we are the executors and we also have an affidavit, signed by Mrs Marsden, to the effect that we deal with all matters appertaining to the land. She was adamant she didn't want to sell.'

'Not sell?'

I know what Dad's thinking: why didn't she tell him and why not sell? They could have done with the money over the years.

'Not to sell,' Richard Bolton confirms. 'We've waited to hear from you since we learned of your wife's death. When we hadn't, and as you are the beneficiary of the will, we thought it prudent to contact you. Especially as this week we have had an enquiry to buy.'

I've kept quiet long enough. 'To buy the land, Mr Bolton?'

'Yes.' He peers at me over his glasses.

'Who from?'

'A firm of builders, Miss Marsden. Called Moorland Investments.' He tilts his head as though asking if I know of them.

'You wouldn't get many houses on two acres, I wouldn't think.'

'No. And it's a greenfield plot set between two rows of houses.' He looks down at the file. 'There is a boundary wall on all sides. As I said, this was once a small market garden. From the information we've had from the solicitor acting for Moorland Investments, the land is neglected and isn't being used, not even as a right of way or public footpath.'

Threading his fingers together, he rests his hands on the table, keeping a steady gaze on Dad. He waits.

Dad says nothing.

Eventually the solicitor says, 'Right. Well, there are a couple of things you need to know at this juncture. Mrs Marsden didn't want to sell when she inherited. We did advise her at the time that it was prudent, especially as it is a greenfield plot of land, and she might not get such a good offer again. But she was adamant. There is a letter in the file stating that, dated the same day as the will was signed.' He scans the file. 'Two years ago. As I say, we have this week received a letter from this company's solicitor again, asking us to approach the owner of the land to see if they are amenable to sell.' He leans back in his chair. 'Of course, there is nothing you can actually do until the will has gone through probate. But I did take it upon myself to apply to Companies House for the details of Moorland Investments. There are three directors: a Mr Matthew Alderson, a Mr Barry Learoyd...' He pauses. 'And a Mr Stephen Birch. Your son-in-law, I believe?'

'Yes.'

'So Stephen knew the land belonged to my mother?' I ask.

167

Did Angela? Is this why she hasn't turned up today? Because she and Stephen Birch have been putting pressure on Mum to sell? When Mum was ill? How could she? Yet, even as I think this, I can't believe my sister would do that. Is that what the bullying is about? She's refused?

Mr Bolton nods. 'The company has known for quite a while, so it would be correct to assume Mr Birch has known as well.' He looks embarrassed. 'From land searches, probably. Their solicitor would have been able to find that out easily enough.'

I swallow. 'Why do they want to buy that particular piece of land?'

'Because the land they own, that they want to develop, around a thousand acres in all, is at the back of Mrs...' He pauses, looks at Dad. 'Now your plot of land, Mr Marsden, and has been granted building permission. With one proviso. A safe access onto the main road. And the only access available is this small plot.'

Dad wriggles about in his chair, looks completely bemused.

'As I said, you'll not be able to do anything for a while, Mr Marsden.'

The solicitor waits. I wait, watching my father, hoping he will say something. But he doesn't. The clock ponderously ticks until, at last, Richard Bolton stands and holds out his hand to Dad. 'Well, I think that's all for now.' He smiles at the two of us in turn. 'I'll make sure everything we have discussed today is written down and sent to you.'

Dad doesn't speak until we're on the bus for Micklethwaite. Then he says, 'I think I need a pint.'

Although the outside has been repainted and there are colourful purple and white hanging baskets on either side of the door, it doesn't look as though the inside of the Swan has been touched since the fifties. The long mirrors behind the bar reflect the pine-seated alcoves and the nicotine-stained Gainsborough prints. Dark maroon velvet curtains match the carpet, which sticks slightly to the soles of my shoes as we walk in.

We sit at a table by the window with our drinks. Dad almost empties his beer glass before he speaks. 'What a rum do.' He wipes the foam from his top lip with the back of his hand. 'I just don't know why she never told me about it.'

'Perhaps she just thought the land wasn't worth anything.'

'Aye, 'appen.'

'Odd that it's Stephen's company that wants it. Angela's not said anything, has she?'

'Not to me.'

'She must know. Surely?'

Dad pushes his bottom lip out. 'Dunno. She doesn't ever mention owt about him when she visits. She knows how me and your mum felt about him. I told yer, Mum was really upset when she came back already married to him. Couldn't get her head around it at first. Same as me.' He picks up his glass, looks inside it and puts it back on the table.

Did Mum know what Stephen is like with Angela? 'I'll get another,' I say. 'Same again?'

'Thanks, love.' When I stand, he says, 'I never did like the bloke. Especially when I found out what he'd done to you. Your mum wanted Angie to come back and live with us after she told us. But she wouldn't. It really upset Eve,' he says quietly, as though talking to himself.

I say, 'One more, then we must get back. I need to talk to Angie.' I realise I've used her childhood name for the first time since I came back.

He calls after me, 'I'd sell to anyone other than that bugger.'

Waiting to be served, I watch Dad through the mirror. I can't get over how old he looks, old and worn out. So different from the man I've remembered over the years. I can't leave him here on his own when I go back to Wales. But what can I do? I need to talk to Angela.

Is it possible Stephen Birch has been taking it out on Angela because Mum wouldn't sell that land? And what will happen if Dad sticks to his word and won't sell either?

Chapter Fifty-eight

Lisa

I wake up knowing I need to talk to Barb but I don't want Dad to hear me. So I can't use the house phone. Standing on the landing at his door, I hear the rumble and crackle of his breathing. He's asleep at last. He was awake and moving about all night. He's been worried since we got back home yesterday.

It's only eight o'clock when I leave the house, but Barb and Chris are sure to be up. Charles the second will have been screeching away for the last two hours, strutting around and shaking his shiny black tail feathers.

There used to be an old-fashioned telephone box on the corner of Oak Drive and Sycamore Avenue. Not anymore. I remember Belinda's brother Ben, being dared by his mates to lift the receiver and, when the operator answered, say, 'Get off the line, there's a train coming'. We ran off, screeching with laughter, Angie and Ben holding me in the air between them when I couldn't keep up. Goodness only knows who we were running from. Still makes me smile now.

The June sun is already high, bringing a few people out: a dog walker with a reluctant German shepherd plodding behind him; a couple of children bouncing around on space hoppers; a front door open, letting the loud pop music float into the air; three old ladies chattering and dragging shopping baskets on wheels.

I'm sure I passed a telephone box along the main road to the village. I just hope it's working and that it'll take the phone card I'm clutching in my hand.

When I pull open the door, the sour smell hits me. There's a mound of dried leaves and rubbish on the floor. I wipe the handset and the buttons with a tissue and prop the door open with my foot. Next time I'll go to the post office and use the phone they've got on the wall there.

Barb answers on the second ring; she sounds breathless.

'I just ran from the shed,' she says. 'The fox got through the fence last night, but luckily we heard the commotion and none of the hens were taken. We're just mending it.' A simple comment but I'm suddenly homesick. 'So, how are things with you?'

'We had a letter from a solicitor about Mum's will.'

'Right.' I hear a scrape of a kitchen chair on the stone floor and a rustle as Barb sits down. 'Go on.'

'We didn't know anything about the plot of land Gran and Grandad Rigby left her...'

Silence. Barb says, 'Our parents died many years ago. They left me some money – it helped set up the small holding here with Chris – and Eve the piece of land. It wasn't a problem for either of us.'

'I know it's nothing to do with me, Barb, but she didn't even tell Dad about it.'

'I know.' I heard her clear her throat. 'I think, at first, she thought she and your dad would be able to build a house for you all on it. But that didn't work out...'

I could tell there was something she wasn't saying.

'Why?'

'I honestly don't know, petal. I know they went through a rough patch when you were small,' she adds. 'Your father got a bee in his bonnet about emigrating to Australia round about the same time. And, even though there was some sort of scheme between our government and theirs, they never had enough money to actually go.'

'There would have been if she'd sold the plot of land.'

'Yes, but Eve didn't want to go.'

'So she didn't tell him about it?'

'No. I suppose that's why.'

More festering secrets below the surface of my family.

Through the trees, I see a man walking along the footpath to the telephone box. He hesitates when he sees me, waits a few yards away. I let the door close so he can't hear. The sour smell hits me; it's even stronger in the cramped space.

171

'Lisa?'

'I'm still here. Sorry, I was thinking.'

The man lights a cigarette. But even though he looks in no hurry, I feel rushed.

'There's someone waiting to use the phone, Barb. I only wanted to know what you knew. We found out that Stephen Birch's building firm tried to buy it from her and she refused.'

'I'm not surprised. Are you?'

'No. But now the solicitor has told us his firm have renewed the offer, and Dad has taken the same stance as Mum. It worries me. He's not well enough for any more stress...' I stop.

'And you're wondering how all this will affect your sister.'

Has Barb deliberately said 'your sister' instead of her name? A reminder of who Angie is?

I don't answer. I can't talk about that to Barb right now. Instead, I say, 'I can't leave until I know what Dad's going to do.'

The man outside drops his cigarette end and swivels his foot on it.

'And I need to go now. Like I said someone's waiting to use this phone box.'

The line buzzes in my ear while I wait for her to say something.

'Let me talk to Chris,' Barb says eventually. 'Give us another call tomorrow? And don't worry, love, I'm sure, between us, we'll sort something out.'

'Thanks, Barb.' The familiar relief, knowing they will help, floods through me.

As I leave, I nod my thanks to the man for waiting. I won't talk to Dad about any of this until I know what to do. And, however I feel about believing that Angie knew all about Mum's plot of land, I need to tell her what the solicitor has said and how Dad feels about the news.

Chapter Fifty-nine

Angela

The quivering begins deep inside her and swells until the skin on her arms puckers. His footsteps are soft on the cream lounge carpet, whisper on the wooden floor of the dining room. Slow, sly steps. The handle of the kitchen door moves. Angie forces herself to focus on the bowl, to watch her shaking fingers sift the flour and margarine. Even so, she jumps when the door bangs against the wall.

He's staring at her.

'Stephen?'

His stare is hard, his top lip pressed tight across his teeth.

The air between them sizzles. The muscles in her legs tighten, ready to move, to put the table between him and her.

'Stephen? What is it?' She blurts out the words, following his slow gaze around the kitchen.

'What do you think?' He raises his eyebrows. 'Huh?' He takes three steps towards her. She moves to the side, pretending to look for something in the drawer by the sink. She sees his sneer in the corner of her eye.

'I'm making a steak and kidney pie,' she says. 'Your favourite.'

The pulse in her neck throbs so hard she thinks he must surely see it.

'Fuck the pie.' His voice is a low monotone. He tips his head to one side. 'Anything to tell me?'

He moves faster than she expected, knocking the plastic bowl of flour off the table. It bounces onto her foot, the contents scattering. Reaching over, he grabs hold of her wrist and pulls her so close she can feel his breath on her cheek.

'What happened? You think it funny? Huh? Want me to beg?' His grip is so tight, it's pinching her skin.

'You weren't in last night.'

'I've been here all morning. Waiting to see what you had to say for yourself.'

'Please, Stephen, let go, you're hurting me.'

'*You're hurting me,*' he mimics, in a high-pitched whine. 'Would have thought, you being a fucking whore, you'd be used to a bit of a slap-around.'

He pushes her against the sink, twisting her round, forcing her arm up her back until she hears the crack of bone in her shoulder. 'So? The will?'

The pain and nausea hit her at the same time. If it weren't for the weight of him pressing against her, she knows she would fall to the floor.

Chapter Sixty

Lisa

With no answer at the front, I go around to the back, even though the mad dog next door is throwing itself at the dividing fence, snarling and growling. The first time I came here, Angie told me the owners have no control over it.

Unlike me, my sister has no fear of dogs. At least she hadn't when we were younger.

I remember being cornered by a large mongrel with froth dribbling from its jaws when I was about six and taking refuge in the telephone box, crying in sheer terror. My sister poked at it with a stick until it turned on her, giving me the chance to run for home. She'd had to jump up over a wall to escape it. Another memory to chip away at the armour of bitterness I wear against her.

I hop from foot to foot, waiting for her to open the door. I step back to look at the upstairs windows; I wouldn't put it past her to be peering through the curtains at me again. But not today. I take a deep breath. The Alsatian manages to get its front paws on top of the fence.

There's no point in shouting above all the barking. I lean sideways to peer in at the kitchen window.

And that's when I see her – with him behind her. She has her eyes closed and is bent over the sink. Twisted. He looks red-faced. Until all at once he's smiling. The loud laugh he gives sounds forced.

'Ah, Lisa, you caught us at it.' He runs his fingers through his hair. 'Just having a quick cuddle.'

He waves, says something I can't hear, and Angie looks panicked. Her eyes are wide as though she's blinded by a harsh light. But then she blinks and looks relieved.

I ignore him. 'I've been knocking for ages on the front door, Angie. Can we talk? You didn't come to the solicitor's. I've come to tell you what he wanted.'

I see him say something. She turns back to him.

'Everything all right, Angie?' I'm speaking to her but I'm looking at him.

Chapter Sixty-one

Angela

'Lisa!' The relief slackens Angela's mouth. She hears Stephen curse. 'Fuck!'

'I did knock.' Lisa raises her voice. 'Can you answer the door?'

Stephen gives her a wide smile and a casual wave. But when he swings around on his heel, he glares at Angela, his mouth barely moving. 'Didn't go, huh?' He scuffles his feet through the flour and margarine. 'Get rid of her. We need to talk.' He slams the door behind him, walking the mess on his shoes through the house, his footsteps no longer stealthy as he goes upstairs. He'll be watching from the study.

Wincing, she slowly eases her arm down until it's almost straight by her side. The pain is excruciating and she can't help a whimper. She tries to roll her eyes in pretend exaggeration.

'Sorry, Lisa, I didn't hear,' she says in a loud voice. She thinks, *Please don't go*. She makes a show of searching with her good hand along the shelves, knowing he probably has the key in his pocket. 'I've lost the back-door key.'

Stephen will have hidden it, his usual trick when he wants to put her on edge. She should have made something up about the solicitor. 'I'd lose my head if it were loose.'

Lisa glances upwards to Stephen's study window. 'We should talk.'

Angela cups her right palm under her left elbow, taking the weight. *Yes*, she mouths. 'Not now,' she calls, loudly enough for Stephen to hear. *Oh, please. Please, don't go away*.

'I'll come to the front door.' Lisa calls above the dog's continuous baying.

'No. No, it's all right. Sorry, I'm up to my eyes in it this morning.' She tips her chin towards the kitchen, hoping Lisa understands to go to the front door.

'Angie!' Lisa's eyes flick upwards again. 'Five minutes?'

'No, sorry.' Her shrill giggle contrasts with the nod of her head. She points to the ceiling and mouths, 'Yes. Please.'

Lisa nods.

Her sister's footsteps fade down the path. Angela can hardly think straight for fear. What if Lisa hasn't understood and really does leave? He'll come downstairs; it'll all start again. She sits down, resting her arm on her lap. Anticipating fingers on her throat, like yesterday.

But then his phone rings out: *The Charge of the Light Brigade*. She hears him answer, the genial chuckle, the smooth, mellow tones as he speaks. Then movement.

Angela stands quickly. She fetches the brush and pan and, squatting, begins to sweep up the pastry mix, ignoring the deep, sharp pain. He's coming down the stairs. She listens even as she works, every nerve in her body alert.

A slight draught lifts a line of flour, the front door bangs shut.

He's gone. Trembling, she falls backwards, sits on the floor and weeps.

Chapter Sixty-two

Lisa

I'm not leaving before I see Angie, to make sure she's okay. She doesn't answer the doorbell, but I'm sure she wanted me to stay. I know there's something wrong with what I just saw. He wasn't giving her a hug; I could swear he was hurting her.

I don't know what to do, so I'm hiding behind of one of the neighbours' garden walls in the hope Stephen leaves the house.

When I see him come through their front door, the relief makes me gasp. I crouch down, clench my teeth when I hear the way he casually chats on his phone as he gets in the car. The engine starts.

When I'm sure he's gone, I go back around to the back of the house and look though the kitchen window. It's odd: she's sitting on the floor, and she starts when she sees me. Her face is pale in the bright sunlight and her expression is familiar. I've never seen her like this before but it's a look I've seen often with my work, in other wives. She looks terrified.

I push at the door; it's still locked.

'Angie, can you unlock the door?' She shakes her head. 'Front door then?'

I go back to the front. It's ages before I hear the fumbling scrape of the lock. We stand, looking at one another. Her mascara runs in black trails down her cheeks.

I move towards her, but she steps back, an instinctive movement. She stumbles to sit on the stairs.

'What happened?'

She gives a strange lopsided shrug. Her face and hands are covered in flour. Her arm hangs oddly by her side.

177

'What's wrong with your arm?'

'Not sure. Think I've bent it funny.'

I don't believe her for a minute but say no more. For now.

The kitchen is in chaos. There's flour all over the place and a mixing bowl on its side against the dining-room door. This wasn't an accident.

She drops to her knees and struggles to reach the dustpan.

'Leave that.'

'No. I can't.' She surprises me. 'If you get a cloth and the bleach from the cupboard under the sink, I'd be grateful if you could start wiping the worktops.' She keeps her head down.

'No.' As gently as I can, I put my arms around her and lift her to one of the chairs, dragging it out with my foot. 'Sit. What's happened?'

I kneel in front of her. I touch her thin shoulder, and hear a low intake of breath. The utter misery in her eyes shocks me. I don't think I can deal with whatever this is. We need Mum.

The grief hits me and we're both sobbing and gasping. I'm rocking her, and she's letting me, although I must be hurting her. Yet when I try to pull away, she won't let go. I'm babbling, 'Let it all out, don't bottle it up, love, there, there.' Stupid useless words.

Until, finally, it's over. In the silence, I hear the dog still barking.

'Bloody dog,' she says. We laugh, loud gales of laughter that go on and on until there's only the gulping hiccups of hysteria.

Angie is holding her arm.

'Are you okay?'

'No.'

She winces when I ease off her cardigan. I've done enough first aid courses to know I'm not going to fix the odd way her arm sits in her shoulder joint – sort of square, instead of round. It's starting to swell. 'Can you move it?'

She shakes her head. 'It hurts.'

'I bet it does. You need to go to hospital.'

'No!' She won't meet my eyes.

I leave that for now, even though I know she'll have no choice. 'What happened?'

'I told you, I think I've bent it funny, somehow—'

'And now you can tell me the truth, Angie. I'm not blind. I saw something was going on between the two of you, and it wasn't nice. Despite him trying to cover it up.'

'Don't.'

I look around. 'Any brandy?'

'In the cabinet in the dining room. But it might be locked.'

It is. And perhaps that's best. She needs proper treatment, perhaps an operation. I make a coffee. 'So what happened?' I ask again.

'Nothing really.'

'Something must have?'

'He didn't know I didn't go to the solicitor's.'

'I'm sorry if I made things worse for you.' I cradle her hand in mine. 'It didn't occur to me that you wouldn't tell him.'

'I almost did go, you know. I got as far as the offices.'

'So, this...' I point to her shoulder. '...is my fault.'

'No, it was already happening when you arrived. It wouldn't have made any difference.' She closes her eyes, tight shut.

I take a breath, stifle the anger.

But then she takes me by surprise. 'You knew, didn't you? You knew from the moment you saw him at the funeral. What he is?'

'A bully? A liar?' My insides flip. 'Yes.'

'I've been avoiding you.'

'I know.' And I know why now, having seen what was happening earlier.

'I knew you'd want to talk about – Robert. I'm sorry.' She's looking steadily at me now. 'I've been ashamed. I was then, that's why I ran away. I was frightened the truth would come out. I couldn't face Mum and Dad, seeing what they were going through...'

'But you also left home because you thought I'd be able to come back.' I force a smile to try to show her I understand.

'I was – still am – a coward.'

'No, you're not.'

'You don't know the half of what I've done.'

'None of that matters.'

There's too much to say, too much to drag up from the past. What's happening now is more important. I will talk to her about the years we lost. But not right now, when she's admitting she's with a man who controls and hits her. This is what we need to deal with.

'Don't worry about that for now.' She doesn't argue when I say, 'I'm going to call a taxi.'

Chapter Sixty-three

Lisa

At first, we don't say much. I'm aware that every movement of the taxi causes her pain. My anger and exasperation are growing. She sees herself as weak when he's the coward.

'We should report him to the police. I've seen enough bullies, men and women, to know they don't stop until...' I don't finish what I was going to say. So often it ends in ever more extreme violence or death. My skin prickles.

We're whispering, each aware of the listening driver. He looked in curiosity at us when we climbed into his taxi and I remembered that my sister is well known as the wife of the local councillor.

'No one will believe us.'

I'm not so sure, remembering the dislike of Stephen at the wake after Mum's funeral. 'Why? As far as I can see, he's not that popular.'

'He is on the council. He's done loads of popular business deals, that he's made sure have been reported in the press, even on local television.'

'He hasn't done much for Dad's estate.'

'It's considered an eyesore. Old houses that cost too much to repair.' Angie grimaces with the pain. 'I'm guessing they'll bulldoze the lot and build new houses, eventually.'

No doubt Stephen's firm will do the building. What a scheming bastard the man is. 'I still don't think people like him.'

'He's built an image for himself. Got a bit involved with local charities.' Not something I expected, until she added, 'Whenever they're in the local newspaper.'

'Sounds about right.'

We pull up outside the double doors of the hospital. It takes a few moments to manoeuvre Angela out. I pay the taxi driver and tell him not to wait. I pay him extra to go to Dad's house with a note to tell him that Angie has had a bit of a fall, so we're just getting her checked over. No need to tell him the truth. The last thing he needs is more worry. And I don't think I'll be back with him in time for tea.

The A&E waiting room is packed. Every one of the brown seats is taken and people, in various stages of distress and impatience, line the walls. Despite all the bustle of the nurses, it looks like a losing battle, with more patients arriving than leaving. There is a fug of body odours and cleaning fluid.

After registering, I spot one solitary plastic chair in the farthest corner and make a beeline for it, getting there just before a large man with a bright orange beard, who harrumphs at me.

'Sorry.' I smile at him. 'It's not strong enough to take his weight, anyway,' I say to Angie, out of the corner of my mouth after he's gone. That makes her giggle. 'You sit on it.' I pull the chair further away from the wall, careful not to brush against her.

'We can share?' She perches on one half and pats the seat, putting me on the opposite side from her injured shoulder. 'Here.'

'Okay. I guess we'll have a bit of a wait.'

She groans under her breath. 'I can't be here long, Lisa. Heaven only knows when Stephen will be back and if I'm not there...'

'We're here for as long as it takes, Angela. You can't carry on in this state.' I must have spoken louder than I meant to because one of the nurses spins round as she passes, eyebrows raised. I hiss, 'There's never an excuse for violence, Angie.'

We sit in silence for a while before I say, 'Do you want to tell me what you know about the land?' I feel the shock flow through her. 'You knew about it, didn't you?'

'I'm sorry.'

'Stephen told you.' It's not a question. 'Before or after you were married?'

'Afterwards. You have to believe me, I didn't know before. Honestly, Lisa.'

I nod. 'Okay.'

'He wanted me to persuade Mum to sell to him – to his firm. But I only asked the once; it really upset her, so I refused to ask her again. We had lots of … fights about it.'

Looking at the state she's in now, I can guess what she really means.

'Mum never mentioned it to me.'

'No?'

'No.'

'She wouldn't sell to him.' Angie leans against me, her head on my shoulder. Her breathing sounds shallow. 'It made him very angry. Sorry, I need some fresh air.' She tries to stand, almost overbalances.

'Sit back down.' I catch hold of her, turn in the chair and push the small window behind us further open. 'It's hurting more? Your shoulder?'

'A little.'

When I glance across, there's a line of people waiting at reception.

She tilts her head against mine. 'What will happen? About the land?'

'It'll be Dad's land once it's all gone through probate. Which may take a while, so, for the time being, there's a bit of breathing space. But he's saying the same as Mum: he won't sell.'

'Can't you persuade him?'

'He's adamant.'

'This is going to cause more trouble.' Her voice wobbles. She's frightened. 'It's awful. It's all so awful. What's going to happen?'

If Stephen was angry before, he'll be raging when he finds out Dad will refuse as well. An icy ripple moves along my spine. 'I'm not sure.' I don't add that I know the person who will suffer most is her. And I don't know what to do about it.

Chapter Sixty-four

Lisa

We're sitting outside A&E, waiting for our taxi to arrive. Lights flashing, ambulances spew out paramedics, people on stretchers, in wheelchairs; a bustle of activity ignored by a man and woman standing nearby, smoking. There is an air of normality around us, yet nothing about today has been normal.

I ask the question that's hovered on my lips for days. 'Why don't you leave him?'

'What?' Angela sounds startled. She looks towards the couple, who have stopped talking and seem to have developed an interest in us.

I move closer to her.

'You could come and live with us in Wales. Barb would love that. We could ask Dad to come as well.' Even as I say it, I know what Dad's answer would be. Still, there would be nothing to stop Angie.

She gives me a long look. 'I can't.'

'Why not?'

'I just can't. And I can't tell you why. You wouldn't understand.'

'Try me.'

I see the woman shuffle a little closer, head tilted towards us. I glare at her. She takes a last drag on her cigarette, drops it and stamps on it, before going back into the hospital. When the man follows, we are on our own.

Angie says quietly, 'I did something when I was in Manchester.'

She takes in a long breath. 'I've never talked about it. I was – I earned my living...' Her mouth works, forming her next words. 'I was an escort.'

It takes a second or two for what she has just said to sink in.

'You mean...?'

'Sshh! Yes. I'm not proud of it. But...' She lifts her chin. 'It sort of happened...'

'Did Mum know? Dad?'

'No! No.' Now she won't meet my eyes. 'He'd be disgusted with me. They both would have been so ashamed of me. I couldn't face that.'

'Oh, Angie.' I take hold of her hand.

She pulls away. 'I don't want your pity.'

'I'm – it's not... You should have told me. You could have written to Barb and Chris. They would have helped.'

She shakes her head. 'No, at first I was too ashamed, and then – well, time went on and it was too late. I got – I got used to it, you know?' There's a glint of defiance deep in her eyes. 'I made a lot of money and it became a way of life. I was good at it, actually, was friends with a lot of – some of them. That's how Stephen met me. I was with someone at a sort of corporate thing he was hosting. He didn't know what I did. What I was. Then.'

I caught hold of the word. 'Then? He knows now?'

Angela gives a small nod. 'He kept coming to my flat until he wore me down. I know, I know,' she adds. 'But I thought he'd changed. Then he kept going on and on about getting married and moving back to Micklethwaite, making things right with Mum and Dad. I thought he cared.' Tears slide down her face. I hand her a tissue. 'He was very insistent about that, you know? Making things right with them. I didn't understand...'

'He wanted you to get Mum to sell the land to him.' It sounds harsh. But I can't help that. I wonder how long it took my sister to understand that. 'It must have been driving him mad. Her refusal was holding up his plans.' I know I sound bitter.

'After that first time, I refused. I told him I wouldn't do it again. That made him so angry. But then it all got worse; six months after we were married and moved to Micklethwaite, he found out about what I really did in Manchester.' She's crying now, loud, rasping sobs.

I put my arms around her. 'Oh, Angie.' I hate Stephen Birch. I can't begin to imagine the terror she's been living with. 'And then this started? This violence?'

She nods, small, rapid movements. 'Yes.'

'You can't carry on like this.' I swallow against the slime of nausea in my throat. But what can she do?

Chapter Sixty-five

Lisa

When we stop outside Angie's house, the red sports car is already parked on the road.

'Stephen's home.' If it's possible for her face to go even whiter, I swear it does.

'Don't worry.' I help her shuffle out of the taxi. Her arm is in a triangular bandage. 'How does it feel now?'

'Better.' She's looking up at the windows, biting the skin on the side of her thumb. 'He'll hit the roof...'

'He won't be the only one,' I say, grimly.

'Don't, Lisa. Don't cause any bother.'

'He caused the bother when he dislocated your shoulder.' It will take me a while to forget that loud pop as the doctor rotated her arm to reset the joint. 'It's okay, I won't say anything.' Unless he starts.

Which is just what happens. I have only just turned the key and helped her inside when there's a shout from upstairs.

'Where the hell have you been? I come home and the bloody kitchen's still in a sodding mess and no sign of any food.'

Stephen is standing at the top of the stairs. He's wearing a dark blue blazer with an open-necked, pale blue shirt and navy slacks. Obviously he's been corporate entertaining while we've been at the hospital.

'Well?'

It's as though he hasn't noticed Angela's arm. Or seen me.

Angela seems incapable of speaking, so I say, 'We've been to the hospital. With your wife's dislocated shoulder. You know, Stephen, the shoulder you dislocated by twisting her arm behind her back?'

When I put my arm around her waist, Angie is quaking so hard the vibrations run through me. Or is it me trembling? Even so, I glare at him, challenging him to answer.

'Bollocks!' He gives a loud scoffing sound and moves down a couple of stairs, sliding his hands along the walls. 'Always playing the martyr. Always looking for attention.'

My sister gives a moan and moves closer to me. Despite the pulsing in my throat, I give him one more scowl before I say to her, 'It's okay. Let's finish up cleaning the kitchen.' I lead her through the lounge into the dining room.

'Here, sit down.' I pull out one of the chairs. 'I'll get a glass of water and you can take a couple of the tablets the doctor gave you to help with the pain.'

'I'm all right. Honest. It hardly hurts now.'

Even so, she can't hold the glass without spilling the water and when I hold it to her lips, her teeth make little clicks against the glass.

'You need to lie down.'

Angie looks towards the kitchen. 'It's a mess in there.'

'I'll do it. It might not be to your standard.' I smile. 'But I'll do it.'

She doesn't return the smile. 'I don't want to be upstairs...'

With him there, I finish her faltering sentence in my head.

'Okay. You can sit here and watch me. Make sure I'm doing it properly.'

While I'm cleaning, he's banging around in his study, but, to the relief of both of us, he stays upstairs. Every now and then I glance at Angie. She's much calmer; the tablets must be doing their work. Less than an hour later the kitchen is spotless.

'You're out on your feet,' I say, drying my hands. 'Come on, let's get you to bed. See if we can make you comfy.'

This time she doesn't argue.

While I'm helping her into bed, I hear him go downstairs. Which suits me fine.

He's making a cheese sandwich when I walk into the kitchen, a smouldering cigarette in an ashtray on the table.

'I know what you're doing.' He points the small knife at me. I wait. 'You're plotting with her. Putting the kibosh on me – the company getting that land.' He cuts slices of cheese, each time letting the blade snap noisily on the plate.

'Dad's land.'

'And when he's gone, my ... *my* wife will have a share of it.'

A shiver runs over my scalp. I won't say he doesn't frighten me. But I'll not let him see it. I raise my chin and stare straight at him.

'Are you threatening my father?'

He puts the knife down, raises his hands, palms outwards. Grins. Sniggers.

'What, me, *Miss,* er, whatever it is you call yourself these days?' He takes a step towards me. I force myself to stand my ground. He's so close I can smell his aftershave, mixed with stale cigarettes. 'Know this, *Missy*, no one gets in my way.' I see his fist clench. 'You try, and you'll regret it.'

'We'll see.' I tighten my own fists and lower my voice to what I hope matches his. 'And now you listen to me, Stephen Birch. If you ever touch my sister again, I will make sure the whole town, especially the council, know what kind of man you are. I'll blow your whole world apart. Just keep that in mind.'

I spin on my heels and walk away from him. The skin on the back of my neck crawls, as though I can feel his hatred boring into me. At the bottom of the stairs, I wait a moment, listening. All is quiet.

When I walk down the path, my legs want to give way under me, but I know he'll have come to the window to watch me, so I pull back my shoulders and march. I only hope what I've said will stop him from hurting my sister.

Chapter Sixty-six

Lisa

'Your mother wouldn't sell to him, so I'm sure as hell not going to.'

Dad's having a lie in. I perch on the end of his bed. We've already discussed my sister's so-called fall, and I've persuaded him not to go and see her today, and said that I'll call in later, after I've found a hairdresser in Barnsgate to cut my hair. It's the easiest excuse I can think of.

'It sounds as though you could name your price, Dad. Think what you could do with the money.' The last thing I want is to help Stephen Birch, but if getting his own way means he'll leave Angie alone, I must at least try to persuade Dad.

'I'm not interested in the money, love.' He pulls at the pillows behind his head and shuffles up the bed into a sitting position. 'I'm not going to let him profit from something I do. I couldn't.'

I give an inward sigh. But at least I know what I'm dealing with now. There's no point in upsetting him by telling him how bad things are with Angie. Not until I've sorted something out. Though what, I haven't a clue.

'So, what are you going to do?'

'Nothing.' His mouth is fixed in a grim line. He tips his chin as though expecting me to challenge him, but I don't. He's never been one to change his mind.

'Okay.' I pat his feet through the covers. 'Like I said, I need to go out for an hour or so. I'll call on Angie later, so don't worry about her. You'll be all right?'

'I'll be fine.' He smiles back at me. Cat jumps up on the bed, stretches, pushes at Dad's hand with his head and purrs. The image stays in my mind as I leave the house.

There have been a few times lately when I wish I'd come to Micklethwaite in my old Mini; it would certainly make getting around easier. Unless – until I can persuade Angie to leave Stephen Birch, I know I'll have to see her every day. If only for my peace of mind. I'll call Barb on the way to the bus stop. I can't keep what's happened to Angie from her.

The phone box doesn't smell any better. Old, left-over fish and chips lie in newspaper on the floor. I really should have used the post office telephone.

When she answers, Barb doesn't give me time to say anything. Her first words worry me.

'Chris and I talked things over. What do you think about him getting in touch with Sandy's husband, Alan?'

'What for, Barb?'

'Don't you remember him talking to us at your mum's funeral? He's the editor of the local newspaper in Barnsgate. He's bound to have reporters who could look into Stephen Birch.'

It's so tempting, I almost agree without thinking. It might destroy Stephen once and for all. Get him right out of Angie's life. And mine. The excitement makes me gasp and I instantly regret it when the rancid stench of the fish hits me.

But getting a reporter involved could be dangerous. What if someone finds out and tells him? That could easily make things worse. For Angie. For Dad.

'I'm not sure, Barb.' I should tell her how bad things are for my sister, but she doesn't give me a chance.

'It could give us a hold.' She sounds excited. 'A reporter would dig up if there's anything dodgy about Stephen and his firm?'

'Let me think about it, Barb.'

'We'd be fighting fire with fire, love. You said you wanted to find out what was happening. You can't stay there indefinitely; you've a job and a life to get on with here. And it worries us, thinking about you going up against him on your own...'

In the silence that follows, I'm sure I can hear Charlie crowing away in the background, and all at once, I wish I was home. 'I don't know...'

'Look what he did to you. However long ago it was, it will show people what he's capable of. A liar stays a liar.'

'Yes, but if that comes out, it will also make things worse for Angie. I was just going to use it as a threat to stop him trying to get hold of that plot of land. To leave us alone.' To let Angie go.

'Well, I wouldn't be surprised if he gave a few backhanders to get on the council. And I'd like to see what he's been involved in since—'

'So would I, Barb, but I can do—'

'No, petal, we don't want you to do anything on your own.'

'But asking someone who works on a newspaper? A reporter?'

'Just think about it will you, Lisa?'

She's not going to let this go. 'I will, I promise. So, which paper is Alan editor of?'

I hear a rustling of papers. 'The *Barnsgate Chronicle*. I said I'd run it past you before giving Chris the go ahead.'

'Can you give me some time, Barb?' I push the door open slightly with my foot, trying to let in more fresh air. 'I need to talk to Angie about this.' I'd really like to get her away from him before anybody started what my aunt is suggesting. This is taking things to a whole new level. And out of my hands.

'Okay, but please don't leave it too long; like I said, we don't like to think of you trying to do things on your own. I really, really don't trust him. It worries me to know your sister is there on her own with him.'

'I know.' I've decided not to tell Barb what's happened. I wouldn't put it past her to report Stephen's assault on Angie to the police. Instead, I say, 'I'm on my way to see her now. I'm giving Dad time to think about things.'

'Will he sell the land to Stephen?'

'No. He thinks he's being loyal to Mum. Anyway, I've left him in bed; he's having a rest today.'

Her voice changes, softens. 'How is he?'

'I'm worried about him. He doesn't look well.' Which is a bit of an understatement. 'Look, let me have a word with Angie and we'll take it from there. If she's okay with it, I think we'll need to meet the reporter, see what kind of person they are. See how we feel.'

'Well, Alan says he's a straight-up kind of chap. But I understand. It'll be your decision in the end, whatever Angela says. You've got a job on your hands to make her see what needs to be done about Stephen.'

'I know.'

'Like I said, Chris and I would be happier if you left it to someone else to find out if there is something dodgy going on...'

'I promise I'll get back to you later.'

There's silence on the other end of the line. I look down at a scruffy black and white terrier sniffing the door. It can probably smell the fish and chips. I feel queasy.

'I'll have to go, Barb. We'll talk later, yes?'

'Okay, *cariad*.'

I check my watch. If I run, I can just catch the ten o'clock bus.

Chapter Sixty-seven

Angela

Angela's skin is clammy. After a sleepless night, she's exhausted and afraid of the day in front of her. She struggles to sit up, taking the weight of her bandaged arm as best she can. She listens; all she hears is the swoosh of her own pulse.

Stephen spent the night in the spare room. She has stayed in bed until she heard the bang of the front door. At least he left her alone this morning, and now he's gone out she can feel easier. Or has he? It could just be one of his games.

She needs to go to the bathroom. The door handle squeaks and the floorboards under the thick carpet creak as she crosses the landing, step by careful step. In the bathroom, the lavatory seat is up and it slips out of her fingers when she lowers it. The loud snap makes her stand still. Listen again. But there is no shout, no sound of feet thumping on the stairs. Her husband is not in the house.

Afterward, standing undecided on the landing, she tries to remember if Lisa had said she would call over today. Last night is a blur of pain and fear.

She's thirsty. She'll have to go downstairs. Hand under her elbow, supporting her aching shoulder, she takes each tread carefully and shuffles through to the dining room. There's a pile of post next to a full ashtray on the table and she spreads the envelopes out. As usual, nothing for her: an electricity bill in Stephen's name, and what looks like an account from his wine merchant, and one from the hotel. She bites her lip; it'll be for their mum's funeral.

She picks up the ashtray to take it into the kitchen but puts it back when she notices a cream envelope on the floor. Half kneeling, she tries to pick it up with her free hand, but it slips along the wooden floor until it's under the table. The name on the front is blue, fancy italics. His solicitor. Kneeling fully and leaning forwards, she manages to touch it lightly with her forefinger and slide it towards her. The flap is torn but the letter is still inside. Sitting back on her heels, Angie hesitates.

She's seen envelopes from his solicitor hundreds of times over the years, so why does this one worry her? But it does. Stephen wants that land. Her dad, like her mum, is refusing to sell it to him. If this letter is anything to do with that, there'll be more trouble and that frightens her. Just how far will he go to get his own way?

Curling the tip of her finger under the flap, Angela can see the documents inside.

The same fears are back. Has Stephen definitely left for work? Is this a set-up, to catch her looking at his post? Angela moves around until she's sitting and waits, listening. Nothing.

Focussing on the envelope again, she shakes it, hoping the letter will fall out, but it's stuck. She shakes it harder. She tries to hold it between the sling and her body, grasp the letter and pull.

The doorbell rings.

She freezes. *Stephen*. It can't be him, she tells herself, he would use his key. But she can't move. It rings again, sharp and harsh.

'Angie, it's me.'

A sob of relief threatens to choke her. 'Lisa?'

'Yes. Are you okay? His car's not here, so you're on your own?'

'Yes. Yes! Just a moment.' Angela drops the letter, grabs the seat of the nearest chair, and hauls herself to her feet.

When she finally opens the front door, she sees the way Lisa's eyes widen.

'I know, I look a mess.' She puts her hand to her hair. 'No make-up and what-have-you.' She stands to one side to let her in. 'Don't worry about your shoes.'

Lisa stops prising her shoes off. 'You're not my sister. What have you done with her?' The words are accompanied by a slight smile that doesn't alter the worry in her eyes. She touches the sling, reaches round to the knot at the back of Angie's neck, and asks, 'Is it rubbing?' before adding, 'Did something else happen last night?'

'No.' She leans against Lisa. 'Just glad you're here. I don't know what to do. There's a letter from his solicitor...' She waves her hand towards the dining room. 'On the floor.'

'It's open.' Lisa picks it up. 'He left it here?'

'Yes. But I haven't read it. I can't get it out of the envelope.'

'Do you want me to?'

'Yes.'

Lisa unfolds the paper and skims through it, then reads a second sheet.

'What is it? What does it say?'

'The first letter just tells Stephen that Dad won't sell. The second is from our solicitor...'

'What does it say?'

193

'It's clear enough.' Lisa reads, '"We refer to your correspondence of the 5th inst. regarding your proposed purchase of the plot of land, previously known as Bardsley allotments, situated on Bardsley Road, Barnsgate. We have been advised by our client, Mr Eric Marsden, the present legal owner of the plot (subject to probate), that he wishes to decline your offer, and does not intend to offer the plot for sale now or in the near future. We understand that the financial offer made by you has no bearing on our client's decision in this matter. Therefore, further negotiations with a view to increasing the sum proposed would not induce our client to change his mind..."'

The unease in Lisa's face matches the anxiety Angie feels.

'Why do you think he left the letter here ... opened?'

'I don't know. Give me a minute.'

Angela waits, too exhausted and overwhelmed to think. Since Lisa came back into her life, things are moving too quickly, and in a direction she can't deal with.

'We need to get you dressed.' Lisa ushers Angela towards the stairs. 'Now!'

'Why?'

'We have to get to Dad's. I think that's where Stephen will have gone. We need to go. We need to go now.'

Chapter Sixty-eight

Lisa

I feel as if we're falling into a trap that Stephen Birch has set, but I can't work it out. I've seen this vulnerability Angie tries to hide so many times in my work. The ability of one person in a partnership to control, through moods, manipulation, or physical harm, and Stephen Birch is a controller. I get the feeling he's trying to control me and Dad too. We're in the way of him making money. Knowing he's been thwarted yet again will have made him angry.

Angie's car is far heavier to drive than my nippy little Mini. Angie isn't sure about the insurance, which doesn't help. I'm gripping the wheel and I can hear her shallow, anxious breathing. She's terrified and I'm furious. We don't speak.

We get to the estate, bouncing over the potholes. She's hanging onto the strap above her door, uttering small cries.

'Sorry,' I say. 'You all right?'

'I'm fine.' She's holding her arm close to her body.

I'm lucky we haven't met any other cars; I'm all over the place, avoiding the bigger surface ruts, trying to look out for other vehicles coming from the smaller avenues.

Nearer Dad's house, my heart jumps when I see the flash of a red sports car on a side road as we pass. My imagination is in a spin.

The front door is wide open and Cat is sitting, upright and still, in the hallway.

'Dad?'

'Dad?' Angie stands close behind me.

My scalp prickles. I step around the cat on tiptoes and push the living-room door with my fingertips. The radio is whistling as usual; he never seems to notice.

'Dad?'

He's lying on the floor at the side of his chair.

'Oh God.' Angie clutches my arm.

I can't move. Then I hear him groan and I shake her hand away and I'm on my knees beside him.

'Dad? What is it? What's happened?' When I crouch lower, I understand. 'He's had a stroke.'

'Oh God.' Angie says again. She collapses onto his armchair.

His eyes are closed but I can see the left side of his face is sagging, his mouth open, saliva dribbling out. He makes a noise, slightly lifts his right shoulder.

'Don't try to move, love.' I fumble for his hand, which is trapped under him, and squeeze his fingers. His skin is cold and clammy. 'Stay still. Angie, phone for an ambulance.'

She doesn't move. Her eyes are blank.

I scrabble across on my knees to the phone and dial the emergency number. 'I'm here, we're both here, Dad.' For all the good my sister is. I stop myself. I know that everything that has happened over the last day has been too much for her. 'It'll be okay.' I'm not sure whether I'm talking to her or Dad.

He's not moving. It feels like ages before I hear a voice.

'Which service do you require?'

'Ambulance. Ambulance. It's my dad, he's had a stroke.'

The woman's voice is careful when she takes the details of our address and asks me to describe what's happened. I'm screaming inside: *Hurry up, just bloody hurry up.* My heartbeat is in my throat.

Dragging the phone with me, I get back to him, as close as I can.

'Hang on, Dad, the ambulance is on its way.'

'What shall I do?' Angie is leaning forward, rocking. 'What shall I do?'

'There's nothing we can do. We have to wait.'

She nods, holding her hand under her elbow. She grimaces. The paracetamol she took earlier should still be working but the rush to get her into her jeans and a jumper probably hasn't helped.

'You okay?'

She nods again.

I lie down alongside Dad, stretching the phone cord so far I'm afraid it will come out of the wall socket. The woman is still talking but I can't take in what she's saying. I hear myself making soothing murmurs as I hold my father close.

Cat is there as well, tucked behind Dad's shoulder.

And then the siren, doors banging, voices, feet swift and heavy on the path.

I'm pulled to one side, the phone taken out of my fingers. Cat runs away, leaping up onto the windowsill.

The rest of the day is a blur: sitting with Dad in the ambulance, waiting with him on a stretcher, doctors and nurses bustling in and out doing various tests. Then we're sitting by his bedside on a long ward with lines of beds on both sides. All the while, we're watching him struggling to swallow, to breathe, attached to various tubes and wires, his face ashen.

Eventually there are different nurses, different smiles of sympathy and words of encouragement. One of them, seeing Angie's arm, is kind enough to sort out another sling to replace the crumpled one and give her more painkillers.

Angie's been asleep for an hour when I stand to stretch my legs. I look through the windows. The sky is pitch black. The hospital grounds are deserted, the lamps throwing orange pools of light on the glistening tarmac, and rain has settled in for the night.

My movement wakes Angie. She glances first at Dad and then me, indecisive, anxious. 'How is he?'

'No different. Look why don't you go back to Dad's? Sleep there tonight?'

She shakes her head. 'It'll makes things worse.'

'How? How could things be worse?'

I wish she could stay away from Stephen forever, but there's nothing I can do about that right now. My priority is Dad. My head aches. There's been nothing to do for hours, except to watch and wait. Perhaps it is best she goes home. Would she be safe?

'Best I go home...'

'He might...'

'He won't. Not now he knows you've seen.'

I'm not sure. 'Even after a day like today? After getting that letter from his solicitor's?'

'Especially after today.' Angie speaks with more determination than I've heard in her voice all day. 'He'll be wondering what's happening. It'll be killing him not knowing. Sorry,' she adds hastily, glancing at Dad. 'Bad choice of words. But honestly, I'll be fine.'

I see a glimpse of the old Angie in her face when she looks up at me.

'If you're sure…?'

'I am.'

'How will you get home? We left your car at Dad's.'

'Taxi?'

'Of course!' I'm not thinking straight. 'You go, then.'

She goes to the bed, kisses Dad's forehead. I hear her whisper, 'I'll see you soon.'

We hug. 'Be careful. Look after that arm.'

'I will. Let me know if…' She gives a sideways tilt of her heard towards the bed. 'I'll be back tomorrow.'

I still worry that she's putting herself in more danger.

Chapter Sixty-nine

Lisa

When, at last, I go to find a phone, my footsteps echo on the empty corridors. I find a phone booth on the wall and feel sick when I dial Barb's number. As soon as I hear her voice, I can't swallow down the sobs.

'Lisa? What is it? What's happened?'

'It's Dad,' I manage between gulps. 'He's had a stroke. He's in the General. I think he might die…'

'I'll come up.'

'Yes. No. I'm being selfish. There's nothing you can do, and there's too much for you to do at home.'

'Is Angela with you?'

'She was, she's gone home for the night.'

The silence on the other end of the line stretches out.

'How are things there?'

I lie. 'Okay. As much as they can be with that pig of a man.'

'Don't underestimate him, Lisa. Have you thought any more about what I suggested?'

'I haven't had a chance to be honest, Barb.'

'Of course not. But don't leave it too long, will you? Chris and I would feel a lot happier if you weren't trying to deal with this on your own. Especially now.'

She's right. I can hear her breathing. Waiting. 'Okay.' I make the decision. 'Let me know when to meet him.'

There is a long sigh. I'm guessing it's one of relief. 'Good,' she says.

'What's his name, Barb? '

A moment of hesitation. 'Watson,' she says, 'Ben Watson.'

The brother of the girl who was once my best friend.

Chapter Seventy

Lisa

I haven't told Angie I'm meeting Ben Watson. Worrying about Dad has kept me awake for the last two nights, and I'm not even sure how much to tell anyone. Has Barb's friend asked Ben to look into Stephen's business dealings for a story, or has he stressed that it's a personal matter and it's a favour? I hope it's the last or all hell will be let loose.

Is he expecting to be paid? I suppose I should offer.

If Stephen gets himself in the local newspapers with anything he does for charity, Ben must already have had some contact with him. I know they hated one another at school, partly because of Angie. I'm betting that hasn't altered.

The café is busy, but I see a couple leaving a table in the corner by the mullioned window and, having ordered a pot of tea for two, I grab those seats before anyone else can.

The bell above the door rings and a man bursts through. He's tall with thick blond hair that flops over his forehead and is just a little too long. As he weaves his way through the tables, his grin makes laughter lines around his eyes. There's no mistaking him, he's an older version of the Ben I used to know.

'Well, well, Mand ... sorry.' He stops shrugging off his jacket and slaps his hand to his forehead. 'Sorry – Lisa.' He dumps his briefcase on the chair, slings his black leather jacket over the back of it, and leans over to kiss my cheek. 'Long-time no-see. How are you?' He picks up his briefcase and sits opposite me, smiling. I'd forgotten how he has the same large pale grey eyes and long lashes as Belinda. I remember how I always used to think how unfair it was for a boy to have eyes like this. 'You okay?' he says.

'Fine. Well, that's debatable, I suppose...' I grimace. 'But it's lovely to see you again. I didn't know how long you'd be, so I thought a pot of tea would be better than coffee. I took a chance...'

'That's great. Do you want me to pour it?'

'No, I'm on it.'

He waits until I push a cup across to him. He helps himself to two spoonfuls of sugar and stirs. 'Like the good old times, seeing you,' he says and then frowns. 'Sorry!'

'Don't be, there were some good times. Before...'

He holds my gaze. 'You were okay afterwards?'

'I was. More than okay, to be truthful. I'm glad I moved.' It's strange to be talking to him. 'It feels odd to be back, though. I was only supposed to come for Mum's funeral and then go back home.'

'I was sorry to hear about your mum. I liked her.' He nods.

'Thank you.' I'd imagined it would be difficult seeing him after all this time, but it's not.

'Actually,' he says, 'I did see you on the day of the funeral. I was in the Chapel of Remembrance with my son.'

'That was you? I didn't see, the light was so dark. Why didn't you say anything?'

'It's a place for private moments.' He drinks, carefully placing the cup back in the saucer. 'It was – for my son, Daniel, and me – it was the first anniversary of my wife's death.'

'I'm so sorry...'

'It's all right, you don't need to say anything.'

'I didn't know.'

'Why would you?' He rubs his nose.

There's an awkward pause. We haven't walked the gradual path from child to adult together, and it feels odd, being forced to share something so private.

To my relief the café door opens, and a group of women bundle in, talking over one another, fussing to choose a table, taking off coats and hooking them on the coat stand by the door.

It breaks the silence and I say, 'How long have you been a reporter?'

'About six years. I came to the *Barnsgate Chronicle* straight after Uni. You?'

'Social services. I look after families. Most of my work is with children.'

'You enjoy it?'

'Yes. Most of the time it's rewarding. Can be frustrating, even upsetting. But it's what I've always wanted to do, work with children.'

And it's there again: that pause, that memory that I know we must be sharing.

'I felt it could be something I could give back. After...'

He starts to say something. Stops. Coughs. Says, 'How long are you here for?' Whatever he was going to say, he's clearly thought better of it.

'Like I said, I was supposed to go back after the funeral. I wasn't expecting Dad would want me to stay but...'

I picture the woman I am at work – strong, dependable, can-deal-with-anything Lisa. When I decided to come back to Micklethwaite, I was worried all the old fears and insecurities would return. But it hasn't been like that at all. 'Well, Dad and I are okay now, we've talked. But, otherwise, things are difficult, Ben. I can't turn my back on Angie and my dad, especially not now, after his stroke.'

'Alan told me some of what's happened: your father's house, the land that was your mum's, how Birch has been after it for a long time—'

He's not wasting any time. I can see a gleam of anticipation in his eyes. I must make it clear this is not going to be a story he can publish. Not yet, anyway.

'I just need to know what Stephen Birch has been up to, for my own sake. For Dad and Angie.'

'I understand, Lisa. I know what you want me to do.'

'Thank you. Dad and I didn't know about the land. Mum never told us. I hate thinking what Stephen might have been doing, trying to wear her down to get his hands on it.'

I'm sitting across from this man I last saw as a boy and somehow I trust him. 'I can't stop thinking how Mum bottled all that up for years. Did all that cause her illness? It makes me furious.'

'It must.' He leans across the table, hesitates, and lightly touches my hand with the tips of his fingers.

I realise my hands are in fists, so tight my nails are cutting into my palms. I need the pain to help me keep all my grief and anger inside.

'And, because he's not got his own way, he's bullied Angie.'

His hand covers mine. Large hand, long, strong fingers, short, clean nails. I'm surprised by how comforting it is, his skin on mine and at first, I don't notice how quiet he's gone.

He takes his hand back.

'He's bullying Angie?'

'Yes. He's making her life a misery.'

'I must say, I was surprised when she came back to Micklethwaite with him in tow. And them married.' His face seems to close up.

It's strange hearing him say her name. I wonder if he still has feelings for her.

'I'm sorry, Ben...'

'In the past, love. Way in the past.' He pulls a notebook and pen out of his jacket pocket. 'Right! I've already done a bit of digging around. More of the same?' I nod. 'I'll see what I can find out about the deals he's involved in? What Moorland Investments has been up to? His council involvement? That kind of thing?' He's scribbling while he speaks, covering the page with bold writing.

'Yes. Is that okay?'

'It is. But, Lisa, if this turns out to be a story my readers will want to know, we'll have to have a rethink.'

Not what I want to hear but what choice do I have?

'As long as we talk about it first?'

'Of course.' He smiles at me. His eyes crinkle at the corners.

'And you will be...'

'Careful? Soul of discretion, promise. Give me a few days to see what I can dig up. If he's been involved in any funny business, I'll find out.' His tone is hard.

He stands up at the same time I do. He's quite a bit taller than me. He leans forward and briefly kisses my cheek again. 'Good to see you after all these years, love. And I hope you father gets better soon.'

'Thank you.'

'He's a nice chap, your dad, I've always liked him. I've seen him once or twice in the Swan and he always passes the time of day with me.'

I watch him squeeze his way past the two tables of chattering women and give me a quick wave before leaving. I can't help but smile. However many years have passed, whatever problems have brought us here, I'm glad I agreed to see him. My earlier instinct to trust him is even stronger now.

I must tell Angie what I've started. I'm frightened what the repercussions will be of going after Stephen. But imagine the triumph if we could see him get his comeuppance!

Chapter Seventy-one

Lisa

As I expected, Angie's horrified. She's furious I've brought Ben into this and terrified that if Stephen finds out he's being investigated, she'll pay the price. Her shrill whisper bounces off the walls of the empty hospital lavatory.

'Why him? You know what they think about one another.'

'I think Ben's professional enough to keep their old rivalry out of it.'

'You think Stephen will?' She's incredulous. 'Honestly, Lisa, I don't believe you...'

'I'm sorry, I should have told you, but I'm sure he'll be careful. It was Barb's idea. Chris's friend Alan is his editor. He recommended Ben, says he's a good reporter.'

'What do you expect him to find?'

'I don't know. Something. Anything that can give us some control. There's bound to be something shifty. He likes his own way; you know that only too well.'

'And what about me? What do you think will happen to me if Ben does find something and puts it in his newspaper?'

She touches her shoulder. The doctor told her to keep the sling on for at least two weeks, and I know she still finds it painful. It must make her feel vulnerable.

'More of this? I can't take much more, Lisa.'

I stop myself telling her to come and live at Dad's. I must go home sometime; she'd be no safer there.

'Do you think I haven't thought of that? I made Ben promise he won't print anything.' (Well, at least not right away, but I keep that to myself.) 'He's doing this as a favour to us. To Dad. To you and me.'

'He's a reporter, Lisa. If he finds something, he won't let it drop.'

'Anyway, Stephen won't know it's anything to do with either of us—'

'It isn't. It isn't anything to do with me.' Her face drains of colour. 'What if Ben finds out about me? About Manchester?'

I hadn't thought of that. All I can say is, 'I'll keep you out of it as much as possible, Angie.'

She shakes her head. 'I don't know, I'm...'

'Scared.' I finish the sentence for her. 'I know, love, I know. Come on, let's get back to Dad. You never know, he might be on the mend.' If only.

There's no proof that Stephen was there when Dad had his stroke and left him on the floor. But I keep remembering that red sports car on the avenue near Dad's house. I can't get it out of my head.

Chapter Seventy-two

Angela

Over the next few days, Angela can't stop thinking about Stephen's part in what happened to her father. She's almost sure he'd been at the house before they arrived.

She's moved into the spare bedroom to sleep, yet still lies awake each night, staring into the shadows, alert to every movement on the other side of the wall. If she does sleep, she wakes up with her jaw aching from clenching her teeth.

They don't speak, but she senses him watching her. Every part of Angela quivers with expectation of trouble. When he's somewhere else in the house, she strains to hear where he is. She's afraid, but it's a different kind of fear to the one she's used to. The anxiety she's lived with for almost three years has stepped up into a nightmare of worry for her family as well as herself.

'You going to the hospital, again?' Stephen appears at the bedroom door, a cigarette between his fingers.

Angela gives a jolt of shock. As soon as the front door slammed, she'd pushed back the duvet and reached for her clothes. Yet here he is, up to his old tricks: pretending to leave the house, creeping up on her. She hurries to dress, struggling to zip up her jeans and pull on the already buttoned-up cardigan she's been wearing for two days now. Her only thought is that he's blocking her escape; she can't get past him. The sunlight on the landing behind him gives a distorted image of his size.

When he moves, she takes a step back and stumbles over a file on his side of the bed. She glances towards the window. The curtains are still closed. There's no one to see her. To help.

'I saw the letter from the solicitor the day my father had his stroke.' Angela didn't know she was going to speak. But the words, the implied accusation, come out anyway. She sees his hand tighten to a fist as it drops to his side. She's gone too far.

He crosses the room so fast she has no time to get away. Pain shoots through her shoulder as he fastens his fingers around her throat. He shoves her back against the bedside table and pushes his face near hers. The acrid taste of tobacco smoke fills her mouth, as she stretches her neck up, twisting, gasping with the agony the movement causes, trying to drag air into her lungs.

'You, dear wifey, will stay out of my business. You hear? Interfere in any way and you'll be fucking sorry. You and that bitch sister of yours. You'll be very, very sorry.'

He squeezes Angela's neck one final time before stepping away.

'I'll be home at one for my lunch. Be here.'

She slumps to the floor, coughing, supporting her arm. He picks up the ashtray and empties it over her head with a laugh. Cigarette ends trickle over her jumper into her lap and she closes her eyes against the cloud of ash.

She doesn't move, waiting until she hears his car start, the crunch and squeal of tyres.

She struggles to her feet. Picking up the ashtray with her good arm, she hurls it across the room. Shards of glass scatter when it smashes against the wall.

Chapter Seventy-three

Angela

When Angela arrives at the door of the side ward, Lisa is standing by their father's bed.

'Where've you been?' She gathers her coat and handbag off the chair.

'I couldn't get away.' Angela can't tell Lisa what Stephen did. She's too ashamed.

'It's turned ten. I'm meeting Ben.' She keeps her voice low, casting a quick glance at their father.

'Again?'

'Yes, again. I'm sorry, Angie, I need to go.'

'Lisa, I'm sure Stephen knows something's going on.' Angela grabs Lisa's hand. She must make her listen.

'Why? What's he said?'

'I can just sense it.'

'He hasn't hurt you again?'

'No.' Not really, she thinks. Nothing he hasn't done before. 'It's fine. You go.'

'I'll be as quick as I can. And I'll let you know what Ben says.'

Her last words bring back the hatred on Stephen's face. What will he do when he finds out about Ben Watson?

Angela rests her head on her father's hand, which lies so still on the bed, and murmurs the ineffective words of comfort she repeats every day, never sure if they're for him or herself. She wishes they'd been closer, but there's no changing the past. She knows he's never forgiven her for Lisa, his favourite daughter, going to live in Wales. Because she *was* his favourite, Angela has always known that.

Lisa has spent more time with their dad in the last month than Angela has since the day she admitted the truth about Robert's death. The way her father looks at her resurrects the constant guilt lurking inside her.

Sooner or later, she and Lisa will have to talk about Robert. What happened, the lies, all the barriers that came between them for so many years. It's up to her to start breaking them down. But every time she wants to, something happens to stop her. And she's grateful. But not for this. Not for this happening to her father.

Dad makes a gasping sound. Tears are leaking from the corners of his eyes, trailing down to his pillow.

'Hush.' She fumbles in the pocket of her cardigan for a tissue and wipes his face. 'It'll be okay, Dad, you'll be okay.'

He opens his right eye. The left is closed by the drooping eyelid.

'It's me, Dad. Angela. Lisa will be here later.' Why does she need to say that? She knows it's not her he wants.

He takes in a faltering, lopsided breath, his eye fixed on her.

She forces a smile. 'Hi.'

The fingers on his right hand quiver. He wants her to hold them. But when she does, he pushes at her.

'What is it, Dad?'

His stare is hard, the tears a steady flow. When she tries to wipe his cheek again, he makes an angry noise and jerks away.

'Dad?' Angela's eyes smart. 'Don't. I'm sorry...' She doesn't know what she's sorry for, except for everything. 'I don't know what to say. I... Stephen...'

He runs a slack tongue along his lower lip, makes a hissing sound.

And Angela knows. She nods, forces herself to ask, 'Stephen?'

He lowers his chin slightly, struggles, makes the same sound.

'I'm sorry, Dad, I don't understand. Stephen? What about him?'

He grunts. She sees the effort he makes as he lifts his arm to let it flop onto his chest. Then he opens his right eye and stares at her, and she understands what he's trying to tell her.

Chapter Seventy-four

Lisa

'I didn't know this place existed.' There's drizzle in the air when I get out of Ben's car. The light wind lifts my hair. It's cool for July and there are goosebumps on my arms. I pull my cardigan out of my shoulder bag and put it on.

I'm hoping Ben has found out that Stephen Birch is up to something dodgy. If he has, Angie'll need help to deal with it. We'll have to decide what we do.

'Thwaite café.' I read the sign on the wall. 'Very pretty.' The small building has hanging baskets, laden with colour, either side of the door and a long, narrow bed of pink and white fuchsia shrubs in front. Looking across the lake, I can see the lines of trees in the park. 'I'd forgotten how close Micklethwaite and Barnsgate actually are.'

'You can swim across.' Ben smiles. He hauls his briefcase off the back seat of the car and squints against the rain. 'Shall we go in?'

Inside, the café is immaculate, all stainless steel and glass. Facing the lake is a complete wall of windows from floor to ceiling. We're shadowy reflections in the glass and the shivering surface of the water, grey like the sky.

'No idea this place existed,' I say again, looking around. The pale orange floor tiles contrast with high-backed, dark green booths and the gleam of the stainless-steel counter.

'It didn't until five years ago. Couple of entrepreneurial lads took a punt on it. The place was an old hut before.'

'Well, it's lovely.'

'Where would you like to sit?' Ben hoists the strap of his briefcase onto his shoulder. 'Coffee?'

'Please.' I choose a booth at the far end of the room. There are only another couple and two women in the booths as I pass. I don't know them, which is a relief. He's a well-known local reporter. Being

209

seen with him would be sure get the rumours started. It wouldn't take long for Stephen Birch to hear.

I sink into the leather seat and rest my elbows on the table, looking out. Thwaite Lake is really a man-made stretch of water, filled by small streams that trickle down from the land surrounding Thwaite Mansion, a derelict, stone monstrosity of a place that Angie and me used to cycle to when we were kids. Memories come flooding back, bringing an overwhelming sadness.

When Ben puts two large green cups and saucers on the table and sits opposite me, I say, 'The last time Angie and I went to the mansion, I was about ten. She bet I would be too scared to sneak out of our house and ride up there on our bikes in the dark.' I smile, thinking about it. 'There was a full moon, so I didn't feel too bad, until we went into one of the outbuildings and disturbed a load of bats. Scared me to death. She just laughed.'

'She always was the gutsy one of our crowd.' He stirs his coffee. 'But I also remember how she always used to look out for you.'

Until the time she didn't. I almost say the words out loud. I feel my smile wither. 'She's changed.'

'I gathered that from what you said last time.'

'So, the sooner we find something that will get her away from him, the better. Have you found anything?'

'Not really. I just wanted a catch-up today, let you know I'm still digging around. I'm sorry. I've been asking, and there are plenty of reports of his erratic temper on sites. He's well known for losing it—'

'Bullying.'

'Yeah. But no one wants to come out and say it in public. They all want to keep their jobs, especially now, with the country being in the state it's in. It's an employers' world, that's for sure.' Ben shakes his head. 'I did manage to get some background though, stories of him sacking blokes at the drop of a hat, things like that. And a couple of years ago he held up a project for a month. One site went on strike because he threw a spanner at a man and the contractors did nothing about it. Apparently, the unions were involved but it all got hushed up and the men went back to work.' He drums his fingers on the table. 'Rumours and second-hand stories. But we'll get there, Lisa.'

I'm hoping it doesn't take Ben that long. But I say, 'Thanks for keeping me up to date, anyway.'

'I just wish there was more.' He has a resolute set to his mouth. 'There will be, though, you can bet on it. We'll get the bugger!' He picks up his cup, gulps at his coffee, grimaces. 'Shall I get fresh...?'

I check my watch – eleven twenty – and hesitate.

'I can give you a lift back to the hospital afterwards.'

'Sure?'

'Yeah. It'll only take ten minutes.'

'Okay. Thanks, I will. Angie's with Dad.'

When Ben returns, carefully carrying two more coffees, he says, 'How is your dad?'

'Not good.' I've wondered whether to tell him my suspicions about Stephen being at the house when Dad had the stroke but, without proof, what's the point? Unless Dad recovers enough to tell us what happened, we'll never know. Asking the neighbours if they'd seen anyone going into the house has drawn a blank. I blink away the image of my father lying so still in that narrow hospital bed.

He puts his fingers over mine and stills the agitation in me.

'It must be hard. You're staying at his place?'

'Yes.' I shrug. 'I couldn't afford to stay in a B&B.'

He stifles a yawn. 'Sorry.' He gives a short laugh and rubs the heels of his hands into his eyes. 'I'm bingeing on coffee today to keep me going. Dan's had me up half the night.' His smile is weary. 'And he didn't want to go to the childminder this morning. Since his mum ... since we lost Sally, he gets a bit clingy.'

'How old is he?' I hadn't asked the last time, but now Ben is talking about his son and wife, it feels okay. And I want to know a little more about him. I'm more comfortable in his company than I've ever been with any other man. Despite what we're actually here for.

211

'He'll be three in October.'

So little to have lost his mum. 'It must be hard for you both.'

I'd said too much, it was too personal, I can tell from the way Ben shakes his head. 'We're fine. He's a grand kid. It just takes a bit of juggling sometimes.' He sits back on the seat, stretching his neck. 'And Belinda looks after him quite a lot as well.'

He looks uncomfortable, so I say, 'How is she? Belinda?' My one-time best friend.

'Married. With four kids. Two sets of twins. All boys.' He smiles. 'In her element; she adores them. And Dan.'

'Goodness!' I make an attempt at a casual laugh. 'She has her hands full.' I don't really want to talk about her. The misery of losing her friendship startles me in its sudden intensity.

'She's a brilliant mum.' There's a hint of compassion in his eyes. 'She was always sorry what she did, you know...'

I lower my chin, pretending not to understand.

'Dropping you as a friend after the two of you being inseparable from being little.'

I raise my shoulders, trying to appear unconcerned. 'Kids fall out, Ben.'

'Worst thing she did, getting in with that crowd with Karen Webb, as was,' he adds. 'Sutton she's called now. Doing a stretch in Styal for GBH. Robbing an old woman.' He sniffs in an expression of distaste. 'Not a surprise, eh?'

There's nothing I can say. 'Who did Belinda marry?' I ask.

'Bloke off Clegg Avenue on the estate, Connor Phillips. Nice enough, but our Belinda runs rings round him; he's too quiet for his own good.' He cups his hands around the mug of coffee. 'She said to say hello when I told her we were meeting.' His eyes search mine; there's a kindness, a concern in his expression. He's still the same as he was as a boy. Friendly and empathetic. Nice.

I nod. 'Say hello back from me, will you?'

I'd only asked about Belinda through curiosity. The hurt lurches back. Even having Jayne as a good friend in Ponthallen doesn't quite replace what Belinda and I had. I wonder if it's the same for everyone, that intensity of a best friend in childhood, never really replaced by later ones with other people.

We drink our coffee in silence. Rain clatters on the window. The drizzle has become a downpour. Through the glass, the lake is pockmarked. A man in a business suit runs in, bringing with him a rush of air and the noise of the rain hitting the ground.

'You okay?' Ben says quietly.

'Yes. It's just...' I spread my hands, palms up.

'I know. At least I think I know. All this must be hard for you.'

All this? 'Coming back here is certainly not what I expected, that's for sure.' I know I sound tetchy, but I don't want to talk about it.

He persists, his voice soft. 'Everybody's been okay with you?'

It's not a question I'm expecting. So when I reply, 'People that matter,' my voice wobbles. I'm annoyed with myself. 'It's never something that goes away, you know.'

He looks at me, his eyes searching my face. 'I understand. It can't. When something happens like that, it's something we have to live with.' I wonder if he's thinking of his wife. Should I ask?

But then he takes me by surprise by taking hold of my hand and saying, 'There have always been rumours, you know, Lisa.'

'About?'

'About what happened to your brother.'

I stiffen. 'I don't really want to...'

'Not when you first left Micklethwaite. Later...'

'Ben...' I try to speak evenly but the tremor in my voice increases. I rest my head against the firm back of the booth, trying to get strength from it. It doesn't help. I can't do this. I need to leave, get away. 'Ben, I don't... This isn't what we're here for.'

'No listen, Lisa. Please.' He shakes my fingers insistently. 'Later, the rumours started. People began to wonder if it hadn't been you. As he got older, we all saw what Stephen Birch was capable of. Like his father, he's a nasty piece of work. The policeman who took his statement that day...'

PC Radon. I'll never forget his name.

'He's retired now. But well before I went to uni, I remember his wife telling Mum that he didn't believe Stephen. That he thought it was him who'd pushed your brother's pram down that ginnel. Just because he could. And that his father covered it up with the help of someone higher up in the police.'

I'm so tempted to just nod, as though it's true.

When I don't speak, Ben leans back as though stepping back from the danger this conversation holds. 'Sorry.' He takes his hand away. 'I thought I should tell you.'

'Thank you, Ben, but, honestly, there's nothing to be done about it now.'

'I wanted you to know, that's all. I hope you don't mind?'

'No, it was kind of you.' It won't stop the nightmares. Or the guilt. It's something I live with. What Ben has said isn't the truth, yet it could be the one thing that will ruin Stephen Birch. If I chose to lie. But I won't. Because it would destroy Angie as well.

Chapter Seventy-five

Lisa

Ben drops me off at the end of the road to the hospital. When I tell him not to go into the grounds, he doesn't argue; I guess the place brings back some bad memories for him too.

Angela's hopping from one foot to the other when I come through the entrance to the main ward. 'Where've you been?'

'How's Dad?' I look over her shoulder.

Angela glances back into the room. 'He's been okay.' Even after all the years apart, I recognise that expression, the slightly startled look, avoiding eye contact.

'Sure?'

Dad's lying still, covers up to his chin. Is he asleep? I go to him, put the back of my hand to his forehead. He takes a deep breath but doesn't wake.

'He became agitated, so the doctor gave him a sedative.'

'Why? What happened?'

'Nothing. They said it just happens sometimes, after a stroke. Look, I need to go.' Angela takes her jacket from the end of the bed, shrugs it over her shoulders.

There's something wrong, something other than her having to get home before *he* does.

'Bugger him. He knows where you are.'

'I can't. It keeps the peace—'

'Such as it is.'

'It's easier for me to still make his meals. I don't sit with him, but it stops more rows if I just make something for him to eat.'

'I would have thought that gives you all the excuse you need not to do a bloody thing for him.' I point at the sling.

'Yes, well... At least being at the house means I can see what he's doing.'

'I don't like you being there.'

'I'm not ready to leave yet, Lisa.'

'When will you be?'

'I don't know. When he can't hurt any of us anymore. You don't know what he's capable of.'

'You're saying that to *me*?'

She blushes. 'Sorry! I'm sorry. Give me some time. Give me until we find something that will make him see he could lose everything. And then...'

'And then?'

'Then I'll leave. I promise.'

Chapter Seventy-six

Lisa

As soon as she's gone, I go to the door and catch the eye of one of the nurses in the main ward. 'Excuse me.'

'Yes?' She smiles absently whilst studying a clipboard. 'Can I help?'

'My sister says my father became stressed?'

'Ah, I'm sorry, I don't know; I've only now come on the ward.'

I move to one side so the nurse can come in to study Dad's notes. 'No, there's nothing to say why. Just that the doctor gave him a mild sedative.' She lifts his arm, checks his pulse. 'He's fine. Just sleeping. Which will do him the world of good.' She pats my arm. 'Would you like me to bring you a cup of tea?'

'No. But thank you.'

Next time Angie comes, I'll make sure she tells me why Dad got so worked up.

Dad's been sleeping for the last hour and a half; it must have been quite some sedative the doctor gave him. I've used the time to write some letters: to Barb, to Jayne, to my line manager, asking for extended leave. I have no idea when I'll be going back to work.

When I glance up at my father, his eyes are open. 'All right, Dad?' I rest my writing pad and pen on my lap.

He blinks slowly. And makes a sound, like a word but not quite.

'Don't try to talk, love,' I say. 'Just rest.'

He moves his head on the pillow. He mumbles the same sound again. His eyes close and open in a long blink. The right-hand side of his face, the side that's almost normal, contorts. He shakily points at me.

'You want to say something?'

A twitch pulls the right corner of his lips downwards.

'No?' It's tough, trying to understand. 'You remember where you are, don't you? And why? The stroke?'

Once more, the slow movement of his head. He touches the bed, pulls weakly at the top cover, as though trying to get it nearer to him.

It strikes me what he wants. I lean forward and put my ear close to his mouth. After a few garbled sounds, he says the word. My breath catches in my throat. I stare at him.

'Stephen? He was with you?' My insides feel hollow. I knew it!

He closes and opens his eyes. He struggles to move under the taut sheets, shifting from side to side, trying to lift his head from the pillow, making noises.

'Did he come to see you about the land? Try to get you to sell. Did you argue?'

'Hmmmm...'

'Badly?'

'Hmmmm...' He closes his eyes again. It looks like too much effort to keep them open.

I hesitate.

'He threatened you?'

A tear trickles from the corner of his drooping eyelid. I fumble for my hanky in my bag. Wipe it away.

'It's all right, Dad. You're safe now. He won't come near you again.'

I must find a way to get Stephen Birch out of all our lives. For good.

Chapter Seventy-seven

Angela

Angela hesitates before putting her key in the lock of the front door and takes a deep breath. She has two choices now: she can either pretend this morning didn't happen, which would suit Stephen, or she can challenge him. She walks through to the dining room.

217

'Where've you been?'

Stephen has pulled the chairs from under the table and is sitting on one, his feet on another. With his shoes on. His black shoes on the fawn seat. They will leave a mark.

He sees she's noticed, and his sneer deepens. How she hates that expression. And how it frightens her.

'Where've you been?' he says again. A bottle stands next to an almost empty glass. He leans forward, pours out more. He flicks long ash from his cigarette towards the ashtray. It misses and lands on the table in a pale grey smear.

'You know where I've fucking been.' The words come careering out of her mouth, loud and aggressive. Filled with the contempt and hatred she's felt for him for years.

He looks stunned.

The room fills with a stillness so palpable, physical, she feels if she reaches out she'll be able to clutch it in her hands. Only for a second.

He rushes at her. She turns to run but it's too late. He's holding her, shoving her into the door frame.

'My arm. Don't...'

'Fuck your arm. Who the hell do you think you're talking to?' He jabs his middle and forefinger into her forehead. The back of her head bumps hard on the wood. It hurts.

But something is happening to Angela. The thick hatred is hardening.

She remembers that day he confronted her about her life in Manchester. She'd prostituted herself – her body, her choice. His anger, his violence, was only because he felt his power, his aspiration to dominate the world around him, was potentially threatened. There is nothing he won't do to protect his reputation. No one he won't hurt. And, right now, she's the only one he can hurt.

He prods her forehead again. She feels dizzy, sick. She must make him stop.

'Dad told me what you did.'

He freezes. But only for a moment before he grabs and shakes her. The pain in her shoulder makes her whimper. The air is filled with their breathing: his heavy with glee, hers with fear.

He leans backward, raises his arm. It makes him slightly off-balance, and she sees this. Her chance. She brings one knee sharply upwards, straight into his groin.

He falls to the floor, holding himself. 'Bitch!' he gasps. 'Dirty, whoring bitch.'

Angie jerks away.

'Dad told me you were there the night he had his stroke. You'd had that letter from the solicitor. You knew Dad wouldn't sell to you.' Even though terror is spreading like water through her veins, she forces herself to keep her eyes on his. 'I know what you did.'

He struggles to scramble to his feet and grabs out at her. With a small scream, she runs, taking the stairs two at a time. Locking herself in the bathroom, she leans on the door. The pain in her shoulder is hot and throbbing.

He's coming up the stairs. She won't get away with what she's just done.

The first crash against the door knocks her into the room. Her legs give way. She sits on the side of the bath, watching the door bulge with each kick.

Chapter Seventy-eight

Angela

The door holds, and he gives up in the end. Angie waits until she hears Led Zeppelin blast from his car radio, followed by the squeal of tyres. Creeping out, she drags two spare duvets and three pillows from the airing cupboard and locks herself back in the bathroom.

It's dark when she wakes. Flinching, she pushes herself into a sitting position, her back against the side of the bath, and listens.

Something woke her. She waits, wrapping one of the duvets tighter around her. He's crashing about, banging doors, and she tenses when she hears him charge unsteadily up the stairs and cross the landing.

The loud thuds on the door make every nerve inside her jolt.

'Still in there? Stupid cow!' More thumping. 'Going to bed now. But I'll be waiting. Think on. I can wait.'

Chapter Seventy-nine

Angela

Angie wakes with a start to a loud noise. Cautiously moving her aching arm and half sitting, she listens. She can't hear movement downstairs.

She jumps when banging on the front door starts again. 'Angie? Angie!'

Lisa! Angela raises up on one elbow and tries to focus her bleary eyes at her watch. Almost twelve o'clock. Impossible.

Everything aches when she sits up. The bathroom swirls. Closing her eyes makes the dizziness worse.

'Angie.'

It sounds as if Lisa is at the front of the house. Holding onto the door handle, Angie slowly turns it, still conscious that he could be hiding. No sounds other than the low pulsing in her ears. She crosses to the bedroom window and struggles to open the curtains.

Shielding her eyes from the midday sun and oblivious to the neighbours, Lisa shouts, 'You okay?'

'I'll come down. I won't be a minute.' Her voice is a croak.

Chapter Eighty

Lisa

It's ages before the front door opens. She looks dreadful: her eyes sunken, underlined with dark shadows. She's still dressed in yesterday's clothes.

'What happened?' I knew I should have come here last night. 'Are you all right?'

'I am now.' She covers her forehead with her hand. 'I have a shocking headache. How's Dad?'

'Same, according to the nurse who answered the ward phone earlier. I'm on my way there now. What happened?' I ask again.

'I'll tell you later.'

'Him?'

'Mmm...' She pulls her cardigan tighter around her.

'I'm sorry, I should have come to check on you. Where is he now? Work?'

'I presume so. Are you coming in?'

'No.' I'm worried, but if she doesn't want to talk about it, there's nothing I can do. 'Look, you get back to bed. I'm meeting Ben again tonight. He rang to ask if we could both go, but I think it best I go on my own, with you the way you are.' At least then she won't have to explain to Stephen where she's going. Or have him follow her. There's nothing I would put past my sister's bastard of a husband.

Chapter Eighty-one

Angela

'Fancy a walk? Along the path in the park?' Stephen leans against the kitchen cupboard, his arms folded.

Angela is shocked by his manner; it's as though nothing

happened yesterday. Aware that he's watching her, she keeps finding things to do so she doesn't have to face him. He's up to something.

'A walk?' She can't remember the last time they went out together. She can remember them walking hand in hand by the lakeside once. Or is it only something she wished for? 'I don't think so, Stephen.' After what happened, you must be joking.

'I've rung a couple of times. Why didn't you answer, if you were here?'

Six times. Six times to check up on her. She won't apologise for not picking up his calls. 'I was here. I must have been having a nap.'

'So you haven't seen anyone?'

'No.'

'Nobody?'

'No.' She's afraid he will contradict her, tell her he saw Lisa come to the house. It wouldn't be the first time he'd spied on her. 'I've made a lasagna.' She faces him. 'Do you want to eat now?'

'No, I told you, I'd like us to go for a walk. I'll get changed out of this suit and we can go for a walk.' His voice is determined. 'We need to talk.'

'About?'

'Just things.'

'I'm not talking about that land.'

The familiar darkness clouds his eyes. Then he gives a short laugh and claps his hands. 'Come on, let's move it. Catch the last of the sunshine. It'll do you good.'

He won't give up when he's in this kind of mood.

'So you believe me?' It's the third time he's asked in the last hour. 'As soon as I read the letter from the solicitor, I phoned Matthew and Barry and arranged a meeting to see if there was any other way that we could get access for the new estate.'

'And is there?'

'No, we've looked at that hundreds of times over the years and there's no way. I'll admit I was furious with your father. And I still don't understand what the problem is. But I was nowhere near his house.'

Angela wishes he would shut up. She's sick of hearing his voice.

'I can't help, Stephen. Dad's too ill.' She watches him out of the corner of her eye.

'Suppose – just suppose, he doesn't get better...' He catches hold of her hand. 'That bit of land would be yours...'

'Oh, come on!' He's unbelievable.

He persists. 'It would be yours.'

'And Lisa's.'

'Yes, okay, and hers.' The grip on her fingers tightens. 'You'd sell to our company, wouldn't you? Think of the money, our money, I've ploughed into the project. It would be in your own interest.'

When had it become *our* company, *our* money? 'Stephen! I can't, I won't think about that. You can't expect me to.'

Her stumble over a gnarled tree root on the path isn't an accident. He touched the side of her foot, catching her shoe.

'Whoops! Watch your step, Miss Clumsy.' His manner is jokey, but still a warning. 'If it wasn't for me always looking out for you, I don't know what you'd do.' He laughs. 'Probably kill yourself, one of these days.' Pulling her close, he turns her so they are facing the lake, standing on the edge of the steep banking.

The sun is sinking low. The trees' reflections stretch and waver over the lake, the water blood-red.

'You need to believe me,' he says. 'Okay?'

Chapter Eighty-two

Lisa

'One shandy.' Ben puts the glass in front of me on the small round table and sits down, a pint of beer in his hand.

'Thanks.'

There's a low buzz of conversation and a lingering haze of cigarette smoke. The setting sun has turned from scarlet to a pale orange, casting golden light on the walls opposite, glinting on the bottles and glasses above the bar. A line of people, mostly men, have their backs to us, laughing, lifting pints, chatting to the woman who's serving. I take a sip of the drink, cold in my throat.

'That's good.' The muscles in my shoulders ache. Twisting my neck from side to side helps. Ben is studying me, and I stop moving, self-conscious. I take another drink of the shandy, and look at him over the rim of the glass, raise my eyebrows. 'What?'

'You look tired out. How's your dad?'

'Not much different. We were hoping for some improvement. I thought he was getting some speech back a few days ago, but they think he had another slight stroke the night before last.'

'Are you still sleeping there?'

'Not every night. Most though.'

'There's nothing you can do, Lisa, only make yourself ill. And then you'll be no good to him when he comes out.'

He says when, not if. I'm grateful for that. I hope he's right.

A door opens and I hear the click of pool being played, a shout of laughter before it closes. We're surrounded again by muted conversation.

'Are you sure you don't want something to eat?' Ben nods towards a blackboard with the menu. 'Or crisps? Peanuts?'

'No, honestly, thanks.' I don't have much of an appetite.

'What's your favourite food?'

I have a flash of homesickness. 'We've just discovered Chinese. There's a new Chinese restaurant opened in Ponthallen; I've been with Barb and Chris.'

Ben grins. 'You'll not get that in here.' He's looking at the board. 'It's pie night tonight: steak and kidney, chicken and mushroom, meat and potato.'

'Haven't you eaten?'

'Oh, yes, Belinda made me something when I dropped Dan off. He's staying with her tonight.'

I don't say anything.

'Another?' Ben empties his glass in one gulp, indicates my own half-empty one.

'No, I'm fine, thanks.'

'Mind if I do?'

'Not at all.'

I watch him go to the bar. He speaks to one or two people, is slapped on the back while he orders his beer. He's well known in Barnsgate, obviously. I see a few curious glances my way. I pick up a beer mat and pretend to read it until he's back with me.

'Cheers.' He drinks.

'Is this your local?'

'As much as it can be, I suppose. I don't come in much since...' He looks around. When I follow his eyes, I notice the curious stares. 'Sorry about that. I haven't been in here with anyone else but Belinda's husband before tonight. Nosy lot.'

I swear there's a hint of a smile hovering around his lips.

I take another sip of the shandy. I'm annoyed to feel the heat in my face for feeling slightly pleased at the implications of his words.

'I've found something that looks dodgy about the Bardsley Road site.'

The sudden change of subject makes me choke. 'Really?' I lean forward. 'What, Ben?'

He reaches down to his briefcase and takes out a buff-coloured folder.

'I called in a couple of favours from someone.' He taps the folder. 'It's all in here.' He takes out three sets of bank statements, paper-clipped together. Accounts belonging to Moorland Investments, Stephen Birch, and Angela Birch. I study them. Some date back to 1977. I don't understand what I'm looking at.

'How did you get hold of all this?'

'Don't ask. I've promised to keep quiet about that, so I'm not sure how we could use these legally. In fact, I know we can't. But it's a start.'

'What does all this mean? What do these prove?'

Ben separates them. 'I've marked the entries, see? Ignore the bank statements for the company for now. Look at Birch's and then your sister's. There are two payments made each month but not always on the same date: five hundred pounds each time.'

I'm confused.

'What am I looking at?'

'Those payments are eventually all paid into the same accounts. I won't say how I found out who the recipients were. Their identities were well hidden.' He sits back and grins at me. 'But I found out who they belong to. Councillors Watts and Wrigley, no less.'

Two of the men at the Grove Hotel the day of Mum's funeral. 'I still don't understand.'

'Look.' Ben taps the top of one pile. 'These are from Moorland Investments' bank account.' He moves his finger onto the next. 'This is one of your brother-in-law's accounts. And these...' He picks up the statements. 'Are from an account in your sister's name. It's this account that the five hundred pounds goes from to the two Tory councillors. The money has gone from here.' He goes back to the firm's statements. 'As a limited company, it's a legitimate payment to Birch because he's a director. It's for his salary, bonuses, expenses and so on. So that's all above board. I only asked my source for these as a paper trail. And we see the same figures here in his account. But following it through to your sister's account—'

'Angie's involved in this?'

There's a moment between us, a precarious silence.

'I don't believe it. She wouldn't.' Unless she was coerced.

He hesitates. 'I don't know.'

'She can't have been. I remember her telling me he dealt with all the money. He gives her housekeeping and she has to manage on that.' I can hear the quiver in my voice.

'Would you recognise her writing?'

'I don't know.' I haven't seen Angie's writing for years. 'I used to, but it must have changed since then...'

He sniffs. 'There are these.' He rummages through the briefcase and pulls out a couple of old cheque stubs. 'Belonging to your sister's account.'

There's a sudden tightness in my chest, a mix of anger and guilt that I'm half-believing what he's saying.

'How did you get those?'

'Like I said, don't ask.' Ben's watching me closely. 'But do you recognise the writing? And the way the figures are written?'

The letters are large, cursive, elaborate loops spread across the stub.

'No. It's not how she used to write. My sister's writing was tiny. Unless she's completely changed it.'

There's something niggling at me, something I'm trying to remember. It comes back to me in a flash: the note I saw in Angie's kitchen that day. I can see it clearly. *Windows this morning.* And then the flamboyant *S.*

'But I have seen this writing before. This is Stephen. It's his writing,' I whisper. The relief courses through me. 'He must have been forging her signature on the cheques.'

'That certainly muddies the water.'

'Why was he giving money to the two councillors though?'

Ben shrugs. 'My guess, initially, was bribery to get on the council. It might be to keep them quiet, or to get planning permission on the land where the company want to build the new estate.'

The housing estate that won't get built unless Stephen's firm can get their hands on Mum's plot of land.

'Are the other two in Moorland Investments, Matthew Alderson and Barry Learoyd, involved?'

'I don't know; it was only Birch I was after. But it will involve them if it all blows up. Even if they don't know, it still benefits them.'

'Is it enough?' I ask.

'Enough to ruin his reputation if it's made public.'

That's not what I mean. Would it be enough to force him to give Angie a divorce with a share of what she's entitled to? Enough to get him off Dad's back about the plot of land?

I can see the gleam in Ben's eyes, the anticipation of a good story for his newspaper.

'You want to publish, don't you?'

He leans forward, catches hold of my hand. I can't help looking across the room. Nobody's watching.

'I can't. I've stuck my neck out to get my hands on all this. Alan, my editor, couldn't cover for me if he found out how I did it. Let's just say it wasn't on the right side of the law. Anyway, tempting though it is, I wouldn't. Not until everything is sorted for your family. I promise.'

'Thank you.'

'I wouldn't do anything that would harm you – or Angie.' He threads his fingers through mine, an intimate gesture, but I don't find it intrusive.

Then I think about him saying, 'or Angie.' And I can't help wondering if he still holds a torch for her.

Chapter Eighty-three

Lisa

It's odd, being alone in the house. A house that no longer feels familiar, whose floorboards creak in a different way from those at home, whose cistern in the bathroom bubbles and sighs in a way I don't remember from my childhood. The noises outside are different as well: when I first came to bed, cars rumbled past, a motorbike's engine revved again and again, and people shouted, laughed. Now there's a deep irritating rhythmic bass coming from somewhere. At home, in Ponthallen, there is only the sound of the birds settling, the odd squawk from the hens, the rustle of trees and, if the wind is in the right direction and the tide's in, the faint hiss of the sea hitting the rocks around the cliffs.

Cat must be missing Dad because he's on the bed at my feet, a bit like a hot-water bottle.

I'm mulling on what happened earlier. Even though we were hoping that Ben would find something murky about Stephen or his company, the bribery has shocked me, and I'm not sure how to tell Angie. It would have been easier if she'd been with me at the pub. She didn't look a bit well, though. I'll go round to see her tomorrow. Hopefully, by then, I'll have worked out what to say. And what we're going to do about it.

Chapter Eighty-four

Angela

'Who was that?'

'What?' She's sitting at the bottom of the stairs.

'I said, Who. Was. That. On. The. Phone?' Stephen exaggerates what he's saying, stepping down on a tread with each word.

'No one.' Angela doesn't want to tell him. She can't stop shaking.

'Secret lover?'

'Don't be stupid.'

She hears the swift steps, feels his grasp on the back of her neck.

'The hospital. It was the hospital.' The grip lessens.

'And?'

'Dad's gone. He's died.' She jumps up. 'And, if you don't mind, I'd like to be on my own.'

She waits to be hit, but Stephen's only response is to stamp back up the stairs.

She doesn't want him to hear her telling Lisa. Going into the kitchen, she takes the receiver off the extension phone. Words are jumbled in her mind. Taking in a long gulp of air, she dials the number.

'He died around midnight,' she says, once the shared gasping sobs settle to the occasional hiccup. 'They rang me as the next of kin;

they only had my number, they said.' Angela pre-empts Lisa's unspoken question. 'One of the nurses found him when she was doing her rounds. He was alive at half past nine... The nurse said we can see him tomorrow.' Angela looks up at the round wall clock. It's two in the morning. 'Later today...'

Lisa's sobbing again. An almost forgotten feeling starts somewhere inside Angela. 'Look, I'm coming over.' She needs to be with her sister, to comfort her. Ignoring the wobbly protests from the other end of the phone, she puts the receiver down.

The nurse had said she was sorry for her loss. It's Lisa's loss as well. 'There's just the two of us now.' Angela tightens the belt on her dressing gown and takes her car keys from the hook.

When she pulls up and sees Lisa waiting at the living-room window, she remembers she hadn't told Stephen what she was doing.

Chapter Eighty-five

Lisa

I was halfway down the stairs when the phone rang. The moment Angie said my name, I knew.

Angie's coming to the house. She'll have told him, of course. I bet his only thought will be that he can now get his hands on that land, he can bully Angie into signing it over to him. Well, he'll have a shock. I won't let her. If I do nothing else, I'll make sure of that.

Why am I even thinking about the bloody plot of land? Because as soon as I stop, there's this great, gagging sob fighting to get out.

'What will we do about Cat?'

Angie is sitting on the stairs, her arms around her knees. We can't talk any more about what's happened and are casting around for safer, more mundane stuff. I'm comforted by her being here; a half-forgotten sense of being protected.

The cat is winding his way around my legs. Every now and then he looks up at me, opening his mouth in a silent yowl. 'Oh no! I forgot to feed him when I got back from the hospital last night. Dad will ... would never forgive me.'

'He'd understand.'

I rinse out the cat's bowl and open the tin of food. It smells so strong. Some sort of fish, Cat's favourite, my father told me the first time I went to the corner shop for it. No point in getting anything else, waste of money, he won't eat it, Dad said.

Cat has jumped up on the worktop and is doing his best to get at it before I can squash it with a fork into his bowl. Dad would laugh; he had a daily battle like this. And it's this thought, this overpowering image of my father, with his grey, morning-mussed hair, crumpled striped pyjamas and bare feet, making sure that Cat was fed before he even got his own breakfast, that breaks me. Once I start, I can't stop.

'It's all right. It's all right.'

Angie is holding me so tightly I can hardly breathe.

'Lisa, Lisa. Please. You're frightening me.' There's panic in her words.

'Sorry. Sorry.' My teeth are chattering. I once read about someone in shock whose teeth chattered, and I couldn't imagine it. But it's happening to me now. The violent shaking inside me blurs everything.

'Come on, sit down.' She leads me to one of the old wooden kitchen chairs. The legs screech on the tiles as she drags it out. 'Sit here, I'll get a glass of water.'

I bend forward, wrap my arms around me, try to suppress the trembling.

I hear her opening one door after another. She doesn't know which cupboard the glasses are kept in. But I can't help. I wonder if I'm having a nervous breakdown. There's a loud whooshing noise in my ears that makes me lightheaded.

'Whoa! You're going to fall off the chair.' Angie's gripping my arm with one hand and holding a glass to my mouth.

The water's cold, soothing, sliding down my throat. When I've taken a couple of gulps, I push the glass away. She lets me go and wipes my face with the tea towel she'd thrown over her shoulder. It's the one Mum brought back from one of her stays with us. *A Present from Ponthallen* is written in red above a yacht on wavy blue lines. And two fat seagulls.

She sits back on her haunches. 'What was it?'

'Cat,' I say. 'Cat and Dad.' I clench my teeth.

'Cat's okay. He's sitting on the windowsill. See?' She points to his silhouette against the dawn sky.

She doesn't understand. She can't understand.

'I know. I know. I'm sorry. It's just...'

'That we've lost our dad.'

'And I remembered something. From when we were kids. When I wished Dad wasn't – well, wasn't my dad. And it's made me feel bad...'

She's waiting for me to carry on. Her face has no sign of shock, just curiosity. I say, 'Do you remember Belinda Watson's father?'

'Ben's dad?'

Of course, that's how she would remember him. She was never away from their house at one point.

'Yes.'

'Not really. Except that he was a big jolly man. Always told jokes. Always lovely with his wife, cuddled her a lot. That used to embarrass Ben.' She puffs out a small laugh that makes her face light up. 'Their house that smelled of baking and beeswax furniture polish. His mum was always baking, cleaning—'

I cut in – she is building a picture that isn't true.

'It was all a pretence.'

'What do you mean?'

'Once, Belinda came to school with the side of her face swollen and red. She told the teacher she'd bumped into her bedroom door, but at break time, when we were sitting in a corner of the playground, away from everyone else, she started crying. She said her father had been on night shift—'

'Didn't he work for the *Barnsgate Chronicle*?'

I push on. I need to get this out. 'He did, a security guard or something. Anyway, she said she got up early to make a brew for her mother and she'd already put the tea leaves in the teapot when her mum shouted downstairs that she shouldn't; what was in the caddy was the last of the tea until her father gave her the housekeeping for shopping. But she'd already put the leaves in and poured hot water on them. She scooped them back in the caddy, thinking they might dry out by the time he came home and made himself a pot of tea. He went mad. Her mother said she'd done it and he hit her. Belinda tried to stop him.'

Angie's mouth opens. 'He hit them?'

'Yes. She said he often did. And that he didn't allow her mum any money of her own. Or to go anywhere on her own. And that, sometimes, if he went out at weekends, he locked them in the house.'

'That's horrible.'

'Did Ben ever say anything? You were older. Didn't you notice anything when you went to their house?'

'No!' She stopped. 'Wait. There was one time. The autumn half term, if I remember...' She twists the tea towel in her hands. 'Ben had a black eye, well, it was turning green and yellow, you know? But you could still tell it had been nasty. He said he'd been in a fight, which I thought odd because he was always such a gentle lad. You don't think it was...?'

'Possibly. Probably. I didn't ever go to Belinda's house after what happened to her. I couldn't believe that a man that I'd thought the perfect dad was so horrible. And that's what upset me. It came to me when I was with Ben yesterday. I remembered how much I'd wanted to see Dad when I came here last month, even though I was scared he'd reject me. Even though I'd resented him over the years, for turning his back on me when...'

'I know. I'm sorry.' She's crying. 'But at least our dad wasn't a bully.'

'I know.'

All I can think is that, really, I lost Dad years ago. And it's too late now.

Chapter Eighty-six

Lisa

'Ready?'

I nod, then shake my head. I feel like I'll never be ready to face that, first Mum, now Dad, are no longer here.

It's eight o'clock and we're standing outside the hospital. Nurses, their faces pale, strained, are pouring out of the double doors, some greeting the nurses going in, some seemingly too tired to speak. Change of shift. I didn't realise we were so early.

We've driven straight from Dad's house. Angie has borrowed some of my clothes, with the jeans rolled up at the ankle and the blue cotton t-shirt hanging awkwardly over her sling. We'd had a slightly hysterical giggle over the bra and pants before she declared she didn't care what she looked like, she wasn't going home to get dressed.

'Ready?' She tugs at my arm.

'He just looked asleep, didn't he?'

We're sitting in the car in the hospital grounds. Neither of us wants to leave. I don't think we know what to do.

'Peaceful,' I agree, blowing my nose. The distortion from the stroke had gone from his face. We'd both kissed him, held his hand. I won't tell Angie, but it wasn't like touching my dad; the cold, waxy skin wasn't him.

As if she knows anyway, she says, 'He's with Mum now, Sis.'

She hasn't called me that since I came back to Micklethwaite. It sets me off again, and we're holding onto one another. I think we both know that we can mend what was destroyed so many years ago.

Chapter Eighty-seven

Angie

'Where the hell are you? Buggering off in the middle of the night.' He's shouting. 'I've been ringing and ringing—'

'I know. And I don't want to talk to you.'

Angie holds the receiver away from her ear until he stops ranting. She feels calm. Or perhaps, after everything she and Lisa have done today, she's incapable of dragging out any more emotion.

'Stephen, my father died last night. Lisa and I have had to register his death and arrange a meeting with the undertaker. For once, just for once, will you stop thinking about yourself.'

'You fuckin' bitch. Fuckin' get back to this house now. Or I'll bloody come and get you.'

She puts the receiver down. Then the trembling starts.

Chapter Eighty-eight

Lisa

It's dark outside. When had it become dark? With the curtains closed, the bars on the electric fire giving out an amber glow and Cat on my lap, the room feels safe.

'Can we talk? There's something...'

I sit up at the hesitant tone of her voice. 'Okay.'

'I've been thinking about something that happened not long after we were married. I'd pushed it to the back of my mind. But talking about Dad and about Belinda's dad last night brought it back.' She's biting the skin at the side of her thumb. 'About the way he kept control of Ben's mum?'

'Awful.'

'About a year after we were married. About money. About the house.'

'Your house?'

'Yes.' She stops nibbling. There's blood seeping out of the side of her nail.

'Let me get a plaster for that.'

'No.' She presses her hand on my arm to stop me getting up. 'Let me say this?'

'Okay.'

'When we were married...' I see her swallow and I nod to encourage her to continue. 'Stephen suggested we put my name on the deeds of the house – so we were joint owners.' She speaks quickly. 'I said, then I wanted to put my savings into the house, so it really was mine...'

I can't help the gasp that escapes from my mouth. How could she have been so daft?

'He didn't argue—'

'I bet he didn't!'

'He said he was grateful, that I was generous. That it would free up some money to go into the business, and to help his campaign to be a councillor. And I know what you're thinking, Lisa, but I'd been independent for years.' She pauses. She closes her eyes. 'I let Stephen have all the control of the money, without even realising it. And later, I was too frightened to ask. Too scared of what he would do, all the time.'

I search for the right way to ask my next question.

'You said, talking about Ben and Belinda's father had brought something back? About the house?'

'Yes. No. What I meant was, talking about how he kept their mum short of money. It set me off thinking how I've let Stephen do the same to me. And *that* reminded me about something I found. Something I stupidly forgot about because it was the same day Stephen found out what I was, how...'

'How you earned your living in Manchester.' I speak as softly as I can. It's not up to me to judge.

'Yes.'

236

'What did you find?'

'An envelope with a bank book and some bank statements – in my name. I haven't got an account of my own, and yet this statement showed thousands of pounds in an account in my name, with money paid in and out every month.'

'And you knew nothing?'

'Nothing. The cheque stubs weren't in my handwriting.'

'So the signatures were false?' Hadn't that occurred to her? 'You could have got him into a lot of trouble.'

'I wasn't thinking straight, Lisa. Not then. And anyway I was too...'

Scared. I don't say it. Now's the time to tell her what Ben has discovered about Stephen and the bank accounts. I've dithered too long. And after what she's told me, I think this is the right time.

'Listen, love, there's something I need to tell you...'

Chapter Eighty-nine

Angie

The room seems to shift around Angie, bucking and twisting until she thinks she will vomit. She curls her fingers inside the sleeve of the thick woollen cardigan she's borrowed from Lisa.

'What do I do?' The enormity of her husband's deceit and lies is slowly sinking in. She's ashamed that she's been so gullible. 'How could I not know what he's been doing?'

'If he took over all the finances, how could you know?'

'I was always careful with my money before.' Angie shakes her head. 'I've been such a fool.'

'No, he's an expert liar. We both know that.'

'What do I do?' she repeats. 'I must go home sometime. Do I tell him I know? How do I explain how we found out? Tell him about Ben? Then God knows what'll he do.' Her stomach's flipping over and over at the thought. She pulls her knees tight up to her chest.

She's listened to Lisa's awful revelations with increasing awareness that she doesn't know anything about Stephen's life outside the house. That she never has. And that she has accepted everything he said and did, because it was easier to do that than to face up to his anger.

'I'll come with you. We'll tell him together.'

'Would you?'

'Of course. And then we'll tell him you're leaving him, getting a divorce and expecting a decent settlement.'

'He'll fight that. He'll fight me getting any money out of him. And he'll tell everyone how I earned a living in Manchester.'

She can't help picturing those early days: the grim, almost derelict terraced house, the tiny, fetid room she shared with other girls, whose names she's long forgotten, the demands and cruelties of so many men. She's tried to tell herself what she did wasn't a choice but a means to an end. She survived that life until she clawed her way up to a better one.

'So then we say we'll tell the world that he was one of your ... clients?'

Angela considers this. 'Yes.'

'And see how his so-called mates on the council like that. And we'll let him know that we'll blow the whistle on all his shenanigans.' Lisa picks up the bottle of Merlot they've been sharing. 'Dutch courage?'

'I shouldn't.' Angela holds her hand over the top of the glass, before taking it away to allow Lisa to empty the bottle into it.

'Why not? We're neither of us going anywhere tonight.'

'I'll have to. You heard him. He'll only come here.'

'Right, then, we'll go together. I'll phone for a taxi. He wouldn't dare do anything if we have somebody with us.' Lisa stood, a little unsteady. 'And besides...' She laughs. 'You probably will look better in your own clothes.'

Angela manages a smile. She's not as confident as Lisa that having a taxi driver with them will stop Stephen. 'I guess I will. And—' She stops abruptly. There's a knock on the front door.

'Lisa? It's me, Stephen. I thought I'd better come over to see how Angela is. I was worried. Thought she might want me to take her home.'

'Stephen,' Angie whispers. 'I knew it. Someone must be out there, watching him. He wouldn't be pretending to be so nice otherwise.'

His words, controlled, falsely concerned, fade away. Angie and Lisa strain to hear the muttered conversation.

'Mrs Mullins,' Lisa says. 'That's Mrs Mullins's voice.'

They hear the neighbour's door close with a sharp click.

'She's gone in. God knows what he's said to her.' Angie can see the fury in the set of Lisa's mouth.

'Angela? Come on, open the door.' Wheedling. 'Love?'

Angie jumps and fights the impulse to scream when there's a series of thundering bangs on the door.

'Open this fucking door. Now! Open it, or I'll break the bastard down.'

She remembers her mother saying, 'Someone's walking over my grave', and shivers.

'What shall we do?'

'I'll go.' Lisa strides to the door, her face grim.

'Don't open it. Please.'

'I won't.' Lisa raises her voice. 'If you don't stop that right now, I will call the police.' She had to bellow over the constant racket he's making. 'Do you hear me?'

'I'll kill her. And you! I'll fucking kill both of you.'

Angie's heart is pounding, her breath rasping in her throat. 'Lisa...'

Lisa holds up her hand. 'It's okay. Listen.'

In the silence that follows Stephen's rant, there are other noises: people's voices, car doors slamming, men shouting, footsteps.

'He's brought some of the other neighbours out with the racket he's making. Listen, they're telling him to leave.'

They stand, frozen, staring at one another.

He gives the door a violent kick. It shakes, the letter box rattling. Then the flap opens, and Angela sees the tips of his fingers. When he speaks, his voice is malicious. 'I can wait.'

Chapter Ninety

Angie

The taxi's engine is running. As is the clock, ticking up the pounds, but Angie feels safer knowing the driver is watching her. She suspects Lisa has instructed him to, no doubt with a small incentive pressed into his palm.

She's packed a suitcase with only the few clothes she's chosen herself over the years. Nothing else. She puts it down to close the front door.

There's a sharp hoot of the horn from the taxi and Angela sees the driver point to the entrance to the street.

Within seconds, Stephen parks his sports car in front of the taxi and gets out. He runs up the path. It takes all her strength to stand her ground.

'So! Here at last.' He looks around. 'No bitch sister to protect you?' He pushes his face at hers.

'I'm on my own, Stephen.' She's waited until he came home for lunch and has made sure she's standing on the path, hoping he won't touch her if the neighbours could see. 'I'm leaving you.'

'Like hell. Get back in the fucking house.'

'No. I won't be going into that house ever again.'

'I'll make you pay. I'll tell everyone what you really are. Whore. You'll be sorry.' He sneers. 'You won't last a day without me...'

'Yes, I will. I'll have a completely better life without you.' Angie's angry with herself because she sounds panic-stricken.

'Listen to yourself, you stupid cow. Right!' He clasps his hands

240

together. 'You've made your point. You're pissed off at me for coming to the bitch sister's place last night. Now...' He reaches towards her. 'Back in the house.'

Angela steps back. She knows, if he manages to take hold of her, she'll be hustled back indoors with no chance to escape.

'You okay, miss?' the taxi driver shouts from his car.

Stephen swings around. 'Mind your own pissing business.' He speaks before he sees the man, all solid six foot four of him. Angela sees the muscles in Stephen's jaw tense. 'Last chance.' He speaks through gritted teeth. 'Or you'll leave with just the clothes you're standing in.'

'I've got all I want in the way of clothes already. As for anything else – well, I'll get what I'm entitled to.' Before he can say anything else, she adds, 'You see, Stephen, I know about the fraud: the accounts, the bribery, the way you've been forging my name. I'd like you to think about the implications of me, oh, and Lisa, knowing all that. And having the proof.'

She sidesteps him, noting, with satisfaction, his slackened mouth, and walks down the path with her bag. She hopes her legs will hold her upright until she gets to the taxi.

The driver opens the door. 'Good on you, miss,' he murmurs when she climbs in. 'Back to your sister, eh?'

'Please.'

When the taxi pulls away, she doesn't look back.

Chapter Ninety-One

Lisa

Angela insisted she would go to the house on her own this morning. Having slept on the revelations about Stephen's fraudulent business dealing and his threats, she got up determined to go and get her things. There was no arguing with her; it was like having the old Angie back.

Even so, when I found out the taxi driver is the son of one of Dad's friends, I explained everything to him, and he promised he would keep an eye on her.

I'm trying not to worry about her.

There's a knock on the front door. It's the last person on earth I expected.

'I hope you don't mind?' Ben Watson frowns warily, making the lines on his forehead deeper.

'No. Not at all.' I poke my head out of the door and look left and right. Sure enough, there are one or two neighbours looking curiously our way. Mrs Mullins next door waves and mouths, 'You all right?'

I smile and nod. 'Thanks.' I step aside to let Ben in.

'Can I get you a cuppa?'

'No, I'm fine, thanks.'

He chooses one of the wooden chairs by the window. 'It's years since I've been in here. Looks...'

'Different,' I offer. 'I know. It was a bit of a shock for me when I first came back. Dad let things go a bit over the last few months.'

'They must have been married a long time, him and your mum.'

'Yes.' We're skirting around something; I can feel it. 'Is everything okay, Ben?'

He gives a small start, almost as if he isn't quite ready to reveal his news. 'I found something out...'

'About Stephen? About the company?'

'Depends...' He digs into his bag. 'Here...' He comes over and gives me an envelope.

I take it, trying to read his face.

'What...?'

'Just look inside.'

I tip two photographs into my hand.

The first is a close up of Stephen. He's in a dark blue suit, pale blue shirt and a navy tie, standing next to a woman. She's stunning. Tall and slim with smooth olive skin and black hair piled up in a huge knot, with a few tendrils carefully arranged to fall on either side of her face. Her eyes are dark and framed by long lashes.

She's wearing a red business suit, fitted jacket with shoulder pads and straight skirt, and a white v-neck blouse.

It looks like a promotional photograph. 'Is she something to do with his business? Or the council?'

'I don't think so. Look at the other photo.'

It's taken at the door of a house. The woman is in a floaty dressing gown. Stephen is in jeans and a white t-shirt. He's holding his jacket flung over his shoulder. They're kissing. Properly kissing. Not a peck on the cheek, but a 'just been to bed but now I must go – reluctantly' kiss.

I can't take my eyes off the photo. My face is hot, yet I'm freezing.

Ben places his hand lightly on my shoulder. 'You okay?'

'I don't know.' I clear my throat. 'Who is she?'

'She's called Rachel Henshall. I've been following him.' Ben's voice is guarded. 'Sometimes it's the only way to... I thought maybe if I could see who he meets, it might lead to something. I'm sorry, I didn't expect this.' The warmth of his hand calms me. 'She's an estate agent and lives in a village on the other side of Barnsgate. That's where I took the photo. More like a hamlet. One pub. I asked in there. The woman behind the bar was very chatty but she said the only thing she knew was that they were a couple and had lived there for about three years, but they don't go in the pub, don't join in village life. She said that one of the neighbours had told her the husband works away a lot.'

'You think...?'

'It appears so. I'm sorry, Lisa. I know this must be a shock. I've seen him go to that house a few times. And I've seen him with her, as you can see. One time he stayed overnight. That's when I took the photo.' He sounds apologetic, almost upset. I think he's upset for Angie. I wonder if he still has feelings for her.

'I thought he couldn't be any worse...' I can't stop the sharp huff of disgust.

243

Ben takes the photos from me. I'm suddenly aware of his closeness. He clears his throat. 'And there's something else.'

His tone changes. When he looks at me, there's a glimmer of excitement deep in his eyes. 'She's also a shareholder of Moorland Investments.'

Chapter Ninety-two

Lisa

I'll be glad when today is over and we can grieve for Dad – and Mum – on our own.

Nursing my fourth mug of coffee since six a.m., I stand at the kitchen window watching a bank of misty-grey cloud building up over the moors. It's growing, casting light and dark shadows on the land. It's going to rain.

I can't stop thinking about those photographs. I'm not sure what to do. I'll have to tell Angie, I know that. But when? I know she says she's left him, and I'm so glad about that, but it's yet another deception.

This last fortnight has gone by in a blur. I've been dreading today. We dealt with all the practicalities of the funeral. We've contacted Dad's friends and told his neighbours. It filled the days. The nights simply need to be got through as best we can.

Stephen hasn't been near since Angie left him. But I don't trust him. And if he turns up at the crematorium today, I don't know what I'll do. It's like living on a knife edge, waiting for his next move.

He'll be champing at the bit to find out what's happening to the plot of land. Well, he can stew. Dad didn't leave a will, so it will be a long time before anything can be done about that. To be frank, it's nowhere near the top of our priorities.

And now there's this business about another woman, involved with Stephen both personally and in business, from the look of things. Poor Angie. I wish Barb could be here. But Charles II got under Chris's feet, tripped him up and he's broken his leg. I don't like thinking I'm not in Ponthallen to help them.

If someone had told me three months ago all this would have happened, I wouldn't have believed them.

My stomach growls: too much coffee and no food. I'm not hungry but I need to eat. If I make toast for both of us and take it up to Angie, perhaps I'll feel more like it then.

I check my watch; we've got another two hours before the hearse arrives.

Chapter Ninety-three

Angela

Looking back, Angie remembers little of the day, even less of the service. She does remember Lisa holding her while they sobbed in the car following the hearse, the rain pounding on the roof. In the crematorium, they stood side by side holding hands. When Lisa wrapped her fingers around hers, it struck Angie that it had taken the death of both their parents and her husband's viciousness to bring them back together.

The worst part of the day was being in the crowded pub afterwards, with the smell of wet coats, cigarettes and beer. She watched the smoky, smeared scene she saw in the long mirrors on the wall behind the bar as if she wasn't really there: people milling around, sitting in the alcoves, greeting each other, a constant movement of indistinct, black-clothed shapes.

Beyond the half-drawn maroon curtains, rain streaked the windows, distorting the day outside. Each time she moved, her shoes stuck to the stained carpet. When the landlord brought pies and sausage rolls from the kitchen and people began pressing her to eat, she thought she would throw up.

245

She saw Ben, and for a moment she wondered what her life would have been like if she'd married him instead of Stephen.

Mostly, she remembers needing to get away from all the faces. People chatting and laughing until they saw her watching, then the sudden shift into pseudo-sympathy, she thinks resentfully. She'd been grateful when Lisa suggested they quietly left the pub.

Lisa has been subdued since they got back to the house.

They were both glad when they could change out of the damp clothes they'd worn all day and put on pyjamas and dressing gowns, even though it was only five o'clock. After making a cup of tea and feeding Cat, Angie has left her alone with her thoughts.

They doze in the armchairs, but, to Angie, there is a frisson of something in the atmosphere. Once or twice, she has caught her sister studying her, as though she's going to say something.

'Are you okay, Lisa?'

'Tired. And sad, obviously. It dawned on me we are now orphans.' Lisa heaves a self-deprecating sigh. 'Sounds daft, huh?'

'No. Not if that's how you feel. You have lost them both...'

'And you.' Lisa looks surprised. 'They were your mum and dad too.'

'Yes. I just feel ... I always felt that they preferred ... loved you more than me, you know? Even before...'

'No!' Lisa sits straight in her chair. 'That's not true, Angie. Not at all. Is that what you felt?'

'Yeah, always.' Angie watches Cat stretch, yawn, curl up again. 'Especially after...' She wipes her fingers across her eyes. She hadn't realised she was crying. 'After they knew...' She can't look at Lisa. 'What really happened...'

Lisa leaves her chair, drops onto her knees in front of Angie.

'Oh, love, that's not true. That's so not true.' She touches Angie's cheek. 'Mum worried so much about you... Look at me. She worried, especially when she didn't know where you were. And she worried about you when you were back here and married to...' She smiles. 'I'll tell you something, shall I?'

Angie moves her head against her sister's fingers.

'I always felt they both favoured you, even before we lost Robert. Don't you remember how Dad always said you were the sensible one and I was scatty? Which I probably was.' They both laugh. 'And I always felt Mum loved you best because you were the eldest and a girl. I always believed she wanted a boy when I was born...'

She stops. Their mother had finally got her wish. And then... Angie can't help the image that comes into her head. It must be the same for Lisa.

Lisa sits back. 'Weren't we daft!' She smiles. 'They loved us both the same.'

'I wasn't really jealous of you, you know.' Angie is anxious for her to know that. 'I just accepted it.'

'And me. Because you were my big sister. And you always looked after me. I thought you were the bee's knees.' Lisa giggles.

'And you were my little sister. I've always loved you.'

'Big hug?'

'Big hug.'

Rain patters on the window. Angie looks across the room. 'It's gone dark. I'll draw the curtains.'

'I think Dad would have enjoyed his day, all his friends there,' Lisa says as Angie sits down again. 'But I'm glad it's over. I should think you are as well.'

'I am. Will you ring Auntie Barb, to let her know how it went?'

'Perhaps tomorrow.' Lisa stops stroking Cat, who's now purring quietly on her lap. She runs her fingers the length of him, from head to the end of his tail. 'At least *he* didn't turn up.'

And there it is, the fear that has hovered over the two of them all day.

'Did you think he would?'

'Didn't you?' Lisa grimaces.

'Yes. If not at the service, then at the pub. Every day, over the past fortnight, I've thought he would come banging on the door again.

I feel sick every morning when I wake up. I don't know what to do, Lisa. But I do know I can't carry on like this, in this limbo. I need to decide.'

'There is something we can do, you know.' Lisa stops. 'I know it's absolutely too soon for me to be saying this, but ... when it's the right time, after probate is granted, we could sell the plot of land to Stephen's company...'

Angie is shocked by the determination radiating from Lisa.

'You don't mean that.' She feels a dropping sensation in her stomach. 'How can you be talking about that today, Lisa? How can you?'

'Neither Dad nor Mum would want you to carry on being miserable, love. They'd see it as a way for you to get away from Stephen.'

'I don't know. It's... Mum held on for so long. She hated him. She'd hate it if we gave in. Dad would be the same...' There's a pause. 'It'd feel so wrong for us to give in...'

'I told you, Barb said Mum had her own reasons for not selling, besides hating your husband. Because they were struggling in their marriage, thinking of going to Australia, but that's not important now. And Dad wouldn't sell, because he thought he was being loyal to her.'

'I know that.' Angie can't think straight. 'But...'

'But nothing. We'll be able to do whatever we want once probate goes through. There's nothing to stop us getting the land valued. Then, when the time comes, we can sell at a price we choose. Ben's already given me the name of a valuation surveyor.'

'You like him, don't you?' Angie sees a flush of red colour her sister's cheeks. She'd expected to feel envious if she was right. But she doesn't.

'He's a good friend...'

'But you'd like it to be more?' Angie prompts.

'No! Well, perhaps. But he only lost his wife last year. And, anyway, we live in different parts of the country. Long distance relationships don't work...'

248

'Eighteen months ago. And they can – and do.'

'That's not what we're talking about, Angie.' Lisa looks as if she's trying not to smile, the corners of her mouth pulled in. 'You're trying to change the subject. Listen, Stephen and his mates at Moorland are desperate to buy. You could open your own account. You'd have your own money.'

She's right. Angie knows she's right. It's just frightening.

'You'd have freedom,' Lisa urges. 'Which is what Mum and Dad would want; they'd want you to be well away from him. Especially now.' Something changes in Lisa.

'Lisa? What do you mean, *especially now?*'

Lisa moves in her chair. Disturbed, with a squeak of displeasure, Cat jumps down and stalks into the kitchen. 'It's something that Ben's found out…'

'What?' Angie is frightened. 'What's Ben found out?'

Chapter Ninety-four

Lisa

My heart is hammering. The white-hot rage I felt when Ben first told me about Stephen's mistress, adding yet another layer to my anger at the viciousness, fraud and dishonesty he's been getting away with for years, rises up again. Grief is the only thing I should be feeling right now, and I resent even having to think about Stephen today. But what he's done to my family, to my sister, what he's still doing to her, makes me determined to expose him for what he is. One way or another.

'What? Lisa? Please, you're frightening me…'

'Sorry, love.' I was trying to work out how to start. 'I should have told you before now.'

'So tell me.' She leans forward, clasping her fingers.

'You might hate me for telling you this.' What if she already knows and puts up with the situation?

'Go on.' She sits higher in the armchair, lifts her chin.

'Ben was looking for more shady dealings with Stephen or with Moorland Investments. He's been following Stephen...'

Angie is still. She hasn't taken her eyes off me.

'Stephen has another woman.' Should I have worked up to that? It's so cruel. I wait for her reaction, expecting denial, anger.

But all she says is, 'I'm not surprised. He hasn't touched me for the last three years.' Her voice is steady. 'Not since he found out I worked as an escort.' She lifts her hands as though in acceptance. Then she gets up, goes to the electric fire and turns a couple of switches. 'Surprising how chilly it is. You wouldn't think it's supposed to be summer.' When she straightens up, her back to me, she says tightly, 'How old?'

'What?'

She whirls around. 'How bloody old is she?'

So she's not as calm as she looked. I'm glad. 'I don't know. Please don't shout at me, Angela, I'm only telling you what Ben found out.'

'I'm sorry.' She rubs angry tears away. 'I know I said I wasn't surprised, but it's being taken for a fool, you know?'

'I know. Come and sit down, please.'

'I'm all right.' She folds her arms. There's a calm determination to the set of her features. 'What's her name?'

'Rachel Henshall.'

'Henshall? I know her. Or know of her. I've never met her, but I've heard him mention the name. She's something to do with Stephen's firm. The estate agent that deals with the sales of Moorland's builds.'

'And also a shareholder in Moorland Investments.'

She flinches. 'I didn't know that.' She looks down at her hands. 'Gets better, doesn't it?'

'I'm sorry.' I wait. Except for the ticking of the clock and the scrape of Cat's tongue as he cleans his fur in the doorway, there's silence. There's not even any noise from outside on the avenue.

Angie presses her hand to her forehead. 'How long has it been going on? Did Ben find that out?'

'No. But if she's a shareholder, perhaps quite a while.'

'Which came first, eh, shareholder or lover?' It's a bitter laugh. 'So, where does she live, this Rachel Henshall?'

'Why?' I'm afraid. 'You're not thinking of finding her? Are you?'

'*Why?*' she repeats. 'Don't you think I have the right? Where does she live, Lisa?'

What good would it do? Still, I tell her, 'It's called Hirstridge, a village on the other side of Barnsgate. Why would you want to go?'

Angie comes to sit beside me. 'She needs to know I'm going to cite her in the divorce proceedings. When I divorce Stephen on the grounds of adultery, I'll be naming her as the other woman.'

Chapter Ninety-five

Angela

'So, is that what you want to do?'

'Yes.' Angie tries to calm herself with deep breaths. Her mind has been spinning over the last hour or so. It seems Lisa has asked that question a million times.

She doesn't know when the hatred and fear of her husband really began. Was it when Stephen discovered how she'd lived in Manchester and the beatings started? Or was it before? As soon as they were married? As soon as he started pushing her to persuade her mother to sell the land to him? When she realised why he'd been in such a rush to marry her: to help his business?

She'd been a fool to plough all her money into their house. How had she ever believed she'd be an equal partner in the marriage?

She gets up to draw the curtains, shutting out the light and the evening rumbling of the estate life. 'I think you're right. We should sell the land. Will we use the solicitors in Barnsgate?'

'Yes, I think that's best; it's the firm Mum used, and they know all the details.'

'Do they deal with divorce as well?'

Lisa paused. 'I should think someone in the firm will.'

'Then they can handle mine.' Chilled, she rubs her forearms. 'I know it'll be hard...' An understatement: it will be horrendous. But with her sister by her side, she can do it.

'You feel strong enough?'

'Yes. But first I'm going to see Rachel Henshall.'

Chapter Ninety-six

Angela

'According to Ben, it's that one.' Lisa points.

It's a small row of six slate-roofed cottages, some with multicoloured flowers in window boxes, one or two with tubs of fuchsias or geraniums by the front door. Unlike most of the others, whose stonework is painted in various colours, the cottage they are looking at is in its original, unpainted sandstone, the door and window frames pale wood.

'Right,' Angie says. A thread of nerves burns through her whole body.

'Want me to come with you?'

Angie grips the car door handle. 'No.' She glances at Lisa, sees the anxiety on her face. 'I have to do this.' It's quite a while since she challenged anything in her life. She forces a smile. 'I need to do this on my own.'

She crosses over to the cottage, her legs trembling. She knocks and sees the venetian blind downstairs move.

It seems an age before the door opens.

'Can I help you?' There's a half-smile on the woman's lips, caution in her large brown eyes. Angie thinks Rachel Henshall knows who she is.

She's wearing a purple suit with a pale mauve blouse under the fitted jacket. Dark brown hair piled high on top of her head. Her feet are bare, the nails a shiny purple.

Rachel Henshall glances down at them and gives a low, deep laugh. 'Excuse my feet, I've just come in from work.'

Angie can't help wishing she'd made more of an effort with her own clothes. Even if she didn't have the now grubby sling, even with her newish jeans, blue cotton t-shirt and matching cardigan, she can't compete with the sophisticated woman standing in front of her. Yet, she still feels she has the upper hand.

'I'm guessing you already know who I am, Miss Henshall. I'm Angela Birch.' She doesn't know what she expected to see when she said her name, but it wasn't confusion. 'Stephen's wife?'

'Oh. Oh, yes, of course.' Rachel looked past her, glancing up and down the road. 'You'd better come in.' She moves to one side, holds the door back. Her fingers are long and slender, nail varnish purple, matching her toes. 'The lounge is first on the right.' The woman's casual acceptance is infuriating.

The room is small but tastefully decorated: white walls with one painting, a sunset, red carpet, red and black swagged curtains, a glass-topped black ash coffee table alongside a pale leather suite. Classical music is playing low from an Amstrad hi-fi tower in the corner by the window. A square glass vase of red roses is on the coffee table.

The sight of them is a shock for Angie. Red roses were always the flowers Stephen brought for her every week in Manchester. Not Mr Bloody Original, then. She's unsure whether she feels contempt or pity for the woman she was, who allowed herself to be duped by him.

She's startled when Rachel speaks.

'May I get you a cup of tea? Coffee?' She's standing by the door, giving an appearance of easy control.

'No, thank you.' Angie is mortified to hear her voice tremble.

She looks around. There's an open wooden staircase in the far corner. Leading to the bedroom, she presumes, feeling acid rising in her throat. She swallows.

Rachel says, 'Why are you here, Angela?'

'Can't you guess?' Surely she knows? But Angie's thrown by the question, her prepared speech forgotten.

A faint frown appears between Rachel's eyes. Her voice hardens. 'Look, I'm not going to play games. Either tell me why you're here or you leave my house.'

'I'm here about my husband Stephen.' The trepidation evaporates. 'The man you're having the affair with.'

'Why do you care? You're estranged anyway. He's told me all about the two of you having separate lives.' Rachel's voice is strong, belying the slight quiver of her lips.

'That's what he says?'

'Yes. And I believe him. You're never at his side when he's been entertaining clients, or at any council occasions.'

'Because he doesn't want me there. Hasn't for a long time.' Angie takes in a long breath. 'Anyway, I'm only here to tell you you're welcome to him. I'm divorcing him. And I will be citing you as my grounds for the divorce.'

'What! You can't do that.'

'I can and I will. If you don't like it, sort it out with him.'

The thought scares her. How will Stephen react?

Angie hesitates but feels she must say this. 'But be careful, Rachel. Stephen doesn't like to be crossed. I know. I've been on the receiving end of his temper – and his fists.'

'You're saying he's hit you?'

'Yes. Often.'

''I don't believe you.'

Angie raises her shoulders. 'That's up to you. I have no reason to lie to you. I'm getting out of the marriage.' She can tell the young woman is shaken. 'I'll go now. I only wanted you to know what I intend to do.'

She pauses again, knowing what she's about to say could rebound on her. But she's beginning to feel slightly sorry for Rachel Henshall, another woman Stephen has deceived.

'There is something else, something I think you really should know. You act for Moorland Investments? Your estate agency?'

'Yes. Well?'

'Well, I think you should look carefully into their books. Especially Stephen's part in any dealings.'

'What do you mean?'

'I've said enough. I only came to tell you about the divorce.'

Angie tries to hold onto every shred of dignity she can as she opens the front door.

Lisa is waiting for her on the pavement. 'Come on, love.' Her arms around Angie, she guides her across the road.

They don't look back.

Chapter Ninety-seven

Lisa

On the way home, Angie doesn't stop crying. I can't get a word out of her. But it's as though she knows she's started a ball rolling, and now she's scared of the repercussions. When I help her out of the car, she's shaking so much I almost carry her to the door.

'Everything all right, Lisa?' Mrs Mullins is on her step. 'Anything I can do?'

I've seen over the last fortnight her enquiring looks when she sees Angie here all the time. She's good-hearted and has kept an eye on Mum and Dad over the years. And she's been kind to me since I came back to Micklethwaite. But just now, all I want to do is get us both inside.

'No, thanks all the same, Mrs Mullins. It's good of you to offer but we're fine. Bit of an upset tummy, that's all.' Angie's whole body is shuddering in my arms. 'Come on, love, let's get you in the house. I'll make a cup of tea.'

'No.'

'Something to eat?'

'No.'

'Glass of wine it is then.'

I found some tinned tuna in the cupboard and eventually managed to get Angie to eat a little of it with some salad. It's about all either of us could manage.

We're sitting in the back garden on the deckchairs, nursing a glass of Merlot each. Cat is on my lap, his soft purr vibrating through him and me. It's eight o'clock but, although the sun is low above the far moors, there is still a soft warmth to the air.

'On days like this, after all the rain recently, I always think what a strange country we live in, weather-wise: so cold the end of last month, now proper August weather.'

I'm only talking to break the silence. Angie only agrees. 'Uh-huh.' I shut up.

I haven't a clue what she's thinking or what she'll do. And I don't know what I can do to help, other than suggest she comes to Wales with me. With Mum and Dad gone, there really isn't anything to keep her here. We could comfort one another and Barb and Chris in Ponthallen.

Barb! Trying not to worry her, knowing how difficult things must be, looking after Chris and the smallholding, I still haven't told her what Stephen's been up to. I should.

I close my eyes, lean back. Many times since I've come back, I've wondered how different my life would have been if that awful day hadn't happened. Now it's Angie I'm thinking about: what would her life have been like if she hadn't let go of our brother's pram?

I stop myself. It's no use going there. I can't change any of it.

Angie looks as if she's shrunk into the chair.

'It'll all work out, you know.'

There's a slight lift of her shoulders. Encouraged, I try again, pointing towards the fields and moors.

'I do love all this. Remember, the walks we did with Mum and

Dad when we were little, the picnics? Summer holidays, staying with Barb and Chris...'

'Until I ruined everything!' She won't look my way. I'm not going to take her up on that, she has enough to deal with at the moment.

'And sometimes in caravans in a different part of Wales.' I force a chuckle. 'I think holidays were the only times Mum and Dad relaxed. I loved our holidays.'

'I don't remember.'

These last weeks have revealed how different our memories of our younger days are. It makes me sad.

The sky darkens slightly. There's a thin stream of cloud crossing the sun hovering above the horizon. A crow flaps its wings on a branch of the oak tree in the field at the end of next door's garden and takes off with a hoarse cry.

Chapter Ninety-eight

Lisa

The brass hands of the clock on the solicitors' wall tick slowly. The door opens in a rush of cool air and murmur of voices from another office. Angie holds her top lip between her teeth, watching Richard Bolton stride in. Halfway to his desk he halts, tuts and, juggling a bulky folder under his arm, comes towards us, holding out his hand.

'Sorry to keep you waiting, Miss Brooks, Mrs Birch.'

'No worries. It's good of you to see us at such short notice, especially on a Friday. And Lisa and Angela, please.'

He clears his throat. 'Hmm. Exactly.' His face is a pale puce. He settles himself onto the black leather chair behind his desk. 'May I offer both of you my deepest condolences for your loss. I remember your father as an honest, straightforward man.'

'Thank you. He was.'

'Right.' Richard Bolton rustles through the pages in the thick folder. 'My colleague took your instructions over the phone for the agreement to sell the Bardsley allotments. I drew up a contract.'

'We want everything to be sorted out as soon as possible once probate comes through.'

He stares at the open folder.

'You're surprised by our decision.'

'Not my business, of course, but indeed. Considering the history...' He leans forward, his arm flat on the top of the desk. 'Would you think it impertinent of me to ask why? I'm afraid this is just my curiosity.'

I sense Angie shift in her seat. 'It's a personal decision, Mr Bolton...'

'Richard.'

'Thank you. Richard,' she says. 'My husband is not the nicest of men. In fact he's a bully, and the only way for me to get out of the marriage, to divorce him, is for us to sell that plot of land to him. I've recently discovered he's been having an affair.'

'I see. Well, my colleague, Miss Vaughan will be dealing with your divorce. I believe you have an appointment with her afterwards?'

'Yes. At three o'clock.'

'Right.'

I see him glance down at the sale agreement. I say, 'We had the land valued and, as Moorland Investments can't build their estate without the plot, that's the price my sister and I have decided upon.'

'Understood.' He passes the contract towards us. 'In that case, would you please both sign here ... and here...' He waits until we've done as he's asked, and then says, 'As you say, nothing can be finalised until probate comes through, but I see no problem in pre-empting that. Moorland Investments will be made aware of those conditions but I'm sure they will be more than happy to comply. The contract – with that proviso – will be in the post tonight to their solicitors. They will get it first thing on Monday morning.'

'So, if there's nothing else...?' He fixes a steady gaze on Angie and smiles. 'Miss Vaughan is an excellent divorce lawyer; she will serve your interests well.'

'Will you come in with me?' Angie's wandering around the waiting room, stopping to study the various notices hanging on the wall.

'Of course. If that's what you want.'

'Yes.'

She doesn't look at me. She bobs on her heels. It's a nervous habit she's had since we were kids. I remember her fidgeting like this before visits to the school dentist, parents' evenings at Micklethwaite Primary, even waiting in line to be examined by the nit nurse. The last thought makes me splutter with laughter.

Angie frowns. 'What?'

'Remember Aunty Nitty?'

She turns, her face relaxed, and grins. 'God, that woman terrified me. The way she scowled and pushed and pulled your head about. I think she hated kids.'

'And never spoke – just pointed at you when it was your turn to be "nitted".'

She chuckles. 'I'd forgotten we called it that. And that poor lad, Adam Weston, who always wet himself when he waited in line...' She stops. 'I always felt so sorry for him.'

'And me. I wonder what happened to him.'

Angie grins again. 'He's a barber in Barnsgate.'

'No!'

We're both still laughing when the door opens.

'Mrs Birch?' Angie's solicitor looks around fifty, with a round rosy face and a wide smile. 'I'm Sandra Vaughan.'

'Is it all right if my sister, Lisa, comes in with me?'

'Of course. Come in, both of you.'

Miss Vaughan's smile gradually disappears as Angie tells her why she wants a divorce. The woman's gentle questioning teases out the whole state of my sister's marriage and her life.

259

'So, his latest assault on you – you went to hospital?'

'Yes.'

'So there will be a record of that.' She nods. 'To substantiate our claim. Have there been other times when you've needed a hospital visit?'

I see Angie fidget in her chair. 'I didn't go, any of the other times. Mostly it was just bruises. Once he twisted my arm and sprained my wrist, but he wouldn't let me see the doctor...'

Just bruises. I clench my jaw.

The solicitor writes something in her notebook. When she's finished, she says, 'So, besides the physical abuse, he controls you mentally, emotionally and financially. The last could be something we could definitely use, providing you have evidence?'

'There's the fraud!' I can't help myself.

Sandra Vaughan opens her eyes wide. 'Fraud? Is that being investigated? Because if it is, we'll have no—'

'No, it's not. Not yet anyway. We don't want the police to get involved.' I could kick myself for blurting it out. 'This is confidential? Yes?'

The solicitor twists her lips. 'Well, I can't un-hear what I just heard. But, yes, everything is confidential. I think you need to tell me everything. There may be something we can use...'

'Angie?'

My sister is looking increasingly tense. She gives me a desperate look.

I nod. 'Go on.'

'A while back, I found some bank statements, cheque books, cheque stubs.' Her voice is squeaky but grows stronger as she continues. 'In my name. With my signature on some of the blank cheques. But it wasn't my writing, and it wasn't my account... I don't have a bank account.' If that shocks the solicitor she doesn't show it. After faltering for a moment, my sister says, 'There were payments, regular payments to people.'

'Any names?' The solicitor holds her pen, poised to write.

'Is that necessary?' Angie grimaces.

'Humour me.'

'This is two or three years ago. There were sums paid out to the same men. Two of the Barnsgate councillors. They're friends of Stephen's: Councillors Watts and Wrigley. I'm sorry, I don't know their first names.'

'That's no problem. It won't take long to track them down, if necessary. If necessary,' she stresses. 'Do you still have the statements, etc?'

'Well, no. At the time, I couldn't ask Stephen about them...'

'Because she was too afraid of him,' I say.

Sandra Vaughan nods. 'Right. That's a shame. Let's move on, shall we? Anything else?' She adjusts her reading glasses. 'Any unreasonable sexual demands?'

'No, we haven't... He doesn't... He hasn't touched me since he found out about my past.' Angie wavers, glances at me.

'It's okay,' I mouth my reassurance. 'Go on.'

She lowers her face into her hands.

Sandra Vaughan and I sit, silent, waiting for her to speak. Tears leak between her fingers.

I drop my handkerchief onto her lap. 'Here, love.'

She fumbles for it.

Before, the solicitor was writing notes. Now her pen is moving across the paper, but it isn't words she's forming, but various patterns and squiggles. She's giving my sister time to recover. I'm grateful for that.

Angie gives one last shuddering gulp of air and blows her nose. Sandra Vaughan puts her pen down and rests both palms on her desk.

'Would you like to tell me?' Her voice is gentle.

'Before I was married, I was an escort. I needed to...'

'Does that make any difference?' I ask. 'It was before she was married. How she went down that road wasn't her fault.'

'I'm not here to judge, Lisa.' She shakes her head. 'Angela, I'm

261

sure, as women, there are things we all would rather not have done. However, under present law, it is up to individual judges to decide on the settlement of a divorce. Unfortunately not all of them will automatically award a fifty-fifty split of the assets. It's purely discretionary and I'm afraid what you are telling me about your life before you were married, could be construed – and please believe me, I think this is terribly wrong – as giving a husband an excuse for his behaviour.'

'That's appalling...'

'It is.' She holds up her hand as I begin to protest. 'I agree. I am only warning you that filing for a divorce doesn't automatically mean fair shares, so to say.'

'I'll take my chances,' Angie says, 'I just want a divorce. And as soon as possible. Besides we'll still have the sale of the land, whatever else is or isn't awarded.'

'Right,' Sandra Vaughan says, 'there are two ways we can get this divorce for you. You mentioned in your letter you want to cite your husband's adultery and...' She riffles through the folders on her desk. 'Miss...'

'Rachel Henshall,' Angie is quick to fill in the pause.

'Indeed. Miss Henshall, as the co-respondent, but that could prove costly and time-consuming. And, as you say, Angela, the sooner you are divorced the better.'

I'm tempted to intervene but resist. This must be my sister's decision. I can tell she's looking at me, but I keep my eyes on the solicitor, squeezing Angie's hand to let her know I'm supporting her.

'Or we could go for unreasonable behaviour? Which is certainly the case here and probably the easiest to cite. But it's entirely up to you.'

I hold my breath. The sooner Angie can get away from Stephen, the safer she'll be. Knowing how he's manipulated her in the past terrifies me.

After what seems an age, she says, 'If you think that's the best way to get out of this marriage, then that's what we'll do.'

I close my eyes and tilt my head back, savouring the relief.

'I'll draw up the necessary paperwork and get my secretary to make another appointment for you.' Sandra leans back in her chair. The smile has returned.

'Thank you.' When Angie stands, she looks more relaxed and confident than I've seen her since I arrived in Micklethwaite.

And when we leave the building, she grabs me around the waist. 'I did it, Sis,' she says, her eyes wide as though she's surprised by herself.

'You certainly did.' I hug her. 'And we've got the ball rolling with the land sale. So it's onwards and upwards, Ange. Or, as Barb always says, onwards and sideways! I think we deserve a glass of wine to celebrate.'

Chapter Ninety-nine

Angela

Over the years, Stephen's manipulation of her life has grown: the controlling, the violence, the sulking, the wall of silence he keeps up for days, are all layered into it. But, unable to escape, for fear of what he would do, she tried to push it all to the back of her mind, to get through the days, weeks, months as best she could. Yet each beating, each insult, each attack on her confidence, built the festering bitterness she didn't know what to do with. Until now.

She's taking back control of her life. And – the most important and brilliant thing that's happened over these last months – she has her sister back. That's what's made her face up to everything.

And because of yesterday, she can see a way out. She hasn't slept – anticipation and apprehension have kept her awake.

Sleepless, she listened to the sounds outside, the different noises that remind her of her childhood: the faint rumble of trains in the distance, the low traffic on the main road at the end of the estate, the chirping whistles of the starlings at the end of the back garden.

They bring back all the times she shared with Lisa. Adventures, companionship, and, most of all, her sense of responsibility for her little sister. The sibling rivalry, competing for their parents' attention and approval, was never necessary, she knows that now. It partly led to her letting her take the blame for that awful day. But yesterday there had been an unspoken forgiveness from Lisa and it has given her an odd kind of peace inside. Is she finally allowed to stop feeling guilty?

She's ready.

When Lisa comes downstairs at eight o'clock, Angie is dressed, with coat and shoes on. She fidgets from foot to foot. 'I was hoping to be gone before you were awake.'

'What are you doing?'

'I'm going back to the house. There are a couple of things I need to pick up. My sleeping tablets for one.' She falters. 'Shall I tell him what we've agreed to do about the land?'

'I wouldn't. The one thing he'll want to know is how much we want; he'll badger you until you end up telling him. And he'll not be happy about the price, you can count on that. Wait until we can tackle all three of them at once. He won't do anything in front of his business partners.'

Angie hopes her sister is right. She has no great faith in his self-control.

'I should come with you.' Lisa frowns.

'I'll be fine. I just thought telling him might make him accept the divorce, if he knows he's getting his own way about that. But you're probably right. I won't say anything. I'll be fine, honestly. I'll ring when I'm on my way back here.'

Chapter One Hundred

Lisa

She said she would ring. She hasn't.

Last night, an idea started buzzing around in my head, it wouldn't go away, and now I'm exhausted and worried. Cat is as restless as I am and we're prowling around the house, not knowing what to do with ourselves.

I sit in Dad's armchair and Cat leaps onto me, kneading his paws, the claws catching the thin cotton of my dressing gown. I let my gaze wander around the room. The carpet, the worn furniture, the old curtains, so familiar. The house feels different, empty. Earlier I heard the buzz of the children passing to go to school, but now it's mid-morning and quiet outside, except for the occasional car.

But, if I concentrate, I hear echoes of voices. Mum and Dad. Faint, drifting words. Cat raises his head, ears twitching.

'You hear them too, Cat. What are they saying?' I murmur, running my fingers across his back, feeling the bumps of his spine. 'Are they trying to help us, trying to tell me what to do?'

The clock on the mantlepiece clicks. Half past eleven. Angie still hasn't rung. The constant lurch of panic in my stomach is making me queasy. Something's wrong.

I need to get dressed.

Cat growls when I push him off and stalks away, tail high.

'Sorry,' I call after him. He ignores me and stands by the back door. I let him out and he sits on the path, washing himself, his back paw upright. Leaving him to sulk, I run upstairs and throw on my clothes.

Running a comb through my hair and hopping about, trying to put my feet in my sandals, I ring for a taxi. This is no time to be catching a bus.

Chapter One Hundred and One

Angie

'You'll not get a bloody penny. Not from my business. Not from this house.' Stephen's pacing the floor, unsteady. Angie can smell the whisky from the other side of the bedroom; the fumes seem to fill the air. His hands clenched, his face blood-red, he's snarling his words. He's not expecting an answer, Angie knows. His tirade has lasted five minutes, ever since he closed the door, trapping her in.

She grips her handbag on her lap, every nerve in her body alert, waiting for a chance to escape.

'You're nowt but a cheap whore. That's how you'll have to earn your money. Oh no...' He lunges at her. She cowers, ducking her head. 'You're too bloody old and raddled, aren't you? You couldn't give it away.' He straightens up, his body shuddering. He goes over to the window, lifts the catch, takes in deep drags of air.

Now! The voice in Angie's head screams at her to run. She makes herself stand on shaking legs and staggers to the door. The rush of relief is short.

'Oh no you don't.' He's quick. Swinging round, he grabs her arm. The pain from her shoulder jolts through her body.

She screams and slaps at him with the bag. The strap catches him in the eye.

'Bitch!' Blinded, letting her go, he stumbles to the floor, clutching his face. He makes another grab at her. Misses. But then his hand is tight on her ankle, pulling her down.

'Let go! Let me go!' Twisting, she kicks out, feels the satisfaction of connecting with his arm. But he holds on.

'You're going nowhere. Think I'd let you just walk out on me? I'll kill you before I let that happen.'

Cold terror gives Angie the strength to wrench her leg out of his grasp and stagger along the landing to the top of the stairs. His grunts are loud as he follows. She reaches for the banister, but her palms are wet with sweat and her hands slip. He's right behind her. Turning onto her knees, she forces herself to her feet, presses against the wall. Faces him. There's a frozen second before he dives at her.

'I'll kill you.' His roar is followed by her scream.

Chapter One Hundred and Two

Lisa

I hear them as I walk up the front path. At least I hear him. Shouting. There's a scream. I run, bang on the front door. 'Angie! Angie?'

When I run to the back of the house, the door is wide open. There's no one in the kitchen or the dining room or the living room. I wrench open the door to the hall. There's shattered glass on the mat.

Stephen is sprawled at the bottom of the stairs, his head against the front door. When I lean over him, his breathing is faint and shallow, and the smell of whisky hits me. For a split second I'd hoped...

I look up towards the landing. My sister is slumped on the top step, her hands over her face.

'Angie?'

She won't lift her head.

I know I should call for an ambulance. Instead, I step over Stephen and crawl up the stairs until I'm on the step just below her. Gently I pull away her fingers until I can see her face. She's staring down at me, expressionless.

'What happened?'

She doesn't reply. Pushing her fingers into her mouth, she bites on the knuckles.

'Angie, what happened?' I repeat. 'You need to tell me.'

'I don't know.' It was a wail. She sucks in air, preparation for another howl.

'Hush. Hush.'

I need to stop her. If she carries on like this the neighbours will hear. I thrust my hands under her armpits and haul her to her feet. I half-carry her down the stairs but when we get to where Stephen is lying, she refuses to move.

'Don't look. Come on.' Somehow, I manage to lift her over him.

I get her into the living room, but she keeps staring back at him over her shoulder.

'He's dead!' She shudders. 'Is he dead?' She's going to start screaming again.

Kicking the door closed with the heel of my foot, I say, 'No, he's unconscious. He's not dead.' It would have been better for her if he had been.

'I don't know what... He just...'

'Sit here.' I lower her onto the settee. 'Don't move.'

'It's my fault. I tried to escape...'

I grab her by the wrists. 'Listen to me. He fell. I could smell the drink on him, and he fell.'

She's shaking her head. 'I shouldn't have...'

'Angie, I won't let you take the blame for this. It's not your fault. I'll say I was here and I saw the whole thing. He'd drunk so much he staggered and lost his footing at the top of the stairs.'

I hurry to the kitchen and fill a cup with water. 'Drink this.'

She's shaking, but she manages to hold the cup and sip.

'Right. Stay here.'

I avoid the shattered glass when I kneel at the side of him, touch his throat. 'He's still breathing.'

I hear Angie's harsh sobs. I just hope she can calm down before anyone arrives.

'Okay, remember what I've said.' I go to the phone. When the operator answers, I take a long slow breath before saying, 'Ambulance. We need an ambulance...'

Chapter One Hundred and Three

Lisa

I empty Cat's tray, give him an extra breakfast in a way of an apology for not feeding him last night.

'I can't stay, I'll leave the kitchen window open so you can come and go as you please.' I tell him, as he gobbles his second helping of sardines. 'I can't leave Angie too long on her own at the hospital.' She calmed down once all the tests and X-rays were done and the doctors declared no broken bones, just cuts and bruises but, because he was concussed they're going to keep him in for a few days for observation. As far as I'm concerned they can keep him in for a few weeks. The longer the better, if it keeps him away from my sister.

And, while we sat around all night, waiting for the results of all the tests, I did a great deal of thinking; I have a plan. I need to talk to Angie about it. I'm just hoping a few days will be enough to push it through.

Because she's too shaken to drive, we agreed I should go to their house to pick up what Stephen will need. Privately, I think it best if she played the concerned wife. At least in front of the nurses.

I wash my hands, open the canvas bag, check that I've got everything: pyjamas, dressing gown, slippers, toiletries.

'And, if anyone asks, I've told her to say that we found him at the bottom of the stairs when we came back from picking up Dad's ashes.' Cat stares at me, unblinking, licking the fish off his whiskers.

I zip the bag closed and flop down on the chair. It's been a long twenty-four hours and I'm exhausted. Cat leaps onto my lap, pushes his head at my hand. 'Mind you...' I put my forefinger under his chin and tickle him. 'The stink of whisky on him when the paramedics carried him into A&E was so bad, I doubt anyone would believe it was anything but an accident.'

Someone knocks on the front door. 'What now! Sorry, Cat.' I

put him on the floor, drag myself to my feet. I'm guessing it'll be Mrs Mullins wanting to know what's happened.

It's not. I can't believe Stephen's mistress has come to my parents' house. 'How did you find this address?'

'With difficulty,' the woman admits, with a rueful smile, tucking her long black hair behind her ears. 'I hope you don't mind.'

'Have I any choice?' It's taken me only moments to recognise her, even though I've only seen her from a distance. Her voice is musical, cultured. She holds out her hand. 'Rachel,' she says.

'Yes.' I don't reciprocate. 'What do you want?'

'To talk.'

This is the last thing I need. 'I haven't much time. And isn't it my sister you should be talking to?'

'I need to speak to you first. It's Lisa, isn't it?'

I shrug. She's got me on the back foot.

'May I come in?'

I look around. Mrs Mullins and another neighbour are standing nearby, apparently chatting to one another, but with glances in our direction. A group of boys hangs around the small black sports car she's parked on the other side of the road.

It's the same make of car as Stephen's. His and hers, I think, even more bitter for my sister. 'They won't touch it,' I say, seeing her quick frown at the boys. 'They're only being nosy.' I pick up Cat, who is winding around my legs, and move to one side.

We stand in the living room, and I look with fresh eyes at Dad's home. 'I'm clearing things out,' I say, and then I'm cross with myself for sounding defensive.

She doesn't seem to notice the shabby furniture.

'May I sit?'

'Yes.' I put Cat on the floor and he immediately scampers into the kitchen.

'I wanted to say I'm sorry.' She tugs the front of her shift dress over her knees before settling in Dad's chair.

'Shouldn't you be saying that to my sister?'

'I will. I'm going to their house next.'

'They're not there. She's at the hospital. In fact I really need to go there now. He ... he had an accident.' I need to stress the accident bit.

'An accident?' She doesn't ask if it's a bad one, I notice. Neither has she taken the hint that I have to leave.

'He fell downstairs. Yesterday.' Should I elaborate? I decide I will. 'He was drunk.'

'I'm not surprised, he drinks quite a lot.' She threads her fingers together. 'I wanted to tell you both I want him out of my life.' We stare at one another. I don't want any solidarity with this woman. 'I have put all his things in bags. I've given his clothes to a charity shop,' she says. 'But there are a few other things – bits and pieces – in the car that I need to give back to him. Things he bought me that I don't want.'

I sit in the other armchair. 'To stop my sister citing you in her divorce?'

'I haven't done it just because of that.' She holds up her hands. 'Seeing her, listening to what she said...'

'About his abuse?'

'Yes. I had no idea. And I thought they led separate lives; he said that was how she wanted it.'

I can't stop the huff of derision. 'If only! He's Mr Control-Freak.'

'So I've gathered. I've been rather stupid for quite a long time.' She frowns and pushes her hair behind her ears in a self-conscious way.

'He's an accomplished liar.' How many times have I said that over these last months?

'In business as well as in his personal life,' she says. 'As I've found out to my cost.'

I try not to sound too eager. 'Oh?'

'I'm a shareholder in Moorland Investments. I have been for the last few years. When ... when Angela ... I hope you don't mind my calling...?'

271

I shake my head, impatient. Why should I object to her using my sister's name? Just get on with it.

'When she came to my house, she told me that there could be discrepancies in the company. I have to say I was a little doubtful.' Presumably seeing my raised eyebrows, she pauses. 'You have to admit, spurned wife and...'

'Let me stop you right there.' My indignation makes my voice abrasive. 'I know for a fact there are many, as you call them, discrepancies.'

'Yes. I know that now. And, unfortunately, some apparently involve me. But I had no knowledge of what was happening.' She leans forward, forearms on her thighs. 'I found certain documents. Let's say they are questionable in their veracity...'

'Meaning?' I have a feeling I know what she is going to say.

'Bluntly?'

'As you like.'

'Documents and letters with my signature on them. My forged signature. Cheque stubs with my forged signature...'

'Payments to certain councillors? Watts and Wrigley?' I tilt my head. 'Documents and letters about a certain proposed building site?'

Were some of those letters to Mum? I wouldn't put it past Stephen to pretend there were other people pressuring Mum to sell. People she'd have seen as having some authority, like this woman, maybe those councillors as well, whose power would have intimidated her. And yet she'd stuck to her decision. I felt such pride.

'You know about it all?'

'I know you probably found Angela's signature on some as well?' She nods slowly. 'Yes.'

'Also forged.' I let that sink in. 'What will you do?'

Her features slacken in relief. 'Get out as quick as I can. Sell my shares. I don't want my agency damaged by this. And I'm selling the house, moving right away from Hirstridge, probably to the other

272

side of Manchester. I have another branch near the city, so I'll probably buy something near there.' She hesitates. 'I really would like to speak to your sister?'

I glance at the clock; it's time I left. 'I'm going to the hospital now...'

'Can I come with you? We could go in my car?'

'I suppose. They might not let you in the ward.'

'I'll chance it. There are things I need to say to both of them. And I have so much else to sort out.' She rubs her hands over the skirt of her dress, an action that suddenly reminds me of Dad, and I wonder what he'd think of all this. 'Anyway, I came to you this morning because I have a proposition for you.'

It's not what I expected. 'What?'

She pauses slightly. 'As I said, I want to sell my shares of Moorland Investments, and I wanted to ask if you'd like to buy them? I'd sell them to you at a rock bottom price.'

'Why? And why me?'

'Why not?' She shrugs. 'I thought it fair. At first I thought I'd ask your sister, but then...'

'You thought he'd get them off her.'

'Yes.'

'And he probably would. So you thought I'd be a better bet. Even though you don't know me?'

'I saw the way you looked after Angela that day she came to my house. I watched you.' She smiles. 'I don't need the money. I inherited the estate agency from my father and it's doing well. I bought half of Stephen's share just to help him out a year or so ago.'

'Help him out?'

She nods. 'He needed money quickly, said it was a cash-flow problem. I had the means.' She drums her fingers on the arm of the chair. 'So? What do you think? It would mean you'd have an equal say in the company.' She smiles. 'And that would really make Stephen furious.'

That makes it doubly tempting. But I don't know. Do I really want to be involved? 'I don't know anything about the building trade.'

'You don't need to. I only made sure I was getting a return on my investment. I didn't get any more involved than that.' She makes a rueful face. 'Or so I thought.'

'Okay. How much?' I can't believe I'm even asking. When she quotes the figure it sounds reasonable. But what do I know? 'Can I think about it?'

'Of course.' Unzipping her bag, she pulls out a sheaf of papers. 'I brought the latest company figures and share prices, for you to show to your solicitor, just in case you were interested. It would only take a couple of business days to get them transferred to you. And, as I said, I don't particularly need the money. I just want to move on as quickly as I can. So I can let you have the shares at half that price...'

I glance over the first page. 'What would you have done if I'd said no right away?'

'I don't know really. Like I said, my first thought was to ask your sister...'

'And, as I said, he'd have them off her in a minute. Look, I have savings. If, as you say, you are willing to sell them at half this price...' I wave the sheet of paper. 'I'll be able to buy.'

Chapter One Hundred and Four

Lisa

Rachel expertly parks the car between a large white van and a motorbike in the hospital car park.

'Will you be all right getting back?'

'Fine. We can get a taxi.'

We walk to the entrance. Even though I've changed into my favourite dress, I still feel shabby alongside her. She takes long strides, her stiletto heels clicking on the path. She walks as she drives, very quickly. We don't talk. My mind is in a whirl about her offer.

There's a determined set to her mouth when she holds open one of the wide doors and lets me through.

I tell her, 'You go and see if the nurse will let you in.' I've decided she can talk to Angie and him without me being there. 'It's on the second floor, the Oscar ward. I'll wait here.' I sit on one of the grey plastic chairs lined up in the corridor. It's busy, nurses and visitors rushing about. There's a buzz of chatter and laughter.

'It won't take me five minutes.' She walks to the stairs behind the heavy glass door, then comes back, reaching out. We shake hands and smile at one another. 'Thanks for this,' she says.

'You're welcome.' I have the feeling that, under different circumstances, I could have been friends with Rachel Henshall.

Chapter One Hundred and Five

Angela

'Right, that's your checks done.' The nurse pockets the thermometer and straightens the sheet over Stephen.

'Leave it!' He glares at her. 'I'm not a bloody child.'

She tuts. 'Now, now, Mr Birch. Language. You've had concussion and a nasty cut on the head. You need to rest.'

'I need to get out of here.'

'Well, that won't happen for a few days. Concussion can be a serious thing, so please do as you are told. Rest. I'll be back later, and...' She wags her finger. 'Have a little sleep.' She beams at Angie. 'You'll soon have your husband back to his normal self again.'

Angie doesn't look at Stephen. She knows he's glowering from her to the nurse. His irritation is palpable.

'Bugger off, will you.'

'Stephen!' Angie glances around. 'Please?'

'Shut up.' He winces. 'Just get me something for this bloody headache,' he says to the nurse.

She flushes. She's only young. A probationer, perhaps. Sweat glistens above her top lip. 'There's no need for rudeness, Mr Birch. And if you continue like this, I'm afraid I will have to report you.' She hovers for a moment, her cheeks a bright red. 'And you've had all the pain relief you can have for now.'

Angie watches her leave the small room.

'You pushed me.'

Angie jumps, but tries to keep her nerve.

'You were drunk,' she replies, determined not to listen to him.

'Just shut the fuck up.'

'You tried to hit me because I'd told you I wanted a divorce. You slipped and fell down the stairs. You've had concussion and they've put six stitches in the cut on the back of your scalp.' She gets some satisfaction adding, 'You'll also have a lot of bruises.'

'You don't need to look so bloody pleased about that. I wasn't sodding drunk, and you're talking crap. There's no way you'd have the guts to get a divorce.' He sits back against the pillows piled up on the headboard. 'No way!'

'I will.' Angie folds her arms across her waist, hugs herself. 'I told you that's what I wanted and you wouldn't let me leave. And you were downing whisky like water.'

'Nothing new there then.'

Angie twists round in the chair at this new voice. Stephen flinches and gasps in pain. Or shock.

'Hello, Stephen.' Rachel walks in.

'How did you...?' His mouth hangs open. 'Why are you here?'

Angie stares down at her hands, watching her fingers twist. She feels outside this scenario, an unwilling witness.

'I need to talk to you.' It's all Rachel offers, her words precise, business-like.

'Rachel...'

Angie hears the whine. She doesn't want to look at him but can't help watching his features crumple. He's at a total disadvantage, and she can tell he hates it.

'Rachel...'

'This won't take long.' Her tone is hard. There's no sympathy in the way she looks at him. 'I should tell you that Angela and I had an interesting chat a few days ago, Steve.'

Steve? Nobody calls him Steve. Angie jumps when Rachel drops a large canvas bag onto the floor with a heavy thud.

'Your things. Well, most of them. Anything and everything you bought me. The rest went out with the rubbish and your clothes went to the charity shop.' Out of the corner of her eye, Angie sees Rachel flick her hands, as if brushing him away. She wishes she could do the same. 'There will be no need to come round to the cottage ever again.'

'My ... laptop...'

'I've kept that. Well, I didn't think you'd want that to go to the charity shop? Not with what was on it? So I'll keep it safe, for now.'

Angie watches his eyes widen in panic.

Rachel nods. 'I thought you'd understand.' She says this with satisfaction. 'Right. I'm gone.'

Angie feels a light touch on her back. 'And thank you, Angela. You brought me to my senses. I really am sorry. For everything.'

'Rachel... Wait...' Stephen's plea is ignored, until he says, 'The company? Your shares?'

'Oh, yes. I should have known that would be your first concern. I probably should have said.' She nods thoughtfully. 'As I only bought them to help you out and I don't need them, I'm selling them. In fact, I'm selling them cheaply – to your sister-in-law.'

And with a faint hint of perfume, she's gone.

Chapter One Hundred and Six

Lisa

'I think your sister may be following me quite quickly.'

I'd heard Rachel Henshall's heels on the hard floor a while before she appeared. She looks satisfied. 'What happened?'

'I told him I want nothing more to do with him. And that I've sold my shares to you. He reacted exactly as I guessed he would.' She holds out her hand for me to shake. 'Look, I need to get on. There's a lot to do.'

'Thank you.' I don't know what else to say. I wouldn't have met the woman if Ben hadn't found out about her and Stephen. And though it's caused a lot of misery for my sister, in the end Rachel Henshall will help her to get away from him. So I say again, 'Thank you.'

She smiles. 'I should be thanking you. God only knows what could have happened down the line. He not only fooled me about his marriage, but he could have caused me a great deal of damage professionally.'

'What *will* you do about him forging your signature? All the documents, the cheques?'

'I'll get my solicitor onto it. If it will help, I'll make sure he copies you in to anything he sends to me?'

'Please.' That would give my plan a bit more substance.

'Right then. If we don't meet again, good luck.'

I watch her stride off towards the car park.

'I didn't know you were here yet, Lisa.' Angie looks beyond me at Rachel Henshall's retreating figure. 'So you saw her as well?'

'She brought me here.'

She jerks her head in the direction Rachel Henshall has disappeared. 'She sold you her shares?'

'Yes. Well, once it's sorted.' I grin.

'She put quite a show on up there. Angie hesitated. 'She's kept his laptop. Do you think there's anything ...'

'Anything on it to incriminate him? I shrug. 'Maybe.'

We stare at one another.

'It made me remember what he did, why he fell down the stairs. He just went for me. He said he'd kill me, Lisa. And I believed him.'

There's a flicker of remembered fear in her eyes.

'He can't hurt you now.'

Angie links arms with me. 'Let's get out of here. How's Cat?'

'Sulking!'

She laughs.

Chapter One Hundred and Seven

Lisa

'I think I've thought of a way to make sure Stephen agrees to the divorce. Something we can do to get you right away from him. Forever.' I hand Angie a glass of white wine. 'He needs to know that, if he refuses, we have enough on him to ruin him.'

'How can we do that?'

'I have to talk to Ben first. Is that okay?'

She takes a sip of the wine, nods. Her eyes are almost closed. 'I'll take this with me to bed, if you don't mind.'

'No. You go.'

I sit for quite a while, with Cat on my knee, trying to work out my plan, and what to say to Ben. My guess is Stephen's public face is more important to him than his marriage. But, knowing how vicious, how abusive he is, I must make sure my sister is protected.

I want to ring Ben. But it's Sunday, probably the only day he and Dan get to spend together, so I make myself wait until the afternoon. While Angie's resting, I try his number, glad we haven't arranged to have the phone disconnected yet and I don't have to go to the smelly phone box.

He answers on the second ring.

'It's Lisa, Ben.'

'Everything okay?'

'Can we meet somewhere? I need to talk to you.'

'I'll have to bring Dan with me. I've only just got in. We've been to Belinda's for Sunday lunch, and I don't really want to take him back there. It wouldn't be fair on him – or her, actually; her lot are playing her up at the moment.'

'I understand, that's absolutely fine.' It'll be nice to see a 'mini-Ben'. 'Of course you must bring him with you. And can I ask a favour?'

'Sure.'

'Do you use a voice recorder for your work? You know, a Dictaphone.'

'Yeah, top of the range. Why?'

'Could I borrow it, please? Just for a few days?'

'If you need to.' He sounds puzzled. 'What are you up to now, Lisa?'

'I'll tell you when I see you.'

'Okay, I'll bring it with me. But I'm curious…'

'Thank you, Ben.' Everything's falling into place. 'Where shall we meet?'

'There's the park by the start of Thwaite Lake. Just go through the gate, you'll see it. It's only small, but Dan loves it there, and it'll keep him occupied.'

Ben has his son on his shoulders. He is indeed a mini-Ben, with a shock of blonde hair and pale grey eyes that study me when they reach me. I'm sitting at a bench in front of the iron railings at the side of the swings.

The little boy has his arms wrapped around his dad's forehead. Ben has to tilt his head slightly back so he can see me. I can't help laughing.

'This is Dan. Dan, say hello to my friend, Lisa.'

280

I smile. 'Hello, Dan.'

'Hello. I'm two and...' He jiggles Ben's head. 'And?'

'Ten months.' Ben says with difficulty.

'I'm two and ten months. How old are you?'

'Very old!'

He laughs. 'That's not a number.' His teeth are small and very white. He's gorgeous. 'You're pretty.'

'That's enough now. Good boy.' Ben lowers him to the ground. 'Swings or slide?'

'Swing. You come?' Daniel points at me.

'I'd love to.'

I stand watching Ben thread his son's legs into the small chair swing and give it a gentle push.

There are a few other people here: a young woman at the bottom of the slide, anxiously watching a little girl hovering at the top; a couple sitting on one of the other benches, a boy on the man's knee. I wonder if Ben, Dan and me look like a family to them, and then immediately dismiss the thought. Stupid!

'I didn't know this park was here,' I say, trying to let go of a powerful sense of regret. 'Is it new?'

'Newish. The community association raised funds with public donations to build it here after the council turned down the application. We ran a feature on it in the paper.'

'It's great. Wish it had been here when we were little.' I look across the lake. 'When Angie and I were kids, now and then on a Sunday evening, we'd walk here with Mum and Dad. Sometimes, we were lucky enough to see otters swimming near the edges of the lake, hiding under the branches of the willows. Sometimes there were swans, or ducks ... mallards, I think. They were really noisy, especially if someone was feeding them bread.'

Looking across the lake, I can see the café Ben and I went to. I can just make out the red of the hanging baskets.

Ben straightens up in front of the swing.

'More.' Dan shouts.

'No, that's high enough, son.' He looks concerned when he faces me. 'What's wrong?'

Before I can answer, Dan shouts, 'Out.'

When Ben lifts him off the swing, he runs over to the sandpit and plonks himself in the middle, where two small girls are digging with buckets and spades. Twins, I think. The woman sitting on the edge of the sandpit smiles as she hands Dan a spade.

'Thank you,' I say, at the same time as Ben. 'Sorry,' I tell him. 'Not my place...'

'Don't be daft.' He drops onto the nearest bench, still watching Dan but looking relaxed. 'Oh, and here you are.' He pulls the Dictaphone from the inside pocket of his leather bomber jacket and hands it to me.

'Thanks.' I put it carefully into my handbag.

'Going to tell me what you're going to do with it?'

'First, Stephen's in hospital. He fell down the stairs at Angie's house.'

'Or was pushed?' Ben gives a short laugh before squinting at me. I must look shocked, because he sits up. 'God, she didn't?'

'No. No! Of course not. But she told him she was divorcing him—'

'About time!'

I stop, trying to identify the tone of his voice. Relief? Satisfaction? It occurs to me again that he may still have feelings for her.

But then he says, 'No woman should ever stay with an abusive partner; this isn't like in the fifties when they just had to put up with it. Totally barbaric!'

Is he thinking of his own father: the jolly, sociable chap in public who tormented and beat his wife, Ben's mum?

'He went for her—'

'He what?'

'He hit her, threatened to kill her.'

Ben's face darkened. 'Bastard.'

282

'She was trying to get away from him, they were at the top of the stairs, he was drunk. He fell, cut the back of his head, got concussion. He'll be in for about a week, apparently. That's why I need to borrow your Dictaphone. When he does come out, I'm going to be with her when she tells him again. If he threatens her, I can record it, without him knowing. Then at least she has proof of what he's like. She can use it to get her divorce.'

'You'll have to be careful. He could just take it off you. He could hurt both of you.'

'Oh, don't worry.' I touch his hand with the tips of my fingers. 'It'll be hidden in my coat pocket.'

I look past the park railing, through the trees towards the lake. The skin of the water is rippling, and every now and again a sparkle of sunlight on the surface catches my eye. I'm taken by surprise when he closes his fingers over mine and says, 'Good. So, saying that all works, what then?'

I like the feeling of holding his hand and I've forgotten what I was saying. 'What?'

'What happens after that? What will you do?'

'Angie and I need to get away.'

'You'll go back to Wales? The two of you?'

'Yes.'

'I'll miss you.' He looks sad. 'Seems we've only just got to know one another again. Properly, as "grown ups".' He smiles. 'That sounds daft when I put it that way. And I know, it was only for me to help you find stuff on Birch, for me to help Angie get her divorce.' He shrugs. 'But I've enjoyed seeing you. Being with you.'

'And me, Ben.' This conversation is not going the way I expected, but I like the intimacy of it. On impulse I say, 'You could always visit? You and Dan. He'd love the seaside.' My heart is racing under my ribs. Suddenly I know I want him and Dan to stay in my life.

'I'd love that.' He nods towards Dan, who is now covered in sand and still wildly digging. 'He would too. It's time we moved on as well.'

I'm holding my breath.

'Sally would want me to be happy.' Without warning he leans towards me and kisses me lightly on the lips. 'Am I,' he pauses, 'reading this wrong? Too quick?'

'No.'

'Good.' He grins. 'Fantastic, even.'

There's a beat of silence. I breathe steadily, try to bring my heart back to normal.

'You okay? About this?'

'Oh, yes. Will Dan be?'

'I'm sure he will.' Ben looks across to the sandpit. 'Hey-up.' He laughs. 'Here he comes. I thought it wouldn't be long.' He nods towards the gate, where a brightly coloured ice-cream van has started blaring out some sort of a tune.

Dan is wobbling towards us. 'Scream?'

Ben stands, still holding my fingers. Holds out his other hand to Dan. Twirls us around.

'Ice cream?'

'Scream!'

Dan tugs at Ben, who bends down to his height.

'Buy Lisa an ice scream? One to share with you?'

Dan shakes his head.

Ben laughs. 'Hmm, she's not that much of a friend yet then?'

Dan whispers something.

'What, buy one for Lisa and one for you?'

'Yeah.'

'Thank you, Dan.' I join in with Ben's laughter.

'Okay, you two.' Ben straightens up, grinning. 'I know when I'm outnumbered.'

Chapter One Hundred and Eight

Lisa

'He's out for the count.' Ben appears at the door with two glasses.

'He's lovely. A credit to you, Ben.'

'Thanks. Here.' He hands a glass to me. 'Only cheap plonk, I'm afraid, but it's the only thing in the house.'

I take it. 'Thanks.'

He sits down next to me. 'Well, this is a turn up for the books, eh?' He smiles. 'The first time I saw you in the chapel of remembrance, who would have thought we'd be sitting here now?'

'I know.'

'But it's good?' He looks straight into my eyes. 'Right?'

'It's good,' I agree. 'Very good.'

I still have to tell him what we've done, and I'm not sure how he'll take it. Especially as one of the provisos I insisted on at the beginning was that his investigations were kept between us; it wasn't something he could publish. I decide I might as well jump right in. I want to hold onto this moment, the knowledge that this man cares for me, just think about that. But I can't.

'But there are a couple of things I need to tell you, Ben.'

'Oh?' He takes a swallow of wine. 'What's that?'

'The thing is – Rachel Henshall is selling me her shares in Moorland Investments at a rock-bottom price. After Angie told her Stephen had lied to her about them being separated, she did some searches of the company of her own, and decided she wanted to get out. She said she wanted to sell them to Angie—'

'But realised he'd get them off her?'

'Yes. So I was the better bet. I'll only be a shareholder, not part of the company, as it were...'

'Your business.' He tempers the words with a smile. 'Nothing to do with me, love.'

'I just wanted you to know. Because we've also decided to sell the land to them. Hopefully, it will help get Stephen to agree to the divorce. And it will be our last tie here in Micklethwaite.' I see the sadness behind his smile, and add quickly, 'Except for you and Dan, of course. But for Angie, I really mean, her ties will be well and truly cut. Rachel said she didn't get involved with Moorland Investments, so I won't need to. Once probate is sorted, the land will be theirs to do with as they like.'

'And that new estate will be built.'

'Yes.' I pull a face. 'I just hope Mum would understand.'

He dips his head. 'I'm sure she would. I think your mum and dad only wanted what was best for both of you.'

'It's something we only agreed on after ... after Dad died, but I should have told you before now. I'm sorry.'

'Why?' He looks surprised. 'It's nothing to do with me.'

'It is in a way,' I insist. 'You found all those records—'

'You asked me to scout around for anything that would give you a lever to make Birch give Angie her divorce. It was nothing to do with your land. Don't worry about that. Please.' He puts his arm around my shoulder.

'But we're going to see Stephen's partners with the bank statements and cheque stubs that Angie found in her name, and...' I stop.

He fills in the rest of my sentence. 'And you want to show them everything I found. All the fraud, the payments to those councillors, the bribes, the fraudulent use of company funds.'

'Yes. I'm sorry, Ben.'

'Best scoop I have had for a while.' He gives me a sardonic smile. 'Go for it, it doesn't matter. You are what matters to me. There will be other stories.'

'We need to know if they know what he's been doing.'

'Whether they know or not, they'll want to keep it under wraps for the sake of the company's reputation.'

'Then they might accept the price we've asked for.'

'You should get the best price you can.'

'Yes, but it's higher than that surveyor you found for us suggested.'

'So? It's what you deserve.'

'We're hoping, if they didn't know, they'll confront him.'

'You want him pushed out of the company. Revenge, Lisa?'

I hesitate. 'Perhaps. Probably. Yes. For Angie and me. For what he did in the past – for what he's doing to her now.'

'You'll need to be careful. I know the bastard deserves everything you can throw at him, but if he sees what you're doing...'

'I'll be careful.'

'And, you never know.' He grins. 'If it all blows up in Birch's face, I might get an even bigger story out of it.'

Chapter One Hundred and Nine

Angie

Angie and Lisa waste no time. First thing Tuesday morning, they're at the locked gate of Moorland Investments' yard. There's no one around. Various machines and lorries are parked in a line on the other side of the offices.

Angie and Lisa are waiting for Stephen's partners to arrive, with their offer to sell the land. Angie holds her breath, as she always does when faced with the unknown.

A security guard opens the gate to allow a silver Jaguar and a dark blue Rover to sweep in, and the sisters follow.

The two drivers stand by their cars, frowning, waiting to see who they are. From their wary half-smiles, it's obvious they recognise Angie, but their faces are blank when they see Lisa.

'Mrs Birch.' The taller of the two holds out his hand. 'I'm afraid Stephen hasn't come in yet?'

'No, I know, Mr Alderson. He won't be in this week, he's had a fall. Nothing bad,' she adds hastily, pre-empting the question the man had opened his mouth to ask. 'Concussion, cuts and bruises. But they're keeping him in for a few days' observation.' Angie shakes his hand and gestures to Lisa. 'My sister, Miss Lisa Brooks. Mr Learoyd.' She nods at the other man, who barely tips his head in acknowledgement.

Angie's always disliked him. He reminds her of Stephen: self-important, aggressive.

'Please, Matthew and Barry. You've known us long enough.' Alderson smiles but still looks puzzled.

'We have a proposal for you.' They've practised what she will say and she is sticking to the script. 'May we go in?' She gestures towards the office doors, which open automatically.

'Of course.' They usher Angie and Lisa in. 'Coffee? Tea?' They exchange a wary look.

'No, thank you.' Angie gives them a thin smile. 'No doubt Stephen has told you our father died?' She doesn't wait for an answer. 'And that, once probate is settled, my sister and I will own the land you've been hounding our parents about for years?'

'Now look here, we've done no such...' Barry Learoyd has a light, quite high voice, which doesn't go with his stocky figure and close-cut hair.

Angie talks over him. 'We're here to tell you we are willing to sell you the land. At a price. We've had the land valued and the contract drawn up. Last Friday, we went to our solicitor's and signed it. It should be with your solicitor today or tomorrow, so the ball will be in your court. In the meantime...' Angie takes the folder from her shoulder bag. 'We'd like you to look at these.'

She spreads out copies of the records that Ben found – the bank statements and cheque books from Stephen's office – on Matthew Alderson's desk. 'Oh, and there's also this.' She holds out the receipt and photocopy of the certificate Rachel has given Lisa for her shares, her copy of the stock transfer form that's been sent to the tax people and the letter she has written for Lisa to keep, which explains why she has disassociated herself from Moorland Investments.

Lisa says, 'I will be a shareholder in the next couple of days. You'll need to inform Companies House.'

The men grab the papers. Pursing his lips, Barry Learoyd skims through the copies. Matthew Alderson folds his arms.

'Where the hell did you get all this?'

'That doesn't matter. It's all there in black and white.' Angie flicks a hand at the folders. 'There's actually more; Stephen also forged various documents and cheques in Rachel Henshall's name. Her solicitor is looking into that.'

'Can you leave these with us, Angie? Miss...?' Matthew Alderson squints at the letter. 'Miss Brooks?' He leans forward and switches on his computer; the low hum fills the silence. 'We'll need to look at all the records we have here.' He points towards the screen. 'And certainly we will have to consult with our solicitors. This is all highly irregular—'

'And illegal.' Angie keeps her voice firm. 'Except, of course, the document for the transfer of the shares to my sister. I think you'll find everything's in order for that to go through.'

'Eventually,' Barry Learoyd mutters.

Angie fixes her eyes on him and smiles. 'Eventually.' She keeps the smile in place when she turns to Matthew Alderson. 'Yes, we'll leave these with you. They are only copies, of course.'

'Mrs Birch, I can assure you we had no idea what Stephen ... what he was doing. We assure you—'

'Then I suggest you also need to look carefully at your accountant as well as my husband.' Angie tucks the folder back into her bag and follows Lisa to the door.

They stand for a second at the open doorway. They can hear machinery from the yard outside. 'We'd be grateful if you would contact our solicitor about the sale of the land.'

They can barely contain their elation. In Angie's car they look at one another in disbelief.

'Now we wait.' Lisa grins.

Angie is shaking. 'Now we wait,' she says.

Chapter One Hundred and Ten

Lisa

We need to make sure Stephen doesn't suspect what we're doing. At least for the next few days. So Angie has insisted she goes to the hospital at least once every day. I'm not happy about it; I think he needs to know she's serious about a divorce, but, as she says, if he gets a hint of what we're doing, he'll discharge himself before we're ready to confront him.

It's only three days since we saw his partners at Moorland Investments, but things seem to be moving quite quickly; we had a phone call from the solicitor's this morning, asking if we could come in today, and here we are. When the door to the waiting room opens and Richard, the solicitor, peers in, he's smiling. I'm hoping that means good news.

'Afternoon. Please come through.'

We've hardly sat down before he opens a file on his desk and puts his glasses on. I'm trying to keep my breathing steady.

'So...' Richard looks over the rim of his glasses. 'It seems Mr Birch's partners can't get rid of him fast enough. I had a letter from Moorland Investments' solicitor yesterday, and this morning a conversation over the phone with her.' He scans a sheet of paper. 'A Mrs Bibby, a very efficient and pleasant woman...' He coughs. 'It seems there are discrepancies in the company's accounting. Mr Learoyd and Mr Alderson are anxious to disassociate themselves from your husband, Mrs ... er ... Angela.'

'What will happen?' I ask.

'Mrs Bibby has faxed through a copy of the paperwork for the shareholders' agreement. For the transfer of company shares from your husband to the partners. Apparently, they are concerned that the *discrepancies* are kept within house, so the value of the company's stock shouldn't fall.'

'I doubt Stephen will care if they try to buy him out.'

'Unless they threaten to reveal his fraudulent activities, of course. They would, I imagine, make that clear to him. In which case, if he is sensible and sells—'

I hear a derisive sigh from Angie.

The solicitor taps the ends of his fingers together. 'We can only hope that will be the case, of course. But, if he does, he will get the value of his shares at the present rate, which ... er, Lisa, you'll be pleased to know, as a new shareholder, is very healthy.' He unclips a couple of papers and passes them across the desk. 'As you brought the discrepancies to their attention, Mrs Bibby said that Mr Learoyd and Mr Alderson are anxious for you to see the letter stating their intent.

'There is one small problem, however. Although they are anxious for this matter to be resolved as soon as possible, neither partner thinks it expedient to meet with Mr Birch at the hospital. They have reluctantly conceded that they will need to wait until he is at home.'

I draw in a long breath and rub my hand across my forehead. It was what I was hoping for. 'That's no problem.' I keep my voice as calm as I can. I don't look at Angie; out of the corner of my eye I can see her fingers clenching, unclenching. 'No problem at all.'

Chapter One Hundred and Eleven

Lisa

We're on the front steps of Angie's house. We've packed all that Angie wants to take with her and now we're taking a break. Everything's ready.

I'm gazing over the roofs of the houses across the avenue. The sky is translucent silver and the sun an orange ball balancing on the top of the Whiston, a black mound of a hill in the distance.

Cat's in his cage at my side. This morning, when he first went in it, he gave a low yowl of complaint, but since then he's mostly slept, only now and then standing to knead the thick blanket I've put in to keep him comfortable. I'm hoping he'll settle in Wales. Though I do wonder what he'll make of the hens and Charles II. That makes me smile. I hope Angie loves Wales as much as I do.

I haven't told Angie about Ben and me. But she seemed happy enough before with the idea of me liking him, so it shouldn't be too much of a shock.

'This time next week,' I say, 'you'll be settled in at Barb and Chris's. You'll love living there, and you'll feel right at home in no time.'

'I hope you're right.' She leans against me, a smile deepening the dimple in her cheek. 'I might even end up with a Welsh, sing-songy accent like yours.' She huffs a short laugh.

'Cheeky mare.' I nudge her. 'You'll love Ponthallen. It's quieter than around here. And you'll have me there.'

'You don't think we'll want to murder one another within a month?'

I put my arm around her shoulders, squeeze. 'Nah!'

And then the significance of what she's just said hits us and we stop smiling.

She looks up at me. 'You must think I brought all this on myself. On us?'

'No. Not anymore.' I move her hair to one side, kiss her forehead. 'We were children. It was an accident.'

'You were a child. I was sixteen.'

'It was an accident. And you were frightened.'

It's always going to be with us, the memory of that day. For a long time it destroyed our relationship. I punished Angie and she punished herself. But we're together again, and we're strong.

Tomorrow, we'll bring Stephen here and we'll do what we've planned. I have to admit my stomach is flipping over and over at the thought, but we'll do it. We'll be rid of him once and for all.

Chapter One Hundred and Twelve

Lisa and Angie

When they arrive at the hospital, Stephen is already dressed and the nurses are stripping and remaking his bed.

'About time!' He scowls from Angie to Lisa and back to Angie again.

'What's she doing here?'

'I wanted Lisa with me because we have—'

'Don't you mean *Mandy*? *Mandy Marsden*? That's her real name. However fuckin' fancy she thinks she is these days.'

One of the nurses makes a wry face of disapproval. 'Time to go, I think, Mr Birch.'

He pushes past the two sisters without another word.

The journey back to the house is in brooding silence, but as soon as Angie unlocks the front door, he shoves his way past her to the living room and swings round to face them.

'And now you can fuck off,' he says to Lisa. He's flicking his tongue against the inside of his cheek, a sure sign he's worked up. 'I don't know why you're here in the first place.'

Lisa doesn't say anything. She's waiting to see his reaction when he realises he's lost control of her sister.

Cat, in his cage by the side of the settee, gives a small squeak.

'What the...?' Stephen frowns. 'What the hell is that thing doing in my house?' He moves towards it, gathering steam.

Lisa is quicker. She stands in front of Cat. 'He's going to Wales with me.' She picks up the cage and walks back to stand alongside Angie.

'And I'm going with her as well.' Angie's voice is strong, but Lisa sees the slight shuddering of her shoulders.

'Like hell you are.'

'I'm divorcing you. I told you.' Angie's voice has the slightest tremble. 'My solicitor will be writing to you in the next few days.'

There's a slow change in his expression; the flicking of his tongue stops.

Lisa tenses, her fingers on the start button of the Dictaphone. If he threatens or goes anywhere near Angie, she's ready.

Stephen points at his wife, his finger shaking.

'You don't divorce me. You even try to leave, and I'll tell the world what you are. Nothing but a tom, a dirty prostitute. Tell them how you conned me into marrying you.'

'I didn't. But that doesn't frighten me anymore, Stephen. Do your worst. Whatever you do or say in the future won't bother me one little bit.'

He sneers.

Hoping he doesn't hear the click, Lisa presses the start button on the Dictaphone as Angie begins talking.

'We do have something to tell you that might change your mind.' Angie crosses her arms.

He narrows his eyes. 'What're you talking about?'

'We're willing to sell the land to Moorland Investments.'

'Oh yeah? What's the catch?'

'No catch,' Lisa steps in. 'Other than you give my sister her divorce.' She doesn't trust him one inch, so she adds, 'And just to make sure you understand the whole situation, we know all about your fraud. We even know you bribed your way onto the council. I doubt you would want anyone to find out about *that*.'

His face distorts into an ugly mask of hatred and disbelief.

'You'll never get Wrigley and Watts to admit that,' he splutters, his breathing ragged.

He knows what he's just said. Lisa feels a spark of triumph. He's given himself away. She keeps her eyes fixed on him.

'I think you've just admitted that yourself, don't you? So...'

'*So...*' he mimics. 'Think you're so bloody clever, don't you? The trouble is, you've no evidence of any of that. You can't prove a thing.' His lip curls. 'Any more than you'll be able to prove what happened to your stupid mother.'

Something comes into the room, a stale sourness that makes it difficult for Lisa to breathe. She clenches her hands into fists.

'What are you talking about?'

An icy shudder of dread travels along Angie's spine. And all at once, she knows. 'Mum came to the house that day. You saw her.' It isn't a question. She knows. 'What did you do?'

'Bloody cheek, coming to my house when I wasn't welcome in hers—'

'What did you do?' Angie's head is filled with splintered slivers of terror and fury. 'What?' She's shouting.

'Stupid bitch said she felt ill, needed water to take her pills. Asked me for a drink. As though I'd give her anything.' He's shaking his head. 'She didn't get her water, but *I* got her pills. Knocked 'em out of her hand and pushed her out the door.'

Angie's stomach flips. She's going to throw up. 'You! You murdered her!'

'She had a heart attack.'

'Her pills would have stopped that.'

'We'll never know, will we.' Stephen cocks his eyebrow.

'You...!' Angie can't breathe. Her mouth goes dry. 'The police – we'll go to the police...'

'With what? Say what?'

'Angie?' Lisa grabs hold of her sister's arm. 'Leave it. Let's just get out.' She's listened, numb with disbelief and loathing for him. Now she rouses herself. 'Angie!'

Angie shakes her off. She drags air into her lungs. 'And Dad? What did you do to him?'

'Nothing. He took a swing at me. Told him what I've just told you. Silly sod just fell down.' He throws his head back and lets out a loud guffaw. 'Slap bang on the floor.'

'You left him!'

'Not my business.'

'Angie. We're leaving.' Lisa picks up the cat's cage and hauls her sister out of the house.

'I hate you!' Angie twists around and screams back at him, even as Lisa drags her down the path towards her car.

'Get in, love.' Lisa puts the cage on the back seat and ushers Angie onto the passenger seat.

'We can't let him get away with it. I don't care about anything else. We have to go to the police. Tell them what he did to Mum. To Dad. Even if there's no proof, we have to tell them what he's done. Lisa!'

Lisa looks towards the house. Stephen is at the front door. He's waving to them 'Bye.' He's laughing. 'Talk soon.'

'Oh, you will,' Lisa mutters.

She gets into the car, fastens her seat belt. 'Here,' she says to Angie, who's sobbing quietly. 'Hold this.' She passes the Dictaphone to her sister. 'I think we've got everything we need for the police.'

Epilogue

2017

Lisa leans back on the wooden chair, raises her face to the sun and sighs. It's good to feel the warmth on her skin, the slight breeze lifting her hair.

'You tired?'

Lisa turns her head sideways to look at her sister. 'A little.' She smiles. 'But it was a good send-off, wasn't it?'

'Well, you only retire once, and nearly forty years in the same job is quite an achievement.' Angela stretches her legs out in front of her, winces at the familiar twinge in her knees. 'You didn't feel you wanted to carry on another five years?'

'No, I've done my bit.' At least she hopes she has; there was always that small, nagging feeling she owed more. 'And I'll have lots of time to spend with these two now.'

They look at the small figures intent on patting sand into brightly coloured buckets with matching coloured spades.

'He's a miniature Ben, isn't he?'

'He is.' It's strange to see the likeness between her husband and grandson. 'And the spit of his daddy. I remember the first time I saw Dan at his age, perched up on Ben's shoulders. Thomas is his image.' She smiles at Angie. 'No regrets on your part?'

'Good grief, no.' Angie glances over her shoulder at the building behind her. 'It was time for me to bow out. I was glad to hand everything over five years ago...'

Lisa knows her sister is proud to have founded the women's refuge over thirty years ago from the proceeds of her divorce settlement. Of the safety she's given to so many. The house, hidden behind the façade of an office, has saved the lives and sanity of hundreds of women and their children.

'I wonder what happened to him after he'd got out of prison,' she said.

'Stephen?'

Lisa nods.

'God only knows.' Angie shrugs. 'And, quite frankly, I don't care.'

A child laughs, brings the women's attention back to the beach. A little boy runs between two makeshift cricket stumps.

'Go, son, go...'

They watch the small boy celebrate, turning round and round, arms aloft, laughing and kicking up the sand.

'Oh, well done, Robert, well done.'

There is a second of silence between the sisters. They exchange glances. Then each reaches over to the other and they lock fingers.

Acknowledgements

I would like to express my gratitude to those who helped in the publishing of *Sisters*.

To all the staff at Honno for their individual expertise, advice, and help.

Special thanks to Thorne Moore and Alex Craigie, dear friends and fellow authors, for their encouragement and enthusiasm for *Sisters*.

And to Janet Thomas, for her support with my writing down the years.

Lastly, as ever, to my husband, David; always by my side, always believing in me.

*

To find out more about Honno Welsh Women's Press, please visit our website www.honno.co.uk.

We are grateful for the support of all our Honno Friends.